WE HAVE SEEN HIM IN HUMAN AND ANIMAL FORM...

…portrayed on ancient temple walls, in tombs of Pharaohs, on Dark Age gargoyles and in the carvings and stories of tribal peoples from equatorial Africa to the bleak Arctic tundra. He is the spirit possessor who schemes to obliterate our God-given environment, and thus mankind's existence. With the availability and spread of deadly nuclear fission, the ultimate tool to accomplish this goal is at hand.

GREEN DEVIL

Other Books by David Saperstein

RED DEVIL – THE BOOK OF SATAN (BOOK ONE OF
THE EVIL ON EARTH SERIES)

COCOON (PART I OF THE COCOON TRILOGY)
METAMORPHOSIS: THE COCOON STORY
CONTINUES (PART II OF THE COCOON TRILOGY)
FATAL REUNION
DARK AGAIN
BUTTERFLY: TOMORROW'S CHILDREN (PART III OF
THE COCOON TRILOGY)
A CHRISTMAS VISITOR (with George Samerjan)
A CHRISTMAS PASSAGE (with George Samerjan)
A CHRISTMAS GIFT (with James J. Rush)
WOMAN IN THE YEAR 2000 (Editor Maggie Tripp)

GREEN DEVIL

THE BOOK OF BELIAL

David Saperstein

RED SKY PRESENTS

New York

GREEN DEVIL
A Red Sky Presents Book/published by arrangement with the
author

ISBN: 978-1-941015-22-3

Published by Red Sky Presents
A division of Red Sky Entertainment, Inc.

The author gratefully acknowledges the help and inspiration provided by the following: Ellen Saperstein, Rabbi David A. Mersky, Rabbi Noah Hefetz, Mr. Anatoly Shcharansky, Carl Sagan, John Paine, Father Colm Murphy, Susan Schulman, Myron "Micky" Hyman, Catherine Venture, Ivan Saperstein, Esq., and the Book of Mormon translated by Joseph Smith.

And to those who, with their love for our planet, give us the spirit and will to fight for our survival against those among us who despoil, trash, rape, ruin and pollute our common home, our Earth.

For my grandchildren

Shai Laurel

Noa Lev

Eve Meital

Ari David Efraim

May our Earth, and every life upon it,
be peaceful, respectful, joyful, hopeful, healed,
and filled with love.

"Let's be clear. The planet is not in jeopardy. We are in jeopardy. We haven't got the power to destroy the planet - or to save it. But we might have the power to save ourselves."

- Michael Crichton

"If we cannot end now our differences, at least we can help make the world safe for diversity. For, in the final analysis, our most basic common link is that we all inhabit this small planet. We all breathe the same air. We all cherish our children's future. And we are all mortal."

- John F. Kennedy

PROLOGUE

Long before the arrival of the Spanish conquistadors, Yupanqui, the ninth generation leader of the Inca tribe, sat near a cave mouth above a fertile plateau on which his strategic village of Cuzco was located. The young warrior prince was despondent, his mood as black as the moonless Andean night. A small fire burned in a circle of granite rocks.

On a nearby outcropping, the remnants of his warriors licked their wounds while silently observing their brooding prince. On the plain below, sounds of drums and celebration, mingled with the screams of Inca women being raped, filtered up the mountainside. The terror that Prince Yupanqui's men had often visited on their neighbors was now being repaid.

The small fire Yupanqui had built did not warm him. He peered into the darkness and listened as the Chancas, a fierce tribe of warriors from the coastal west, engaged in celebration. Their conquest had slowly moved toward Cuzco, devouring Inca land and enslaving Yupanqui's people. The Inca had fought fiercely, but the Chanca gods were more powerful than the Inca's. The vanquished Inca prince pictured Capac, the victorious Chanca chief, a

1

powerfully built warrior who claimed decadency from the puma, sitting outside Yupanqui's longhouse. He imagined the arrogant chief proclaiming himself "Lord of all the Earth!" as he ordered the older Inca survivors slaughtered and the young ones enslaved, keeping Yupanqui's favorite wife as his own.

As Prince Yupanqui pondered his tribe's bleak future, a shadowy figure emerged from the dark rear of the cave into the fire's glow. It was a large, snow-white puma. The prince tensed and reached for his stone knife as the creature approached, but the puma did not adopt a threatening stance. The sleek, powerful animal's demeanor was somehow comforting as it moved to the other side of the fire and lay down. Its eyes glowed red and bore deep into Yupanqui's soul. Then it turned away from the prince to observe the festivities below.

Thoughts, like whispered words, entered Yupanqui's mind. "Your women have been raped," the puma told him. "Your wives and children enslaved. Your old ones slaughtered." Prince Yupanqui nodded. His shame and frustration deepened.

"I have lost all. I am weak and defeated. I am shamed," he said aloud. On the outcrop below, the warriors saw their prince in conversation. But they could not see the puma. Was Yupanqui talking to spirits or gods, they wondered? Or had he gone mad?

"Not all is lost, Prince of the Inca," the puma hissed, as his black tongue licked his sharp white fangs. "Worship me and I will deliver your people to greatness and riches."

"But are not the Chanca your children?" Yupanqui asked, his fear contained in his left hand, which clutched his bejeweled stone knife, symbol of an Inca prince and high priest.

"Noooooo…" The puma growled, deep and low. "They are no longer mine." The great cat then turned his gaze away from the carnage below and fixated on the young Inca prince. "Victory has made them arrogant. They call themselves lords of the Earth and believe they are strong without me. They are fools."

A small flame of hope was kindled in Yupanqui's heart. Could this beast do what he proposed? Could he turn defeat into victory and make the Inca strong again?

"Worship me," the puma hissed again. "Worship me, and together we shall destroy the Chanca." Yupanqui stood. He reached for his brightly festooned feathered headdress and cape and donned them. Then he stepped to the mouth of the cave, where his warriors could see him.

"Bring me the Chanca woman," he ordered. Manco, Prince Yupanqui's second-in-command, jumped to his feet. His blood pumped fast as he sensed that power had returned to his prince's voice.

"The woman," Manco ordered to a nearby warrior. The man grabbed a naked Chanca slave they had captured in battle. He dragged her to Manco, who grasped her long black hair and lifted her up toward Yupanqui.

"This one, my prince?"

"Bring her," Prince Yupanqui ordered. Manco obeyed, climbing to his prince's cave, dragging the frightened, struggling young woman behind him. When he reached the cave, Manco hesitated at the sight of the puma. His prince had surely gone mad, for this was the god of the Chanca. But Manco was loyal. When his prince gave an order, Manco obeyed. He threw the woman down in front of the fire. Without hesitation, Prince Yupanqui grabbed the woman. He knelt and bent her body backward over his knee. From under his feathered cape, he drew a razor-sharp sacrificial knife. The puma purred, pleased. Prince Yupanqui turned the ruby and emerald knife handle to the white beast and pledged his unwavering obedience and eternal soul to the puma, then slit open the terrified woman's throat with one powerful thrust. Blood spurted into the fire and flowed over the circle of rocks. The puma slid out his wide, black tongue and licked the bright red liquid as the dying woman's heart pumped away her life.

"This pleases me, Prince Yupanqui." The white puma then rose and summoned a spirit from the shadows of the cave. It was the evil sub-prince Beelzebub. The puma's great front paws became two hooded cobras. One embraced Yupanqui, the other Beelzebub. The puma's tongue, dripping with sacrificial blood, licked the man and the spirit, and in one swift motion, Beelzebub entered the body of Prince Yupanqui. "Now you are my prince, and a god to your people," he announced. "A god, and a conqueror!" The puma leaped from the mountain cave above Cuzco, transformed into an enormous black condor. "Follow me, prince of the Inca," the condor screamed. His high-pitched voice echoed up to the snow-capped Andes. "I am Belial, your god!"

Mesmerized and possessed, Prince Yupanqui threw the dead Chanca woman aside and leaped from the cave into the cold, black Andean night, where he had now transformed into a sleek, avenging peregrine falcon.

"Follow me," Yupanqui screeched in high-pitched excitement. "Follow me to victory!" Manco and the startled warriors gathered their weapons and, led by their prince, now armed with talon and beak, descended from the mountain and recaptured Cuzco in a bloody, barbaric victory. The Inca fought fiercely, led by the two avenging birds that tore into the Chanca ranks, ripping flesh to the bone and tearing gaping wounds with their bloody beaks. Yupanqui instructed Manco to capture Capac, the Chanca chief, and keep him alive. Later, when the battle had ended and Yupanqui was once again a man, he dressed in his robe and his headdress of bright, bird of paradise plumage, and before his tribe, eviscerated and beheaded Capac. The great white puma observed the ceremony from the forest. His black eyes glowed until they were blood-red with pleasure.

CHAPTER ONE

A STORM IN THE VALLEY

In 1847, after years of persecution and wandering, the Mormons, then a new and controversial religious group, found sanctuary in the great Salt Lake Valley. Now, after more than a century and a half of peace, the verdant valley that their leader Brigham Young had called "their place" had grown into a burgeoning suburban sprawl outside Salt Lake City. It nestled beneath the majestic Wasatch mountain range, and stretched more than fifty miles, from Bountiful to Brigham City. It was here that more than 75 percent of the people of Utah, mostly Mormons, lived and worked.

The spring snowmelt had begun early. Two of the three great rivers that feed the Great Salt Lake, the Weber and the Bear, were rising steadily to dangerous levels. To make matters worse, a late spring snowstorm was gathering, threatening to deposit twenty new inches on the already record-breaking snow pack. An uneasy tension spread through the area.

Robert Christensen, his wife Carole, and their six children made their home in he valley, farming sixty fertile acres while grazing cattle on another forty. For the past six years the severe winters, and the snowmelts that followed, had taken a toll on their livelihood. Flood followed flood, as though a biblical test had been given this hardworking, deeply religious Mormon family. Robert Christensen's forebears cleared this land in 1872. The farm had been passed down and worked through four generations. Although only forty-three, Christensen always planned for the day when he would pass the farm on to his sons.

"We have a good life in this land," he often told them. "Providing sustenance for our fellow human beings is honest and important work. It is God's work."

It was a mild spring day. Christensen sloshed his six-foot frame across what had once been his best alfalfa acreage. Now it was a swamp from the floods. He slapped at a mosquito attempting to feast through the weather-beaten skin on his neck. He took off his green and yellow John Deere cap, waved it about his head, and then smoothed back his dark blond hair before putting it back on. "More snow up there," he muttered, as he eyed the dark clouds gathering above the Wasatch Range. "That'll mean more water down here, God help us." The weather prediction was for rain in the valley, but he knew that the bulk of the storm's moisture would be deposited on the mountains above as snow. Its melt would flood him out again and render the land useless for another season. Last year he had spent fifteen thousand dollars to drain and grade his fields after the spring melt. Now all that work and expense would be for naught. The new storm brewing could well be the coup de grace. He weighed the cost of leaving this acreage to weeds and muck

7

against the cost of battling the floods. *When,* he wondered, *would the government wake up to the changes in global weather and provide some effective flood control?* The legislature had debated the matter endlessly. So far, the urban majority had won out as they argued that, "spending millions of dollars on an unproven theory that flooding would become a regular event, rather than the anomaly that it is, wastes taxpayers' money." In the end, Robert's Mormon pragmatism reminded him that the best way to get a job done is to do it yourself. He had applied for a loan to construct a flood-control dike. Hopefully, the bank would approve his request in time for him to do the preliminary work that could stave off most of the flooding and erosion.

As Christensen approached the chain-link fence, topped with barbed wire, that surrounded the adjacent property, he took notice of the odd, dome-shaped rock mound. That bit of unusual geology had been eroded another three feet along its sides by the latest flood. The dome's top had first appeared ten years ago when an unusually hot summer caused the Great Salt Lake to drop more than nine feet. The next spring there was severe flooding and erosion. What had first appeared as slight elevation, he theorized, might be the smoothed top of a large rock formation, left behind by a retreating Ice Age glacier. It seemed to rise out of the Earth. As the years passed and the floods persisted, they revealed symmetry about the rock that could have been man-made. With more erosion, it now looked like the dome of a mosque, or perhaps the top of an Eastern Orthodox Church.

He knew the land was owned by a local Salt Lake holding company, Victory Development Corporation, but he had never seen anyone on the property near his farm. Christensen came closer to the fence and scanned the area.

No one was around. Curiosity took hold in his mind. Something drew him to the rock, something that caused a cold shiver to travel down his spine and pump adrenaline into his bloodstream.

Long before the Mormons arrived, the Salt Lake Valley had been home to the Navajo, a proud Indian tribe that had migrated from the north and settled the American southwestern desert regions. They fiercely resisted the white man's onslaught but were eventually subdued. Today, they are the largest Native American tribe, more than two hundred thousand strong. Powerful medicine men, called shamans, still practice ancient remedies and ceremonies, and the tribe tenaciously preserves their Athabasca language. The other major tribe in the area is the Pueblo. There were several small tribes within the Pueblo nation, including the Paronto, a small, shadowy, and secretive sub-tribe who maintain they are the sole true remnants of the once great Inca, Maya, and Aztec empires. Unlike most Navajo, whose religion focuses on the emergence of the first people from worlds beneath the Earth's surface, and living in harmony with the natural world, the Paronto focuses on the spirit world. It is known among Navajo tribal elders that the Paronto pursue dark, unspoken powers that other tribes avoid and fear.

Jim Swain, a Paronto leader, was a day laborer working in the booming construction industry of the Salt Lake area. His rugged features, framed by straight, jet-black hair, left little doubt as to his ethnic background. His profile might be found chiseled into the walls of an Aztec or Mayan ruin. Powerfully built and agile, the thirty-six-year-old was a formidable presence. But his dark, coal-black eyes were what held one's attention. Their gaze was mesmerizing, their impact hypnotic. Swain was not a man to be taken lightly. His look exuded danger, and something more—something almost inhuman.

Swain parked his battered '94 Dodge pickup in a corpse of beech trees on a hill above Robert Christensen's farm. It was chilly and beginning to drizzle. He grabbed the 30.06 Remington from the rack behind him and expertly attached the laser scope to it. He then scooped up the powerful Nikon binoculars from the seat next to him. Thunder rumbled in the mountains. He, like Christensen, was concerned that the storm would bring heavy snow up there, and rain to the valley. But his concern was for very different reasons. Swain checked his jacket pocket where he had stored a full box of ammo, then stealthily crept to the edge of the beeches and dropped to the ground, flattening himself against the damp earth. He had a clear view of the domed rock below. He trained the binoculars on the flooded fields and was surprised to see a man standing there, next to the fence. Swain twirled the zoom knob on the binoculars until he could identify the man. It was the farmer Christensen.

It didn't take much effort for Christensen to slide under a section of the fence where the soil was eroded. The drizzle that had begun a few moments ago became a light rain. He brushed mud from his jacket and jeans and approached the domed rock. A distant flash of lightning caught his attention. He counted aloud, getting to six before the clap of thunder reached his ears. The storm was moving rapidly. He approached the side of the rock, feeling that chill down his spine again. Was it the negatively charged atmosphere, or something else in the rock?

Swain watched Christensen approach the rock. He set aside the binoculars and picked up the Remington, chambering a round. He wound the rifle's sling tightly around his left elbow and placed the elbow on the ground. He lay flat on the ground with his boots turned outward for stability. It was one of he first positions he had learned at the firing range of the Marine Corps Recruit Depot on Parris Island. Christensen was next to the rock, and kneeling. Swain focused the laser sight and put the nosy Mormon farmer's head in the crosshairs, centering on the yellow leaping deer of the John Deere cap. A sudden flash of lightning, followed almost immediately by an earthshaking clap of thunder, startled Swain and caused him briefly to move off his target.

That same clap of thunder brought with it the promise of a deluge. In a moment, Christensen was soaked. A small river was already forming along the rock, carrying with it chunks of the red soil. He stood up and ran for the fence, promising himself a closer look another time. As he moved away from the rock, the air seemed to warm and his body relaxed.

Swain cursed aloud as the rain began to fall in sheets. The ground, already saturated from previous rains, could hold no more water. Rivulets began to form, wending their way down into the valley. More will be exposed, Swain worried. He had to report this information quickly, along with the interest that Robert Christensen seemed to have in this sacred place.

Sheets of cool rain hammered the granite walkway that led from a small plaza to the offices of Nicholas Perez. A bronze plaque near the entrance of the modern steel-and-glass three-story building announced that this was the corporate home of Victory Development Corporation (VDC). Perez was VDC's CEO. His private offices took up the entire top floor of the building. Entrance to the suite required fingerprint recognition and a corneal scan. Much of the work done at VDC was for government agencies, maintaining and overseeing private development of selected federal natural resource properties, mostly forests and mines. A new and secret side of VDC's business involved development of systems for the disposal of the country's growing accumulation of hazardous nuclear waste.

Perez's executive secretary, Raymond Light, an intense, swarthy, humorless man, was the only one present on the top floor of the VDC building. Light's real name was Ramón Luz. He, like Perez, had come to the United States from Cuba. Luz met Perez while they both were detained and interned in Miami awaiting rulings from the Department of Naturalization and Immigration. The nerve center of Perez's office was its computer/media room, taking up one-quarter of the top floor. Raymond Light sat in front of three flat wall monitors. On this stormy day, Perez was in Washington, D.C., meeting with senior officials from the DOE, the Department of Energy. Light used a headset while computer-searching and passing on, via secure satellite telephone, the data that Perez required.

Perez was not a member of the Church of Jesus Christ of Latter-day Saints, but he was overtly civic minded, and politically well connected to several Mormon leaders. Nothing about the ageless man's appearance said high-powered businessman. He was slight of stature, barely five feet three inches tall. He weighed no more than 130 pounds.

His complexion was pale and pasty. His steel blue-gray hair was close-cropped. He was someone who could pass by unnoticed. And yet, to anyone meeting Perez, his presence was charismatic and unforgettable. Despite his diminutive size, many women found his persona intoxicating. His mother was from Belarus, his father from Peru. They met shortly after Castro took over in Cuba. She was a petrochemical engineer; he was an adviser to Castro and a close friend of Che Guevara. Both, it was rumored, died in a Cuban prison, where they were serving life sentences for treason. The story Perez told was that he had come to Florida on the Mariel boatlift. After being granted political asylum, Perez moved to Salt Lake City.

"The latest number we have is forty-six point six tons of high-risk nuclear waste material ready for storage," Light reported. He heard Perez repeat the amount to someone nearby.

"Is that all the states, or just the contiguous ones?"

"That's all of it—Alaska and Hawaii included, Mr. Perez." Again there was a pause as information was relayed.

"Very good, Raymond. Is there anything else?" Light double-checked that the phone was still in scramble mode.

"Yes, sir. Swain called. He had some concern regarding the…uh…the farm next to the dome."

"What concern?"

"Erosion. We're having more rain here, and a heavy snow in the mountains. The Bear River is approaching flood level. And the farmer seems to have taken an interest in the…uh…the area too."

"What kind of interest?"

"He was observed breaching the fence today."

"And?"

Light paused. "He came close, but a downpour drove him away."

"I'll be back in two days. I'll want to see Swain. Tell him to get some men ready. And you go have a look out there yourself. Immediately."

The phone clicked off. Light waited until the scrambler cleared and their proprietary computer program swept the recorded conversation for any sign of a tap or intercept. It signaled all clear.

Light left the computer/media room and quickly walked down the hallway to a locked oak door. He took out an ornate key and inserted it into the lock, slowly turning it 360 degrees. One of the oak panels slid open in front of him at eye level. It revealed a flat blue screen. Light leaned his face against the screen and opened both eyes wide. A dim white light scanned his eyeballs. The door clicked open. The room was dark. The door closed behind him. Light moved across the room without the benefit of any illumination. There was a rustling of clothing and shoes being removed. Then the silence was broken by a high-pitched screech. A window high up on the room's far wall slid open.

A sleek, swift peregrine falcon emerged from the tiny opening in the concrete wall as the rain continued to grow in strength outside VDC's headquarters.. The raptor screeched once again, and then flew off to the north. The window sealed itself shut and disappeared, as though it had never existed.

CHAPTER TWO

A WALK IN THE PARK

The problem of how and where to store America's deadly nuclear waste materials was growing daily. The subject was highly politicized. The continued containment and storage of these potentially deadly materials at nuclear electric generating plants, weapons factories, hospitals, and other nuclear waste sources was clearly inadequate. On the other hand, no politician wanted this hazardous material stored in their state—a classic case of NIMBY (Not in My Back Yard). Even those states, mostly in the vast uninhabited southwestern desert regions, that had explored the possibility of having such a storage facility had encountered stiff opposition from environmentalists as well as the general public. Thus, few politicians were willing to stick their necks out on this issue, even if it meant the loss of jobs, and revenue to strapped state and local budgets.

Nicholas Perez, as a consultant to the Department of Energy, separately wined, dined, and cultivated three key people in the agency's nuclear oversight department. They were

Lincoln Foster, William Claremont, and Bertha Smalls. All were career federal employees who had control over burgeoning nuclear waste materials in the Southwest, where many nuclear power plants are located. He had gained the trust of the three DOE executives by commiserating with them over the impossible problems they faced in finding safe storage. Over time, he carefully introduced a plan that he maintained could help solve the problem. He proposed building an underground pilot facility of his own design. He would prove that it operated efficiently and safely, producing foolproof containers and a storage matrix that would satisfy politicians and critics.

At a quiet dinner in a chic Georgetown restaurant, he offered the final details of his plan to all three executives, proposing that he use his own money, and land in Utah, to build the pilot facility. In return he required that the project be kept top secret, and that when his design had proved successful, he be given the inside track to construct and operate future, larger facilities throughout the country—a contact that would be worth tens of billions of dollars.

"And you three will reap the benefits of a grateful nation, as well as of the nuclear industry," Perez said, stroking the three executives. "You'll be heroes." But he met resistance from the chief executive, Bertha Smalls. She hesitated at his demand to being granted the inside track on future contracts.

"I can dodge any flack, Bertha. I've contributed heavily to the campaign of the current congressional representative in my district, as well as our newly elected junior senator from Utah. Rest assured, I will have their full attention." Perez's solution was well thought out. He revealed that he would build the underground pilot facility in the guise of a water-control project that had already been approved for his land by the Utah Division of Water Rights. Now that floods were again threatening the Salt Lake City area, it was a perfect time to push through all the necessary construction permits. But Smalls, fifty-three years old and an eighteen-year veteran civil servant who had risen to a G-10, a reasonably high pay grade in the DOE, was still not convinced. Like a large percentage of Washington civil servants, Smalls was black. In two years she would be eligible to take her pension and retire, and she didn't want to do anything that might jeopardize that plan.

"I am just not comfortable with this, Mr. Perez," she told him after Foster and Claremont had left the restaurant. "Mind you, I appreciate your offer," Smalls said patronizingly. "I mean, someone has to start to seriously confront this problem. But I've thought long and hard about it, and I believe it must be done under governmental supervision and control. Too many things can go wrong. An accident. Nuclear pollution. Well, you know how delicate the issue is. It can be a deadly business, and mistakes are not easily cleaned up."

"We will bear full responsibility. And it's only a pilot project. If all goes well—and I'm sure it will—the government will step in and take control." Smalls hesitated, then smiled.

"I'm sorry, Mr. Perez. I just can't go along with it."

Perez moved closer to her. He locked his intense, dark eyes on hers. "This is very important to me, Ms. Smalls." His hand moved across the table and rested close to hers. "I know my design will work. And when you retire, I know the industry will show its gratitude with lavish job offers. This can be very lucrative for all of us…" His voice trailed off.

He waited patiently as she weighed the risks. Then she took a deep breath.

"Yes…well, Mr. Perez, I'm afraid not. Lord knows, I'm no angel, but the possible danger of disaster…well, that just has no price tag for me. I'm sorry. I know you mean well."

"Please, Ms. Smalls. No need to be sorry," Perez told her softly. "I completely understand." He patted her hand. "Your point is well taken." She felt a strange sensation. His touch was cold, yet a hot tingle shot up her arm. Her heart beat faster. He smiled, staring deeply into her eyes. She shuddered slightly as a shot of adrenaline surged through her body. "We entrepreneurs can only dream and try to fulfill those dreams. Sometimes we are so anxious, and have such firm beliefs, that we tend to wear blinders when it comes to the pace of progress. Cutting red tape and all that…" He moved his hand away. The intensity of his gaze was gone. He smiled again. "Let me go back to the drawing board and see what I can work out." Bertha Smalls thanked him for dinner and left.

While Nicholas Perez ordered a second espresso and a glass of grappa, and Robert Christensen worried about the punishment that nature was heaping on his farm, Allen Weber, Christensen's brother-in-law, was worrying about the family's farm bank loan as he hurried to a meeting with his bosses. It was six-thirty in the evening.

The Weber family had been members of the Church of Jesus Christ of Latter-day Saints, the Mormon church, dating back to its beginnings. More than eight generations earlier, Peter Weber, a descendant of Dutch settlers, had worked the hard clay soil near Palmyra, New York. He befriended a neighbor, Joseph Smith, Jr., who was to found the Mormon Church. By 1830, Peter Weber was one of Smith's most dedicated followers. When the Mormons, persecuted in New York, moved westward, Peter Weber was a church leader. In 1844, Joseph Smith, Jr., the Church's founder, was killed in Carthage, Illinois, for his beliefs. Two members of the Weber family were also slain in persecutions that followed. In 1847, when the new Mormon leader, Brigham Young, brought his flock west to the Great Salt Lake basin, Peter Weber was a member of the Council of the Twelve Apostles, the fledgling church's governing body. Left undisturbed, the Mormons prospered. Their faith deepened. Their numbers multiplied.

Seven generations later, Allen Weber, a direct descendant of Peter Weber, was being groomed to take a seat on the powerful Quorum of the Twelve Apostles, which still governed much of the Mormon Church's activities. One day, Allen Weber might even become a member of the First Presidency, one of three men who had the final say in all Church business.

Allen Weber had majored in communications and language at Brigham Young University, where he met his wife, Susan Christensen, Robert's sister. Weber graduated cum laude and served his two years of missionary service in Israel, in the ancient city of Jerusalem, at the Brigham Young University Study Center. Upon his return, Susan and Allen renewed their college friendship, and fell in love. They married when Allen was offered a management position in one of the Church's holdings, the Desert Management Corporation.

The storm had finally passed. The setting sun cast long shadows through the glass corridor of Desert Management's nineteenth-floor executive offices located in Salt Lake City's trendy Triad Center, close to the Capitol. Allen Weber hurried to the meeting with Desert Management's CEO and CFO. Aside from being his bosses, both men were members of the Mormon Church's First Quorum of the Seventy, considered, after the Quorum of the Twelve Apostles, to be the next highest authority of the Mormon Church. In other words, they were two very powerful men.

Weber, dressed in his best conservative dark suit, white shirt, and muted tie, walked confidently across the thick carpeting of Chief Executive Officer Dale Richards's office. The imposing sixty-two-year-old silver-haired executive rose from his black high-backed leather chair and extended a friendly hand.

"Good afternoon, Allen." "Rain's finally stopped, I see," he said, glancing out the window.

"Yes, sir. We've certainly had enough." Weber turned to greet Chief Financial Officer Henry Pratt, who had ten years on Weber's forty but seemed much younger. "Hello, Mr. Pratt," Weber said as they shook hands. Pratt, seated in one of two oxblood leather chairs that faced Richards's massive mahogany desk, did not get up.

"Have a seat, Allen." Richards beckoned him over. Weber sat in the chair next to Pratt. "I hear Susan is expecting again."

"Yes, sir." The CEO smiled and nodded his approval. He opened a file on his desk.

"That's nice. Henry, here, tells me that you wish to recuse yourself from the Christensen loan application, but you've also asked that it be given immediate attention."

"Well, sir yes…I did. You see, Mr. Christensen is my brother-in-law and, uh, well…"

"Allen," Richards interrupted. "Did you think we are not aware of that fact?"

"Well, sir, I…" Richards closed the file and smiled.

"If we had any doubt that you would approach this loan differently than any other, well, Allen, that would mean we have sorely misjudged you, wouldn't it?"

"You see, sir, it's just that I've been struggling with the moral aspect of it. Appearances…and I…" Weber realized that there was nothing more to say. "Thank you for your confidence, sir." Richards stood up. Weber followed suit. The kindly CEO walked around his desk, put his arm around Weber's shoulder and guided him toward the office door.

We have complete faith in your business judgment, Allen. And in your morals. I admire your concern for your family."

"Thank you," Weber said as they reached the door.

"I'm glad, Allen. I assume you approve of the loan?"

"I've done the due diligence. It's a good project, and the collateral is solid."

"That's fine. We expect big things from you. I can tell you that people at the highest levels of our little world out here are pleased with your progress." As they shook hands, Weber attempted to muster another "thank you," but a rush of excitement caused it to catch in his throat.

Two days later, Bertha Smalls was found wandering in Rock Creek Park dazed, naked, and bleeding. Her body was covered with bite marks and scratches. Chunks of her flesh had been torn out. Small veins had been severed. She was hospitalized but slipped into a coma. A medical report identified the bites and scratches as inflicted by "a large feline of undetermined species." The coma was as attributed to severe trauma and loss of blood. Her condition was guarded, but it was expected that she would regain consciousness as her body healed.

A local and federal police investigation produced no results. The bizarre story made the network and cable TV news and page three of several East Coast newspapers. It was gone in twenty-four hours. A few days later, D.C. police officials surmised that Bertha Smalls had suffered some kind of nervous breakdown and, while passed out in the park, had been attacked by raccoons and possibly stray cats.

A week later, Nicholas Perez met again at the DOE with Lincoln Foster and William Claremont. Foster had temporarily taken over Bertha Smalls's duties. The men agreed to move Perez's plan forward, keeping the pilot program a secret. Perez never mentioned that Smalls had balked at the plan. He told Foster and Claremont that she had endorsed it enthusiastically. He rewarded the two DOE executives, whom he now called his "partners," with an all-expenses-paid trip to Hawaii, and a promise of bigger and better perks to come. He then returned to Salt Lake City, and a meeting with Raymond Light and Jim Swain.

CHAPTER THREE

RITUALS

Robert Christensen met the two detectives at the front door of his house. They showed their ID. He nodded. The muscles in his clenched jaw twitched.

"We'll take my truck," Christensen said angrily, pointing to his Dodge pickup. Nothing more was said until they had turned off the blacktop driveway onto a dirt road.

"When did you find them?" Detective Sergeant Harold Snow asked. The nineteen-year veteran of the Salt Lake City Police Department sat next to Christensen in the center of the pickup's wide front seat. His partner, Detective Andrea Ruiz, sat next to the open window. It was a warm, sunny day. Ruiz was new to the Special Crimes Unit, having recently passed her detective's test and moved from uniform to plain clothes. She was a Mexican-American whose ancestry was Mestizo, a fiery mixture of Aztec and Spanish. The Mormon church proselytized heavily in Mexico, Central America, and South America. Detective Ruiz was a Mormon convert.

"Just past six this morning. We…my two oldest and I were on our way out to the construction site," Christensen explained. They left the dirt road and cut across a large, empty pasture. "We're building some flood-control dikes and canals at the east end of our property." They crossed a pasture and stopped at a closed iron gate. Christensen got out and swung it open. Beyond, on higher ground, was another lush, fenced pasture. As Christensen got back into the truck, Ruiz observed two figures and a tractor in the distance on the crest of a hillock near a lone live oak.

"My two oldest boys are up there. They're pretty upset. Not a sight for kids to see, but this is their farm too, and I figure they have a right."

Only two of Christensen's seventeen prize Black Angus bulls were alive. They stood apart from their dead comrades and nervously eyed the approaching truck. Todd, fifteen, and Kenneth, thirteen, walked from the tractor to their father's pickup. Each carried a twelve-gauge shotgun.

"You boys okay?" Christensen asked his sons as he got out of the cab.

"We're fine, Dad," Todd answered. He was a handsome boy, tall and fair.

"There are flies all over the place. And it's beginning to stink," Kenneth added. His voice was changing—it cracked, making it difficult for him to form the words. His father nodded and put his arm around Kenneth's shoulder.

"It's okay, son. This is Detective Snow and Detective Ruiz. These are my boys, Todd and Kenneth." The detectives eyed the shotguns. "They know how to use them," Christensen said, the anger clear in his voice. Snow and Ruiz shook hands with boys.

"Okay, Mr. Christensen, let's have a look," Snow suggested. Christensen, followed by his sons, led the detectives to the other side of the hillock, below the live oak. There, scattered in a seemingly haphazard fashion, were the carcasses of fifteen champion Black Angus bulls. The carnage represented the destruction of a line of excellent breeding stock that Christensen had spent ten years building. The two detectives approached the first carcass. As Kenneth had warned, flies were swarming, laying their eggs in the open wounds where blood had flowed and then coagulated. The exposed flesh was already black, except where bone, fat, tendons, and ligaments were exposed. In was only a matter of hours until thousands of pupae would become maggots and begin the process of eating away everything to the bone.

"Holy Mother of God," was all Detective Snow could muster. He was not a Mormon, nor, in fact, a religious man. The stench of death hung over the hillside. He took out a handkerchief and covered his mouth and nose. "Six this morning, you say?"

"Yes, sir." Snow looked at his watch. It was nine forty-five.

"It appears they've been dead for several hours. It must have happened during the night. When was the last time you saw them alive?"

"About six thirty yesterday afternoon," Todd volunteered. "I brought one bull, number four ninety-eight, out here in the trailer with the tractor tow." He pointed to a carcass off to the left. "He'd been at stud on the Crockett farm in Morgan."

"And everything was okay?" Snow asked the boy.

"Yes, sir. They were all here. Seventeen head, grazing all peaceful like." He glanced up at the growing flock of circling buzzards. Ruiz walked past the nearest dead bull to the one the boy had indicated. She snapped on a pair of latex gloves and knelt next to it, but the stench caused her to back away. She took a surgical mask from her pocket and covered her mouth and nose. This bull had been hacked apart like the others. It had also been eviscerated, but its entrails seemed to have been spread out in a circle around it. She then noticed a boot print in the soft soil and glanced quickly at the three Christensens' footwear. All wore heavy work boots. The impression she had found was that of a high-heeled cowboy boot.

"I found a boot print over here," she called to Snow. "We'd best get the crime scene investigators out here pronto." Snow gave her a thumbs-up. She reached for her cell phone and made the call.

"If you don't need my boys," Christensen said to Detective Snow, "they've got school."

"They can go."

The boys drove the tractor back to the house. Since they had missed their bus, their mother would have to drive them to school and explain why they were late.

For the next hour, Snow, Ruiz, and Christensen went from corpse to corpse. They carefully approached each of the remains, looking for any clues the perpetrators might have left behind. Each bull had been ritually slaughtered. Each had different parts of its body displayed. One had had its head removed, another the forelegs, and still another the testicles. Ruiz made notes and sketched the position of each bull in the field. As the ninth was being examined, the CSI, consisting of three technicians, arrived at the pasture by helicopter. Ruiz showed one of them the boot print while Snow filled the other two in on what they'd discovered so far.

As Ruiz began to sketch the tenth dead bull, something caught her eye.

"Sergeant Snow!" she called out, excited. "Have a look here." Snow and the chief CSI walked quickly over to her.

"What's up?" Snow asked. He had respect for the young detective. She was intense, dedicated, and smart.

She showed him her sketch. "I think there's a definite pattern here." She pointed out how the nine bulls that had already been examined were positioned in the pasture. Five of them, almost equidistant apart, seemed to form a circle. But four more, closer together and inside the circle, formed the base of triangles below the bulls. "I roughed in where the rest of the carcasses are," she told her boss, "and when you connect the dots, it forms this!" She showed them a five-pointed star. "It's a pentagram."

"Yeah," Snow muttered. "Ritual."

"Devil worshippers?" Ruiz suggested.

"Maybe. These bulls aren't exactly small animals."

"A ton each, I figure," the CSI remarked.

"So it took a bunch of fired-up people to do this," Snow said. "People with a purpose."

A chill of excitement slithered down Detective Ruiz's spine. This was the kind of detective work she'd dreamed of doing. Then one of the other CSIs called out. He had found a knife inserted in the displayed heart of a dead bull. Snow examined the way it was positioned and had it photographed before asking the technician to remove it and bag it as evidence. He then brought it to Ruiz, who was talking to Christensen and recording the registration numbers of the dead bulls. Snow had some idea of the knife's origin, but because of Ruiz's Aztec heritage, he sought her opinion. Although she immediately knew the design and markings, she initially said nothing, taking her time to examine the knife. It was old, made of stone, with a bone handle. Definitely ceremonial and Native American. She feared where the origins of this knife might lead, and the furor it could cause if, in fact, local tribespeople were to blame. But in the end, she was a professional, sworn to uphold a very strict code of justice, no matter who was involved.

"It's Navajo," she said softly. "Something a medicine man might have."

CHAPTER FOUR

WITH SPIRITS JOINED

Hospital facilities, except for emergency rooms, are usually quiet after ten p.m. At the Washington/Virginia Medical Center, visitors are required to leave by eight. By nine, most medical staff are gone, except for night-shift residents, interns, and nurses, who catch up on paperwork while most of the patients are asleep.

The nurses' station on Five West was staffed by two RNs and a nurses' aide. The aide, Usman Ayub, the proud Pakistani possessor of a brand-new green card, was making rounds with Millie Greenstein, a dedicated ten-year veteran of overworked and underpaid nursing. Five West was a special wing. The nine patients currently there were all comatose—three in the final stages of brain cancer, two with head trauma sustained in an automobile accident, two left for dead from a gang shooting, one on life support from a motorcycle crash, and Bertha Smalls, the DOE executive attacked in Rock Creek Park. All were hooked up to monitors and surveilled by TV. The motorcyclist and the gang members required breathing assistance. The staff kept the IVs flowing, emptied catheter drains, turned patients periodically, sponged them down once a day, and watched for any signs of recovery.

The second RN on duty, Imelda Flores, originally from the Philippines, sat at the nurses' station recording temps, blood pressure, and fluids in/fluids out, and reading notes in the patients' charts left by the last shift. She was so immersed in her detailed paperwork that she did not hear the doctor approach.

"Good evening, Nurse," he said in a deep and resonant voice.

She gave a start. "Oh! Oh, good evening, Doctor." He wore the usual white lab coat, with a stethoscope draped around his neck and a row of pens clipped inside his breast pocket. He carried a silver case the size of a laptop computer. Imelda, who vision was impaired by astigmatism, had on her reading glasses. She could not make out the name on his ID tag. "I didn't hear you coming, Doctor, uh…"

He smiled knowingly. His voice was kind. "The paperwork never ends, does it?"

"No, sir. How can I help you?"

"I need the chart for Bertha Smalls." Nurse Flores switched glasses. Now she could clearly see the doctor's face and ID. He was Michael Genovese, M.D., Department of Cardiology. She swiveled around in her chair and rolled over to the rack of medical charts behind her. Each encased in a metal binder with the patient's name and attending physician on the spine. She pulled out Bertha Smalls's chart and handed it to Dr. Genovese.

"I haven't entered the latest data yet, Doctor," she said. "We're only two here, plus an aide."

"No problem. I'm just looking in on her for a colleague." He smiled, took the chart, and turned to leave.

"She's in five thirty-three. It's that way," Nurse Flores said, pointing in the other direction down the brightly lit hallway.

"Of course. Thank you."

Bertha Smalls was lying on her back. The fluorescent light gave her coffee-colored skin a greenish pallor. A vitals monitor above her bed beeped quietly as it received an update from the contacts attached to her motionless body. An intravenous port had been inserted in her chest, just above her left breast. At the moment, it was providing a high-calorie IV cocktail of fat and protein Her breathing, unaided, was shallow but steady. Her face was calm.

Genovese glanced down the hallway. Satisfied that no one was watching, he entered the room, closing the door behind him. He approached the bed and saw that Bertha Smalls was, in fact, comatose. That would make what he had to do easier. He placed the silver case at the foot of the bed, then raised the Venetian blinds and opened the window as wide as it could go. He turned off the light above the bed. Ms. Smalls was illuminated only by the ambient streetlight from the window.

Dr. Genovese removed his white coat and shirt. His body began to grow coarse yellow and black hair that took on the pattern of spots. His hands became hairy and his nails grew sharp and thick. But it was his face that underwent the biggest transformation. As it became flatter, his eyes grew closer together and glowed red. His nose became a snout, and from his widening mouth emerged long canine teeth and fangs dripping with thick, yellow saliva. More hyena than man, he opened the silver case and took out a clear glass vial that appeared to be empty. But when he removed the cork stopper, a pale blue mist rose out of the vial. He inhaled the mist deeply as though he were savoring the bouquet of a fine wine. His skin glowed red, then turned dark green. The blue mist continued to pour out of the vial. It rapidly filled the room. Bertha Smalls inhaled it. Her skin also turned red and then green. Her body undulated while her hands and feet twitched like a rag doll being shaken. Genovese took out a jeweled-handled Inca sacrificial stone knife. Dried bloodstains darkened its sharp edge.

"I do my master's bidding," he murmured as he placed the knife's stone blade on his hairy wrist. "I obey for his triumph." He slit open his wrist, wide and deep. Green blood gushed out. He raised his arm and passed it over Bertha Smalls's head, bathing it with his blood. The light in the room dimmed.

"Amaimon calls," he growled. Bertha Smalls's body shuddered violently. Her eyelids popped opened. Her eyes rolled back in her head, her eyeballs were black, like a feeding shark.

"Amaimon calls in my master's name, intoned Genovese." Bertha Smalls's mouth opened. Her tongue, now a bright green, slid out of her mouth. A second tongue emerged from underneath Genovese's tongue. It grew long and turned red. It reached down, snakelike, and entwined with Bertha Smalls's tongue.

"Amaimon bids one to enter." Blue-white moonlight appeared as a breeze came into the room, parting the blue fog within. Behind the breeze a formless shadow entered.

"Amaimon calls. Who has come to do my bidding?" asked Genovese. The shadow moved into the gaping wound in Genovese's wrist and disappeared. Genovese's lips and tongue turned inky black. The darkness spread onto Bertha Smalls's tongue, mouth, and lips. Then, as quickly as it had appeared, the blackness was gone, and skin color returned to normal. Her eyes rolled forward into their normal position. Her tongue shrank back into her mouth. Her lips parted, and a woman's voice emerged.

"I am Trisaga, Ruler of Triads, servitor to you, my sub-prince Amaimon."

Nurse Millie Greenstein and Usman Ayub returned from their rounds at eleven o'clock. Nurse Flores was still buried in her paperwork. Greenstein checked the room monitors. Smalls's monitor was dark.

"What's with five thirty-three?

Flores looked up. "Huh?"

"Five thirty-three is dark. No monitor or vitals."

"But there was no alarm," Flores said, concerned. "There's a doctor...uh, Genovese. From Cardiology. He's in there."

Usman Ayub walked over to the monitor. "It seems to be working," he said. "Perhaps it is the camera?"

"Maybe the doc accidentally disconnected it or something," Flores said.

Greenstein's brow was furrowed. "I'll check it out." She headed down the hall.

"How about giving her a hand, Usman? Greeny's not much with electronics." The aide smiled and trotted down the hall after Nurse Greenstein.

A minute later, the call button from 533 rang, shattering the silence. Flores looked up at the TV monitor. It was still dark. She punched in the PA system to the room. "What's up?"

"Call the resident, STAT!" Greenstein shouted. "Then get in here with a crash cart."

Flores quickly paged the resident, then grabbed the emergency crash cart and raced down the hall.

Five minutes later, Dr. David Engelhardt, the resident on call, and Nurse Supervisor Lisa Burgess arrived at Five West. The nurses' station was deserted. Burgess's experienced eyes quickly came to rest on the blank TV monitor for room 533. She checked all the other monitors and vitals screens. All was quiet.

"It's five thirty-three. We'd better get over there!"

As Burgess and Engelhardt entered the room they saw the two nurses and the aide struggling to keep Bertha Smalls in her bed. The patient was wide-awake and gleeful as she evaded their efforts, emitting a mordant laugh that filled the room and echoed out into the hallway.

Six time zones away, at the lush Papakea Beach Hyatt on the island of Maui, Lincoln Foster and William Claremont sat at the outdoor bar enjoying their third piña colada. They had played a round of golf on this last day of a splendid week, compliments of their "partner," Nicholas Perez. Their wives were in their rooms, primping for the last night of dining and dancing before returning to Washington. Their golfing partner, Raymond Light, Perez's business associate, drank with them. The two DOE executives were relaxed, well on their way to a late-afternoon buzz.

"How about we do the sauna and a massage?" Light suggested.

"Sounds like plan," Claremont said.

"A damned good one," Foster added. "Maybe I'll get that Danish girl again. She has great hands."

"And a happy ending," Claremont added.

The three men laughed lasciviously. Light reached for the house phone and reserved private massages for his guests.

Twenty minutes later, with their fourth drinks in hand, the trio headed for the health spa. Light carried a laptop-sized silver case exactly like the one Genovese had with him at the Washington/Virginia Medical Center.

Light had made an arrangement with the masseuses, by way of a generous cash payment ahead of time, that guaranteed that Foster's and Claremont's massages would be deep and thorough, meaning the two women would ply their sexual favors generously.

When they were finished, the masseuses left the naked DOE executives on cots, covered with sheets, and warm towels wrapped around their heads and necks. Both men were still slightly drunk, and now satisfied and relaxed.

"How was it?" Light asked them as he entered the room, setting the silver case on a side table that held various scented ointments and clean warm towels.

"Excellent," Foster said, his voice muffled by the towel.

"Beyond remarkable," Claremont added in a muffled tone.

Raymond Light smiled. "That's great. We've got some time. Enjoy the rest. I'm going to take a sauna."

"Right," Foster said.

"Mmmmmm…" was all that Claremont could muster. Both men's eyes were covered by the warm towels, so they did not see Raymond Light. He opened the door of the sauna and removed his white terry robe. But he did not enter the hot, redwood chamber. Instead, he opened the silver case, took out a clear vial, and removed the cork. A green mist rose from the vial. He put it under his nose and breathed in deeply. In the transformation, Light's fingernails grew long, like the talons of a raptor. His hands extended out, ending in long, grasping claws. Long, golden feathery quills grew through his skin from within his body, until it appeared that he was robed in them. His face twisted and stretched as his eyes moved to the side of his narrowing head. His nose and mouth melted into a menacing, curved yellow beak. Clutching the vial in his talons, Light, now resembling a man-sized peregrine falcon, approached the two men, who were now asleep on their cots. He poured the green mist onto their face towels and stepped back. Both Foster and Claremont stiffened as they inhaled. Then they began to shudder and shake, slowly at first, then more and more violently, until the towels and sheets that covered them were tossed aside, leaving them naked. Their mouths opened as if to scream, but no sound emerged. Their skin turned a fiery bright red, then blackened and scabbed. Light, the falcon, went into the sauna with a second vial, and poured its contents onto the hot sauna rocks. They steamed and sizzled, filling the sauna and the room with a thick fog.

"I do my master's bidding," the falcon said in a shrill, high-pitched voice that resounded in the silence of the room. Its sound pierced the ears of Foster and Claremont, and they screamed. "I obey for his triumph," Light said as he

stood between the two DOE executives, who were now awake but unable to move. The overhead light dimmed. "Amaimon calls in my master's name. Amaimon calls and bids two to enter." Two formless, shrouded figures moved out of the sauna and waited in its doorway. "Yes!" the falcon screeched. "Yes!" He bent over Foster, whose eyes revealed the terror he felt. "You will be first." Light bent closer and grasped Foster's head in his massive claw, lifting the terrified man off his cot. In one swift movement the falcon tore open Foster's chest with his beak. "Enter!" the falcon screeched. One of the figures crossed the fog-filled room, dissolving into a dark liquid substance that filled Foster's gaping chest wound. The skin closed. The wound disappeared. "Who has come?" asked the falcon.

A raspy voice emerged from Foster's lips. "I am Hacamuli, the spirit that withers life, sub-prince Beelzebub." Then Foster slept.

Raymond Light, the falcon, then repeated the same process with Claremont. And when he asked who had entered, the response was, "Orgosil, the spirit of tumultuous events, sub-prince Beelzebub." Claremont too slept.

Later, when they both awoke, neither remembered what had happened after their massages. All they knew was that they were extremely grateful to Raymond Light for arranging their late-afternoon trysts.

When Claremont and Foster returned to their rooms, their wives were cross that their husbands were a little drunk. At dinner, the men were loud, curt to the waiters, and uncommonly playful toward their wives. But they were demure when it came to Light. What their wives would never know was that within their husbands' bodies there now dwelled spirits called upon by, and beholden to, the sub-prince, Beelzebub.

CHAPTER FIVE

CONSTRUCTION

Flooding from the rain and snowmelt turned out to be less than expected. Robert Christensen's fields were spared more erosion damage. The rivers receded. With the loan in place, Christensen's plan was to have the new dikes and flood-control canals finished in time to put in a crop of alfalfa and corn. But as word of the ritual animal killings spread, and the police made no arrests, several contractors who had bid on the project were reluctant to commit. In addition, Nicholas Perez's Victory Development Corporation announced it was accepting bids on a huge flood-control project of its own on the property adjacent to Christensen's farm. Since this was a much larger and more lucrative job, contractors rushed to get in their bids, leaving Christensen in limbo. Within a few weeks, Perez's project had leased all the best equipment and hired the most experienced contractors and workers in the area. No one was left to work for Christensen.

Robert Christensen was of tough pioneer stock, and not a man easily defeated or denied. Angry and frustrated, he called his brother-in-law, Allen Weber, and made an appointment to meet at Desert Management's offices the next day.

The two men sat across from each other at a polished teak table in a small private conference room. The window faced the mountains, where the last remnants of snow were receding under the bright Utah sun. Weber wore a blue serge suit, white shirt, and light blue tie, while Christensen was dressed in a blue-and-black plaid shirt, dark brown corduroy pants, and construction boots. His worn leather windbreaker was draped over the back of his chair. The contrast in dress made clear the difference in their lives.

"Nicholas Perez is a well-respected businessman in this town," Weber told his agitated brother-in-law. "I mean, what can I do? He simply made better offers to the contractors."

"You've got it all wrong, Allen," Christensen replied angrily. "There's more to it. The police aren't that interested in finding whoever slaughtered my bulls. But someone's putting out rumors about satanic cults. So people get nervous. And this Perez shows up, throwing big bucks around. I'm thinking maybe he had something to do with it. You take my meaning?"

Weber knew his tough-minded brother-in-law could be volatile at times. He now saw he was building up a case against Perez and VDC, and sensed it could get out of hand. And the fact that Weber's bosses, who also did business with Perez, surely wouldn't help matters. "I wouldn't go there, Bob."

"No, I guess you wouldn't," Christensen remarked sarcastically. Weber shook his head and shrugged.

"I'm sorry, Allen. I didn't mean to...I'm just upset. So where are we? I mean, I can't do the job myself—that is, the boys and me. We can't run the heavy equipment and…" His voice trailed off.

"We're family, Bob. Your loan is good. It'll be there for you. I hear by early winter Perez will have his project done and—"

"No, he won't," Christensen interrupted. "He's got six subcontractors out there with more than fifty workers. Whatever he's doing is big."

"He's doing flood control, like you. Hey, maybe it'll help your situation."

Christensen laughed and shook his head. "Help? He's going to take care of his own land. My guess is that it'll actually mess with my drainage and add to my problems."

"I can't respond to that, Bob."

Christensen sighed deeply. "Okay. Here's where I am, Allen. I've lost my Angus herd. It has to be rebuilt. That takes time and money. The two bulls I have left are a start. Without the dykes and canal I can't risk planting my fields. That means I lose feed, plus a cash crop. So I'm… I'm…" Christensen threw his hands up in disgust. "I'm in a box."

"I called Nicholas Perez's office this morning," Weber announced. That got Christensen's attention.

"You did? Why didn't you tell me up front? What did he say?"

"I thought I might work out some kind of sharing of facilities. But they were rigid." Christensen's shoulders sagged. "Perez was away. His VP, a guy named Raymond Light, says they have a time constraint in the approvals they got from the Division of Water Rights. I'm sorry, Bob. Their attitude was classic—business is business, Light told me. Nothing personal."

"It's always personal, Allen." Christensen stood up. "Well, I've got my own time constraint. It's called survival. I'll go out of state if I have to. You say the loan is good, right?"

"Yes. Of course."

It took a month for Robert Christensen to locate a qualified general contractor. He found one in Phoenix, Arizona. Flatbeds loaded with heavy earth-moving equipment began to arrive at the farm, along with operators and laborers. Under the arrangement, the workers would stay in tents on the site during the week and at the Hilton in Salt Lake City on weekends. Christensen's costs were increased, but he felt that could be offset by a bumper crop of alfalfa. And the good news was that his flood-control project was under way.

The next week, before Perez's construction was about to begin, his primary contractors had abruptly been given radically different plans. Instead of surface dikes and canals as originally bid, construction was now to be a half-mile deep-tunnel, dug at a thirty-degree angle, leading to a huge man-made chamber. Rather than have floodwater evaporate or be channeled into the Great Salt Lake, the new plan was to divert and conserve as much as possible to hold for local irrigation. In effect, Perez announced, they were creating a huge cistern.

"I was told that Christensen plans to dig his first canal adjacent to the dome," Raymond Light told Perez as they entered the tunnel to inspect the progress. The mouth had been hardened with prefabricated reinforced concrete slabs. A gravel bed for a service road and rail tracks was being laid in the tunnel that was already nearly one hundred yards down into the Earth. The shaft was illuminated by powerful mining lights strung above a conveyor that transported subsoil and rock up and out of the shaft. It was loaded onto dump trucks and moved to another part of the property.

"Have you spoken to his contractor?" Perez shouted above the din of the conveyor.

"Yes," Light yelled back. "He's straitlaced. A Mormon, like Christensen. Nothing to do there.""Any chance of accidents?" Perez asked slyly.

"That is always possible, Master. But I am concerned about your, uh…I mean, with a canal so close to the tunnel, a bad flood could draw attention to it and, well, we might have some problems."

"Yes, I understand," Perez hissed. "Swain told me the farmer was nosing around a while back. The man could be a problem." He stopped. They had descended as far as they could. Ahead, a massive three-bit rock-cutting machine poured ground rock and subsoil onto the conveyor-belt system trailing behind it, appearing like a tormented sculpture of a steel Triceratops. It blocked their way. "Look how far we've gotten," Perez said brightly. He watched the machine grinding into the earth. "At this rate, we will be able to bring in nuclear waste material sooner than we planned." He turned to head back up to the surface.

Once clear of the site, and alone in Light's car, Perez pondered the Christensen matter, as he called it. *Something has to be done. Swain had a chance but, well, maybe it was for the best, then. Gather your brothers to us. With things moving along so well, I think it's time we dealt with this bothersome Mormon.*

CHAPTER SIX

MEDICINE MAN

When detectives Snow and Ruiz attempted to speak to the Utah Navajo Tribal Council about the knife they'd found on the Christensen farm, they were referred to the council's attorney, Taro Heart. She was a sharp, knowledgeable, Harvard-educated lawyer, and protective of her tribe's rights. The detectives showed her the picture of the knife and described how it had been buried in the bull's heart. In her thirty-one years on Earth, she had not seen anything like it, or the way it had been used.

"Stone, isn't it?" Heart asked.

"Yes," Snow answered.

Heart examined the picture carefully. "It looks to me like one of those Inca or Aztec ceremonial knives they used for ceremonies. Human sacrifice, I think."

"We suspect it might be Navajo," Ruiz said. "I'm of Aztec descent. Many Navajo rituals and designs are derived from the Aztec. You think a medicine man may have one?"

"I couldn't say," the young lawyer responded. "But I can tell you that I've never seen or heard of any Navajo doing what you describe. We revere nature and all animals."

Snow leaned toward Heart with a friendly smile. "Would you know anyone we might talk to about this knife and the, uh…the rituals?" During his years as a cop he had occasionally become involved with the dominant tribes in the region—Hopi, Apache, Pueblo, and Navajo. He knew that medicine men or women were very powerful in Navajo society.

"It could belong to almost anyone," Heart answered defensively. She was not going to be conned into letting these cops poke around the reservation. "In fact, they sell copies of knives like that right here in downtown Salt Lake. So any tourist could have done it. Maybe if you had fingerprints…"

"It was clean," Ruiz offered. "But it looks authentic, don't you think?"

"Like I said, Detective Ruiz, slaying of animals, the way you described—that's just not something a Navajo would do."

Snow then took the actual knife, sealed in a plastic evidence bag, and placed it next to the photo on Heart's desk. "Look, counselor, we're not accusing anyone here. Someone is probably trying to frame the Navajo. We need information. We need your help."

Heart turned a practiced eye on the knife in the bag. "I appreciate your concern. May I keep this picture?" she asked.

"Sure," Snow answered.

"Thank you," she said and stood up, signaling that she had nothing more to say. "I'll be in touch."

A few minutes after the detectives left her office she telephoned Jimmy Tellman, who flew the tribal plane, a twin-engine Cessna, between Salt Lake City and the Navajo reservation near the town of Bluff, in the far southeastern corner of the state. She asked if she might hop a ride down there.

Jacob Yahze was a "Hatali," a medicine-man chanter. The Navajo, the second largest tribe in North America, after the Cherokee, number more than a quarter million. Most Navajo reject the white man's religions. The Utah Navajo bands, and their tribal brothers and sisters in Arizona and New Mexico, understood that Jacob Yahze possessed great magic and wisdom. He was a conjurer who knew the old ways, the old stories of tribal mysteries, origins, spirits and cures.

As Taro Heart climbed the hill to where Jacob Yahze lived, she was acutely aware of the sounds around her—the sounds she had grown up with. City living muted the natural sounds of the living Earth. A horned lark's song—sweet music to her—was interrupted when two ruffed grouse flew up from the long grass beside the path. Below, in a backwater of the San Juan River, a noisy flock of wood ducks, on their way to their breeding grounds of northern Canada, banked in for a rest. Taro inhaled the sweet fresh air. *How different, she mused, from the atmosphere of Salt Lake City that was fast becoming one of the most polluted urban areas in the country. What a paradise this land must have been before the white man invaded and destroyed it.* At the thought, the beauty around her assumed a melancholy pall.

As she reached the crest of the hill and saw Jacob Yahze seated in front of his hogan, facing west into the setting sun, her appreciation of nature's beauty returned, and she was uplifted.

Yahze's hogan, a traditional Navajo dwelling, was made of pine logs, brush, and earth. A smoke hole in the center of the ceiling admitted a shaft of light to the dark, cool interior and acted as an escape for a fire's smoke. When Jacob Yahze saw Taro Heart, he rose gracefully from his place on a traditional Navajo blanket. His fluid motion belied his. He wore jeans, cowboy boots, a bright red and yellow shirt, and a black ten-gallon Stetson. From the hatband sprouted three large silvery-white tail feathers from a golden eagle. Their color matched his long, braided hair. The Hatali's wrists and neck were encircled by ornate silver and turquoise jewelry. His polished belt buckle, also finely worked silver, reflected the golden late-afternoon sunlight. His coal black eyes focused on Taro Heart. A broad, kindly smile creased his face.

Jacob Yahze had been educated as a chemical engineer, and also held an MBA from Stanford. At the age of thirty-eight, while working for Exxon in Dallas, Jacob was summoned home to the reservation by his ninety-four-year-old father, Hash'ke. The old shaman knew that his days were numbered. According to tradition, the knowledge and powers the old man possessed would pass from father to child or would be lost to the Navajo forever. Hash'ke told his son that the time was approaching for Jacob to take his place as medicine man to the people. Although the request was powerful, it was not a demand. Hash'ke had encouraged his son to see what life was like outside the reservation before he had to assume his tribal duties. But both men also understood that this time would come. The position of medicine man carries great responsibility. Jacob had prepared for this day. For the next two years, Hash'ke revealed his secrets and the sources of his powers. He arranged for Jacob to meet with other shamans, especially those of the Haida and Tlingit tribes, far to the north in Canada and Alaska. The Haida had strong spiritual contact with nature and with the Old Ones, known as Sasquatch and Yeti, who still roamed the solitary high forests. The Tlingit could call upon their ancestor's powerful spirits. Jacob brought greetings from his father, and amulets of turquoise and buffalo horn as gifts. The Haida and Tlingit shamans shared many secrets and rituals with Jacob. They introduced him to the spirit world of the north, and to a few of the Sasquatch, who passed through their territory during the time of their mating.

Hash'ke had died peacefully one autumn morning twenty-six years earlier after completing an antelope chant with his son. Jacob Yahze, Navajo medicine-man chanter, had served his people faithfully from that day to this.

"Ahhh," Jacob said as Taro approached the hogan. "You grow more beautiful each time I see you." She smiled and blushed. He was very much a grandfather figure to her, and she knew she was one of his favorites. "I am encouraged to see that big-city law has not etched a frown or furrow on that beautiful brow." As she approached, he reached out and embraced her, patting her back softly through the buckskin jacket she wore.

"I'm glad to see you, Jacob Yahze," she said respectfully. "You look well." He let her go and took a step back, studying her face.

"I *am* well. And you, I can see, are troubled."

"Yes, sir." He motioned her to sit on his blanket.

"Then you must tell me why."

He sat stone-faced as she related the events on the Christensen farm and her visit from the police. When she finished, she handed him the photo of the knife buried in the bull's heart. Jacob studied it for a long moment and then handed it back to her.

"It is very old. Fashioned like those from the time of beginnings. The Diné—the first people. You know the story?"

""Of course," Taro said. He smiled, nodded, and told it anyway.

""It is the end of May. Dotso, the eighth month of our year. It is the time of Ayei'ne'denaiyote—a mixture of rain and spring snow. Like now." Jacob spoke perfect ancient Athapascan. Taro did not, so he translated those words as he went along. Jacob was not a man who wasted time, so Taro knew that the story had a purpose from which she could get a clue to bring back to the Salt Lake police. "Nlchi'dilqil, the Black Wind," Jacob continued, "is its feather. The grass grows a dark green. The antelope drop their young. Nlchi'litsui, the Yellow Wind, shakes the Earth, and it thunders. The flowers come forth and plants open their leaves. In this time, the First Man called four holy boys to him. He sent the White Bead Boy, the one we know as Dawn Boy or the Rock Crystal Boy, to the mountain of the East, Sis na' jin; the Turquoise Boy, the one we know as Daylight Boy, to the mountain of the South, Tso dzil; the Abalone Shell Boy, the one we know as Twilight Boy, to the mountain of the West, Dook oslid; and the Jet Boy, the one we know as Darkness Boy or Obsidian Boy, to the mountain of the North, Debe'ntsa."

As Jacob spoke, Taro recalled the first time she had heard this story. She was seven years old. It was wondrous to a child to know how her people, and the part of the Earth they lived in, came to be. Later, after she was educated in the white man's schools, the magic and power of the story left her. The outside world and the white man's law pulled her away from her own myths and origins into those of the Judeo-Christian world. As she listened to Jacob Yahze, she was transported back to her roots, to a foundation as solid as the ancient red bluffs carved by the San Juan River below them. Jacob was preparing her for something that would require solid, immovable strength.

"They fastened Sis na' jin to the earth with a bolt of white lightning. They covered the mountain with a blanket of daylight, and they decorated it with white shells, white lightning, black clouds, and male rain. They placed a white-shell basket on the summit, and in this basket two eggs of the hasbi'delgai, the pigeon. They said that the pigeons were to be the mountain's feather; and that is why there are many wild pigeons in this mountain today. And lastly they sent the bear to guard the doorway of the White Bead Boy in the East." Jacob took Taro's right hand and clasped it between his own. "Now listen to this part, for it will tell you something of what you have brought to me." A cold shiver traveled down Taro's spine, causing her to shudder. The medicine man squeezed her right hand, and warmth flowed into her body, calming her.

"Tso dzil they fastened to the earth with a stone knife. They covered this mountain of the South with a blue cloud blanket, and they decorated it with turquoise, white corn, dark mists, and the female rain. They placed a turquoise basket on the highest peak, and in it they put two eggs of the blue bird, doli. Blue birds are Tso dzil's feathers. They sent the big snake to guard the doorway of the Turquoise Boy in the South."

Turquoise, white corn, dark mists, and female rain, Taro repeated in her mind. She glanced down at the picture of the knife. The handle was turquoise; the carving, corn, mist, and rain! Jacob then let go of her hand and breathed deeply. He smiled and completed the story by telling what the First Man and the First Woman did for the other two boys and their mountains. When he had finished, the sun was about to set. The light was now a deep orange; the air held a slight chill.

Taro lifted the picture. "The knife is the same as the Turquoise Boy's, isn't it?"

"Yes."

"Was it a Navajo who did this?"

"I do not believe so."

"But why point the blame toward us?"

"Someone very evil was there." Jacob took the picture of the knife in his hand. "He is telling us that he has great power to lift mountains in the south, and to destroy food, water, and life."

"And he knows we will tell the white man this?" she asked.

"Yes. But he also knows that the white man will not believe as we believe, and will not trust us."

"I met with the detectives on the case. One's blood flows from Aztec, she says. I trust her. Will you tell her what you just told me?"

"Yes. This evil one uses a ritual knife to cast suspicion, but I believe he fears us."

"And if the police don't listen to you?"

Jacob smiled and, reaching behind him into the hogan, brought out a fetish doll. He took the picture of the knife and placed it on the blanket, then put the doll on top of it. The picture faded away until there was only white paper, which turned to fine powder and blew away. "They will listen to us." Jacob closed his eyes. As the sun set, he chanted:

"For Tso'dzil, the mountain of the South,
the plan was made. The plan was made
in the home of the First Man.
The planning took place on the top
of the Beautiful Goods.
They planned how a strong Turquoise
Boy should be formed; how the Turquoise
Boy should be formed, and how the
Chief of the Mountain should be made.
How he should be made like the
Most-High-Power-Whose-Ways-Are-Beautiful.
All is beautiful where I dream.
I dream amid the Dawn and all is beautiful.
I dream amid the White Corn and all is beautiful.
I dream amid the Beautiful Goods and all is beautiful.
I dream amid the Mixed Waters and all is beautiful.
I dream amid the Pollens and all is beautiful.
I am the Most-High-Power-Whose-Ways-Are-
Beautiful,
And I dream that all is beautiful."

It was a chant that celebrated the beauty and nurturing bounty given to humans by the Most-High-Power. But as Jacob sang of the Earth's beauty, he knew—and Taro feared—that it would take much more than chants from this distant hill to keep the evil from destroying it. When he had finished, Jacob rose and helped Taro to her feet.

"Time is our enemy. This evil I sense grows." There was urgency in voice. "Jimmy won't be flying our Cessna back north until tomorrow afternoon. We will take my Rover and drive to Salt Lake tonight. Call the police and tell them we will be there in the morning." Taro had never seen the shaman so agitated. It frightened her.

CHAPTER SEVEN

NIGHT VISITORS

The two black Cadillac Escalades turned off their lights as they approached the domed rock. There was enough light from the quarter-moon to see the fence beyond. Six men emerged from each SUV and silently gathered around Nicholas Perez. They were all dressed in black jump suits and wore black U.S. Navy watch caps and black military combat boots. Raymond Light and Melvin Plotter, another of Nicholas Perez's trusted assistants, stood silently on either side of their boss. Plotter was, in fact, the same man who had infused the spirit Trisaga into Bertha Smalls, when he posed as Dr. Genovese. Aside from those three, the rest of the men were Paronto. Jim Swain pointed out the place along the fence under which Robert Christensen had slid to look at the domed rock. Perez ordered two men with shovels to dig there and enlarge the opening.

A half hour later the visitors had crossed Christensen's fields and scouted around the dark farmhouse. Then they split up and moved toward the house in three teams.

The first, three men led by Raymond Light, approached from the front. They stayed low to the ground while crossing the driveway, then into the shrubs and up over the railing onto the front porch.

The second team, three more men, led by Melvin Plotter, came across the field into the tree line, then over a split-rail fence, across the patio, and up to the kitchen door, at the rear of the house.

The last team, two Paronto led by Jim Swain, cut the phone and cable lines and disabled the electrical main line leading into the house.

Inside the house, Mike, the Christensens' Border collie, opened one eye and lifted an ear. Something was moving on the porch. He got up and sniffed the air. Then he turned toward the kitchen as another faint sound of footsteps caught his attention. He growled and trotted off to inspect.

Downstairs, Light forced the front-door lock open and slipped inside with his team. Mike heard them enter and turned his attention from the kitchen to see who was there. He growled and bared his teeth as Nicholas Perez stood in the front doorway. Perez held an Inca stone sacrificial knife in his left hand. His face was expressionless in the faint light. His eyes, black and cold, fixated on Mike. He returned Mike's snarl by baring his own canine teeth, which had grown into long fangs. Mike charged at Perez.

The dog's bark, followed by a whimper, woke Robert and Carole at the same time. They sat up in bed and listened, but the house was silent. Carole reached to turn on the lamp on her night table. It didn't work. Robert tried his light, with the same result.

"Power's out," he said, getting out of bed.

"That was Mike barking, right?" Carole asked.

"I think so. Maybe the kids woke him up. A midnight snack," he said, putting on his robe and checking the clock radio on his night table. It was 2:47 p.m.

Plotter's team was in the kitchen. He drew a Ruger 9mm pistol from a pocket of his jumpsuit. The three Paronto with him carried machetes and an ax. They moved stealthily into the dark house.

As his two lieutenants and their teams gathered around Perez in the living room, they heard the door to the Christensens' bedroom open. Perez pointed the knife toward the sound. He slashed it through the air, signaling for the men to get to work.

CHAPTER EIGHT

A SAVAGE ACT

Jacob Yahze and Taro Heart had driven four hundred fifty miles through the night to Salt Lake City in Jacob's ancient but serviceable Land Rover. The shaman was talkative and told Taro more Navajo legends about the Diné, the first people, and how the world was given to them. "But with that gift came responsibility for the Earth's well-being," Jacob said. "The white man has no respect for our Earth or its living creatures, or our water and air. He leaves his dirt everywhere. He condemns his children to wallow in it. This is an old, sad story. The white men have rich and powerful religions, but none that forbid greed. And this greed thoughtlessly destroys nature. My great-grandfather died fighting the white man for our land. My grandfather made peace with the white man and starved on the reservation. My father turned to the old ways and tried to preserve our language, our land, our ways, and our people. And now, with power to destroy all life, and only greed as his god, the white man's worship of wealth has allowed great evil, which he does not understand, to arise and flourish."

Jacob Yahze spoke these same words to the two Salt Lake City detectives.

"We appreciate your coming in to see us," Detective Snow told the Navajo shaman. He looked at Ruiz and rolled his eyes as if to say, *Do we really have to listen to this lecture?* But the young detective did not respond to her partner's silent complaint. "So the knife is genuine?" Snow asked.

"Yes, it is, Detective Snow. It is very old."

"Who might have such a knife?" Ruiz asked. She was suspicious of his all-too-concise answer, sensing that he was withholding something important.

"No one that I know. No one on the reservation. And it is not from our museum at the Hatathli Center and Diné College in Tsaile, Arizona, either."

"Any idea where it might be from?" Snow asked. His years of experience questioning witnesses told Snow that this man would not volunteer information unless asked the right questions.

"An archeological site," Yahze answered. "Or perhaps a private collector."

"Indian artifacts are a big business, you know? Especially from our graves," Heart added, with a tone of sarcasm.

"What about the way it was used, Mr. Yahze?" Snow asked as he gestured to the photo of the bull's heart with the knife buried in it. "Does that represent anything meaningful to you?"

Yahze took the photo in hand and examined it closely. His face was as impassive as chiseled granite.

"Do you have the knife?" he asked. Snow passed the knife, still wrapped in the clear plastic evidence bag, to

Yahze, who held it gingerly. It had been dusted for fingerprints and examined for human blood. None had been found. "Can you remove it from the bag?"

Snow broke the seal on the bag and handed it to Yahze. The shaman slid the knife out onto the table. It rattled as though a small earth tremor had occurred and then spun until the point came to rest, aimed at Snow.

"Step away," Yahze shouted to Snow in a loud, commanding voice.

Startled, Snow stepped aside. Yahze began to chant softly. He took out the same fetish doll he had used on the photo at his hogan and placed it next to the knife. The knife began to spin until it stood upright on its handle. Then it soared straight up like a rocket launched from its pad. Snow, Ruiz, and Heart followed it with their eyes as it buried itself, up to the hilt, in the ceiling of the interrogation room. Yahze's eyes were closed. He chanted in Athabaskan.

> "I walk with beauty.
> On the trail marked with pollen may I walk,
> With grasshoppers about my feet may I walk,
> With dew about my feet may I walk,
> With beauty may I walk."

His voice grew stronger. The knife glowed bright green.

> "With beauty before me, may I walk,
> With beauty behind me, may I walk,
> With beauty above me, may I walk,
> With beauty under me, may I walk."

Yahze slid the fetish doll directly under the knife and chanted even louder. The green glow turned blue. The knife began to slide out of the ceiling.

> "With beauty all around me, may I walk,
> With old age wandering on a trail of beauty,
> lively, may I walk."

The knife, suspended in mid-air, turned from blue to yellow.

> "With old age wandering on a trail of beauty,
> living again, may I walk.
> It is finished in beauty."

Then, as the chant ended, the glowing stone knife disintegrated and fell as a shower of dust onto the table.

Snow gasped. "Mother of God!"

"She cannot help you with this evil," Yahze uttered solemnly. "Now I would like to go to the place where the animals were slaughtered."

Snow drove the unmarked Jeep Cherokee. Yahze sat in front with him. Ruiz and Heart sat in back. The tension in the car was palpable. When Snow tried to extract an explanation about what had happened with the knife, the shaman demurred.

"In good time you will understand. First I must see the place where the knife was used." It was a command, not a request. Snow decided to be patient.

It was late in the afternoon by the time they reached the Christensen farmhouse. Snow pulled into the driveway and parked.

"I'll see where Mr. Christensen is," Snow told the others. "We'll have to go out to the site in his pickup," he said, gesturing toward the vehicle parked alongside the house. The senior detective walked onto the porch and up to the front door. He rang the bell. No one responded. He knocked. Still no response. He tried the door, but it was locked. He noticed scratch marks around the lock, then walked along the porch and peered through the bay window into the living room. No one was there. No lights on. No sign of anyone. It was quiet. Too quiet. He walked to the end of the porch and peered around the side of the house. Then he saw something that sent adrenaline coursing through his body.

Andrea Ruiz had worked with Snow long enough to know the signs. She saw him lean over at the end of the porch, then straighten up quickly and reach inside his jacket. She knew he had unsnapped his holster. She quickly got out of the car. Taro Heart started to follow, but Ruiz stopped her.

"Stay here, please. Both of you, she said to Heart and Yahze. She joined Snow on the porch. "Problem?"

"Something's up. There a dead dog around the side of the house," he said. The truck's here. They've got six kids. It's too damned quiet." Ruiz unsnapped the holster of her sidearm, a 9mm Glock automatic, moving stealthily to keep the action from Yahze and Heart in the car. "Go around back that way," Snow said, pointing to the far side of the porch. I'll cut around the other way and have a look at that dog. Be careful."

The two split up and cautiously worked their way to the rear of the house. In the distance there was the echoing caw of a crow. Snow knelt next to the dead dog. It had been beheaded.

As she moved toward the rear of the house, Ruiz kept her body pressed against the cedar-shake siding. Her peripheral vision caught some movement above her. There were five or six buzzards circling.

Snow left the dog and chambered a round in his gun. He too had heard the buzzards.

When Ruiz came around the end of the house onto the patio, she froze in her tracks. She had never imagined she would ever confront such a sight.

She gasped. Then she shuddered and briefly closed her eyes, hoping the vision would go away. It did not. "Oh my dear God." Snow came over to where she was standing, his gun drawn.

"Jesus!" he muttered.

They both approached the awful scene before them. The entire Christensen family was dead, laid out naked on the flagstone patio at the rear of the house. Robert and Carole had been slaughtered, like the bulls, and were lying head to head at a forty-five degree angle. They formed the top of a pentagram. Each had body parts removed and displayed on their chests. The six children appeared to have been attacked by wild animals. Their naked bodies were scratched and torn. Chunks of flesh had been ripped out as though fed upon. The remains of the four oldest, three boys and a girl, formed the other points of the pentagram. The remains of the two youngest, girls two and four, were positioned in the center of their family. Each had a shiny golden object hung around her bloody neck. On closer inspection they appeared to be golden book pages or plates, covered with strange picture writing that the stunned detectives could not decipher. The little girls' eyes were open. Their expressions of horror and fear were unmistakable.

Moments after they discovered the murders, Jacob Yahze appeared beside the detectives, with Taro Heart behind him. He said he had been drawn to the scene by children's cries of anguish.

"These are very young and strong spirits," the shaman said sofly. "They do not know what has happened to the bodies they dwelt within."

Snow was in no mood for supernatural babble. He was about to cut Yahze off, but Ruiz put her hand on her partner's arm and gestured for him to wait. Then Yahze started to walk toward the crime scene.

"Hold on. You can't go there," Snow said sharply.

"Of course," Yahze said, stepping back. "Forgive me. It is just that the very young ones continue to cry for help." Yahze's words sent a shiver down Snow's spine. *Could this Navajo actually hear and see spirits or ghosts?* The harsh reality of the carnage that was spread out before him clicked back in. This case was going to be huge. Mystical speculation would fuel what he knew would be a media frenzy. But right now he had business to attend to and procedures to follow.

"Call this in, Andrea," he told his partner. Ruiz had recovered her equilibrium, but she knew that her life would never be the same. She focused on procedures and headed for the car. "And grab our evidence kit," he called after her. "Pull out some gloves, evidence bags, and the camera. I'm going to have a closer look at those gold things around the kids' necks."

"Take care, Detective Snow. They appear to be old and powerful holy objects," Yahze warned. "But I have never seen such things used this way before."

Snow recalled the weird incident with the knife that morning. He had written it off as hypnosis of some sort, or a magic trick. He wanted to believe anything but what he saw, or thought he saw. In any case, he felt the shaman was sincere in his beliefs, and he did have useful knowledge. Maybe he could be of some help.

"You know these things?"

"The ones I knew of were in old books with stories about holy men and their gods' laws."

"How were they normally used?"

"In holy rituals. But these have evil around them—like the stone knife, only stronger. It is defiant. It mocks us."

"Us?"

"Humans." The way Yahze said the word left no doubt that he believed something inhuman was responsible for the carnage laid out before them.

"You think this was done by some kind of animal?"

"I don't know what did such brutality—and to children." Yahze spoke with deep sadness in his voice. His use of the word "what," and not "who," was not lost on Snow.

CHAPTER NINE

MEDIA ZOO

Allen Weber heard the news on his car radio while driving to a client's office for a meeting. He immediately called his wife's cell phone. She was due to deliver their third child in five weeks and was at the obstetrician's office for a sonogram. He said nothing about the murders but told her that his afternoon appointment had been canceled so he was free to see the sonogram with her. Then he telephoned the obstetrician and explained what had happened. The doctor agreed to keep Susan isolated until Weber arrived.

When Weber walked into the examination room where Susan was waiting, ostensibly for her husband so they could see the sonogram together, she took one look at him and knew something was terribly wrong.

"The children! Are they all right?" He sat next to her and took her hand. He was shaking.

"Our kids are fine. But…" The words stuck in his throat. "Oh God, Susan." He paused. "It's Bob and Carole … the children. All the children … " He broke down and wept, burying his face in her swollen bosom. She gasped and held on to him tightly, then wailed mournfully, rocking back and forth. That brought the doctor and his nurse running. Susan had to be sedated for the sonogram, after which the doctor ordered bed rest and suggested that Weber hire a full-time nurse right away, until at least a week after the funerals.

As soon as the news hit the national airwaves, the entire country was in shock, and those in the Salt Lake area were frightened. There were maniacs on the loose! Where would they strike again? Was this a hate crime, aimed at Mormons?

The media quickly slipped into their usual feeding-frenzy mode and turned Salt Lake City into a television zoo. At the height of their mindless and endless coverage there were seventy-two TV and cable trucks beaming the same story. It was all filled with speculation, rumor, and spin that went up to satellites and down into the world's living rooms, bedrooms, and kitchens. The slaughter of the Christensen family was chopped into sound bites and buzzwords that turned the tragedy into an event.

"Mormon Massacre" was what CNN dubbed the event. Each story they broadcast was preceded by the title superimposed over a darkly lit photo of the great Mormon Tabernacle, accompanied by somber music so relentless that it grated on the ear.

The police withheld several facts about the murders, including the positioning of the bodies in an inverted pentagram, and the strange golden objects found hanging around the young girls' necks. Snow and Ruiz were initially the lead detectives on the case, but the commissioner of the SLCPD, under pressure from the mayor and the governor, demanded a task force.. This required that a captain or someone higher on the chain of command be in charge. As the publicity mounted, and before the Salt Lake police were able to organize their task force, the U.S. attorney general declared the case under federal jurisdiction, and the FBI moved in.

Because of their excellent education, high degree of ethical and moral training, and patriotism, Mormons account for an inordinately high percentage of FBI agents. And because every Mormon man must serve two years of missionary service overseas and speak foreign languages, the CIA also recruits heavily among them. When the public relations committee of The First Quorum of the Seventy, an important ruling body of the Mormon church, heard about the Christensen murders, they immediately contacted the Salt Lake City FBI office. The ritual killings, they concluded, struck at the heart of their beliefs. To the committee, this was a sign of hatred and prejudice rearing its ugly head once again. So it was that the political clout of the Church of Jesus Christ of Latter-day Saints caused the case to be federalized. To solidify the attorney general's move, coordinated leaks to selected media suggested that there were suspicions that these brutal murders might be a terrorist attack, and thus a threat to national security. This tack could also allow use of the so-called "terrorism laws" that many legislators deemed a direct threat to constitutional law and the guarantee of basic freedoms.

Of course, Detectives Snow and Ruiz thought differently. The Christensen murders were no foreign terrorist attack. And if Jacob Yahze was right, it involved something inhuman.

CHAPTER TEN

EVIDENCE

While the FBI and police organized their forces, a team of forensic specialists flew in from FBI headquarters in Washington, on one of the bureau's jets. The special agent in charge, Michael Benjamin, was a twenty-five-year veteran whose areas of expertise were hate crimes and ritual murder. He was made aware that there were elements within the Mormon church who were at odds with the current leadership. Oblique death threats had been made. On the chance that the crime had been committed by people who belonged to that church, the attorney general had hand-picked Benjamin for the job because he was not a Mormon.

Benjamin, by his own admission, was a nonpracticing Reform Jew. He was fifty-five, married, with three grown children and seven grandchildren. Because of the number of people murdered, and the bizarre arrangement of the bodies, Benjamin knew there had to be more than one perpetrator. The two major clues—the arrangement of the bodies as an upside-down pentagram, and the golden plates found hanging around the necks of the two youngest children—were clearly significant messages.

Benjamin debriefed Snow and Ruiz. They filled him in on the earlier animal slaughter at the Christensen farm and the details of their discovery of the murdered Christensen family. The two detectives had agreed not to relate either Jacob Yahze's announced contact with the spirits of the dead children or the knife episode. Benjamin then asked Yahze and Heart in for questioning. They related what they had seen but said nothing about the evil Yahze had sensed, nor his mention of the spirits of the children.

Benjamin also contacted an old local friend, Professor Lyman Goode, chairman of the Department of Anthropology at Brigham Young University. The professor examined the small gold plates found on the younger children. This was done at the Wallace F. Bennett Federal Building in Salt Lake City, where Benjamin's task force had set up shop.

"The cuneiform engraving is excellent and quite well preserved," Goode told Benjamin as he studied the first plate through a magnifying glass. Snow and Ruiz, who were present to answer any questions the professor might have, watched and listened intently. "I'd say these are Sumerian. Or perhaps Assyrian." He looked up at Benjamin. "You remember our discussion about Joseph Smith and how he described what he was instructed to do when the angel Moroni—"

Benjamin interrupted him. "I remember, Lyman. Now please translate the golden plates. That's why I called you. The Book of Mormon was written on plates like these, right?"

The professor smiled at his friend's impatience. "Yes. Of course, they were returned to the messenger after Joseph Smith had translated them and written it all down. They have never been seen since."

"Do you think these two plates are … ? I mean, did someone find them?"

"No. Revelation of such things would never come this way, with the murder of a family … of children. If you ask me, I think they are something else; something to taunt or confuse. Perhaps to point you in the wrong direction."

"Toward the Mormon church," Snow said. Professor Goode nodded. *First the Navajo, now the Mormons,* Snow thought.

"Nevertheless," Goode continued, "if you have no objection, I'd like a friend of mine to have a look at these. He lives in Israel, but I happen to know he is in New York now, at Columbia University, giving a lecture series on ancient Judea and Samaria. He's an expert in ancient tongues. He might be able to give us a translation and perhaps a clue as to where these originated."

CHAPTER ELEVEN

THE JERUSALEM CONNECTION

Three brutally emotional and heartbreaking days after the murders, Allen Weber was finally able to have a quiet, reflective moment. Susan had been given a mild sedative and was asleep. The full-time nurse, a pleasant grandmotherly woman in her mid-sixties, kept their two children occupied while his wife napped. The local police, acting on the request of Weber's boss, Dale Richards, had moved the media feeding frenzy back three blocks from the Weber residence.

Richards, part of the secret and powerful inner circle of the church, had made a promise to Weber. "The full power of our church will be directed toward solving this horrible crime. We have friends in high places, Allen, and I assure you that they will not rest until the killers are brought to justice."

Weber mixed a tall iced tea and stretched out on a chaise in the backyard. Though the weather was threatening rain, it was a mild day, and the fresh air felt good. He was emotionally drained, but he knew he must gather his strength for the funeral. The service would be held at the Tabernacle. Thousands were expected to attend. The bishop from Christensen's ward; a Melchizedek priest; the bishop for Utah; and Fairchild Ballard, the president of the church, were all going to speak. But the service had to wait until the coroner and the FBI forensics unit completed their examination of the bodies. It was hoped they might be released by week's end. They would then have to be prepared for viewing in the chapel prior to the service.

Weber closed his eyes and, as he had every time since hearing about the murders, tried to picture the Christensen family dead. Word had been leaked that the bodies were arranged in a ""ritual fashion." He remembered how his brother-in-law had described the way his slaughtered Black Angus bulls had been found. What had he said? *Their carcasses were arranged ritualistically, in the shape of an upside-down star— a pentagram.* Weber wondered whether the Christensen family had been positioned that way too. But his mind's eye could only picture the family alive and happy, especially the children. That image tore at him. His eyes filled, and tears rolled down his cheeks. He wiped them away with the back of his hand.

"Be strong," he said aloud.

Robert Christensen's voice came back to him. He recalled the conversation about Nicholas Perez luring contractors and equipment away for a purpose. Was there any validity to Robert's suspicions?

As the executor of the Christensen estate, Weber knew the farm would go to his wife. He suddenly felt an urge, and on the spur of the moment, he telephoned Detective Snow and told him he wanted to go out to the farm to begin an inventory. Snow cleared it with FBI Special Agent

Benjamin, who said that as it was still an active crime scene, the forensics team would supervise Weber's visit.

Laurie Kosloski, M.D., who had been an FBI agent for seven years, led Benjamin's forensic team on the Christensen murders. While the three other members of her team concentrated on the murder scene, buildings, and fields around the farmhouse, Kosloski zeroed in on the autopsy evidence developed by the Salt Lake City coroner, Dr. Abel Finkler. She was especially drawn to the wounds that had been so savagely inflicted on the victims. Finkler had identified two distinct types: razor-sharp slashes that cut deep and clean, and jagged rips and tears, as though someone had plucked out chunks of flesh, sinew, and even bone. They were similar to the wounds—initially thought to have been made by animals—that had been reported on Christensen's Black Angus bulls. She identified the number and variety of wounds to Benjamin, and they agreed that there had to be more than one perpetrator, probably several. Kosloski suggested that the killers might have used actual animal parts such as claws, fangs, and beaks as weapons. That led Benjamin to focus on ceremonial and hunting tools used by Native Americans. He knew that an ancient sacrificial stone knife been used on the dead bulls. Finally, the coroner had found a strange amulet inserted in the heart of Mark Christensen. These were strong clues that Benjamin vowed to explore aggressively.

The state trooper on duty at the farm's entrance had been apprised of Weber's visit. As Weber slowly drove in, the deserted farmhouse, shrouded in misty rain, seemed to punctuate the tragedy that had occurred there. This place, once filled with activity and the laughter of children, was now gray and still in the failing late-afternoon light. For Allen Weber, the scene was unbearably sad.

The FBI forensic team had finished its work in the house. They had been respectful. Things were neat and in place. Weber wandered from room to room, haunted by images and memories he was unable to shake. He tried to temper his emotions, remembering that he would have to be strong for Susan and the children. Egged on by unseen forces, his grief turned to anger. He silently swore an oath to avenge the brutal deaths of his brother-in-law's family.

The first place Weber decided to inventory was Robert Christensen's office. It was a small room off the kitchen, facing the rear, or north side, of the house. The air there was cool, so it had originally been used for vegetable storage. After their third child was born, the Christensens built an extension onto the house, expanding the kitchen and this room. Bob's eldest son, Mark, got his father interested in computer applications for farming and livestock management. Bob took to the new technology enthusiastically, converting the old vegetable pantry into a computerized office.

Weber started up the computer and searched the files until he found those relating to the proposed flood-control construction. Fax copies of the loan papers he had prepared were there, along with bids on the project from local contractors. Another folder held the bids from the Arizona contractors Bob had solicited after Perez hired away all of the local people. As Weber studied the files intensely, he did not hear Benjamin enter the room.

"Hello, Mr. Weber." The greeting startled him. "I'm Agent-in-Charge Benjamin." They shook hands. "Detective Snow said you might be out here today."

"Oh, yes. Hi."

Benjamin glanced at the computer.

"I'm just looking. I'm the executor and I uh … " Weber's voice trailed off.

"I know Mr. Christensen was your brother-in-law. It's a terrible thing. Terrible. My condolences." Weber nodded.

Benjamin's crime scene investigators, part of the forensic unit, had already gone through the computer files and programs, including all the documents Christensen thought he had deleted, not realizing that they just stay on the hard drive and can be accessed by a major tech person. "Have you found anything that might help us?" Benjamin asked.

"No. I haven't gotten to the, well, the personal things yet. I just… It's hard. It's the children…" Benjamin nodded sympathetically. He took a seat in the wicker chair facing the desk.

"Do you mind if I ask some questions?"

"Whatever I can do to help."

"Was Mr. Christensen a religious man?"

"He was active in our church. Attended regularly. Tithed. Yes, I'd say so."

"Do you know if he had any outside, uh… "Well, let me be direct. Was he interested in the occult?"

"Occult? You mean like ghosts and spirits?"

"Like that."

"No. Bob was a very steady guy.

"You're sure?"

"Yes. Family, farm, church—that was his life."

Benjamin reached into his pocket and took out a small plastic bag. He removed a small, shiny object and handed it to Weber. "We discovered this in, uh...among Mark Christensen's remains." He didn't let on that X-rays had revealed it buried in the young boy's heart.

Weber examined the object. It appeared to be a piece of jewelry, which the Christensens never wore. He looked closer. The piece was a silver dragon. One foreclaw, larger than the other, clutched an onyx. He thought he had once seen an object like this, only larger. He felt a chill, as a memory flooded back to him, wrapped in dread. Onyx was the symbol of the tribe of Joseph, one of the twelve tribes of ancient Israel. Although made of a different gemstone, the dragon was an exact replica of a much larger one he'd seen emblazoned on the sealed door of Satan's tomb in Xian, China, and on a ring worn by that same fallen archangel.

Allen Weber had performed his two years of Mormon missionary work in the Holy Land, helping the Church of Jesus Christ of Latter-day Saints to increase its presence there. Weber had learned Hebrew before leaving for Jerusalem, and while living there, he developed an interest in archeology. He had an affinity for languages and studied ancient Aramaic, impressing his teachers as well as the rabbis and scholars he met. The Mormons believe that at the time of the Babylonian capture of Jerusalem, about 600B.C., the Israelite tribe of Joseph, also known as the tribe of Efrayim or Manasheh, was commanded by God to immigrate to the New World to escape capture. He showed them how to build great ships. They set sail, landing somewhere in South America. The Mormons believe that all the North and South American Indians are direct descendants of that tribe, but over time, they lost their Judaism. Weber spent his spare time in Israel poring over ancient books and scrolls and visited several archeological sites. On one of those trips, at a dig near the Lebanese border, he met a couple, Michael and Anya Gross.

Anya was a Russian citizen and the daughter of Colonel Peter Ilyavich Somoroff (Ret.) of the KGB. The colonel had been instrumental in the hunt for, and eventual capture of, the fallen archangel Satan, now entombed in Xian, China. It was during that secret operation, which involved the KGB, the CIA, and Mossad, that Anya Somoroff, working with her father, met Michael Gross, a special Mossad agent. They fell in love and eventually married. This was before the breakup of the Soviet Union. They chose to make their home in Tel Aviv. Weber and the Grosses became good friends. Through them Weber met a small group of rabbis in Safed, Israel, who followed the teachings of the Rabbi David Ben Zimrah, a mystic. Those rabbis had been key players in the capture and imprisonment of the Red Devil, Shawtan—the Hebrew name for Satan. Two of the sect's members, Rabbi Chaim Malachi, now in Xian, and Rabbi Isadore Vogel, now in New York delivering lectures on ancient Judea and Samaria at New York University, were part of the multireligious group known as The Vigilant.

After returning to America, Weber made a point of keeping in touch with his Israeli friends. As he silently studied the amulet that Agent Benjamin had handed to him, and identified the dragon and the onyx, the jewel of the lost Tribe of Joseph, Weber knew that he must speak to Michael Gross in Israel as soon as possible.

The sun dipped behind the Wasatch Range as Nicholas Perez, Raymond Light, and Melvin approached the smooth, dome-shaped rock. The sandy soil that surrounded it faded from yellow to muddy brown in the failing light. Perez stopped at the side of the rock where it flattened and disappeared under the soil. He knelt, placed his hand on the rock, and made a fist, causing his ring to protrude. As he slid his hand down along the rock, the ring, a carved piece of solid onyx in which a dragon made of emeralds was imbedded, touched the soil and parted it. He bent and drove his arm into the ground up to his shoulder. Light and Plotter exchanged an excited glance as Perez stretched his arm even further down, groping for something.

"Ahhh," he sighed as he made contact. "Here it is." Perez strained for a moment as though he were lifting a heavy object through the sand. Something under the soil clicked. Perez quickly extracted his hand. He stepped back, signaling for his two companions to do the same. They obeyed instantly. The soil rapidly fell away from the rock, like quicksand down a sinkhole, revealing a flight of stone steps that led down under the rock.

"It has been a very long time," Perez said as he descended the steps. Light and Plotter followed eagerly as more of the sandy soil was loosened, exposing a golden door emblazoned with a sculpted bas-relief of an upside-down pentagram. In the center of the pentagram was a jade dragon whose eye was a brilliant ruby. Perez touched the emerald dragon on his ring to the ruby eye on the door. A shrill wail, like the cry of a raptor announcing its presence, emanated from behind the door. The ground beneath them shuddered, and then, with a hiss, like the fiery breath of a dragon, the great door opened inward.

"I am home," Nicholas Perez announced as he entered.

The domed rock was like the tip of a huge iceberg. A structure that extended several hundred feet underground contained a catacomb of interconnected passageways leading to six ornate chambers hewn out of the rock. Each chamber, lit by the wave of Perez's hand, served a special purpose. Some contained charms, implements, statuary, amulets, and a variety of weapons. Some of the chamber walls were covered with writing in Aramaic; others depicted fierce animals in vicious acts of bloodlust. There were libraries of ancient manuscripts and books, and sacrificial chambers that contained the rotting remains and bones of strange animals and giant humans.

Inside the dome, Nicholas Perez became a changed man. As he moved through the chambers, his five-foot three-inch frame seemed to grow with each step. His two servants, Light and Plotter, followed, filled with awe like eager children on Christmas Eve, anticipating what wonderful presents Santa Claus would bestow on them.

As they stepped into the main chamber of the tomb, the largest in the underground complex, Perez waved his hand again and it too lit up. The lighting, which glowed outward through the pale, opaque limestone walls, revealed that this chamber was a grand temple. The smooth golden-domed ceiling was thirty feet high at its apex. At the far end, a regal golden throne, swathed in forest green velvet and encrusted with emeralds, stood on a platform overlooking the chamber. Behind it, a carved upside-down pentagram of ebony framed the chair.

Perez walked solemnly to the throne, stepped onto the platform, and sat down. Light and Plotter fell to their knees and bowed, their heads pressed to the green marble floor.

Perez, their master, smiled. He extended his arms, which became two deadly, hooded serpents. Each reached out to the prostrate forms on the floor and caressed them. Light and Plotter undulated ecstatically, emitting sound of orgasmic pleasure. Satisfied, Perez withdrew his snake arms.

"Here is my throne," he proclaimed defiantly. "Here I am all powerful Belial, whom God cast out to favor the child Jesus!"

His body morphed into the great white puma that had seduced the Inca prince Yupanqui centuries ago. It roared, baring its razor-sharp claws and fangs. Light and Plotter cowered before the great cat as it gazed upon them. Then it slid off the throne and approached. The puma's thick black tongue licked Raymond Light's bowed head.

"Take form, my prince Beelzebub. You are my eyes from above." Raymond Light became a fierce raptor, the peregrine falcon.

Belial then licked Melvin Plotter's head. "And you, Prince Amaimon, are my bite." Plotter became a large, spotted hyena whose powerful jaws dripped yellow saliva. "He who cast me out gave me dominion over this place. Here, I am a god!" Belial proclaimed. The falcon screeched and the hyena screamed praise to their master. The great white puma roared in response.

High above the throne, in the dim light, the word "Yahweh," written in Hebrew, glowed bright for a moment, as if a great eye had opened to let in the light.

CHAPTER TWELVE

THE QUORUM OF THE TWELVE APOSTLES

That same evening, fifteen Caucasian men, all clean-cut and over fifty, met in an inner chamber of the great Mormon Tabernacle in Salt Lake City. They were The Quorum of the Twelve Apostles, the ruling body of the Church of Jesus Christ of Latter-day Saints, directly under the three presidents. They all wore conservative dark suits, white shirts, muted ties, and wingtip shoes. As they sat at the polished mahogany conference table, they might have been the senior executive committee of any large publicly traded corporation. But they were on a far different mission than any corporate board might consider. Three other men were present: President Jeremy Cabot, second counselor of the First Presidency, the third highest officer of the Mormon Church; Peter Horne, a senior bishop from Salt Lake City, and one of the more politically savvy men in the church; and Vernon Flood, a church employee, among whose duties as chief librarian was the safekeeping of sacred church writings and books, some of whose existence was secret even to The

Quorum of the Twelve Apostles. President Cabot called the meeting to order.

"We have an extremely serious and pressing problem to discuss this evening," he began somberly. "You all know of the tragic events at the Christensen farm. President Ballard has tasked me with overseeing our official response to this brutal act. We have taken the following steps." Cabot opened a folder on the table in front of him and consulted his notes. "We have arranged for the FBI to take control of the investigation. The case was federalized on our insistence that it be labeled a bias crime—a denial of civil rights. We also requested that Special Agent Michael Benjamin, who is Jewish and a good friend to our church, be put in charge. That has been done. We asked Agent Benjamin that certain facts about the murders be kept from the public. Some of these would have been treated that way as normal police procedure, but there were other facts that were... uh, shall we say, sensitive to our church doctrine."

"May we know what those facts are?" Bishop Horne asked.

"Yes, Peter. There were two golden plates found on the scene." Everyone in the room was stunned. A reference to golden plates meant only one thing to Mormons—they were connected to Joseph Smith, the founder of their church. These plates, which the angel Moroni presented to Joseph Smith to copy, became the Book of Mormon, the basis of the religion. "They are being analyzed by Professor Lyman Goode under Agent Benjamin's supervision."

"You said this Benjamin is Jewish?" Bishop Horne asked.

"That's correct, Peter. Since most of the local FBI agents are members of our church, we don't want the public to think that we have loaded the investigation, or that we are controlling it. You understand?" Horne nodded, but he was not happy.

"Special Agent Benjamin is sensitive to our needs," Jeremy Cabot said, "and a good friend of Professor Goode's. That's a big plus. In fact, he brought the professor into the case without our even suggesting it." Cabot turned his attention back to the Quorum. "What we have to decide this evening is to what extent we want to open our archives to the investigators."

Several of the men at the table exchanged worried looks. This was an extremely sensitive area for the church. Many at the table knew that the content of certain documents in the archives were religiously explosive. This was especially true in the area of what were called "mystical and supernatural events." That is what the Christensen murders appeared to convey. Kenneth Pace, a longtime member of the Quorum, spoke first.

"In this case, I don't buy into a supernatural event. I believe that someone is trying to stir up the old hatred and bigotry against us. And they are trying to scare us." Several of the Quorum nodded in agreement. "There is no need to use church secrets to add fuel to the fire."

Though many at the table seemed to be of the same mind, the Mormon church is not run as a democracy, nor by majority rule. The true power resides with the president, and everyone at the table knew that Jeremy Cabot was President Fairchild Ballard's man.

"A point well taken, Kenneth," Cabot answered respectfully. "Nevertheless, President Ballard feels we should be prepared, should the FBI be unable to identify and apprehend the perpetrators quickly. To that end, I have asked our chief librarian, Vernon Flood, to join us here today. Vernon is a trusted employee and devoted church member. I've asked him to gather a description of some of the materials that might be of use in this matter. Vernon?"

Flood, who had been sitting in one of the leather chairs that were lined up along one wall, stood and approached the table. He was a tall, thin, bookish man in his early forties who was bright, self-assured, and respectful of his superiors.

"Good evening, gentlemen," Flood began. His voice was deep and resonant, like an old-time radio announcer's. "The two avenues that I have been tasked to explore, namely, the golden plates and the use of the inverted pentagram, found at both murder scenes on the Christensen farm, are symbols well known to us. As far as the plates are concerned, we must assume that they are either forgeries or from ancient Assyrian books that were produced in this manner. But there is no way they can be the holy plates from which Joseph Smith translated and copied our sacred Book of Mormon, for, as we all know, those plates were returned to the angel Moroni when Joseph Smith completed his task. As far as the inverted pentagram is concerned, there is some controversy as to its place in our church. As you know, it has been used in the reconstruction of the Nauvoo Temple, and exists on no other temple. However, it has been used on the history museum across Temple Square from this great edifice. The research on how and why this symbol has now appeared is not yet clear, but one thing is certain: the upside-down star—the pentagram—has long been recognized as the symbol of Satan!"

As he addressed the Quorum of the Twelve Apostles, Vernon Flood knew that any direct threat from Satan against the Mormon church or, for that matter, any organization or individual, was impossible. Flood was a member of The Vigilant, and thus was aware of Satan's entombment in Xian, China.

CHAPTER THIRTEEN

SATAN'S TOMB

The gently sloping mound, covered with grass and wild berry bushes, rose out of the yellow clay soil on the plain below the Tsinling Shan Mountains. It was originally thought to be the site of the four-thousand-year-old tomb of the first emperor of the Zhou dynasty. As it was carefully explored and excavated, it was discovered not to be the emperor's tomb, but something even more extraordinary. Archeologists from Peking University consulted with government officials, who, in an unprecedented move, quietly invited Buddhist and Hindu scholars to the site. They, in turn, contacted the Vatican and a small sect of rabbis in Safed, Israel, to join them. These scholars agreed that what had been uncovered was the tomb, and potential prison, of Satan, one of the four fallen archangels, the major force of evil and darkness in the world.

Not long after Satan's capture in the Soviet Union, imprisonment in the tomb had been made possible by a dedicated group of men and women in the Soviet, American, and Israeli intelligence services and representatives of several religions—Taoist and Buddhist monks, Shiite and Sunni imams, rabbis, Catholic and Shinto priests, African healers, and Nestorian and Eastern Orthodox priests. This group came to call itself The Vigilant.

At any given time, at least two of The Vigilant were present in Xian, close to the tomb. Satan's two sub-princes, Asmodeus and Ariton, and many of his disciples were still at large and active in the world. Their top priorities were to free their master, Satan, and to ruin efforts at peace by fomenting discord, bigotry, and brutality among nations and religions. But if Satan were kept imprisoned in this tomb, the only place on Earth where this was possible, then he was powerless, and his followers vulnerable.

The other three fallen archangels, Belial, Leviathan, and Lucifer, were also at large somewhere in the world, wreaking their own particular brand of evil and fomenting chaos. So, in addition to guarding Satan's tomb, the work of The Vigilant was to seek out these three archangels and their tombs.

Not far from Satan's tomb, life-size and incredibly lifelike terra-cotta statues of warriors, many on horseback, had been discovered. As they were unearthed, they were left in place and studied. Some were eventually put on public display. An estimated six thousand of these statues were originally thought to be an army created to protect the entombed emperor. But their real purpose became known to The Vigilant and to the Chinese authorities assigned to the tomb.

On the day the Quorum of the Twelve Apostles met, a group of Austrian tourists was being guided through the public exhibit of the figures. Not far away, behind a temporary canvas wall, a group of archeologists was excavating several warrior statues. Two of those involved in the dig were Rabbi Chaim Malachi of the Rabbi David Ben Zimrah sect from Safed, Israel, and Father Colm McDonough, a Columban Catholic priest from Greystones, Ireland. Father McDonough was on leave from his work with indigenous peoples on the island of Borneo in Indonesia. Both were members of The Vigilant.

As the Chinese tour guide herded her Austrian charges onto their bus, she noted that one woman was missing.

"Has anyone seen Frau Waldheim?" she asked in perfect German.

"Yes, Ms. Chin," a rotund, gray-haired, rosy-cheeked woman answered, pointing toward the tomb. "She went that way." In the distance, Ms. Chin could see the woman running toward the distant mound. A surge of panic rippled down her spine. Guides had been warned by government officials of Shensi Province: "Never allow your charges to leave the group. Never allow anyone to approach the tomb!"

At the nearby dig, Rabbi Malachi felt a slight tremor of the earth. The others, with the exception of Father McDonough, thought it was a small earthquake, a common event in this part of China. But both men knew otherwise. They unobtrusively separated from the group. As they were about to exit through the rear doorway, the ground shook again. Off to their left, from a group of recently excavated terra-cotta warriors not yet studied or open to the public, an armored figure on horseback, holding a long pike, had come to life. The horse reared up, then leaped out of its place in the ranks. It galloped past the two men and through the doorway. As it raced toward the tomb, Malachi and McDonough followed. Ahead, in the field, they saw a woman running toward the tomb entrance. The warrior sat high in his saddle in hot pursuit. As he closed on the woman, he raised his pike to his shoulder. The woman looked back and saw him. Her arms transformed into two hoofed legs and her head into that of a large goat. She galloped toward the tomb with renewed effort and speed. The warrior extended his arm backward, and in one smooth and powerful motion hurled the deadly shaft. It found its mark in the small of the goat woman's back. She collapsed to the ground, bloodied and perfectly still. At the same time, the warrior and his horse, still on the run, turned back into terra-cotta, then crumbled to dust in the field. Rabbi Malachi and Father McDonough stopped, grasped each other's hands, and prayed together.

"He that dwelleth in the secret place of the most High shall abide under the shadow of the Almighty. I will say to the Lord, He is my refuge and my fortress—my God. In Him I will trust." As they prayed, the goat woman's corpse transformed back into a very dead Frau Waldheim as a slain evil spirit, placed there by Satan's sub-prince Asmodeus, departed her body and the Earth forever.

CHAPTER FOURTEEN

SUSPICIONS

After Special Agent Benjamin left, Weber worked silently at Robert Christensen's computer, continuing to look for clues that might shed light on the murders. He had discovered a flash drive in a pocket of Christensen's work clothes in the barn, but he chose not to tell Benjamin about it. When he accessed it, he found that it contained sketchy research on the Victory Development Corporation, Nicholas Perez's holding company. It also contained an edited genealogical report.

In April 1969, Perez arrived in Key West, Florida, as a seven-year-old Cuban immigrant on a boat with his parents, who were seeking political asylum. His mother was originally from Belarus, now an autonomous republic, but at the time part of the Soviet Union. His father was born and educated in Quito, Ecuador. Another file on the drive was a copy of a public record from the U.S. Immigration and Naturalization Service. It revealed that Perez's mother had been in Cuba as part of the Soviet diplomatic mission, working as a translator of Russian to Spanish. Perez's father was a civil engineer who had been hired by Castro's government to supervise work on an ambitious highway construction project. The two married in Cuba and later adopted Nicholas, whose birth records had been lost. To formalize the adoption, they had to become Cuban citizens. Specific reasons for their fleeing Cuba were not mentioned, other than they were granted asylum as "political refugees." Once they gained that status, the family moved to Los Angeles. There were no official records of either of Perez's parents' families in Belarus or Ecuador.

Weber found it strange that there were no records, since the Mormon church's genealogical archives, the source of Robert Christensen's research, are the most extensive and detailed in the world. Weber reflected on his conversation with Perez about how VDC and his brother-in-law might share local resources for their flood-control projects. Perez had been cordial but uncooperative. Christensen seemed to accept the reality of the situation and went to Phoenix to find a general contractor. But the date on the file indicated that that had occurred before Christensen put the information on the drive. If so, then why was he so interested in Perez's background?

Weber glanced at his watch. It was after midnight--seven a.m. in Tel Aviv. He had planned to call Michael Gross from the farm, where he would have privacy. But now, with the questions he had about Perez gnawing at him, he wondered whether the call might be premature. Was Christensen onto something about the man who owned the land next door? But then the sketch he had made of the dragon amulet after

Agent Benjamin left caught his eye. Weber reached for the phone.

Even half asleep, Michael Gross knew the ringing sound was not his alarm clock. As he grabbed the phone, Anya sat up in bed anxiously. A call this early in the morning usually meant trouble, especially now that Palestinian terrorists had once again begun suicide attacks on Israeli women and children.

"*Kan*?" Gross said curtly. (Hebrew for "yes.")

"Shalom, Michael. It's Allen Weber." Gross was confused, momentarily unable to place the voice or the name.

"*Ma*?" Then the cobwebs cleared. He realized the person on the other end was speaking English. "I mean what. Who is this?"

"Allen Weber. From America."

"Weber?"

"The Mormon. The one you called the reluctant missionary."

Gross remembered Weber with relief. No bombing. No dead women and children.

"Ah, yes. Weber. Allen. Yes. The Aramaic scholar and archeologist. How are you, my missionary friend? Are you in Israel?"

"No, Michael. I'm in Salt Lake City."

Gross glanced at the clock radio. It was 7:05 a.m. Just after midnight in Salt Lake City. "What is wrong, Allen?" Gross's tone of voice changed. He looked at Anya and signaled for her to get on the extension phone in the den. She hurriedly got out of bed.

"You can tell, huh?" Weber said softly.

"Don't you remember? It is my job to tell," Gross said lightly.

"I do. Well…" he paused. "I've got a problem here and I think it might have something to do with things I learned in Safed."

"You mean from the Ben Zimrah rabbis?"

"Yes. About Satan and the Xian tomb."

"Are you on a cell phone?" Gross asked.

"No." Weber understood Gross's concern. *He wondered fleetingly whether the phone on the farm had been tapped, but he dismissed the thought. There was no reason for the FBI to do that. No one lived there anymore.*

"Well, Allen, as far as I know, that, uh, that thing is still where it belongs."

"Good. But something has happened here. In Utah. Something terrible and strange. There are symbols and things that fit a similar pattern." Weber knew he was being vague, but he didn't have proof or a connection that he knew the rabbis in Safed would demand. Still, something deep inside, a feeling he could not suppress, had urged him to make this call. He went ahead and related what had happened on the Christensen farm.

The information disturbed Michael and Anya Gross. They extended their condolences, but their thoughts focused on the possibility of a battle ahead. They knew from the body count of Israelis murdered by Islamic terrorists that entombing Satan had not put an end to that kind of evil in the world. Satan was but one of the fallen archangels banished to an earthly existence.

Then Weber described the amulet, the familiar dragon clutching a stone.

"What kind of stone is in the amulet?" Anya asked.

"I don't know the word in Hebrew, but here we call it onyx." An image suddenly popped into Weber's head. "It was just like one of the twelve stones in the Breastplate of Aaron that Rabbi Malachi showed me in Safed. He called it onyx."

"You are sure?" Michael asked.

"Yes."

"That is the jewel of the tribe of Joseph."

"Yes, Michael. It was onyx. You know that the tribe of Joseph is very important to us Mormons. The Book of Mormon tells us that they were the Lamanites, the remnants of the House of Israel that God commanded to go to the New World."

"The peoples you now call Native Americans, right?" Michael Gross asked.

"Yes. We believe the indigenous peoples of the Americas are the descendants of the tribe of Joseph—the Lamanites."

It was then that Michael Gross knew he would be making a trip to Safed that very day. And while he contemplated that trip, Weber knew he would be paying a visit to the great Mormon Tabernacle downtown.

After their meeting with the Quorum of the Twelve Apostles, Bishop Horne spoke with Jeremy Cabot privately in Cabot's office.

"I'd like to help in this investigation," he told Cabot. "The Christensens were in my ward. We were close friends."

"Yes, of course," Cabot answered. "You should coordinate with Vernon Flood. He will report directly to me."

Bishop Horne then went directly to Flood's office to advise him of his conversation with President Cabot.

"I want to be kept informed of every step of your investigation," Horne told Flood. "If you need to see anyone in my ward, go through me."

Horne's request was more like a command. His tone of voice made Flood uneasy, but he maintained his obsequious demeanor. He had risen to his very sensitive position in the church by understanding that when powerful people thought you were suitably deferential, they tended to drop their guard. This technique had allowed Vernon Flood to gather information that could be of value to The Vigilant.

There were also some strange circumstances in Bishop Horne's background that made Flood wonder just how devoted a Mormon the man was. Flood maintained a quid pro quo relationship with a highly placed contact in the Justice Department and thus knew that Horne was a silent partner is several real estate deals on Native American lands—deals that were under investigation by the federal government. Nothing in church law forbade business and commerce, as long as it was honest and the church received its share via tithing. In fact, many bishops were appointed after having successful business careers. Still, Horne's dealings appeared not to have been aboveboard.

"Of course, sir," Flood told Horne. "I would never think to do otherwise," he said while making a mental note to keep a watchful eye on this nosy bishop who had insinuated himself into the church's investigation of the murders.

Bishop Horne, satisfied that this milquetoast of a librarian was under his control, bade him good-bye.

CHAPTER FIFTEEN

FUNERAL AND FARM

The service for the Christensen family was one of the largest, and saddest, ever seen in the great Mormon Tabernacle. The church's top leadership attended, including President Fairchild Ballard, President Sheldon Cook, First Counselor, President Jeremy Cabot, Second Counselor, and the Quorum of the Twelve Apostles. Over a thousand of the faithful filled the Tabernacle, while another five thousand stood silently outside. Six caskets, including two heartbreakingly small ones for the youngest Christensen girls, were lined up below the pulpit. They were all covered with white lilies. Behind the pulpit platform, the famed Mormon Tabernacle Choir raised their voices in praise of God. Bishop Peter Horne eulogized the Christensen family as one, pointing out their devotion to their church and their community. President Fairchild Ballard spoke eloquently of the Christensens as a model Mormon family, and vowed, "The considerable resources of the church will be used to apprehend those who committed this heinous act."

The Webers, being the Christensens' only close relatives, sat prominently on the pulpit platform. Throughout the service, as each speaker finished, he came over to the Webers to offer his condolences. President Ballard shook Allen Weber's hand, then bent close and asked him to call his office to make an appointment.

"We will take care of things for you, Allen," he said somberly.

Against her doctor's advice, Susan Weber had insisted on attending the funeral. Their parents had passed on, and Robert had been her only sibling. She was calm during the service, but at the internment, when the tiny caskets holding the remains of her two nieces were lowered into the ground side by side, she emitted a wail of grief that echoed throughout the cemetery. Then she collapsed.

The funeral director had the foresight to have an ambulance standing by. Susan Weber was rushed to the nearest hospital. Allen Weber went with her, leaving their two children—Michael, age seven, and David, age nine—in the care of his sister, Grace Weber Miller, and her husband, Ronald. Susan regained consciousness in the ambulance, but her doctor insisted she remain in the hospital overnight.

Bishop Horne visited the hospital later that evening. He expressed his concern and offered his offices for any spiritual needs the family might have. Then he asked what plans Weber had for the farm. At first Weber thought nothing of it—just an innocent question from a man of the cloth trying to be helpful.

"I really don't know, Bishop," Weber told him.

"It seems a burden you should not have to carry, Allen," Horne responded. "What I mean is, well, you're not a farmer, and that farm is a prime piece of land. It will fetch a nice price."

"I honestly haven't given it much thought," Weber told him, wondering why the bishop seemed to be pressing him about the farm.

"Well, I was just wondering. I mean, it must be hard for you to go there, to see where they were all, you know … where it happened."

"It is very hard, Bishop, but I can manage. After all, we know they have gone to a great reward, haven't they?"

"Of course, Allen, of course." Horne glanced at his watch. "Well, I've got to be going. Just remember, my door is always open." He extended his hand.

Weber shook it. "Good-bye, Bishop Horne. Thank you for coming by."

"Of course." Horne hesitated for a moment as he held Weber's hand. He seemed to be gathering his thoughts. Then he smiled. "And when the time comes to sell the farm, please let me know. I have someone in mind who is very interested. I'm certain he would make you an extremely attractive offer."

Weber was now more than curious at Horne's pressing him on the farm, acting more like a real estate agent than a pastor. "And who might that be?" Weber asked him.

"Oh, he's a very well-known businessman in the area. Nicholas Perez. Perhaps you've heard of him. He owns the adjacent land."

"I think I've heard his name mentioned." Weber suddenly became very wary. He wondered whether Horne knew about his conversation with Perez regarding the local contractors and construction equipment he had taken away from Robert Christensen. "Is Mr. Perez a friend of yours?"

"Well, I know him. He's not a member of the church, but he has been generous to our youth programs and homeless shelters." His quick answer sounded defensive to Allen. It was something to wonder about. But he set that aside. His immediate concern was for Susan's well-being.

"Should Susan want to sell the farm, I'll keep that in mind, Bishop Horne. Thank you."

As the bishop walked toward the elevators, Detective Ruiz passed him, coming the other way. Weber recognized her face from the television coverage.

"Hello, Mr. Weber," the young detective said softly. "I'm Detective Andrea Ruiz." She showed him her gold shield. "How is your wife doing?"

"She's okay, thanks."

"Look, Mr. Weber. If you've got a few minutes... I know this is a bad time for you, but I have some important questions, if you don't mind."

"No. That's fine."

"I'm terribly sorry for your loss." Ruiz was sympathetic, but she also had a job to do. Weber appreciated her position.

"Would you like to get a cup of coffee?" he asked. "There's a cafeteria downstairs."

"A soft drink. No caffeine. I'm a Mormon," she told him, hoping to make him more comfortable with her.

"Give me a minute," Weber told her. He walked back to Susan's room and looked in. She was asleep. The full-time private-duty nurse checked Susan's IV. Then she stepped outside of the room with him.

"She's resting quite comfortably, Mr. Weber. The doctor prescribed a mild sedative."

"I'm going down to the cafeteria for a few minutes."

"I think she may just sleep through the night."

"Well, I'll be back in a while," he told the nurse.

"Not to worry. Your wife is in good hands." Weber was certain of that. From the moment she came on the job, this nurse, a serious African-American woman over six feet tall, had taken charge.

As they waited for the elevator, a man in a white doctor's coat with a hospital ID observed Weber and Ruiz. He was Jim Swain, Perez's Paronto henchman and spy. When the elevator arrived, Ruiz and Weber got in. Once the doors had closed, Swain walked down the hall toward Susan Weber's room. His mission was to keep the pressure on these new owners of the Christensen farm until they got the message to sell.

Ruiz and Weber took their soft drinks to a table in the far corner of the cafeteria. Ruiz, who had been acting as a liaison with the FBI task force, had been told by Special Agent Benjamin that Allen Weber had been out to the farm and had used Christensen's computer. She pretended that this visit with Weber was a follow-up to the interview Benjamin had with him at the farm.

"Did the computer contain anything that might be of interest to us?" Ruiz asked. It was late afternoon and visiting hours were ending, so aside from a few nurses and interns on break, the cafeteria was quiet.

"Not really. Mostly stuff about farm operations. Bob was into some management programs."

"Anything else that was special? Different?"

"No." The material about Perez that he'd found on the flash drive crossed his mind. "He had some interest in his neighbor, Nicholas Perez..." His voice trailed off as he gazed out the window. A strong breeze rattled the leaves on a stand of silver birches, causing them to shimmer in the fading sunlight. A moment of melancholy fatigue from the day's events caught up with him.

"What kind of interest, Mr. Weber?"

He turned back to her. *She's pretty,* he thought to himself. *Nice to look at such beauty in this lousy, violent world.* He took a deep breath.

"It seems the man Perez had wooed away all of Bob's contractors and laborers. I had arranged a loan for Bob to do some flood-control construction on the farm." He wondered whether he was being unfair to Perez, involving him in the case by telling the police this. But the bishop's mention of Perez made him go on. "I work for Desert Management as a loan officer. But it seems this guy Perez had a big project of his own. Bob was quite annoyed, as you can imagine."

"Annoyed how?" Ruiz was interested but kept calm.

"My brother-in-law had to go out of state for help. Cost more time and money. Anyway, Bob did some research on the man. Background stuff, genealogy, stuff like that. I can't imagine why."

"Do you know Perez?"

"I spoke to him once about sharing the equipment. He was inflexible. A hard-nosed businessman. That's all."

Ruiz was a good detective. She heard something in Weber's voice that didn't ring true. "Are you sure that's all?" He looked her squarely in the eye for a long moment and decided to trust her.

"Actually, no. I'm not sure. Bob wasn't one to waste his time. And then earlier today, one of the church elders, Bishop Horne—he's the bishop of Bob's ward—came to the hospital." Weber paused as he considered that he was about to involve Bishop Horne in the investigation. Maybe he had been mistaken about the reason the bishop insisted on his selling the farm to Perez. "He said it was a pastoral visit," Weber continued, "but frankly, all he seemed interested in was what I was going to do with the farm."

"Mr. Christensen left the farm to you?"

"To my wife. I'm the executor." Ruiz nodded. "I told him I didn't know what we'd do with it, and he kept bringing up this Nicholas Perez and how he might be interested. It seems he owns the land next to the farm."

Ruiz felt a surge of excitement. "Perez wants to buy the farm?"

"That's what the bishop said."

"Okay. I'll look into it."

"Look, Detective, I don't want to make trouble for anyone—certainly not the bishop. Bob was under a lot of stress and maybe he was clutching at straws." Ruiz studied Weber for a moment. She realized that he had shared a sensitive confidence with her, that he trusted her.

"I'll be discreet. I don't want to get a bishop involved unnecessarily either." She decided it was time to pursue the matter that had really brought her to the hospital. "Mr. Weber, there are two people I'd like you to meet. They are Navajo. They were with Detective Snow and me at the farm when we found the family. I think they might be helpful to the case. They'd like to visit the farm again. I'd like to do that without the FBI getting involved." This was the first inside information Weber had heard about the investigation.

"I have access to the farm," he said, intrigued. His frustration and anger about the murders began to ebb. He felt he was doing something to find the killers. "When would you want to go?"

"How about this evening? After visiting hours, of course."

CHAPTER SIXTEEN

A PLACE OF EVIL

Rabbi Isadore Vogel appreciated the moist hot towel that the flight attendant offered to him fifteen minutes before landing. It had been a long trip, flying to Chicago from Newark, waiting three hours there for a flight to Salt Lake City, only to be delayed another two hours because of a security breach. "These terrorists give me no rest," he muttered to himself when the reason for delay was announced.

Vogel had finished his last lecture yesterday afternoon, and the faculty at NYU had given him a farewell party that went on into the wee hours. He was tired. As he rubbed the towel on his face, the warm moisture evaporated from his skin. It cooled and refreshed him. He mentally played back the conversation he had had two days earlier with his old friend, Professor Lyman Goode, regarding the golden plates found hanging from the necks of those poor murdered children.

The use of the plates, a strong symbol to the Mormon faithful, and the manner in which the family was ritualistically murdered, along with the inclusion of the inverted pentagram in the picture, troubled Vogel. Although there were satanic cults and copycat killers in this troubled world, his experience told him that murder committed with such viciousness portended great evil, and he knew about evil having been involved with Satan's capture in the old Soviet Union. Rabbi Isadore Vogel was a member of The Vigilant.

While Vogel's flight banked for its final approach into Salt Lake City International Airport, Raymond Light escorted Jim Swain into Nicholas Perez's private office. The sun had nearly set. The heavy drapes were drawn shut. The room was dark and cold.

"Did you see her?" Perez asked the nervous Paronto.

"Yes, sir. But there was a private nurse in the room. Then a doctor went in. She has constant attention. I couldn't get close. Too busy. Too many people."

"Yes. Of course. People." Perez's deep voice had a cutting sarcasm to it. "How long will she be there?"

"Overnight. It was just a fainting spell, they said."

"And Weber?"

"He saw the bishop. And then that half-breed cop, Ruiz."

"She was there? Not the FBI?"

"Yes, sir. She was alone. I tried to get close enough to hear what they were talking about, but then he went to the room. I heard him tell the nurse he was going to the cafeteria. Then he went to the elevator, and I thought it would be a good opportunity to ..."

"I understand. Where are they now?"

"After I saw that someone would always be in the room—the nurse and doctors—I went downstairs to the cafeteria. But they were gone."

"Left the hospital?"

"I checked the lobby, then the parking lot. Weber's Jeep was gone."

Perez shifted uncomfortably in his black leather chair. He had felt something strange for a while now—the sensation of a dangerous presence. It pressed down on his chest like a heavy weight. It brought forth distant, unpleasant memories.

"Go to the hospital and finish your work," Perez commanded. "Do it now!" He turned to Raymond Light. "Go with him. Make sure that no one interferes."

Professor Goode and Agent Benjamin met Isadore Vogel at baggage claim. The rabbi and the professor embraced warmly, with the Russian custom of kisses on the cheeks. When they got to Benjamin's car, the FBI agent handed the amulet, still sealed in its evidence bag, to Rabbi Vogel.

"May I touch it?" Vogel asked. Benjamin broke the bag's seal and handed it back to him. Vogel slid the amulet out of the bag onto his palm. He immediately shuddered from a cold, sickening sensation deep in the pit of his stomach. He quickly put the amulet back in the bag and handed it to Benjamin. "You found this in the flesh," the rabbi said quietly. Not a question. A fact.

"How did you know that?" Benjamin asked.

"Best just to believe that I know these things," Rabbi Vogel insisted. "Where?"

"In the boy's heart."

"The heart of a child?"

"A teenage boy."

Vogel sighed deeply and nodded. "I want to see where it happened."

"It's not far," Goode said. "We can get you settled at the hotel and have a look at the plates. Then we can go to—" Vogel raised his hand to interrupt the professor.

"That can wait. Now it is urgent that I see this place. Afterwards it is possible that I will need to make a secure telephone call to Israel."

Weber drove his Jeep Cherokee. Detective Ruiz sat next to him. Taro Heart and Jacob Yahze were in the back seat. They had talked little during the ride to the farm, except to convey their condolences and their concern for Susan. Yahze's voice was soothing, putting Weber at ease. The shaman spoke slowly and deliberately, assuring Weber that the Navajo had nothing to do with the Christensen murders.

"This evil brutality is not something that native peoples do. Even in battle, for most tribes, touching your enemy was more important than killing him. But once, some time ago, when I was with the Haida people in British Columbia, there was a white man who claimed to be a conservationist. He said the Haida had no right to hunt whales even though the government allowed it once a year for religious purposes. He shot a hunting party of nine and gutted them the way the Haida prepared their kill of the whale. He was insane."

At the farm's gate, Weber stopped and got out. The guard had been removed and the only vestige was a posted notice that it was an active crime scene. He unlocked the thick Master lock and slipped the chain open. Then he got back in the Jeep and drove through the gate. Ruiz got out and closed it but left the lock open on the chain.

Before they reached the farmhouse, Yahze sat up abruptly. "Please stop!" Weber stepped on the brake. Yahze opened his door and got out. The sun had set behind the Wasatch Range, but the cloudless sky was still bright orange with the golden light of a late spring evening as the summer solstice approached. Yahze faced east. He began to chant softly and then got back in the car. He stopped chanting for a moment and whispered something to Taro Heart in Navajo. Then he continued the chant.

"He asks that you drive to the east. To a large domed rock," Heart said.

"I don't know any … Hey, wait a minute," Weber said. "Bob mentioned something about a rock. It was at edge of the property, adjacent to his flooded fields. He said water had eroded some of it. But it's not on his land."

"Is it on Perez's property?" Ruiz asked.

"Yes, I think so," Heart replied.

Yahze stopped chanting and pointed to the east. "That way, Mr. Weber. There is a road."

Agent Benjamin was surprised to see that the lock at the gate was open. He reflexively checked his shoulder holster, knowing the Ruger 9mm was loaded, along with three nine-round speed-load clips. He opened the gate and drove through, saying nothing about the lock to Professor Goode and Rabbi Vogel. As they approached the farmhouse Vogel, like Yahze, turned to the east. He frowned. Something disturbed him, and it continued to bother him as they got out of the car and Benjamin fumbled for the key to the farmhouse. As Goode and Vogel waited, the rabbi was drawn to the end of the porch.

"This way, Rabbi," Benjamin said as he opened the door. Vogel stared off to the east. "Rabbi Vogel?"

"What is this way?" he asked the FBI agent, pointing east.

"The farm. Fields. Grazing land."

"May we go there?"

"I don't know if there is a road. My car may not—"

Vogel cut him off. "There is a road. Your car will pass. And we must go now!"

The domed rock was on the other side of a newly erected chain-link fence. Razor wire sat atop it, tight, like huge metal hair curlers. Jacob Yahze, still chanting softly, stared at the rock. The three others stood behind him, waiting for an explanation for what brought the medicine man to this place. Ruiz turned and saw the headlights of a car approaching. Although it was still dusk, and the light adequate, Benjamin had turned them on for better visibility in case there were rocks or ruts to avoid on the dirt road that led to the fields.

"We've got company," Ruiz announced. Heart and Weber turned in the direction of the oncoming car. Yahze continued to stare at the rock as though in a trance.

"This place is evil," he said, repeating the same words he had uttered when he had approached the fence.

"Someone is coming, Uncle Jacob," Heart told the shaman. Fixated on the domed rock, he did not respond.

Detective Ruiz unsnapped the leather guard on her holster and walked up from the fence to meet the approaching car. In the dim light she saw that the driver was Agent Benjamin. Her heart sank. He wasn't going to be happy that she was out here without his permission. But before the two could speak, Rabbi Vogel emerged from the backseat of Benjamin's car and rushed toward the fence where Yahze stood.

Yahze turned as Rabbi Vogel approached. The men gazed into each other's eyes and connected immediately.

"There is great evil here," the medicine man said.

"Yes," the rabbi answered. "I know it. I have seen it before." He looked past the rock to a copse of trees two hundred yards away. It was the same place from which Swain had tried to shoot Christensen. "And we are being watched."

Above, hidden behind the trees, two Paronto, Alex Cherry and John Macack, crouched lower to hide from the two sets of eyes that they felt burning into them from below.

CHAPTER SEVENTEEN

HOSPITAL VISITORS

Swain parked his pickup on a dark side street three blocks from the hospital. Light handed him a sharp stone knife, similar to the one used to kill the Angus bulls on the Christensen farm.

"Stone won't trip the metal detectors," Light told the Paronto servitor. "Be sure that you bury it deep in her womb, and twist." They got out of the truck, donned white lab coats over their street clothes, and stuffed latex gloves in their pockets. The finishing touch was to clip on false hospital IDs. Swain locked the pickup, and he and Light walked toward the hospital.

Alone in his office, Perez grew more uneasy. He rose from his chair and paced back and forth like a caged animal. The rims of his dark eyes glowed with a reddish hue. His breathing was rapid and shallow.

After knocking gently on the door, Raymond Light entered the dimly lit hospital room. The private-duty nurse was seated in a chair, knitting. She put her wool and needles aside and got up as Raymond Light, with a stethoscope draped around his neck, took Susan Weber's chart from the foot of the bed and examined it.

"She's resting comfortably, doctor," she said as she approached Light, and stopped behind him. She was six inches taller than he was. He put the chart down on the foot of the bed and spun around to face the nurse. He lashed out with his right hand, which had become the claw of a peregrine falcon. Caught unawares, the nurse was frozen momentarily, giving Light the advantage. His talons ripped across her exposed throat, severing the carotid artery and trachea. Blood spurted from her neck. She tried to scream, but the only sound was the gurgling of blood pouring into her lungs. She was a strong woman, and though in shock, was able to reach out and grab Light by the throat. Surprised by her strength, he fell backward onto the floor. She held on and fell on top of him. But her strength was waning rapidly. Her grip relaxed as she slipped toward death. Light returned to human form, extricated himself, and quickly checked to see if the ruckus had awakened Susan Weber. Sedated, she was still asleep. Light stood over the dying nurse and stepped on her throat, crushing it. He dragged her back to the chair and propped her up so that she appeared to be asleep. Then he stepped outside the room and signaled to Swain, who was waiting at the end of the corridor.

Susan Weber slowly and carefully opened her eyes as Raymond Light dragged the nurse to the chair. She had heard the struggle. At first she thought it was a dream, but when they fell to the floor, their bodies had bumped into her bed, shaking it. That was no dream. Terrified, she had kept her eyes closed, feigning sleep, and remained still. She heard the attacker drag the poor woman back to the chair and leave the room. At that moment she pushed the nurse call button that was pinned to the sheet near her left hand. It sent a signal to the nurses' station, and opened a two-way intercom. She held on to the call button and kept pumping it with her thumb.

Seeing Light's signal that all was okay, Swain walked rapidly to Susan Weber's room. He opened the door and gripped the stone knife tightly in his right hand. In the dim light he was surprised to see the woman sitting up in bed. Then she screamed at the top of her lungs. That shocked Swain and, for a moment, confused him and froze him in place.

Out in the hallway, Light heard the scream and thought that Swain had made a noisy kill. He cursed the Paronto idiot. Then there was another louder scream that told him the attempt had gone wrong. Light ran to the nearest window and dove out. He transformed himself back into the peregrine falcon and soared off into the night sky.

At the nurses' station, the nurse on duty yelled over the intercom, "What the hell's going on there?"

"He's going to kill me!" Susan Weber screamed back. "For God's sake, help me!"

Swain made a move toward the bed. He raised the knife menacingly. "This is for you, Mormon bitch."

Susan gathered her strength and squirmed out of bed, dragging the attached monitor wires and IV stand across the floor, away from Swain. She screamed again. "Help!"

"Security is on the way, Mrs. Weber," the nurse yelled. Then a man's voice came over the intercom: "And I am armed."

At the sound of the threatening male voice, Swain panicked. As he ran out into the hallway he saw two security guards rushing toward him with guns drawn. He turned the other way and collided with two nurses on their way to the room. The stone knife, which Swain had slipped into his belt, twisted and plunged into his abdomen. It sliced an artery. He fell to the floor, twisting in agony as his blood spurted out like a geyser. He moaned, clutching at the knife and pulling it out. It clattered across the white tile floor, leaving a crimson trail of blood. One nurse pinned him down while the other tried to stanch the bleeding, which had now increased. Swain couldn't have had this accident in a better place. Within moments he was in the bed of a nearby room while two surgical residents and four nurses, surrounded by crash carts and other medical personnel and paraphernalia, fought to save his life.

Susan Weber had gone into shock. She was shaking uncontrollably. A code blue was called and the OB/GYN resident paged. She went into labor. The chief resident arrived and assessed her condition.

"She stays here until the OB/GYN sees her." He saw that in the struggle she had disconnected her vitals hookup and IV. "Get her hooked up again." He glanced over at a security guard who was standing in the doorway. "Did anyone call the police?" The guard reached for his radio.

Susan moaned and cried at each contraction. "My baby. My baby. Please save my baby."

"Get this room cleaned up and ready for a delivery," the chief resident barked to the two interns and three nurses on the code blue team. And someone call her doctor."

The OB/GYN on duty arrived and was briefed by the resident. She examined Susan and concluded that the trauma had threatened her pregnancy.

"Let's get her upstairs. No sedation yet. I want a monitor on her belly, STAT. Where's the sonogram cart?"

A nurse headed for the door. "I'm on it."

The OB/GYN turned her attention back to Susan Weber as she had another contraction. She examined her to see how far she had dilated. As she did, she noticed blood starting to ooze from her vagina. "Okay people, no time for tests. Let's get this bed up to surgery."

Fifteen minutes later the trauma team had Swain stabilized. He was in critical condition. In an operating room three floors above, a Caesarean section was being performed on Susan Weber.

CHAPTER EIGHTEEN

ANGER GROWS

While Rabbi Vogel and Jacob Yahze were observing the domed rock, Nicholas Perez experienced an uneasy feeling. It abated when Raymond Light killed the nurse, replaced by a pleasing sensation that coursed through his body. But when his servitor, Jim Swain, inadvertently stabbed himself with the stone sacrificial knife, Perez shuddered in pain. His body experienced any attack on one of his disciples or servants. The uneasy feeling, coupled with the physical sensations, were distracting him from his plans for the nuclear waste material that would soon be coming from the DOE to his pilot disposal facility.

The peregrine falcon returned to Victory Development Corporation's offices and resumed the form of Raymond Light. His report spurred Perez to action. They went to his office. A false wall behind his desk slid open to reveal a large inverted pentagram. Each point glowed with an eerie light. They represented his five disciples. The top two points were his sub-princes, Asmodeus and Beelzebub. The three lower points were his current disciples, the three DOE executives, Bertha Smalls, Lincoln Foster, and William Claremont. Inside the pentagram, at the base of the star points, were dimmer lights indicating Belial's current servitors: Bishop Horne, and the Paronto—Jim Swain, Alex Cherry, and John Macack. Swain's light was flickering, dimmer than the rest.

"The Paronto fool is dying," Perez told Light. "Now that we have opened my sacred place, we will take care of such matters ourselves." The night buzzer rang. Light turned on the front-door video screen. Alex Cherry and John Macack were at the door. "Let them in," Perez said coldly. A few moments later, the two Paronto were on their knees.

Nicholas Perez paced back and forth in front of them, in a rage. "You should have killed them all," he roared. His open mouth showed bared yellow fangs. His dark hair lengthened and took on the sheen of a puma. "How dare you allow them to come so close to my dwelling place!" His eyes glowed red. "You are not servants of Belial. You are cowards!" He pointed at them. An unseen force drove them to lie prone on the floor, shaking uncontrollably as Perez sent searing pain through their bodies. "You are dung. Human scum." He turned away, disgusted. "Get up, you sniveling animals." The two Paronto struggled unsteadily to their feet.

"We are sorry, master. They saw us," Cherry said. He cast his eyes downward, afraid to look at Perez.

"The two by the fence," Macack continued. "They touched us. I don't know how, but we felt it. It burned."

Perez narrowed his gaze at the two men. "It burned?" He was very interested. "Who were they, these two men?"

"One was a stranger. He came with the FBI agent," Macack told Perez.

"I am sure the other was a medicine man," Cherry said, hoping the information might placate his master. A Navajo, I think."

"Think? You do not think. You obey. Now listen to me carefully. Go and guard my throne—night and day. No one must come near. No one must enter. No one! If you fail me again, you will die in unimaginable pain and agony."

CHAPTER NINETEEN

THE FALLEN ARCHANGELS

The group drove downtown in two cars from the Christensen farm to the FBI's command center. Jacob Yahze and Rabbi Vogel went in Agent Benjamin's car with Professor Goode. They talked about the ritual aspects of the Christensen murders and what the amulet and golden plates might signify. The rabbi struggled with how much he should reveal about the amulet and what he sensed emanating from the domed rock.

"Who do you think those men were who were watching us?" Vogel asked Yahze.

"We were being watched?" Goode asked.

"Yes. From some trees on a rise above the rock," Yahze told him. "I am not sure who they were, but I believe they were there guarding."

"Guarding what?" Goode asked, sensing that Yahze and Vogel knew more than they were revealing.

Vogel smiled. "That, professor, is what we must find out."

Andrea Ruiz and Taro Heart drove with Allen Weber. Because the detective had been so helpful in arranging for Jacob Yahze to return to the Christensen farm, Heart's trust in Ruiz had grown. The feeling was mutual. The conversation on the way into Salt Lake City concerned Susan Weber's health and speculation about who Vogel was.

The group reached the FBI command center and settled in around a conference table. Vogel had decided to explain his presence.

"Professor Goode asked me to come to Salt Lake City because I have expertise in ancient writing, specifically Aramaic. Much of it has been found on metal plates like the ones found with those poor children. But there is more to it than that. The signs left behind at the farm, with the cattle and the Christensen family, may portend something far more sinister than crazed killers or fanatics." His words were chilling to everyone except Jacob Yahze.

"There are four archangels who have fallen from God's grace," Vogel began. Yahze interjected that the evil these archangels represented was part of Navajo belief. "We call them by different names, but their mission of evil is the same. The first is Satan. It is he who stirred up conflict by encouraging bigotry and hatred among races and religions. But, God be praised, Satan has been captured and entombed."

Andrea Ruiz gasped audibly. "Satan?" she asked in disbelief.

"Shawtan is his Hebrew name," Vogel elaborated. It was he who tempted Jesus in the wilderness."

A wave of fright pulsed through the young detective's body.

"Satan's tomb is remote and always guarded." Vogel had decided not to mention the terra-cotta army that guards the tomb, nor anything about The Vigilant. "Since Satan's capture, mankind has struggled to find peace. Satan can no longer interfere, giving tolerance a chance, but only by our own free will."

Jacob Yahze began chanting softly as Vogel spoke.

"Each of the four evil ones has sub-princes that serve him and can call many other evil spirits to do their bidding. They gather human followers—servitors—with promises of riches and power. They are disciples whose souls are lost, but they are capable of stirring up trouble and fomenting evil in their master's name."

"You said there were four fallen archangels," Heart said. "Where are they?"

"Satan has been entombed. The other three—Leviathan, Belial, and Lucifer—still roam the Earth. Each nourishes evil but uses a different approach and means for one common end—the destruction of humanity, and of God's Earth. This is their revenge against God. Blessed be His name, who cast them down."

"How are they different, Rabbi?" Benjamin asked. He was not a religious man. Much of his work depended on science and technology. Yet he found the rabbi's presentation compelling and wanted to know more.

"Leviathan's domain is water. He uses the oceans, lakes, and rivers, and some creatures therein, against us. He encourages the uncaring, the ignorant, and the greedy to ransack our natural resources and food supply, and to pollute. Without food and water, humanity cannot exist."

"So the floods and the evaporation of the Great Salt Lake might be his doing?" Benjamin asked.

"It is possible," Vogel answered.

"And the others?" Goode asked.

"The next is Belial, who attacks us through the corruption of nature. He offers power, through his sub-princes Amaimon and Beelzebub. They call upon unholy spirits to invade greedy and uncaring human bodies to do his bidding. It is said that Belial and his sub-princes can transform into rapacious creatures of the animal world. He demands living sacrifice and pagan ritual. He is the despoiler of the Earth, the polluter of the air and land. His work is everywhere. Our garbage and chemicals are slowly killing us." Everyone at the table nodded their agreement, and Yahze paused in his chanting.

"The last, Lucifer," Vogel continued, "is perhaps the most dangerous of the archangels." Yahze had returned to his chanting, this time a little louder. "His way to our destruction is to foment jealousy, hatred, bigotry, and greed among the nations. He is a sly whisperer, planting suspicions and lies that keep the world in a constant state of anxiety. His subjects are the world's demagogic leaders, mindless terrorists, corrupt politicians, and religious zealots, as well as greedy corporations and businesses and their executives. Lucifer's goal is to corrupt our ideals of tolerance, reason, and decency until humanity devours itself in unthinkably violent and brutal war, slavery, oppression, and, eventually, disease that will ultimately leave the world barren of rational human life and civilization as we know it."

Weber, Goode, Heart, Benjamin, and Ruiz sat in stunned silence as they absorbed Vogel's revelation. They had been given insight into a world that up to now had been shrouded in myth and mystery. But it had suddenly entered their lives with reality as harsh and stunning as the Christensen murders.

Vogel uttered a prayer. Yahze stopped chanting and announced, "I believe we have work to do."

CHAPTER TWENTY

CORRUPTED PLATES OF GOLD

It was past ten p.m. Taro Heart was due in court early the next morning, so she excused herself. Agent Benjamin went to his safe, removed the two golden plates found hanging around the murdered children's necks, and brought them to the conference room. Jacob Yahze had remained to work with Rabbi Vogel and Professor Goode on the plates. Although his Aramaic was rusty, Allen Weber offered to help.

Before they started, while Goode studied the plates, Vogel went to Benjamin's private office and scanned a photo of the dragon amulet. Using a secure FBI computer, he e-mailed it to the leader of his sect, the Ben Zimrah, in Safed, Israel. As he hit "Send," Allen Weber came into the room.

"I did my missionary work in Israel," Weber told Vogel. "That's where I studied Aramaic."

"Where?" Vogel was interested.

"The Hebrew University in Jerusalem. And I went on a few digs near Beersheba."

"An Aramaic scholar and an archeologist. I'm impressed."

Weber closed the door to the office. "I wanted to tell you this alone, Rabbi." Vogel stopped what he was doing. "I know about the capture of Satan, and the tomb in Xian."

Vogel was suddenly on his guard. He glanced at the closed door. Was this seemingly nice young man a disciple? Could he be a servitor? Or perhaps a sub-prince of an evil archangel?"

"On one dig, I met Michael and Anya Gross. They introduced me to Rabbi Levi Lemach ben Abraham, Rabbi Malachi, and the others in Safed. When I saw the amulet I remembered the description of the doors of the tomb."

Vogel relaxed. He was impressed by Weber's sensitivity in not mentioning Xian. He knew the Grosses. They were part of The Vigilant. But, Vogel determined, Weber knew nothing of The Vigilant. He decided to keep it that way, for now.

"Then our coming together here is most appropriate," he told the young Mormon banker. "God moves in such wonderful ways. Now let us see what the professor has discovered about those plates."

While the others were busy, Benjamin took time to talk privately with Ruiz and confront her about going behind his back and bringing Yahze and Heart to the Christensen farm.

"I was pursuing a lead," Ruiz replied. "I didn't think of it as going behind your back."

Benjamin studied the young detective's manner. Her body language told him something different from what she was professing.

"Was your partner aware?" he asked.

"Snow knows what I've been doing."

"I read his report about the knife found in the cattle, and what this medicine man Yahze did with it. Pretty strange stuff, don't you think?" Ruiz smiled. "And what Rabbi Vogel told us isn't? I'd like to see your report to Washington on that."

Benjamin returned her smile. "Touché. They'd probably have me report to our psychiatric consultant immediately."

"Definitely. But there may be something in what he said."

Benjamin paused to consider that. He had been raised in Orthodox Judaism but had long ago abandoned it as irrelevant to American life in the twenty-first century. "You're a Mormon. Are you religious?" he asked.

"No. Not religious. Realistic."

"Archangels and sub-princes conjuring up demonic spirits? That's realistic?"

"I saw firsthand what was done to the Christensen family and their cattle. With what we heard tonight, it sort of makes sense, or at least it creates a rationale for those events. I can almost taste it—this cult from hell-bent on evil."

"Or the ultraconservatives looking to humiliate or disparage the Mormon church?"

"Or the Navajo," Ruiz added.

Professor Goode and Rabbi Vogel determined that the plates were genuine and the language authentic. As the three men translated the Aramaic, they found that the plates contained a corrupted variation of a portion of Chapter Nine of the Second Book of Nephi, part of the Book of Mormon. Instead of praising God, the words mocked Him. Together they translated the first plate:

O the graceless, arrogant, witless God proclaims:
"If the flesh should rise no more,
spirits will invade and become
subjects of the angels who fell from
My presence."

Goode opened a copy of The Book of Mormon and saw the corruption, which he pointed out to Vogel and Weber.

"The author of this knew the original text. He changed a few words to make it seem that God instructed the archangels to invade mankind with their evil spirits."

They translated the second plate:

"And those spirits become devils, angels
into devils, to be shut out from the
presence of God, and to remain with these
four glorious fallen fathers; yea to those beings
who beguiled our first parents, who now
transformeth nigh unto an angel of light
and stirreth up the children of men
unto secret combinations of murder and
all manner of secret works of darkness."

Goode confirmed that the Book of Mormon meant that this spirit invasion was blessed by God, equating worship of the archangels with the worship of God Himself. "The key is this phrase: "yea in glory like unto Himself." For the next half hour the three men discussed the implications of such a corruption. It was so intense that Weber realized he had not called the hospital. He excused himself to to check on Susan.

A few moments later he burst into Agent Benjamin's office in a highly agitated, nearly incoherent state.

"I called to see how she was," Weber blurted out. "There's been an attack. They tried to kill my wife…and the baby. They did an emergency C-section. It's a girl! The baby is okay. but my wife isn't."

Ruiz was on her feet. "Who? Who was it?"

"I don't know. Some maniac with a knife. A stone knife. They got him. He's wounded. Look, I need a fast ride to the hospital. Can you do that? Please?"

"Of course, Mr. Weber." Benjamin was on his feet and moving toward the door. We'll take my car. I have a siren and flashing lights."

CHAPTER TWENTY-ONE

A VOW

Detective Ruiz flashed her ID to the policeman on guard outside Susan Weber's room. She explained who Allen Weber was, but the cop at the door hesitated.

"Let me check with the detective in charge," he told her, and keyed in his radio.

Ruiz was surprised to find that her partner, Harold Snow, was at the hospital, now a crime scene. When the Salt Lake police received the call, they dispatched two patrol cars, with Snow in charge. He put uniformed police on Susan Weber and placed two officers to guard Jim Swain, who was in critical condition and, as yet, unidentified.

"Captain Fuchs asked me to take the call," he told Ruiz, "seeing as I was involved before. How's it going with you and the Feds?"

"It's going okay, Harold." She introduced Allen Weber. Snow let him into the room. Ruiz then filled Snow in on some—but not all—of the details, being careful not to mention any of the fascinating information that Rabbi Vogel had disclosed.

DAVID SAPERSTEIN

Susan was asleep. As Allen approached the bed in the dimly lit room, a voice from the corner startled him. A burly man stepped out of the shadows. He wore a white smock and pants and looked like a male nurse, but Weber didn't see any ID. "May I ask who you are?"

"Allen Weber. Her husband," Weber said sharply, slightly annoyed. "How is she?"

"She's sedated. The C-section went well. But Mrs. Weber was in shock before that and, well, Mr. Weber, there was some hemorrhaging." Weber moved to the bedside and took Susan's hand in his. He brought it to his lips and kissed it. His eyes began to fill with tears.

"Allen?" His name floated up faintly from her lips. "Is that you?"

"Yes, my love. Yes." He dropped to his knees beside her, still clutching her hand and kissing it. "I'm here." She blinked her eyes and then opened them. Allen stood up, bending over so she could see him. "I'm here, love."

"We have a daughter," she said. "I saw her. She's beautiful."

"Yes, I know. They tell me she's as beautiful as you are. And she's fine."

"It was a…" Susan frowned, trying to recall what had happened. "Something… Someone bad. I couldn't… Did they tell you?"

"I know about it. Everything is all right."

She smiled up at him. "Good." Then she gave another frown. "How are Michael and David?"

"They're with Grace and Ronnie. They're good. Happy to have a sister." She smiled again and drifted off to sleep.

"She won't wake up for several hours. I suggest you come back in the morning," the nurse told him.

128

Weber stared at him. Should he leave? A fog of confusion and frustration clouded his thinking.

"We'll take good care of her," the nurse said reassuringly. Weber nodded. "Would you like me to ask the doctor to… I mean, maybe he could give you something to relax."

"No. Thank you. I'm okay." He bent over Susan and kissed her tenderly on the forehead. "Sleep well, my love. God bless you."

Weber spoke to the OB/GYN resident, who assured him that Susan would be okay. "Have you seen you daughter?" she asked.

"No. Where is she?"

"Neonatal intensive care. It's on the fifth floor. Come on, I'll take you up there." The doctor led the way. Ruiz accompanied Weber to the elevator.

"Will you do me a favor?" Weber asked the detective.

"Of course."

"My two boys, Michael and David, are with my sister, Grace Miller, and her husband." He gave her the address in Millcreek, a Salt Lake suburb. "Can have the police keep an eye on them?"

"No problem." As she reached for her cell phone to make the call, Benjamin and three FBI agents, including Dr. Laurie Kosloski, the forensics expert, arrived.

"We'll keep and eye on your wife and daughter," Benjamin assured Weber. "And Dr. Kosloski will have a look at the prisoner and that knife."

Weber thanked Benjamin. The elevator arrived. He followed the resident into it and went up to see his new daughter. She was pink and feisty, and the image of her mother.

The next morning, Weber's promised meeting with Fairchild Ballard was brief. Part of Ballard's function as president of the Mormon Church was to interpret scripture. He was the proclaimed prophet of the church, and thus much like the Roman Catholic pope in his pronouncements and his infallibility. His word was law to the seven million members of the Church of Jesus Christ of Latter-day Saints. After again expressing the church's official condolences—and his personal ones—to Weber, and inquiring about Susan and the baby, Ballard got down business.

"I wanted to speak to you privately, Allen. Your family, going back to your great-grandfather, who farmed next to our blessed Joseph Smith, Jr., has been a very important part of our community. Yours is a great heritage. One that I know you honor."

"Thank you, sir. I try. I have the greatest reverence for my forebears and for their struggle."

"Allen, I want you to know that this tragic business is being pursued with the full power and authority of our government. The officials in charge are good friends of our church. I can imagine the anger and frustration you must be feeling, and your wish for those responsible to brought to justice."

"Yes, sir."

"We must let those best qualified do this work."

"Of course," Weber answered quickly, wondering where President Ballard was going with this.

"Good. Now, I understand that you have been talking with a Navajo medicine man about this. I was informed that the Navajo are possible suspects—something to do with savage implements and weapons." Weber understood.

Someone had told Ballard about his meeting with Jacob Yahze and Taro Heart. As Weber was about to reply, Ballard held up his hand.

"Now mind you, Allen, we hold these people very dear to us. All Native Americans, north and south are, after all, the direct descendants of the Israelite tribe of Joseph, to whom God gave this hemisphere so that his true church might be rebuilt in New Jerusalem, and readied for our Savior's return."

Weber noted how smoothly Ballard had slipped into his role as religious leader. He nodded.

"Nevertheless," Ballard went on, "until these people accept our church as theirs, they are lost pagans who have forgotten their roots, heritage, and obedience to the word of Jesus Christ." Ballard paused and waited for a response, but Weber remained silent. "So do we understand one another?" Ballard asked.

"Yes, sir, we do."

"That's good to hear. As I said, your family is very important to us." Ballard stood up, signaling that the meeting was over. He put his arm around Weber's shoulder as they walked to the office door. "Losing the Christensens that way was devastating. Be consoled that although they are missed here on Earth, they are in glory with God."

As Allen Weber walked down the outside steps of the great tabernacle, its pull on him seemed somehow diminished. He had come face to face with the most powerful man in the church and found his purpose politically motivated. He could understand why Ballard had counseled him to refrain from seeking revenge, but to tell him not to talk to the Navajo about the case only deepened Weber's desire to find, by any means, those who had killed the Christensen family and tried to murder his wife and baby. He made a silent vow.

"No matter what it takes, I will find who did this to my family, and destroy him. And no one—not the church, not the police, not the FBI—no one will stop me!"

CHAPTER TWENTY-TWO

AUTHORIZATION TO SHIP DEATH

With word from their partner, Perez, that the so-called flood-control project was nearing completion, Bertha Smalls, Lincoln Foster, and William Claremont gathered in a secure conference room at DOE headquarters in Washington. Smalls locked the conference room door and told Foster to close the blinds on the windows that overlooked the Washington Mall near the Lincoln Memorial. She turned out the overhead fluorescent lights. The three joined hands. The spirits that had been implanted within them emerged, distorting the faces of their hosts and twisting their hands, limbs, and necks into impossible positions until the three could no longer stand. They were forced to lie down on the soft, carpeted floor. The spirit Trisaga, who dwelt within Bertha Smalls, spoke first.

"Our master announces that the time has come," she said. Her voice was deep, and echoed as though she spoke from within a great chamber. "I, Trisaga, ruler of triads, now call us to action.

"I, Hacamuli, the spirit that withers life, pledge my devotion to our master." This excited, high-pitched voice came from within Lincoln Foster.

"And I, Orgosil," the spirit within William Claremont announced, "pledge the same. These bodies we inhabit are to be used for our master's work. They are as insignificant as the greed that allowed us to enter." Orgosil's voice was soft and pleasing. It belied the evil of the tumultuous events.

"Then we are pledged," Hacamuli said, "and our mission begins."

The three released each other. Their bodies returned to normal. Bertha turned the light back on and they sat around the table as she took a sheath of papers from her attaché case.

"I have chosen three facilities from which to draw those materials that our master requires. We will each carry, by hand, a directive from my office authorizing the shipment of these specified nuclear materials to the new facility in Utah." She passed sets of papers to Foster and Claremont. "I have purposely chosen facilities that house lethal and nonlethal waste materials to make it seem all-encompassing. Move swiftly." The two men glanced briefly at the papers, then took them and left the room.

Lincoln Foster's assignment was one of the three Palo Verde nuclear generating unit in Phoenix. Since the terrorist attacks of September 11, 2001, most such facilities had stepped up their security. Foster's DOE position put him on a top-secret clearance list. He entered the plant with ease and was greeted by the general manager, Harold Cortez, who was used to surprise visits by DOE executives. Foster, wasting little time with small talk, presented Smalls's directive. Cortez studied the papers carefully.

"I thought Nevada was going to be the repository of this material," Cortez finally said. He was a cautious man, a necessary trait for managing a facility where one mistake could result in the loss of hundreds of thousands of lives.

"That was always open to discussion. Congress waffles while these waste materials pile up. I don't have to tell you that is driven by the NIMBY syndrome." Cortez nodded.

"No one wants it."

"Correct. The administration has decided to move forward by proving that there is a safe process."

"That makes sense," Cortez agreed. "Understand that it will take time to segregate the material you list here. Some of it is among the most dangerous we have."

"Of course. How long?"

"Perhaps two weeks."

Foster closed his briefcase and stood up. "Good. I will arrange for the transportation to be here then. You understand that this operation is top secret." Cortez nodded his agreement, but was still uneasy about releasing the deadly waste material.

The day was a cool and damp, normal for this time of year in Richland, Washington. William Claremont had just come through the safety showers and was being helped out of his cumbersome protective suit at Energy Northwest's Columbia nuclear generating station's waste storage facility. He was with Anna Sinclair, the plant manager. She was also a director on Energy Northwest's board. The facility was deep underground and was guarded by an elite detail from the Wackenhut security organization. Like Harold Cortez in Phoenix, Sinclair was nervous about Claremont's request.

When both were out of their suits and had been double-checked for radiation, they were driven back to Sinclair's office in the main plant.

"Bertha never mentioned this to me last December," Sinclair told Claremont. "She might have called with some kind of heads-up."

"That would have been dangerous, Anna," Claremont said in a friendly, personal tone. "The administration has wearied of the "not in my backyard" people, and the tree huggers. They have no plan for what to do with this stuff. Their only response, when pressed, is to stop the generation of nuclear power. You and I know that that is impossible."

"Yes, I suppose that's true at the moment," she said. "But we might also explore other means."

"Of course. But that's Congress's mission, not ours, Anna. Bertha has a green light from the highest levels of the administration. It's time to move forward and begin to deal with this waste material before it gets totally out of hand."

Anna Sinclair was relieved to see something was finally being done to store these waste materials properly. But the fact that Claremont had indicated taking some of the deadliest materials, for what he said was a pilot project, seemed contrary to common sense. Nevertheless, she accepted Claremont's explanation.

The weather in Austin, Texas, a boiling cauldron, was in direct contrast to that of Richland, Washington. A three-week heat wave, with temperatures over 100 degrees every day, had air conditioners on maximum and power at peak demand. Several brownouts had occurred, and many industrial users had been forced to curtail production.

The managers and executives at STP-1, South Texas Project's Unit 1 in Wadsworth, were under great stress when Bertha Smalls made her surprise visit to that large nuclear generating facility. Lyman Ashcroft, the unit's general manager, who had always been tolerant of bureaucrats and their often officious behavior, ushered Smalls into his office. The two had met several time before, and Ashcroft, whose sixty-eight years meant he had been brought up in segregated Texas, considered Smalls a nice black person. But he avoided any social contact with her, such as inviting her to dinner when she was in town.

On this visit, Bertha Smalls seemed very different. Her manner bordered on the gruff and rude when he questioned the wisdom of shipping the materials she required.

"The directive is clear, Mr. Ashcroft. That material—that specific material—will be segregated, containerized as indicated, and ready for shipment in two weeks." He tone was that of a superior giving an order to an underling.

"Well, Bertha," Ashcroft said softly, "y'all can see we've got a bit of a heat wave on our hands. We're stressed and spread thin. Brownouts just about every day now. I just don't know as I can spare the resources to get this done in two weeks. And frankly, like I said before, I have security concerns that are—" Smalls cut him off.

"Security is my problem, Ashcroft." She had never talked to him that way before. It was either Mr. Ashcroft or, on rare occasions, Lyman. "And secrecy. That's part of the security. That means that it's just you and I who know about this. My trucks will arrive at your temporary storage facility after midnight. I will have DOE personnel here to load the materials. Only you and I will supervise. There will be no one else present. Is that clear?"

"It's clear, but I just don't know…"

Smalls leaned across the desk. "Let me put it another way, Ashcroft. If anything about this leaks out, or if the shipment is endangered, like, say, some terrorists getting hold of the materials? I will personally see to it that you are charged with treason."

CHAPTER TWENTY-THREE

A CALL TO THE HOLY LAND

Shortly after Agent Benjamin apprised Rabbi Vogel and Professor Goode of the attack on Susan Weber, they decided to call it a night. There was much to mull over about what the golden plates had revealed. An FBI agent drove Vogel to his hotel, the Prime, which was within walking distance of Temple Square, the site of the great Mormon Tabernacle.

Vogel got to his room and checked the time. Eleven p.m. in Utah meant it was seven in the morning is Israel. He placed a call to Rabbi Levi Lemach ben Abraham, the leader of the Ben Zimrah sect in Safed; ben Abraham had just finished morning prayers.

"Good morning, Isadore. How are you?" ben Abraham asked. Vogel got right to the point.

"I'm worried. Did you get the photos of the amulet and stone knife?"

"We did. We discussed it at great length, but these things are inconclusive. Is there anything new to report?"

"I studied the plates that were found around the children's necks. They are certainly genuine. Very old, to be sure."

"True Aramaic?"

"Yes, Levi. They are corruptions of the original Book of Mormon, twisted to glorify evil."

The rabbi in Safed thought for a moment. "Can you send us the text?"

"Yes. Tomorrow."

"Of course, you understand that for us to commit our forces we need proof."

"Yes. Yes. Of course."

"There was another attempt in Xian," ben Abraham said, changing the subject. "That is the third this month. Satan's followers are getting active."

"That's another good reason to look into this evil in Salt Lake. Perhaps they are trying to distract us."

"Perhaps. Stay there and keep working. Have a good look at that domed rock. If it is an archangel's tomb, please dear God, we might have a chance to confront and capture another of these abominations."

"Yes. One more thing, Levi. There is a man here, a Navajo shaman. He has special powers and knows much about this evil that has emerged here. I respect him and—"

"Isadore?" Rabbi ben Abraham interrupted, "Are you asking to bring him into The Vigilant?"

Vogel smiled. "Yes. Yes, I am."

"Then by all means do it. Without your knowledge, wisdom, and courage, Shawtan's evil might still be in the world. We trust you, my dear friend."

CHAPTER TWENTY-FOUR

THE VIGILANT GROWS

After his call to Israel, Vogel called Jacob Yahze, who was staying at a Radisson hotel near the airport, seven miles away. The two men arranged to meet for a breakfast in Vogel's room early the next morning.

The rabbi began by telling Yahze the details of Satan's capture in the old Soviet Union years ago. It took nearly an hour.

"So you see, it was an effort that involved many people of different faiths, nationalities, and expertise," Vogel explained as he neared the end of the narrative. "None of it could have happened until we knew the location of Satan's dwelling, his resting place in Xian, which under the right circumstances could become his tomb. The people involved in the effort were the core members of The Vigilant, sworn to seek and capture these evil ones. Now there are three remaining fallen archangels, Belial, Leviathan, and Lucifer. Over the years we have added a few select people to The Vigilant. Today I invite you, Jacob Yahze, to join us."

Yahze weighed Vogel's invitation carefully. He believed the story. He knew that he had certain powers, which is why he, like Rabbi Vogel, had felt an evil presence near the domed rock. The other events at the Christensen farm—the plates, the amulet, the stone knives—all pointed to a plot with a purpose as yet unrevealed. It also involved his tribe, his people. Could he bear two allegiances? Might they conflict?

Vogel waited patiently, knowing that Yahze had much to consider. Finally, the shaman nodded and drew a deep breath.

"I am honored to join you, Rabbi Vogel. I will do whatever I can to help." The two men embraced.

Vogel went on to describe the members of The Vigilant and their backgrounds. Among them, he mentioned someone local—Vernon Flood, the Mormon chief librarian.

The small synagogue adjacent to Rose Park Circle in northwest Salt Lake City seemed a safe place to meet. Jacob Yahze arrived first. It was 3:30 p.m. The sanctuary was empty. He took a prayer shawl—a tallit—from a stand outside the sanctuary, kissed the end of it, and draped it around his shoulders. This was not the first synagogue he had been to.

While serving in the army, in the 82nd Airborne, and training at Fort Benning, Georgia, he had met Barry Hertzberg, a tough Jew from The Bronx. Before they took their first jump, Hertzberg had made a nervous comment to Jacob.

"Just remember this, my Navajo chief: While you guys were painting yourselves blue and eating buffalo meat, we

Jews already had diabetes!" They had a good laugh that put them at ease, and the jump went well. The two went on to serve in the same squad in Vietnam. When they mustered out, Jacob went to New York with Barry. They spent a month kicking up their heels in the Big Apple before Yahze went back west to school. Their spree ended on Rosh Hashanah, the Jewish New Year. Jacob attended services with Barry and his family. He always remembered the warmth and peace of the service, and the friendly acceptance by Barry's family and the congregation. Brutally oppressed people have so much in common that differences, such as race or religion, become obscured.

After Jacob adjusted the tallit, he took a white yarmulke from a nearby box, placed it on his head, and entered the sanctuary. The caretaker, a portly Hispanic man in his sixties, with steel-gray hair and broad shoulders, was putting away prayer books. He glanced at Yahze and went back to work. The shaman sat in a pew at the rear of the sanctuary, picked up a prayer book, and skimmed through it. He mused about the Mormon belief that the natives of this hemisphere were all descendants of the Hebrew tribe of Joseph. Had his distant ancestors spoken and written the language printed in the prayer book?

A few minutes later, Vernon Flood came in and sat next to him. Flood had also donned a tallit and yarmulke. Both men observed the caretaker leave the sanctuary.

"Good to meet you, Mr. Yahze." They shook hands.

"My pleasure. You are now the second member of The Vigilant that I have met. And please, my name is Jacob."

"And I'm Vernon—Vern is fine. Perhaps soon you will meet several more of us." The two men then discussed what each knew about the ritual murders and the different effects rippling out from it.

"So the evidence that Navajo are involved is much too convenient," Yahze told Flood when they had traded information.

"Blatantly false, I'd say."

"The FBI's forensic people say the killing at the Christensen's farm was done with weapons or tools made of fangs, claws, and talons. But here's what I'm thinking. What if they weren't tools? What if they were living animals and raptors?"

Flood was intrigued. "You're saying that this could have been an actual animal attack?"

When Rabbi Vogel had secretly called Flood to inform him that he had brought Yahze into The Vigilant, the librarian was concerned. Though Navajo belief encompassed a spirit world beyond, it did not define God, or acknowledge the existence of the fallen archangels. Earth, nature, respect for life, and mankind's place within these spheres were their core beliefs. What the shaman was saying, and the way the cattle and the Christensens were displayed, could not be the work of wild animals. But what Yahze said next opened a new train of thought for Vernon Flood.

"I mean those who are, at once, animal and man," the shaman said. "Rabbi Vogel talked of it when he described these evil archangels."

"Yes," Flood replied. "I have heard such things myself. I was not involved in the capture of Satan. But there was no talk that he, or his sub-princes and disciples, took animal form."

"Perhaps this archangel, or whatever is the evil we seek, is different. Perhaps it had different powers."

"If it is so," Flood said, "then we are up against a force that can appear around us without our knowing."

CHAPTER TWENTY-FIVE

TWO CALLS FOR HELP

While Yahze and Flood were meeting, Vogel returned to the FBI command center to fax a translation of the plates to Rabbi Abraham in Safed. Special Agent Benjamin had news.

"Our forensic people have identified the assailant at the hospital. His name is James Swain. He served three years in the army. Infantry. Marksman. He's a Native American."

"Navajo?"

"No. A small sub-tribe called Paronto. I hope to have more info on them later today. Oh, and Mr. Weber is here. He called asking for you. I told him you were coming in. I hope that's okay. You all seem to be working together."

"Of course. Where is he?"

"The conference room."

Weber was standing and looking out at children playing in a park below. He turned away from the window when Vogel came into the room.

"How is your wife?" the rabbi asked, wondering why the young man was not with her at the hospital.

"Resting comfortably," he answered. "She'll be okay."

"And your baby? A girl, I heard."

"Yes. She's just fine. Let's sit down," Weber suggested. They sat at the table. Weber was in no mood for small talk. His manner was grim and determined. There was a cold intensity in his eyes, and an aura of anger around him. "So what's our next step?"

"Are you all right?" Vogel asked with genuine concern. He liked this young man and was acutely aware that what had been done to his family could prove to be overwhelming at a time when clear heads must prevail.

"I'm all right, Rabbi. Really. I just want to find these killers and bring them to justice."

"We all want that. I pledge my complete attention."

"And mine," Weber assured him.

"Now, Mr. Weber—"

"It's Allen. Please."

"Yes. Allen, I wonder if you might make a copy of the translation from the plates while I make a phone call to our mutual friend, Michael Gross, in Israel."

Michael and Anya Gross were having an early breakfast in their Tel Aviv flat. Vogel brought them up to date on events in Utah and his call to Rabbi ben Abraham.

"You are saying that the Ben Zimrah are not convinced?" Michael asked.

"Not yet, Michael. We need solid proof of what this is."

"Is there anything we can do here?" Anya Gross asked.

"The FBI is checking out this James Swain fellow. When he is out of intensive care I will make arrangements to test him."

"Be careful, Isadore. The Ben Zimrah say that Satan's legions are becoming active. He might be one of them."

146

"Yes. I have heard. I'm calling now because I thought you might have a talk with Andy Taft about this. The FBI and CIA have been cooperating more since 9/11."

Taft was the former defense intelligence agent, now with the CIA, who had also been instrumental in Satan's capture. He too was part of The Vigilant.

"So they say," Gross answered sarcastically.

Michael knew that this so-called increased interagency cooperation, filtered through the U.S. Department of Homeland Security, had become slightly better domestically. But internationally, it left much to be desired. Gross was Mossad, his wife Anya was the daughter of ex-KGB Colonel Peter Somoroff. Andy Taft was CIA; his significant other was Sasha Andreyev, formerly KGB, and now an attaché with the Russian embassy in Washington. All were members of The Vigilant.

"Getting Andy Taft involved is a good idea, Rabbi. I'll give him a call."

Gross placed his call to Taft's Washington apartment using the secure scrambler phone in his office.

"Your timing, as always Michael, is lousy," Taft said. "Sasha and I were just about to open a bottle of Russian vodka and some exquisite Beluga caviar fresh from the Moscow diplomatic pouch."

"I see moving from DIA to CIA hasn't changed your life style. Are you sure it is not drugged?" Gross joked.

"I always used to make her taste everything from the pouch. Old habit die hard. But we're all allies now, aren't we?"

"Most of the time. Well, I won't keep you two from your pleasures."

"You won't, Mishka," Sasha Andreyev said. She was on the extension. Sasha was smart and beautiful, with dark, almond-shaped eyes and the high cheekbones that revealed her mother's Asian genes. "This braggart of an American thinks he can drink half a bottle of Russian vodka and still make love."

Gross switched to Hebrew, which he knew Taft did not speak. "Like I've told you many times, if you want a lover who can also drink, you must try an Israeli."

"What makes you think I haven't? Remember, I was KGB." They laughed together.

"If you two are finished telling state secrets you might tell us what's on your mind, Michael." Taft jokingly scolded both of them. Gross turned deadly serious.

"Not happy news. It is possible that we may have another of those pesky archangels on our hands. Only this one is in America." He filled them in on what had been happening in Utah. Taft and Andreyev were alarmed.

"Do you think Vogel needs our help out there?" Taft asked.

"Not yet. Let's see what he and the Ben Zimrah can come up with. But we thought that you might avail yourself of the considerable assets that some of your friends there in Washington have, and see who this James Swain is. And while you're at it, check out one Nicholas Perez. Your old friend Allen Weber says he's in Washington a lot doing business with the government. He owns the land where that domed rock is located."

"Nicholas, you say?" Sasha queried. "Remember that Colonel Valarian's name was Nickolai." She was referring to the human body that had Satan inhabited when he was captured.

"I had the same thought," Gross admitted. "Let's keep it in mind. But I've kept you from your caviar and vodka long enough." Gross didn't like telephones. He had been wounded once by a bomb that had been planted in one.

"Yes, Michael. That you have. I'll get right on Swain. I've got a buddy at the Bureau of Indian Affairs. And I'll do a sweep of all federal department and agency visitors for the past year. If Nicholas Perez does business with any of them, he'll pop up."

"One more thing," Gross added. "Weber says that a Mormon bishop named Peter Horne has pushing him to sell Perez the Christensen farm. Weber's the executor of his brother-in-law's estate."

"Peter Horne. Mormon bishop," Taft repeated as he wrote the name down alongside Swain's and Perez's. "I'll run him too."

"Shalom," Gross said.

"Shalom," Sasha answered. "Give your lovely Russian wife a kiss for me."

"Shalom, Michael," Taft added. He hung up.

Without a word spoken, Taft and Andreyev set aside the vodka and caviar and turned their attention to this new work of The Vigilant.

CHAPTER TWENTY-SIX

A DEADLY CARGO

The rain began a little after 9:00 p.m. and grew in intensity. It was another unpredictable storm, a result of the year's El Niño effect. By midnight it was hammering the Phoenix metro area, bringing local streams and rivers close to flood stage. The two white tractor-trailers, devoid of any identification markings, cleared the entrance security at Palo Verde's Nuclear Generating Unit 2xs. They slowly made their way along a slick blacktop, led by a black and red security Humvee with mounted flashing yellow lights. The convoy pulled into an empty parking lot adjacent to the underground bunkers where years of nuclear waste material were stored. Bright, blue-green halogen floodlights illuminated the heavy rain, increasing its visual intensity while giving the pristine white trucks an ominous and eerie glow.

Lincoln Foster stepped down from the passenger side of the lead truck's extended cab. He wore a military-type poncho with the hood pulled forward so that his face was hidden. He trotted over to the Humvee, arriving just as the driver, plant manager Howard Cortez, got out and opened a large black umbrella.

"Some night, huh? I thought maybe this rain might flood the roads and hold you up," Cortez said, trying to be friendly.

Foster was in no mood for small talk. For him, the rain was a blessing. It provided cover for the operation. If it kept on for the next few hours they could be loaded and on the road, with the knowledge that the local police and highway patrol would either be cooping somewhere dry or busy with floods and accidents.

"Nothing holds us up," Foster said, coldly. "Let's get to it."

The two men walked toward the entrance to the bunker. Cortez got out his electronic key card and inserted it in the slot to the right of the steel door. A click sounded and a panel slid away, revealing a glass frame that glowed pale blue. He placed his hand on the glass and his palm was scanned. The door clicked again and opened.

"That's that," Cortez said, fatalistically. "You can bring your people in."

Foster waved to the trucks and six men, all Paronto, got out of the extended cabs. All wore black vinyl jumpsuits. Three carried Uzi's. The truck that Foster had been in began to back up toward the bunker doorway.

"Are the weapons really necessary?" Cortez asked, as they entered the bunker.

"Standard procedure," Foster answered. "Now, where is the material we requested?"

The weather in Wadsworth, Texas, was still hot and humid. The hundred-degree heat wave had broken earlier in the week, but nighttime temperatures were still in the high seventies. The humidity was hovering around sixty percent. For the past two weeks, Lyman Ashcroft had personally supervised the preparation for the shipment requested on Bertha Smalls's DOE directive. Most of it was among the most deadly nuclear waste material he had in his possession. Although he was relieved to be rid of it, Ashcroft was still uneasy about the secrecy imposed on him. Twice in the past two weeks he had been tempted to telephone the secretary of energy and question Bertha Smalls's directive. But then the bureaucrat in him took control, and he feared for his job and pension. So he obeyed orders, and when Bertha Smalls arrived with the tractor-trailers, and men to load the materials, it was ready—packed to specifications and sealed in steel, lead-lined drums. As the two unmarked trucks pulled away from the South Texas Project Unit 1, Lyman Ashcroft, the unit's general manager, mulled over the threat Bertha Smalls had made two weeks ago.

"If the shipment is endangered, like terrorists getting hold of the materials, I will personally see to it that you are charged with treason."

He cursed her under his breath. Unaware of the evil spirit dwelling in her, he wondered how he had misjudged her all these years. As the rear lights of the trucks faded into the hot Texas night, Ashcroft muttered, "Good riddance, bitch," and walked to his car. It had been a long time since he felt such dislike for anyone.

The trucks—two from Arizona and two from Texas—traveled at night, taking the less-trafficked routes, trying to lower the possibility of accidents or observation by state police. They also avoided cities, since many had radiation detectors at their truck-weighing sites. Although they had all the necessary identification and paperwork, Perez still thought it prudent to minimize the risk of detection, even though nuclear material was normally shipped this way, in unmarked vehicles. Forty-eight hours later, the convoy from Phoenix neared Salt Lake City. The trucks from Texas were just a day behind them.

The story at Energy Northwest's Columbia Nuclear Generating Station at Richland, Washington, was different from the others. The shipment that the plant manager, Anna Sinclair, was supposed to have ready was not. She had called William Claremont two days earlier to inform him that there had been a minor malfunction in the steam-generating system and she had to divert personnel from packaging the waste material to deal with the problem. When she called, Bertha Smalls was already on the road to Texas. Claremont reached his boss on her cell phone. She immediately telephoned Anna Sinclair.

"I will accept no excuses. Our trucks and people will be there as scheduled. You will be ready for us," she ordered Sinclair, who was already stressed out from dealing with generating problem.

"No I won't, Bertha," she told the DOE executive, who had been a friend for years. "It will be ready in three more days, and that's that."

The conviction in her voice told Smalls's evil spirit, Trisaga, not to argue.

"Very well, Anna," Smalls said, changing to a conciliatory tone of voice. "I understand. Three days. At midnight. I'll let Claremont know. And I'm sorry if I sounded abrupt."

"No problem, Bertha," Sinclair told her. "We're both under a lot of stress. Three days. Midnight. As instructed. I'll be ready."

Bertha Smalls called Claremont from her motel in Austin later that afternoon. Her voice was that of Trisaga, leader of Triads. Claremont, as the evil spirit Orgosil, listened obediently.

"Three days and she will be ready. A small but annoying delay. Our master is displeased. But his wishes are that we do not make it an issue. After you have the material, dispose of her. Make it look like an accident away from the plant."

Three weeks after she mysteriously disappeared, Anna Sinclair's decomposed body was recovered from the Columbia River, miles downstream from her home. It appeared that her car had been pushed off the road by a rock slide.

CHAPTER TWENTY-SEVEN

HOSPITAL VISITS

Susan Weber's recovery and recuperation was going to take time. Aside from the physical effects from her C-section, there was the lingering trauma from witnessing her nurse's murder and Swain's attack. The doctors prescribed rest and therapy. They suggested she be moved, with her new baby daughter, to the Carlisle Clinic in the mountains near Park City. Allen Weber asked Agent Benjamin that Susan have FBI protection, which was arranged. Allen's sister and brother-in-law, Grace and Ronald Miller, would keep Michael and David Weber in their home. Acting on Detective Andrea Ruiz's request, the Salt Lake City police arranged for the boys and the Millers to have round-the-clock protection.

A few days before Susan left the hospital, with the baby, named Ruth, Bishop Horne paid her a visit. He was delighted that she was recovering and advised her that the Mormons in their ward were praying for her.

"Thank you, Bishop," she said, genuinely touched. "That's very kind of everyone. Please tell them I said so."

Her state of mind was fragile, but she vaguely remembered that Allen had said something about Horne's inquiring about selling the farm. *Had Allen said something about being suspicious?* Susan strained to recall that conversation.

"Will you be going home soon?" Horne inquired.

"No. The baby and I will be going to a clinic for a while to rest."

"Oh? Where?"

"In the mountains. Park City, I think."

"Do you know the name of the clinic? You have many friends in the congregation who would like to send flowers or maybe visit." She tried to recall the clinic's name.

"I'm sorry. I can't remember. You might ask Allen. He'll be here this evening."

"I guess he's busy with the farm," Horne said. The details of her conversation with Allen about the bishop's interest in the farm started to come back to her. He began to move closer to her hospital bed. "Allen told me you would want to sell the farm." His tone of voice was making her uncomfortable. "After all, it must be a disturbing burden to have to deal with," Horne continued as he neared her bedside.

Now that's not true, she thought, feeling uncomfortable as his body reached the bed. Susan knew that they had made no decision about selling the farm, especially to Horne's friend Perez. She wanted Bishop Horne out of her room.

"Did he tell you I have an interested buyer?" the bishop asked.

Susan's heart beat faster. She slid her finger over to the nurse call button under the covers and pushed it. Outside in the hall, the FBI guard had also been summoned. When the nurse came down the hall, the guard was already up and had quietly entered the room. The agent assessed the situation. Mrs. Weber seemed okay, if a little pale. The bishop, a cleared visitor, was next to the bed. Too close.

"Are you all right, Mrs. Weber," the agent asked.

His voice startled Bishop Horne, who, concentrating on Susan Weber, had not heard the man enter the room. Horne spun around, looking too startled and guilty for the agent's liking. He moved to Susan's bedside quickly, insinuating himself between her and the bishop.

The nurse entered the room. "Is there something you need, Mrs. Weber?" she asked, also moving close to the bed.

As Horne backed away, the nurse spoke to him. "I'm sorry bishop, but Mrs. Weber needs her rest now."

As he left, the FBI agent never took his eyes off him.

In another part of the hospital, in a locked ward guarded by the FBI and the Utah State Police, it was determined that Jim Swain had recovered enough to be interrogated. Special Agent-in-Charge Michael Benjamin read the prisoner his Miranda rights. Two other agents were present, one operating a video camera.

"I have nothing to say," Swain announced. "I want my attorney." Then he grinned arrogantly into the camera.

Benjamin produced the stone knife that Swain had fallen on. "We were just wondering why you tired to kill yourself, Mr. Swain."

The Paronto's expression changed. He turned away from his interrogator and buried his face in his pillows. Benjamin had hit a sore spot.

"Suicide after murder. That's the current hallmark of a terrorist," Benjamin continued. He was an experienced interrogator. Swain turned back to Benjamin. The FBI agent saw a momentary flash of hatred in Swain's eyes. Suicide was a sensitive issue with Native Americans, as many, segregated by white Christian society, had moved away from their heritage and drifted toward hopelessness and suicide. But not the Paronto, who had long ago sworn their allegiance to a dark power. The hatred that Benjamin saw told him that it could be used to manipulate this killer. He backed off for now, determined to return soon, but this time he would have Jacob Yahze and Rabbi Vogel with him.

CHAPTER TWENTY-EIGHT

SHAFT OF DEATH

The shipment of nuclear waste material from Richland, Washington, finally arrived at Perez's flood-control site. The other convoys from Arizona and Texas had come, off-loaded, and gone. Before returning to D.C., Bertha Smalls and Lincoln Foster had received a generous monetary reward from Nicholas Perez, and his gratitude in the form of physical pleasure for Trisaga and Hacamuli, the spirits that dwelt within their bodies.

William Claremont's shipment was off-loaded at three in the morning by several Paronto, supervised by Nicholas Perez and Raymond Light. Claremont received his reward and an extra moment of pleasure for his spirit, Orgosil, for eliminating Anna Sinclair.

After Claremont departed to join Smalls and Foster in D.C., the Richland material was transported on diminutive rail cars from the mouth of the so-called flood-control tunnel, down nearly a half mile to the main chamber, which was originally a limestone cave that had been greatly enlarged. With this final shipment—mostly spent nuclear fuel rods and deadly medical isotopes—there was nearly four tons of deadly nuclear waste material in the chamber.

"We will leave the canisters sealed until this is complete," Perez told Light as they inspected a deep shaft at the rear of the chamber. Perez turned on the lights that illuminated the shaft. It was only eight feet in diameter, slanting down and away at a steep thirty-degree angle.

Light peered down and saw that at around one hundred yards the shaft curved away, its end hidden from view.

"How far down is it, master?" he asked.

"Nearly a half mile to the underground river that flows into the main aquifer."

"When do we do it?" Light asked eagerly. He felt a thrilling rush course through his body. His master had given him a reward.

"In due time. I must be sure that we act when there is maximum release of water from the main aquifer that feeds the Colorado River basin. The fools monitor for bacteria and chemical agents but not for radioactivity. When contaminated and diluted to nearly undetectable amounts, our nuclear poison will flow into the system and be used by tens of millions for drinking, bathing, cooking, and, best of all, irrigation for California's farming industry. Radiation will slowly build up in the population, the soil, and the food chain until it eventually blossoms into a nationwide health problem. From that comes death and economic destruction." Light listened rapturously as Nicholas Perez expatiated on his plan.

"How much more of the waste material will we need to bring?" Light asked.

"What we have here now is enough for this system," Perez answered. "But our servants, led by Trisaga, will arrange shipments to be dispersed into aquifers in other parts of the country. The effective half-life of the lethal waste material is ten thousand years. In other words, once out in the water systems, ten millennia will have to pass before its potency is diminished by just half." Perez grinned, revealing his teeth as they lengthened and yellowed. His eyes glowed red. "And by then," he continued, "little or no life, much less human life, will exist in this hemisphere." He flamboyantly flicked the switch. The deadly shaft went dark.

CHAPTER TWENTY-NINE

A SERVANT'S END

Washington, D.C., is not a good place to keep secrets. Andy Taft, having worked in the intelligence community for more than twenty years, had solid contacts in all branches of government and access to a very high level of the Washington surveillance apparatus. With his CIA clearance, it was easy for Taft to find out who Nicholas Perez visited in the nation's capital. It took a little longer to get information on Jim Swain from his contact in the Bureau of Indian Affairs.

"He's a full-blooded Paronto," Taft's contact finally reported. "They are a sub-tribe of the Pueblo. They claim to be direct descendants of the Aztec. They're a small group, maybe fifty or sixty. They have been offered tribal access to Pueblo reservations but choose to live apart. They have made no claims on us and hardly do any business with the bureau. Jim Swain is a leader of sorts, though they don't have an official chief or medicine man. He works in construction. Most of them do, for a company called Victory Development. That's about all I can tell you."

That was not much to go on. However, the information about Victory Development did link the Paronto to Nicholas Perez.

"The FBI made an inquiry about Swain several days ago. They got the same info I'm giving you, except I didn't mention the Victory Development thing."

"How come?"

"They don't share so freely with us, so I figure turnabout is fair play. Sorry there isn't more, Andy."

Taft thanked his friend. If the FBI hadn't yet made the Victory Development connection, it might give The Vigilant people in Utah a leg up on Swain and Perez, since Taft's sweep of government agencies showed several recent visits by Perez to the DOE.

Bertha Smalls, a G-12 level executive, was Perez's contact point there. She held a sensitive position in nuclear waste management. Her dossier revealed the strange circumstances of her being attacked by an animal in Rock Creek Park and her miraculous recovery. Taft perused the DOE organizational charts and found that her immediate subordinates, Lincoln Foster and William Claremont, had had contact with Perez while Smalls was in the hospital. They took on the oversight for development of nuclear waste disposal programs in her absence. Taft decided it was time to meet Bertha Smalls and, he hoped, Foster and Claremont in person.

"Sometimes a direct question from an unexpected place, like the CIA, can rattle the cage a little," Taft told Sasha, his Russian girlfriend.

"Then rattle, my darling, and we will see where these little birds fly."

The type of stone knife Swain used had now shown up twice; in connection with the Christensen's cattle mutilations and Swain's attack on Susan Weber. Agent-in-Charge Benjamin believed the stone knife was more than just a way to fool the hospital's metal detectors. And his forensics expert, Dr. Kosloski, suspected that knives like these might also have been used in the Christensen murders.

Seeing Swain's reaction to the mention of the knife and suicide, Benjamin brought Jacob Yahze and Rabbi Vogel to see the prisoner the next day. While Benjamin and two other agents were setting up a video camera, Yahze and Vogel remained outside.

"I told you I won't talk to you without my lawyer present," Swain told Benjamin. The Paronto leader was feeling better, sitting up in bed. He had just finished a meal of eggs and toast. This first solid food was a sure sign that his wounds were healing well. "I demand you get out," he barked.

The FBI agents ignored him. "Things don't look good for you, Swain," Benjamin said. The Paronto assassin sneered. This man was a fool. He had no idea of the power Perez possessed.

He imagined that at this very moment his master was making plans to free him.

"You've got nothing on me. I was trying to help that poor woman. I saw the killer run. He dropped that knife. I tripped and fell on it."

"Besides the assault on Mrs. Weber," Benjamin responded, "we now have a match on your boots, putting you at the scene where Christensen's cattle were slaughtered."

"So you think I killed some cows," Swain said arrogantly. "So what? Maybe they had mad cow disease and I was doing the community a service." He chuckled at his own joke.

Benjamin glared at Swain, but as a successful interrogator, he felt satisfaction inside. His prisoner had taken the bait.

"I wouldn't be making jokes right now, Mr. Swain. This is no longer a local matter. I don't think you were there killing the cattle. I know you weren't. And bias crimes are the jurisdiction of the federal courts. No plea bargains or flexible sentencing there." Swain stopped grinning.

"What bias crime?"

Benjamin didn't answer him directly. "Local connections won't help you now. All you have to look forward to is hard time in a maximum-security prison. But before I turn you over for arraignment, there are a few people who want to meet you."

"Well, I don't want to meet them," Swain said.

Benjamin signaled for Yahze and Vogel to come into the room. Yahze came in first. Swain eyed him suspiciously. The Navajo shaman was dressed in a beaded antelope-skin jacket bound at the waist by a rattlesnake-skin belt whose buckle was the fanged snake's head. His buckskin pants ended draped over fine-tooled leather boots. His headband was bright yellow with a stunning black nine-pointed star centered over his forehead. Golden eagle feathers hung down from both sides of the band, framing his long, gray hair that was woven into pigtails.

"Hello, Brother," Yahze said in the ancient Aztec tongue. Swain's reaction was immediate.

"Get him out of here!" Swain's voice quivered with fear. He was so distracted and upset that he did not notice Rabbi Vogel slip quietly into the room and stood behind the FBI agent operating the video camera.

Yahze took a Navajo fetish doll from his jacket pocket and held it out in Swain's direction.

The Paronto saw the doll. His eyes widened. "No. No. Take it away." He curled up in a fetal position. "Take it away," he whimpered.

Rabbi Vogel observed Swain's reaction with great interest.

Nicholas Perez was in his office with Raymond Light and Melvin Plotter, discussing the timing for the release of the nuclear waste material, when a light within the pentagram behind his desk began to flicker.

"Aieeee," Perez called out and shuddered as a sharp pain ripped through his chest. He spun around in his black leather chair and looked at the flickering light. "Someone attacks us. They are with Swain."

In the hospital room, Benjamin and the two agents watched in awe as Yahze placed the doll on Swain's chest. The Paronto shook uncontrollably. His eyes rolled back in his head so that only the whites were visible. His teeth chattered and his arms and legs flailed about, throwing off his blanket. Vogel began to pray quietly in Hebrew. Yahze held his hands out over Swain's body, raising and dropping them like a puppeteer until his motions seemed to control Swain's undulating body. Blood began to ooze from beneath the dressings on his wounds. Then Yahze raised his voice and chanted in Aztec:

"He made it. He made it. He made it.
At the place where the people
Emerged from the underworld,
Near the Lake of Emergence, he made it.
He made it with the female wood and the male wood.
He made it with the Black Mesa rock.
He made it with the hard river rock.
He made it with the help of
The-Most-High-Power-Whose-Ways-Are-Fearful ..."

Perez felt the pain being inflicted on his servant Swain. He stood and discarded his suit jacket. Stains of blood appeared and spread in the same places on his body as they had on Swain's. Perez raised his arms. The pentagram lifted off the wall and hovered above his head. Light and Plotter fell to their knees as their master's head morphed into that of the Aztec serpent god Quetzalcoatl. Its yellow-beaked mouth, surrounded by shiny blue and green scales, opened and emitted a hiss that sounded like a deep, gasping sigh. A brilliant reddish orange glow burst from Swain's flickering light within the pentagram and connected with the serpent's eyes, and they glowed red.

Swain's eye whites also began to glow red.

Yahze's chants became louder and stronger and were joined by Vogel's prayers.

"We beseech You, our Lord, to protect us from this evil, as you did Abraham, Moses, and Isaac, Rebecca and Leah," the rabbi called out.

Agent Benjamin and the two other agents were dumbstruck. But the agent operating the video camera had the good sense to keep recording, covering all the activity and grabbing close-ups when he could.

The fetish doll began to shrivel and burn. Pieces of it were sucked into Swain's gaping mouth. As he choked and gasped, his chest heaved, swelling to an impossible size so that it looked as if it might burst.

In Perez's office, Quetzalcoatl drew a deep breath, sucking the shaft of light from the pentagram into his being. Along with it came smoke and pieces of the burning fetish doll. The serpent-god gagged and hissed as it swallowed the burning debris.

Blood flowed from Swain's eyes, ears and mouth. The blood oozing from his wounds turned black, emitting a foul odor that sickened the FBI agents in the hospital room.

Swain's light inside Perez's pentagram burst into a bright, blood-red color, then turned black, flickered, and finally was extinguished. The serpent-god's head changed back to become Nicholas Perez.

"He is taken," Yahze said softly. "Taken to his death."

"Dear God," was all Benjamin could muster. Yahze took the charred remains of the fetish doll, crushed them in his hands, and sprinkled the ashes over Swain's limp body.

Vogel joined Yahze at the bedside. Both men carefully examined Swain's remains. They quietly removed Swain's hospital gown and the bandages. They wiped away the red blood and the black blood. They lifted his arms and legs and turned the body over on its stomach, peering and touching, seeking something. "The mouth," Vogel suggested. Yahze pulled Swain's lower jaw downward so that his mouth was open. Vogel bent close and probed inside it with his finger. He found the sign of the dragon tattooed under Swain's tongue.

"He is marked," Yahze whispered to his fellow Vigilant member.

"Please bring that over here," Vogel said to the agent with the camera. After the dragon tattoo had been video'd, Vogel withdrew his finger. "I will need a copy of everything on a DVD," he told Benjamin.

The disk would be given to the Israeli consulate in Salt Lake City and flown by courier to Washington, D.C. That same night it would be transferred to the Israeli diplomatic pouch to Jerusalem. The tape would be with the Ben Zimrah in Safed within sixteen hours. It was done in this manner, rather than as an electronic transfer, to avoid any possibility of interception.

CHAPTER THIRTY

THREE VISITS

Taft picked up some additional information about the movements of Bertha Smalls, Lincoln Foster, and William Claremont. The fact that these three executives were responsible for the storage and disposal of nuclear waste—some of it highly dangerous, some of it with weapons-grade potential—sent a chill down Taft's spine. He also got the D.C. police report about the attack on Bertha Smalls in Rock Creek Park and tied that to the story that Michael Gross had related about the animal-like attacks on the Christensen family. When he tracked the three DOE executives' latest movements, he discovered that they had made visits to three separate nuclear facilities, in Arizona, Texas, and Washington State. Before confronting the three, he decided to visit the facilities. Palo Verde was first.

Howard Cortez studied Andy Taft's CIA ID carefully. The DOE had pulled some surprise security checks at Palo Verde Unit 2. But the CIA had never been involved, and the tests were usually in the form of a mock attack. He handed the ID back to Taft.

"Domestic is a little out of your bailiwick, isn't it, Mr. Taft?"

"Not these days, Mr. Cortez. Homeland Security talks to everyone these days." Taft smiled.

"Please sit down," Cortez said, gesturing to a chair in front of his cluttered desk. "Pardon the mess. The paperwork never ends."

"That's why I'm here," Taft responded. "I'd like to talk to you about Mr. Lincoln Foster's visit here a few weeks ago." Cortez couldn't control the flush of shock that the CIA agent's request caused. He felt his face redden as adrenaline coursed through his body.

"Foster?"

"Yes. DOE's Lincoln Foster. Two weeks ago," Taft said. Cortez's reaction confirmed Taft's suspicion that something was going on. The plant manager's shoulders slumped. His head drooped down as he avoided eye contact with Taft.

"I told them it was impossible."

"What was impossible?"

"Keeping that kind of shipment a secret."

Taft spend the rest of the morning gathering evidence and making copies of the directive and shipping manifest for the materials that Foster had taken from the plant's storage facility in the middle of the night. He thanked Cortez for his cooperation.

"I'm glad it's off my chest. I'm no good at intrigue."

"You did fine, Mr. Cortez. If there's anything else you remember about that night that might give us a clue as to the destination of the shipment, please call me." He handed Cortez his card.

"Well, there is one thing," Cortez said hesitantly. "The men he had with him … they were all, well, not your typical DOE types."

"In what way?"

"I'm a Mexican-American. Third generation. I have some Indian ancestry. Toltec. I think those people were of Aztec ancestry. That's what they looked like."

"How many did you see?"

"Six. Plus Foster. And they were heavily armed."

The next stop was the South Texas Project's Unit 1 in Wadsworth, Texas. Armed with evidence from Arizona, Taft's went directly to the point with Lyman Ashcroft, the unit's general manager. He showed Ashcroft the Palo Verde material and asked to see his. Since Ashcroft had not questioned why the CIA was involved, Taft decided to bluff.

"I know Bertha Smalls was here, and I know she came in the middle of the night," he stated, "and I know she took highly dangerous material from your unit."

"She had the papers. She had the authority. What's the problem?"

"The problem is, where did it go?"

Ashcroft shrugged. "She didn't tell me. But I'll tell you what she did say. She said she would charge me with treason if anything happened to the shipment."

"Why would she say that?"

"I'm thinking 'cause she knows I don't like her. I imagine she thought I might up and tell someone." He paused and stared at Taft. "So what's the problem? That bitch do something she wasn't supposed to?"

"I can't say," Taft answered. "But I would like copies of all the paperwork involved."

Lyman Ashcroft pushed his chair away from his desk and stood up. "That, Mr. Taft, would be my great pleasure."

Anna Sinclair's body had been discovered shortly before Taft arrived in Richland, Washington. The police were treating her death as an accident. The evidence indicated that a rock slide had forced her car off the road and into the Columbia River. The acting plant manager was cooperative and opened the files for Taft to copy the paperwork on the shipment William Claremont had supervised. The high grade of the material in this shipment disturbed the CIA agent. Because of Perez's Cuban communist background and the strange lack of information about his parents, Taft began to suspect that Perez might be involved in terrorist activity. Perhaps he was gathering material for a dirty bomb—an explosive device that could spread deadly radioactive material in a heavily populated urban environment or at a critical facility. And perhaps, Andy Taft speculated, Anna Sinclair's death was no accident. It appeared that Bertha Smalls and her cohorts at the DOE had a lot of explaining to do.

CHAPTER THIRTY-ONE

POKING THE DOE

The activity level at midsummer in Washington, D.C., is like the weather—slow and sultry. Because of vacations, most government offices are lightly staffed. Congress, which seldom convenes for more than one hundred days a year, is, of course, in recess. The president is usually vacationing or traveling. Only tourists fill the capital's hot, humid streets and cool, air-conditioned museums and public buildings.

Andy Taft chose the time just before lunch to present himself to Bertha Smalls at the Department of Energy. He had gone past the building guards without being announced by flashing his CIA ID and throwing them a knowing wink.

He waited until Smalls's secretary went to lunch, then walked into her office and presented his ID.

"May I have a minute?" he asked Smalls. The evil spirit, Trisaga, Ruler of the Triads, stirred uneasily within her. She was not consciously aware of the spirit's presence. It became alert.

The ID was official. Smalls invited him to sit down. She was wary. The CIA was not an agency that interfaced with her domestic jurisdiction. But she was also curious.

"How may I help you, Mr. Taft?" she asked politely, but with the officiousness of a long-entrenched bureaucrat. Taft took out a file he had prepared, filled with a half ream of extraneous paper to make it look thick. He opened it, studied something for a moment, and then looked up.

With the evidence he had gathered in Arizona, Texas, and Washington State, and the involvement of three DOE executives with Nicholas Perez, Taft had decided to play it as though he knew where the shipment had gone.

"It's about Mr. Nicholas Perez," Taft began. "Do you know him?"

"Yes I do," Smalls answered calmly.

"Then you know he is originally from Cuba," Taft said. *So that's why he's here,* Smalls thought.

"He is an American citizen," she said.

"Oh, yes. Of course. That's not really...well... You see, this is rather a delicate matter..."

"Delicate? In what sense?"

"It's about some shipments of nuclear waste materials to Mr. Perez."

"Yes," Smalls said matter-of-factly. She had taken the bait, deciding Taft knew the connection. She was not going to play games with the CIA.

"It seems they were authorized in your name, along with, uh... " He glanced down at his papers. "Yes. Here it is. Mr. Lincoln Foster and Mr. William Claremont." At the mention of those names, the spirit Trisaga focused on Taft.

"That's correct. They both work for me."

"The manifests of shipment list the material as low-grade. But as far as we can determine, other than serving as a collecting point for some low-grade medical isotopes, the facilities where the shipments originated produce only spent fuel, which, as you know, is quite high-grade. In fact, much of it is weapons-grade material." Smalls smiled and nodded.

"Yes. Well, Mr. Taft, I'm sure there's some mistake. We never move that kind of material without authorization from our Nuclear Regulatory Agency. I believe what happened is just a paperwork glitch. Perhaps a typo. The low-grade material that was moved was mostly medical and industrial isotope waste. It was just gathered at those sites to be placed in special secure travel containers to a storage site that Mr. Perez's company has prepared for this purpose. It is all contracted under the jurisdiction of my office."

"Ahhh," Taft said, leaning back in his chair and smiling. "So that's it. Well, Ms. Smalls, I surely am relieved."

"Good. May I ask why the CIA is involved here?"

"Of course. It's part of our cooperation with the Department of Homeland Security. Our interest, and theirs, is to keep weapons-grade materials out of the hands of our enemies. So when a Cuban national, uh, ex-national, but with, shall I say, a questionable family background, pops up on the radar and nuclear materials are involved, we're interested. But you've explained it. We'll just backtrack the paperwork and find out who was sleeping on the job." Taft got up and shook Bertha Smalls's hand, which he found was cold and sweaty. Her body language was stiff and uncomfortable. *Squirm,* he thought to himself as he walked out, closing her office door behind him a little more forceful than necessary.

CHAPTER THIRTY-TWO

SURVEILLANCE

The FBI inquiry into Swain and the Paronto at the Bureau of Indian Affairs yielded the same information Andy Taft received: Swain was a Paronto. His employer was Victory Development Corporation. That, plus the information Robert Christensen had in his computer regarding VDC, and Nicholas Perez's Cuban background, led Agent-in-Charge Benjamin to order round-the-clock FBI surveillance of VDC and its key officers, Perez and Light.

Tracking devices were installed on Perez's and Light's cars. Their phones were tapped and their e-mail and Internet use monitored. Perez was followed every day to his property, which was gated, walled, and guarded by armed Paronto. It was noted that he drove to the site of his flood-control project and went underground. The Department of Justice asked Homeland Security for satellite observation of Perez's property, but it yielded in the way of information. Benjamin considered sending agents disguised as workers at the Utah Division of Water Rights to check on the progress of the flood-control project. He wanted to know what Perez was doing behind his closed gates.

CHAPTER THIRTY-THREE

FOR SALE

Allen Weber was beginning to feel frustrated at being left out of the loop. He toyed with the idea of telling the FBI about Bishop Horne's interceding on behalf of Nicholas Perez to buy the farm, and Bob Christensen's suspicion about the VDC executive. But each time he called Agent Benjamin, he had to leave a message, and it always took a few days for the agent to call back.

Determined to keep his vow of finding the Christensens' killers, Weber decided to probe by himself the only slim leads he had: Bob Christensen's suspicions about Nicholas Perez, and Bishop Horne's interest in the sale of the farm. He called the bishop and told him he was moving forward with the sale of the farm. Horne controlled his surge of delight.

"I think it's a wise decision, Peter. Would you like me to call my friend?"

"You mean Mr. Perez?"

Horne was surprised that Weber remembered the name. "Why, yes. As I told you, he owns the adjacent property."

"Can you set up a meeting?" Horne knew Perez didn't like meeting with people outside his close circle of associates.

"Don't you have an agent handling this, Allen?"

"No. I've decided to handle it myself. We can meet at the farm or in town. Whichever you find convenient."

"Give me a few days and I'll see what I can do."

Weber sensed that Horne was unsure of something. Was the bishop's end of the deal loose? Was he afraid of Perez? He decided to press the issue. "I can't promise it will still be on the market then."

"Can you tell me what you're asking? I can pass that on and perhaps get an offer." Horne knew Perez would pay handsomely for the farm.

"No. I'll want to discuss that in person, if and when we meet." Weber's tone was strong and final.

"Very well, Allen. I'll see what I can do. Good-bye."

There was no "Thank you for calling" or "How's Susan?" But Weber was not surprised. "I'll bet you will," Weber said aloud to himself after he had hung up.

As Weber had imagined, Horne called back in less than an hour. Perez had agreed to a meeting at the farm. Weber told the bishop that he would be available at seven thirty that evening.

It was a warm summer's eve. The last of the livestock had been sold and moved off the farm. The Christensens' personal belongings had been packed. Allen Weber sat on the porch with Taro Heart, whom he asked to be there. He had told her only that he had arranged a meeting to sell the farm, and asked that she sit in as his lawyer.

DAVID SAPERSTEIN

Bishop Horne and Nicholas Perez arrived in separate cars. Horne was alone, Perez came with Raymond Light. Introductions were polite.

"It's such a nice night," Weber said. "We—our family and the Christensens—loved to sit outside on evenings like this." He gestured to a grouping of wicker porch chairs he had arranged. Everyone took a seat.

"It's a beautiful house," Horne said.

"Yes. It was always a home filled with love and children's laughter." Although he was answering Horne, he looked at Perez. The man was unmoved. His expression was stony and his body language stiff and uncomfortable.

"Do you have an asking price?" Raymond Light queried.

"Not exactly," Weber answered. His gaze remained on Perez. "Don't you want to look around?" Perez finally spoke.

"Why?" His voice was deep and penetrating. His eyes, shiny black coals, bore into Weber. Allen felt an icy hand grip his heart. He fought off the fear that Perez had conjured in him.

"This land has been in my wife's family for generations. I want it to go to someone who appreciates and respects the work and care that went into it. So anyone not interested in that, well, that speaks volumes to me." Perez moved in his chair, making the aged, -beaten wicker groan. It was the only sound heard for a long moment. "And because of what happened here to my family, to the children, I want to know this farm will be respected and treated as the hallowed ground it has become."

"Now, Allen," Bishop Horne began nervously, noticing Perez's discomfort. "That's a bit presumptive of you.

180

Hallowed? I mean, after all—" Weber lifted his hand and cut him off.

"With all due respect, Bishop Horne, that's what's most important to me." Taro Heart knew enough to understand that Allen Weber was up to something more than selling the farm. "So, if Mr. Perez is still interested, we can take a ride around in my Cherokee." Perez eyed Weber for a moment and then got up.

"Of course, Mr. Weber. Forgive my insensitivity. Please. I understand completely." He turned to Light. "Raymond, we're going to be longer than I imagined. Take my car, and go back to the office. Bishop Horne will drive me back to town." He had not asked the bishop. His words, an order, were not lost on Weber or Taro Heart.

The FBI team assigned to follow Perez and Light told Benjamin that they had come to the farm in Perez's car, but that Light had left alone.

"You guys hang in there. I'll send a car to intercept and follow Light. Let me know when Perez leaves, and with whom. This guy is beginning to really interest me." He hung up and wondered what Weber was up to.

The tour of the farm took an hour. It was dusk when they drove across the barren alfalfa fields to the site of Robert Christensen's now suspended flood-control project. Other than a few drainage ditches and the beginnings of a canal, there was little more to identify it as a construction site. Weber stopped near the fence and got out. The others followed. The domed rock was visible in the gathering shadows beyond the new, formidable fence that Perez had installed.

"This is where my brother-in-law had started his flood-control project. But of course you're familiar with that, Mr.

Perez. You'll recall that we spoke about it." Weber's tone was sarcastic and combative.

"Yes, we did. We are doing one too. I told you that. The topography in this area is prone to flooding. Good soil, but unreliable in the spring."

"He had to go to Phoenix to find a willing contractor and equipment," Weber continued, ignoring Perez's remark. "But you knew that, Mr. Perez, didn't you? You knew a lot about what Bob Christensen was doing."

Perez glared at Weber. "What do you want, Mr. Weber?" he asked impatiently.

"Why did you try to stop by brother-in-law from completing his flood-control project?" Weber asked angrily. Taro Heart now understood what this was about.

"You are way out of line, Mr. Weber. I never tried to stop anything." Weber, a tall man, moved closer. He towered over Perez.

"Am I, Mr. Perez?"

The sun had set behind the mountains, leaving the four of them standing in a deepening purple shadow.

"You don't want to sell this farm, do you," Perez said. Weber only smiled. Perez turned to Heart. "Isn't that correct, Ms. Heart?"

"I really don't know, Mr. Perez," she answered truthfully. Perez then glared at Bishop Horne.

"Then why bring us all out here, Allen?" Horne asked, nervously. "I don't understand you." The bishop was visibly upset. "This is most embarrassing."

"I meant what I said back at the house, Bishop, about respect and the hallowed memory of my family." Weber gazed at the domed rock as he spoke. "I think Mr. Perez understands."

"You think I should have helped your brother-in-law?
Perez asked. "That I should have, as you suggested on the
phone, shared my assets. Well I didn't think so then, and I
don't now. Nor do I take lightly being brought out here and
scolded by one of Desert's clerks. I know a lot about you,
and your pioneer family. But you know nothing of me. Keep
your wife's farm, Mr. Weber, or sell it. It is of little
consequence to me." He turned to Horne. "If you will get
your misguided congregant to take us back to your car, I
have other, more important, matters to attend to."

Nothing was said on the way back to the house. The
atmosphere in the Jeep was icy and tense. By the time they
got to the farmhouse it was almost dark. No good-byes were
exchanged. Bishop Horne was obviously very nervous.

As Perez got into Horne's car, he glared at Weber, who
was walking away. Taro Heart saw it. She thought she saw
his eyes glowing red, and his lips parting and curling
upward. For a brief moment, Nicholas Perez seemed more
feline than human.

CHAPTER THIRTY-FOUR

A CALL FROM ISRAEL

The cell phone in Isadore Vogel's pocket vibrated with insistence. He was in the room that Michael Benjamin had set up for Professor Goode, Jacob Yahze, Allen Weber, and Rabbi Vogel to continue their study of the golden plates. The rabbi looked at his phone. He had a message to call Rabbi Levi Lemach ben Abraham in Safed.

Vogel excused himself and went to a small office down the hall that Benjamin had assigned to the group and where there was a secure FBI landline. Vogel placed the call.

"We have reviewed the videotape you sent, Isadore," said Rabbi ben Abraham, leader of the Ben Zimrah and a member of The Vigilant. "It is both revealing and disturbing."

"What have you determined, Levi? Vogel asked.

"This was a servant, a disciple—we think an important one. But he was not a sub-prince or archangel."

"Whom does he serve?" Vogel's heart was beating rapidly at the thrill of what he had discovered—an evil one confirmed.

"Ahhh, my dear Isadore. That is the question. We do not believe it is Satan. He was marked with the dragon, as you so aptly discovered."

"Yes. Under the tongue."

"As you may recall, Satan marked his servants with a backward C. It is possible this one, this Indian Swain, was close to either Leviathan or Belial."

A surge of adrenaline made Vogel shudder and sent a wave of nausea through him. Belial or Leviathan. Might this lead to another fallen archangel to confront?

"Your choice to bring the shaman into The Vigilant was a wise one. Investigate the one Swain worked for."

"Nicholas Perez?"

"Yes. And those close to him. Try to get a close look at that domed rock you told us about. If the Shaman sensed evil, there is the chance that it may be an unholy gathering place, or a tomb. Meanwhile, we will prepare here to aid you."

"Thank you, Levi." Vogel stiffened with purpose. "There is one more person that I will need to help us. He is a close relative of the slain family. Allen Weber. I believe you know him."

"Weber. The Mormon missionary who studied Aramaic in Jerusalem and went on digs."

"Yes. He can help us. He is well connected in his church. He knows the area and is very motivated."

"I imagine he is. Michael Gross told us about him while you were on your way to Salt Lake City."

"A small world, Levi."

"Yes, Isadore. Do what you think prudent. Gross also decided to involve our friends Andy Taft and Sasha

Andreyev. They are doing some investigating in Washington. I suspect Mr. Taft will soon call you."

Andy Taft is involved, Vogel thought. *CIA. Sasha Andreyev. SVR, Russia's Foreign Intelligence Service, which took over that area of the old KGB. Michael Gross. Mossad. These were all people in The Vigilant, and all who shared the experience of capturing and imprisoning Satan. If that was the case, the Ben Zimrah must be fairly certain an evil archangel is lurking nearby, in Utah, Arizona, New Mexico, or Nevada, at a spot, called the Four Corners, where the four states met.* Vogel now believed the hunt was really on.

"I look forward to his call, Levi."

"Remember, Isadore. If a fallen archangel is close, you know what you may be confronting. Be very careful, my dear friend."

CHAPTER THIRTY-FIVE

MORE THAN A ROCK

"Be careful." Those were the words Andy Taft had uttered to Rabbi Vogel after informing him about Nicholas Perez and the deadly nuclear waste that had been shipped to Utah in the guise of low-grade medical and industrial isotope waste material. Jacob Yahze and Vernon Flood, also members of The Vigilant, listened on speakerphone in the office Agent-in-Charge Benjamin had provided in the FBI command center.

"Getting to that rock is now our top priority," Vogel told the others after Taft had hung up. "We need to know what is there. Also what Perez is up to with the nuclear materials."

"Taft said the FBI has not made the connection yet between Perez and the DOE," Flood remarked. "If we told Benjamin, perhaps he could arrange for a search warrant."

"I'm not sure that's the best approach, Vernon," Vogel said. He was not sure Benjamin would be as sympathetic to The Vigilant's mission as to his assignment to solve the Christensen murders.

"I agree," Yahze added. "I am wary. With our tribe's long and bitter experience with the federal government, there's one thing I do know. Once the FBI moves in, it will be with a heavy hand. This kind of action could alert a fallen archangel—or his sub-princes, if that is what we have here. We should listen to the warnings from Mr. Taft and Rabbi ben Abraham."

"You're right," Vogel agreed. "We need to get close to the rock by ourselves. And for that we will need Allen Weber's cooperation."

The four men watched silently as Allen Weber guided Robert Christensen's pickup across the barren field toward the fence. It was past dusk. The truck's lights were off. The smooth top of the domed rock, which loomed ahead of them on the other side of the razor-wired fence, was deep purple in the fading light. Yahze, who sat in the front seat next to Weber, strained to see if anyone was near the rock. Vogel and Flood, in the back seat of the extended cab, also peered out at the darkening terrain.

"We should go on foot from here," Yahze suggested. The men got out as quietly as possible. They removed two shovels, a pick, a crowbar, and an extendable aluminum ladder from the flatbed of the truck.

When they were about fifty yards from the fence, Jacob Yahze raised his hand, indicating for the others to stop. He knelt down, quietly placing on the ground next to him the pick and shovel he carried, and signaled for the others to follow suit.

"There is someone watching the rock," he whispered. "Two or three, I think. Let's have a look. Leave the tools here."

Yahze led the others as they stealthily approached the fence, keeping as low as possible and using every rise, rock, and bush as cover. When they got as close as they dared, they were disheartened. Four men, armed with automatic weapons, were guarding the domed rock.

"Paronto," Yahze whispered. Vogel and his cohorts would have to find another way to find proof for the Ben Zimrah to expose Perez's connection to evil. The shaman was about to suggest that they back off when headlights raked the area. The four men flattened themselves to the ground and remained motionless. A sleek black Mercedes SUV pulled up next to the rock.

"That's Perez's car," Weber whispered to the others as it stopped and the headlights went out. A small man got out. He was alone. Two of the Paronto rushed to the man's side, guarding him the way the Secret Service might guard a president. The man did something with his hand alongside the rock. It was too dark for the four observers to see exactly what he did. They heard a whooshing sound, like sand spilling down a chute. The man then walked to the front of the rock, the side closest to the fence, and paused. He stared in the direction of the four hidden men.

A shiver tore down Weber's spine. "It's Perez," he whispered. Yahze, Vogel, and Flood studied the diminutive man whose gaze scanned the Christensen property. The three exchanged a look that confirmed what they all felt. Evil permeated the night air, its source the man Weber had identified as Nicholas Perez.

Perez turned away from the fence and appeared to walk down into the earth and under the rock, disappearing from view. The Paronto guards took up defensive positions, with their weapons at the ready.

Yahze waited a moment, then indicated that they should crawl back one at a time, pick up their tools, and leave.

"I will watch," he told them. "If you hear an owl hoot, it is my warning to freeze and stay low." Flood went first, then Vogel, then Weber. When Yahze saw they were all at a safe distance, he crawled away. But even as he moved away from the rock, the evil presence stayed with him.

As Weber drove the pickup back to the farmhouse, feeling his way in the dark with only the light of a quarter moon to illuminate the terrain, Yahze revealed what he had sensed about Perez.

"I too felt an evil presence," Vogel said after Yahze had finished. Flood concurred.

Allen Weber listened and pondered his own feelings in the presence of Nicholas Perez. *Yes,* he thought, *evil is the correct term. And ruthlessness.* Their confrontation in at the fence left little doubt his mind that doubt that Nicholas Perez was responsible for the murders the Christensen family.

CHAPTER THIRTY-SIX

DINNER FOR SEVEN

Later that same night after the incident at the rock as the four men discussed their next move, Andy Taft called again. He shared the proof that Lincoln Foster and William Claremont were part of Bertha Smalls's covert nuclear waste operation with Perez. Taft suggested that Foster and Claremont might be the key to discovering who Swain's master was, and where. Vogel related how Perez had the domed rock guarded.

"Remember, Isadore," Taft warned, "we discovered that the sub-princes and their master usually keep some servants close. But others are distant, assigned to do their evil bidding. Getting their hands on that waste material seems about as evil as it can get these days."

"You are thinking about a dirty bomb?" Vogel asked.

"In a place like Utah, the center of an entire religious group," Taft answered solemnly.

"It would be a devastating blow to our church," Flood said quietly. "A disaster."

"If we can tie those two DOE guys to Perez," Taft continued, "I think we might find a way into his organization, his land, and that rock."

During this conversation, Weber remained silent. Although he had been accepted as part of this group and of their investigation of Nicholas Perez, this talk of sub-princes and archangels had never been clearly explained to him. Neither had the relationship among Taft, Vogel, Flood, and Yahze, four men with very diverse backgrounds and vocations who were focused on one mission. He knew nothing of The Vigilant.

"Foster and Claremont dine together once a week at the same restaurant," Taft said. "That may our opportunity."

Two days later, Rabbi Vogel and Allen Weber were seated in a quiet French restaurant, Nuit et Jour (Night and Day), located on the second floor of a Georgetown brownstone in Washington. It was an expensive, out-of-the-way bistro, offering excellent cuisine and an impressive wine list. Their table was near that of the two DOE executives.

Taft, Flood, and Sasha Andreyev were parked downstairs in a nine-seat custom black Lexus SUV, the vehicle favored by the CIA. Sasha, a trained driver, sat behind the wheel with the motor running.

When Foster and Claremont finished their meal and signaled for their check, Vogel did the same. As they left the restaurant, Foster and Claremont passed Vogel and Weber's table. The rabbi became dizzy. His vision was blurred for a moment, and then cleared as the two men walked away.

"Bad spirits," he told Weber, "and powerful. They will be difficult. Are you ready, my friend?" Vogel asked as he keyed his cell phone to alert Taft.

"I've been ready for this a long time," Weber answered.

When the two DOE executives emerged from the restaurant onto the quiet Georgetown street, Vogel and Weber were a short distance behind them. Sasha drove the Lexus up and parked directly in front of the brownstone. Taft got out and opened the rear door, as though he was letting a passenger out. Foster was only a few steps from Taft. Claremont was slightly behind his partner, looking for a taxi.

Vogel rushed up from behind and pushed Foster into the arms of Taft, who shoved him into the Lexus, where Flood rammed the needle of syringe filled with a strong sedative into his neck. Simultaneously, Weber grabbed Claremont from behind, while Vogel grabbed him from the front. Taft, now out of the Lexus, joined in, and the three men rapidly shoved the confused Claremont into the rear seat, now empty, as Flood had pulled the drugged Foster back to the third row of seats of the customized Lexus. As Claremont entered the SUV, head first, pulled by Taft and pushed by Weber and Vogel, Flood leaned over and rammed the needle into his neck, emptying the remaining sedative, a curare derivative, into the struggling man's neck. Its effect on the brain was immediate. Claremont collapsed into Taft's lap. Weber jumped into the rear seat and Vogel into the front passenger seat. Doors slammed and Sasha hit the gas pedal. The Lexus screeched away into the night. The entire operation had taken less than fifteen seconds.

CHAPTER THIRTY-SEVEN

COMING OUT

It was just past midnight. The District and the surrounding bedroom communities were quiet. This was an early-to-bed, early-to-rise part of the country.

In the bedroom of a suite at the Holiday Inn in Crystal City, Virginia, across the Potomac, the last item that Jacob Yahze placed on the round wooden table at the foot of the bed was a polished piece of brilliant turquoise. Next to it were three other symbols required for the ceremony.

One was a clay bowl, kiln-fired blue and yellow and filled with white corn kernels, a hybrid developed by the Navajo centuries ago. Next to it, a grinding stone on which a small mound of dried boysenberries and two bluebird eggshells had been placed on two strips of wet birch bark. Finally, a crystal jar of clear water, gathered from the first spring rain. These were all the physical ingredients the shaman needed.

Yahze wore his beaded antelope jacket and headband with the nine-pointed yellow star emblazoned on it. Eight feathers from a golden eagle dangled from the headband on either side of braided gray hair. A long necklace of bear claws and orca teeth hung down to his waist.

The bed had been pulled away from the wall and placed in the center of the room. The curtains were drawn, the windows closed and locked. The only illumination came from candles made of rendered buffalo fat that also scented the room.

Lincoln Foster and William Claremont were now awake, bound and gagged, lying side by side on a king-size mattress that was covered with heavy plastic sheeting. The bedding had been removed. They were blindfolded and naked under an ancient Navajo blanket decorated with blue clouds and a mountain covered with snakes.

Sasha Andreyev sat in an armchair near the door to the suite's living room. Andy Taft stood next to her. He held a 9mm Glock automatic in his right hand.

Vernon Flood came out of the bathroom wearing a long white robe over his street clothes. In his hand he held a leather pouch, its neck tied with a red silk ribbon.

"I'm ready, Jacob," Flood told the shaman.

Yahze glanced over at Rabbi Vogel, who was positioned with Allen Weber in front of a long chest of drawers along the wall opposite the drawn curtains. The rabbi turned to view the screen of a laptop. Hooked up next to it was a video camera that Weber operated. Vogel spoke to the camera.

"Can you see everything clearly?"

A response came back immediately.

"We can see perfectly, Rabbi." It was Michael Gross. He was in Safed with Rabbi ben Abraham, viewing the hotel room via a secure CIA satellite link to Mossad.

"Good." Vogel turned to Weber. "No matter what happens, keep that camera aimed on the bed." Weber nodded. Vogel turned to Yahze. "We are ready, Jacob."

Yahze began to hum softly. He picked up a stone pestle and crushed the boysenberries, bluebird eggshells, and birch bark strips into a paste on the grinding stone.

Vernon Flood walked to the head of the bed. The headboard had been removed, replaced by a small nightstand. He opened the leather pouch. It was lined with red velvet. Inside were two parchments mounted in ivory frames. One was black, the other white. Yahze finished grinding the paste.

"Let them see," he told Flood. The blindfolds were removed. Foster and Claremont glared at the people in the room with palpable hatred. In the next room, Sasha Andreyev, a former KGB operative who had witnessed many horrible deeds in Moscow's infamous Lubyanka prison, shuddered. Taft felt the evil too. He took Sasha's hand to comfort her, and himself.

Yahze stared into the hateful eyes of his captives.

"They covered this mountain with a blue cloud blanket and decorated it with turquoise, white corn, dark mists, and the female rain." Yahze began. As he spoke, he gestured to the elements before him. "They placed a turquoise basket on the highest peak, and in it they put two eggs of the bluebird called Doli. Bluebirds are Tso dzil's feather. They sent the big snake to guard the doorway that no spirit might enter." Then, one by one, he lifted each item on the table. "Turquoise from the highest peak; white corn from fields that nourish; female rain, the water of mother spring that brings life; and dark mist… " The shaman put a match to the mixture of ground boysenberries, bluebird eggsshells, and wet birch bark. A wisp of dark smoke wafted up and spread over the blue cloud blanket. "Tso dzil, the Abalone Shell Boy, the one we know as Twilight Boy, is of the mountain of the West—our mountain. He was fastened to the earth with a stone knife." Yahze took from his pocket a stone knife similar to the one used on the Christensen farm. He raised it above the two captives plunged it into the mattress between them, and began to chant.

The rent in the mattress widened. A loud hissing sound came from within, as though a large snake were sheltered underneath. Foster and Claremont arched their backs as the mattress began to heat up beneath them. They twisted and began to moan. Their mouths opened and long green tongues emerged, flailing about like snakes without eyes or scent, tracking as snake tongues might search for prey. The snake image on the Navajo blanket, shrouded in the dark mist from the smoldering grinding stone, came to life. Foster and Claremont writhed in pain. The blanket snake opened an enormous mouth and roared, sucking in the two men's tongues, yanking the prone Foster and Claremont up into a sitting position. The two DOE executives howled in pain. Yahze stopped his chant abruptly.

"We have them," he yelled to Vernon Flood.

Allen Weber was stunned. It took all the self-control he could muster to keep from running out of the room. What kind of madness was this? His body trembled. He could barely keep the camera steady. But he held fast, sending the startling images halfway around the world to Israel.

"And I beheld multitudes of people who were sick," Flood said aloud, "and who were afflicted with all manner of diseases, and with devils and unclean spirits." The Mormon librarian's stentorian voice filled the room as he read from the parchment framed in ivory. Black liquid oozed from the captives' mouths and spread onto the plastic covering.

"The evil comes forth," Yahze announced as he lifted the turquoise over the two men on the bed.

Flood continued reading from the parchment. "Therefore the spirit of devils did enter into them and take possession of their house." Foster let out a wail that shook the room. Claremont joined in with him. "And these shall be cast out into outer darkness!" The wailing of both men turned into a single, ghostly, sickening lament, like a mortally wounded animal. "There shall be weeping and wailing and gnashing of teeth, and this because of their own iniquity," Flood shouted as he pointed to Foster and Claremont.

The dark liquid turned blood-red and spread farther onto the plastic covering around them. Yahze pulled the blanket away to reveal that the entire plastic cover on the mattress was covered with the foul liquid. The snake, which had remained hovering over the two men with their long green tongues held in its mouth, released them.

Allen Weber gasped, rapidly sucking in air, trying to understand what he was witnessing and fearful that he might faint. But he kept the camera steadily trained on the bed.

"The spirits are out," Yahze announced as Foster and Claremont fell back onto the bed, motionless. Their tongues retreated back into their mouths. The snake slid to its place on the blanket that had fallen onto the floor and became inanimate once again.

The dark red fluid continued to spread as though it were alive, rippling and coursing around the inert bodies like arms seeking to envelope them.

"Shall we send them away?" the shaman asked.

"Yes. But first we must know them," Flood answered. "The angel Moroni spoke of knowing evil when he gave the holy golden plates to John Smith. We must know this evil's name so that we may destroy it." Flood took the parchment and read, "Now this is the state of souls of the wicked, yea, in darkness, and a state of awful, fearful looking for the fiery indignation of the wrath of God upon them; thus they remain in this state, as well as the righteous in paradise, until the time of their resurrection." The dark red liquid began to dry and turn to a reddish-brown powder. "You are called now by name, for until that is done resurrection shall forever be denied." The liquid was gone. Flood threw the parchment into the rusty powder and it immediately turned into a black, powdery ash. "I command your name before God almighty!"

Yahze began to hum and chant. Rabbi Vogel repeated the Sh'ma, the ancient Hebrew prayer, "Hear, oh Israel, the Lord our God, the Lord is One."

"Reveal yourselves!" Flood bellowed. The ash swirled and encircled the unconscious men on the bed. Then it settled and formed names, in ancient Aramaic, on the foreheads of Lincoln Foster and William Claremont.

"Hacamuli," Vogel said as he pointed to Foster.

Allen Weber stepped forward to get a closer view of the writing.

"And this is called Orgosil," Weber said, translating the words on Claremont's brow.

Yahze pulled the stone knife from the mattress. The ash swirled again and disappeared.

"They are gone," the shaman announced.

"Yes," Flood agreed. "But there are scores and scores of such spirits that the archangels and their sub-princes may call forth and command." Foster and Claremont stirred. Dazed, they opened their eyes and began to weep.

Sasha Andreyev and Andy Taft, who were standing in the bedroom doorway, relaxed but continued to clasp each other's hands. They glanced over at Allen Weber, still operating the video camera. His face was ashen. They both smiled at him.

"Quite a show, huh?" Taft said. "Your Aramaic is still excellent." Weber managed a sheepish grin, but his expression was one that said, *What have I gotten myself into?*

Later, as Taft and Weber cleaned up the room and put the furniture back in order, Sasha and Yahze tended to the two DOE executives, who were still in shock. Taft arranged for them to be moved to a secure government psychiatric facility, where they would be isolated and treated.

In the suite's living room, Isadore Vogel and Vernon Flood spoke with Rabbi ben Abraham via the secure satellite hookup. The Ben Zimrah leader, who was now in a chamber deep below the walled, six-hundred-year-old compound, had witnessed the entire ceremony. Michael Gross, who had recorded it in Israel, operated the camera that was focused on Rabbi ben Abraham.

"You did well, Mr. Flood," Rabbi ben Abraham said. "As did Shaman Yahze. Isadore, as I said before, your judgment was excellent in asking Jacob Yahze to join The Vigilant." The leader of the Ben Zimrah was a serious man, not prone to giving praise easily.

"Thank you, Levi," Vogel responded.

"Do you know these spirits, Rabbi?" Flood asked.

Rabbi ben Abraham indicated for Gross back up and widen the camera's view. Inscribed on the four walls of the chamber, made of yellow Jerusalem stone, were the names of the four fallen archangels. "Each wall is devoted to one archangel," Rabbi ben Abraham began. "Satan the north, Belial the west, Leviathan the south, and Lucifer the east. Each has the names of their sub-princes inscribed beneath theirs, and beneath that the names of the spirits that served each sub-prince." The strong light on Gross's camera revealed the names in ancient Aramaic, chiseled into the Jerusalem stone. Below each archangel's name were their sub-princes—Asmoseus, Ariton, Beelzebub, Amaimon, Magot, Piamon, Astarot, and Oriens. And beneath those, the names of hundreds of evil spirits that served them.

In the center of the room, lit by oil lamps, was a table on which a magnificent blue and purple robe was spread. On top of that was a golden breastplate with twelve jewels set into it, each representing one of the twelve tribes of Israel. Reuven: ruby; Shimon: topaz; Levy: beryl; Yehudah: turquoise; Yissakhar: sapphire; Zebulun: diamond; Dan: jacinth; Naphtali: agate; Gad: jasper; Asher: emerald; Yosef: onyx; and Binyamin: –jade. A golden miter, gold chains and clasps, and other garments of white—trimmed in gold and blue—surrounded the breastplate. These were the robes and vestments of Aaron, brother of Moses, and the first priest of Israel. They were discovered in an ancient tunnel beneath the Temple Mount in Jerusalem by Sholem Asher, a noted archaeologist. He secretly brought them to Rabbi ben Abraham because he knew that the Ben Zimrah sect understood the power the vestments and robes contained for combating evil and protecting Israel.

"The spirits you drove out of those unfortunate men are servants to Asmodeus and Beelzebub," Rabbi ben Abraham said as he walked to the Western Wall and pointed to their names. "This is the wall of Belial, despoiler of the environment. The one called Hacamuli was the spirit that withers. It destroys the life that nurtures us. Our food. The other, Orgosil, was the spirit of tumultuous events, the harbinger of environmental disaster. These two are usually alone. But they were brought together, perhaps with others. They may be part of a dangerous plot. We must locate their masters, the sub-princes Amaimon and Beelzebub." His hand and the camera tilted up to the sub-princes names on the wall. "And when we do, we must destroy them."

"We will start immediately," Vogel said.

"We will not rest," Flood added.

"You say these two men had a supervisor?"

"Yes. A woman in the government. Bertha Smalls. The one said to have been attacked by an animal in the park."

"You must find her. Her body may harbor one of these sub-princes. If that is the case, be very careful. It will take more than what you three have done today to destroy it. These are powerfully evil entities that you seek."

"We will be careful," Vogel assured Rabbi ben Abraham.

"There is one more thing. Amaimon and Beelzebub make their own deadly mischief, but they in turn are controlled and beholden to another. Of that one, be warned and extremely wary"—Rabbi ben Abraham's hand gestured up to the top of the chamber's Western Wall—"for he is the archangel Belial, fallen with his three brothers from God's grace. His only desire is to foul the Earth and destroy all of our Lord's creation, but especially mankind."

CHAPTER THIRTY-EIGHT

SPIRITS DEPART

While the ceremony to exorcize the spirits Hacamuli and Orgosil from the DOE executives was taking place, Raymond Light was with Nicholas Perez in the underground chamber where the nuclear waste material had been deposited. The shafts leading to the aquifers had been opened. All that remained was for the steel and lead containers to be opened, and their contents, mostly highly radioactive spent fuel rods, sent down the shafts into the aquifers. Perez had determined that four Paronto could do the job in two weeks. As they discussed who was expendable to assign the task—for whoever did it would surely be dead from radiation poisoning within a few days—Raymond Light, whose body harbored Beelzebub, sub-prince to Belial, was struck with a gut-wrenching sickness. He doubled over, then fell to the ground, writhing in pain.

"Who is it?" Perez demanded.

Light had sensed his servant spirits Hacamuli and Orgosil. The ceremony to drive them out of Foster and Claremont had begun. He started to bleed from his nose and ears, and had difficulty speaking. "They have captured my servants, Hacamuli and Orgosil. They use the power of the ancient Shaman and another. A Mormon, who uses his words!" The pain increased. "They move to expel my servants from the men you bid me to give them."

"Who dares to do this?" Perez asked. His eyes began to glow red and his teeth yellowed into fangs. He too was beginning to feel the expulsion of the two spirits from the service of his sub-prince.

"I cannot see!" Raymond Light screamed. "I cannot stop them." His tongue, that of Beelzebub, long and black, shot out of his mouth, licking wildly at the air as though he were gasping for breath. Perez pulled Light up on his feet. The tongue retracted, but black ooze still dripped from his mouth. "They are destroyed, master. And their names are known." Perez was furious. He paced back and forth in front of the deadly nuclear waste.

"A Navajo, a Mormon, and a Jew dare to do this? I felt them watching my home. Puny mortals. I will crush them. But first we must gather power. I will call to your brother, Amaimon. He will send Trisaga, in the woman Smalls's body, to me."

Bertha Smalls, possessed by Trisaga, was still disturbed by the visit from that arrogant CIA spook Taft, but she had not yet contacted Perez about it. She knew that this was a delicate time for him because of the waste material shipment. Plus, she knew she was being watched, and she believed her caution would be appreciated. Trisaga ached to meet Belial one day, as it had been promised by Amaimon. When the call came from Melvin Plotter, who identified himself as an associate of Nicholas Perez, Trisaga was excited. Plotter ordered Smalls to come to Perez.

"You must leave your office immediately. Go to Dulles Airport. There is a ticket for you on American Airlines to Dallas and an America West flight from there to Salt Lake City. I will meet you at the airport."

"Is anything wrong?" she asked, hearing the anxiety in his voice. "The shipments? Are they okay?"

"Do not question. Just come!" He abruptly hung up.

Smalls—with Trisaga, Ruler of Triads in control—gathered the papers detailing the transfer of the nuclear waste material shipments and left her office. On the way out, she hesitated, considering whether to stop by and alert Foster and Claremont, but then thought better of it. If she were finally to meet Belial, they would be jealous. She was in no mood for grousing from underlings now.

Fifteen minutes after she left DOE headquarters, Andy Taft and two trusted CIA operatives arrived to arrest her. Flood, Vogel, and Weber were waiting in Crystal City to perform the exorcism. If she was possessed like Foster and Claremont, who were in a psychiatric clinic operated by the CIA, then The Vigilant now had the means to drive out the spirit. Finding her gone and her files disrupted, Taft put out a request through Homeland Security to scan all transportation leaving the Washington area.

Three hours later, Bertha Smalls popped up on a flight manifest to Dallas with a connection to Salt Lake City. Taft notified his cohorts in Crystal City.

"We will have to get the FBI involved now," he told them. "I don't have the resources to track her. My scope of operation in the country is limited. And with that nuclear material floating around, we'd better gather our forces and get some help."

Taft then called FBI Agent-in-Charge Michael Benjamin. He introduced himself, made all the connections that Benjamin needed to know—Smalls, Foster, Claremont, Perez, nuclear waste, Utah. He suggested that Smalls be followed from Dallas to Salt Lake. "Let's see who meets her and where they go."

CHAPTER THIRTY-NINE

A BISHOP TAKEN

Rabbi Vogel remained behind in the national's capital. He needed to consult with others of The Vigilant in Safed, and to plan the next moves. Andy Taft informed them that after his conversation with FBI Agent-in-Charge Benjamin, he was satisfied they had a strong ally.

Vernon Flood flew back to Salt Lake City with Jacob Yahze and Allen Weber. They discussed Weber's encounter with Perez, which Bishop Horne had arranged. Weber discussed the confrontation at the farm in detail with Flood, who was especially interested in the bishop's subservience to Perez.

"Horne approached me after the Council of the Twelve Apostles meeting," Flood told his companions, "insisting that he be involved with my investigation into the murders of your family, Allen."

"So you think his relationship with Perez might be more than as just a friend?" Weber asked.

"I'm not sure. He's a political animal and might just be cultivating Perez for his money and connections."

"Or maybe he's been possessed to serve Beelzebub and Amaimon, like Claremont and Foster," Yahze suggested. They agreed that it was time to test the bishop's loyalty. Flood called Horne and told him there were new developments in the Christensen case. They made an appointment to meet in Flood's office in the Tabernacle, later that afternoon.

It was another hot summer afternoon in Salt Lake. The air pollution, one of the worst in America, hung heavy and brown over the city. This penchant for man-made ecological nightmares was one of the reasons Belial chose to make America his home.

Bishop Horne coughed as he ascended the white steps of the great Mormon Tabernacle. After sixty-seven years, he had much in common with inner-city children all over the country. He was developing serious asthma.

"Got a summer cold?" Vernon Flood asked as he escorted the bishop to a special room deep underground below the massive tabernacle.

"No. Just a drip," Horne answered. He took out his handkerchief and blew his nose. Flood noticed that the brown mucus was specked with blood. They reached the door to the room and Flood took out a set of keys to open the three locks.

"What is this place?" Horne asked.

The door swung open and Flood gestured for the bishop to enter. Flood did not answer, but indicated that the bishop should sit in a chair in the center of the plain, windowless room. It had a white pine floor and painted white walls. A gold light fixture hung from the white ceiling above the chair. Large armoires were placed along three of the walls.

Another door, closed, was in one corner. The door through which they had entered swung closed and locked. Flood then went to one of the armoires and opened it.

"There are several similar rooms on this level. They are part of my domain as chief librarian of the church," Flood said as he removed two items from the armoire and placed them on a small table a few feet in front of Horne, who had sat down. He then stepped in front of the table, blocking the bishop's view. "What business do you have with Nicholas Perez?" he asked the bishop directly. His deep, resonant voice was accusatory and firm. For a moment Horne was confused. He had expected to be informed about the Christensen murders.

"Excuse me? What are you talking about?"

"Nicholas Perez. You brought him to Allen Weber to buy the Christensen farm. Apparently you were quite insistent."

Bishop Horne got control of himself. "What business is that of yours?"

"It's a simple question, Bishop. Let me ask again. What is your relationship with Mr. Nicholas Perez?"

Horne stood up and glared at Flood. "And I said that is not your business, librarian." His tone was condescending, implying that Flood should know his place. Flood turned to the table behind him and picked up a black gabardine jacket with black buttons. He turned back to Horne, holding it lovingly in his hands.

"Do you know what this is, Bishop Horne?" Flood asked softly. Horne did not answer. The garment made him feel a little queasy. "It is the jacket worn by the Prophet Joseph Smith on the day he was murdered by a mob of bigots in Indiana."

Horne stood and stepped backward, knocking into the chair and falling onto the floor. He felt increasingly ill. A cold sweat, followed by nausea, swept over him. He was so distracted that he did not hear the corner door open or see Jacob Yahze and Allen Weber enter. Flood proffered the jacket to the cowering man.

"Would you like to try it on, Bishop Horne?"

"No! Take it away!"

"We thought not." Flood placed the jacket back on the table and picked up a piece of aged paper encased in a glass frame. He turned and raised it so that Horne could see. As he did, Horne fell to his knees. "This is also a great treasure, Bishop Horne, left in the keeping of this humble librarian. It is a page from the original Book of Mormon. The actual translation of the holy plates brought to Joseph Smith by the angel Moroni."

Horne's illness turned to panic. He sensed danger behind him as Jacob Yahze and Allen Weber approached. Yahze held a fetish doll in his outstretched hand. The doll began to smoke as the shaman came closer. Weber moved to the bishop's other side. Using the chair for support, Horne struggled to his feet. With an armoire behind, Yahze and Weber standing on either side, and with Flood in front, Horne was trapped. As Flood turned to put the holy paper back on the table, Horne saw an opening. He bolted for the door through which they had entered. None of the three men in the room moved to stop him. He reached the door and grabbed the worn brass knob. It would not turn. He jiggled it and pulled at it, but it was bolted shut.

Horne turned and faced Flood, Yahze, and Weber. He looked on them as his tormentors. The bishop's eyes glowed red. His tongue slid out of his cruel mouth, long and black, flicking in and out, like a reptile. His upper lip curled, baring pointed yellow teeth.

"You are vermin. Rodents that I will devour," he growled. His voice was strong and menacing. He moved boldly toward the three men. "Jesus-loving scum and a savage."

Although steeled by his observation of what had happened to Foster and Claremont in Washington, Allen Weber saw something even more menacing in Horne. Perhaps it was because this time he was closer to the evil, or perhaps it was because Horne, as a bishop in the Church of Latter-day Saints, was a man he had once respected and revered. Now he appeared to be something to be reviled and repelled.

Yahze's smoking fetish doll burst into flames as Horne came closer. The shaman dropped it to the floor, which distracted Horne for a second. Weber's fear was succeeded by anger and frustration. It released the fury that had been building since the Christensen's murder. He seized the opportunity and rushed toward Horne. The bishop, sensing the attack, turned away from the burning doll to face Weber just as the young Mormon hammered Horne's jaw with a crunching right hook. Stunned, the bishop collapsed to his knees.

"He is one of them," Yahze said. "But, I believe, not a spirit like the others. Look," he exclaimed, pointing to the fetish doll. It had stopped burning but had not been consumed.

Weber paid no attention to the shaman. Hatred blocked his senses. Horne's jaw was slack, possibly broken. Blood dripped from one corner of his mouth. Weber raised his hand to deliver another angry blow.

"No, Allen!" Flood shouted as he stepped in front of Weber. The librarian held a syringe in his hand. "We need him intact."

Later that night, after Bishop Horne had been bound and sedated, Vernon Flood telephoned Rabbi Vogel in Washington with the news of what had transpired.

After driving out the spirits Hacamuli and Orgosil from the bodies of Foster and Claremont, all of which had been observed by The Vigilant members in Safed, Vogel spent time with the DOE executives in recovery. The two men remembered nothing of their possession, other than that Raymond Light had been with them in Hawaii when they first began to feel what they describe vaguely as "different." They recalled some blackout periods, and that their wives complained of strange behavior. Both men were afraid of Bertha Smalls and neither had a dragon sign tattooed under his tongue. The news that Bishop Horne appeared to be possessed by a stronger entity disturbed Vogel. He contacted Safed again, and Rabbi ben Abraham agreed to send Vogel one their most valuable possessions.

"From what we saw, Isadore," ben Abraham said, "these spirits, controlled by Amaimon and Beelzebub, indicate their presence in Salt Lake City. And where they are, Belial cannot be far. Our Mormon and Navajo brothers possess great strength, but I fear all of you will need greater protection. I will send Michael Gross to deliver Aaron's breastplate to you. It will arrive in Washington tomorrow morning on El Al.

CHAPTER FORTY

AN ANCIENT SHIELD

It was time for Andy Taft to head for Utah. Sasha Andreyev would follow if her services were required. Before leaving Washington, Taft met with Bill Jenkins, the Director of Central Intelligence. The two men were career operatives who had the deepest respect for each other. Jenkins was aware, through a top-secret, eyes-only file, of Taft's involvement in the capture of the archangel Satan.

"Benjamin's onto the Smalls woman," Taft told his boss. "She was met in Salt Lake by a guy who works for Perez. Name's Light. Raymond Light. I ran a book on him. He's a Cuban refugee. His real name is Ramón Luz. And like Perez, he got political asylum. He checked Smalls into the airport Ramada. She's been sitting there for two days. Benjamin has assembled an assault team. They're ready to go." Jenkins smiled to himself. The director knew that he wasn't getting the full story. One never did with Taft.

"Okay, Andy," Jenkins said. "Do what you have to. Do you have what you need?" Taft's clearance level gave him access to the full power and facilities of the agency.

"I've picked a few of my trusted soldiers and three top techies here to back us up."

Jenkins nodded his approval. "You're on your own on this, Andy. Understand?"

"Yes, sir." Taft got up. The director extended his hand. The two men shook.

"Good luck and Godspeed."

While Taft made final preparations at CIA headquarters in Langley, Virginia, Rabbi Isadore Vogel met with the Mossad agent Michael Gross in a small, secure conference room adjacent to the Israeli ambassador's office at the embassy in Washington.

Gross broke the seal on the diplomatic pouch and produced a key. "I must tell you that carrying this treasure out of the country was nerve wracking," he said as he unlocked the pouch and extracted a leather case, handing it to Vogel.

The rabbi took it gingerly, placed it on the table, and carefully opened it. Inside was a light-blue velvet cloth that he folded back, revealing the gold breastplate of Aaron, set with the brilliant jewels of the twelve tribes of Israel. Vogel nodded and drew a deep breath. Then he rewrapped the breastplate in the velvet cloth and closed the case.

"Thank you, Michael. Now let us pray that its power will protect us against Belial."

Sasha drove Andy to the Israeli embassy, where they had a reunion with their old friend Michael Gross. But it was brief—Taft had a CIA jet standing by. A half hour later he and Rabbi Vogel were airborne and on their way to Salt Lake City. Throughout the flight, Vogel kept the leather case containing Aaron's breastplate on his lap.

CHAPTER FORTY-ONE

IN EVIL'S LAIR

Activity was observed at the airport Ramada in Salt Lake City. Raymond Light arrived and went to Bertha Smalls's room. When they both emerged from the hotel and drove away, two FBI teams followed, taking turns as the primary tail. When it became clear that Light was heading for Perez's property, Benjamin was notified. The gate there was a reinforced steel barrier that slid into an opening in the surrounding ten-foot-high stone wall. The wall was topped with sensors and protected by razor wire. From the time the nuclear shipment arrived, the gate had been manned twenty-four hours a day by Paronto. They allowed Light's car to pass. The FBI teams kept their distance and reported in.

Benjamin had received clearance to have an FBI helicopter equipped with sophisticated surveillance cameras track Perez's movements, so he knew that Perez was on the property with an unidentified man. . The FBI chopper crew observed and photographed Light and Smalls entering the opening under the domed rock as they had done earlier.

In the throne room, the large central chamber under the rock, Nicholas Perez greeted Bertha Smalls. The spirit Trisaga was comforted by his words while Smalls, unconscious of the spirit dwelling within her body, was in awe of this strange underground cavern and of Perez sitting regally on a throne in front of her. No one had yet told her why she had been ordered to leave Washington abruptly.

"You have performed excellent service," Perez told her. "The nuclear materials are secure and will be processed."

"Thank you, Mr. Perez," she said, believing that he was her partner. "I am confident, as are Foster and Claremont, that your pilot project will be a resounding success. But why am I here?"

"They are dead," Perez said dryly.

"Dead? I don't understand. Who is dead?"

"Claremont and Foster."

Smalls was frightened. Her breathing became rapid. She felt faint.

"Dead? When? How? I saw them just a few days ago."

"Well, they are dead. They were killed. We seem to have attracted some enemies."

"Enemies? I'm sorry, but I don't understand."

Perez grew impatient. "Who have you told about the shipments?"

"Told? Why, no one... well, there was a man. A CIA agent. He came to my office on a fishing expedition."

"What did he want?"

"He asked about the shipments being fuel waste materials when they were listed as medical and industrial isotopes. I explained that they were medical and industrial waste and that the paperwork was correct. He had been to the plants because he knew what had been shipped. I told him I'd look into the matter with the plant supervisors. It was an error in the paperwork. I was going to tell you. But please, what happened to Foster and Claremont?"

Perez decided she had outlived her usefulness to him. He would have to make other arrangements to obtain more nuclear waste material when it was needed.

"You are an incompetent fool," he told her. "Did you think the CIA would buy that lame response with such vital materials involved? Idiot!" Within her, Trisaga was now uncomfortable. He could only control Smalls when directed to do so by his master, Amaimon, who was not present.

"Now, just a minute," Smalls said. "You can't talk to me like that." Perez stood up. His voice deepened.

"You chose to withhold important information from me." He raised his fist and shook it accusingly. It became a hooded king cobra that rapidly grew and coiled in midair. Smalls was mesmerized. The serpent opened its mouth and sprang at Bertha Smalls's throat, sinking its deadly fangs into her carotid artery. She fell backward, mouth wide open in a silent scream of pain. For the moment, Trisaga was trapped within the dying woman.

"Bring me the other," Perez told Light. "I will give Trisaga a new home myself." Moments later, a bewildered Professor Lyman Goode, the Aramaic scholar who had originally called Rabbi Vogel to examine the golden plates found around the Christensen children's necks, stood before Nicholas Perez. He was the other man the FBI chopper had observed with Perez. "I have been very philanthropic toward you and your work, Professor. Now it is time to pay back."

Goode was confused by Perez's words, and by the strange underground place he had been brought to. The antiquities and artifacts in the chamber were amazing—

masks, weapons, headdresses, and statues and carvings of grotesque creatures and gods. He could only guess at their origins. The throne that his benefactor sat upon was solid gold—probably once occupied by an Inca or Mayan king. And the great dragon seal he had seen on the door must be from an ancient Chinese dynasty. But there was a dead woman on the floor. Who was she? The man sitting on the great throne in front of Goode seemed very different from the Nicholas Perez who had so generously funded his local digs and those in China, Kenya, and Israel. And, he wondered, what Perez meant by "pay back."

He was about to ask about it, and about the dead woman, when he suddenly became tired. His arms grew heavy. His feet seemed fastened to the stone floor. He he began to have a vivid daydream. Or was he hallucinating? He imagined he saw Perez transform into the Aztec serpent god Quetzalcoatl. Perez's assistant, Raymond Light, became a sleek but large peregrine falcon. It was a fantastical dream with strange chants, and blood that turned red and green and black, all caught up in a swirling, dark, pungent mist.

As Goode dreamed, his body became the host of the evil spirit Trisaga, Ruler of Triads, beholden no longer to the sub-prince Amaimon but to the ultimate master, the archangel Belial.

Goode's first task was to dispose of Bertha Smalls's body. Light, now known to the spirit inside the professor as the sub-prince Beelzebub, led Goode to a smaller chamber that housed all manner of ancient weapons of the western hemisphere's early natives. Light placed a Mayan war ax in Goode's hands and instructed him to hack Smalls's body into pieces and then burn it on a jade altar as an offering to Quetzalcoatl.

Later, in the throne room, Perez and Light, now returned to their human form, discussed how many Paronto would need to be sacrificed while opening the fuel rod containers and dispersing the deadly waste into the aquifers. Suddenly, Dimirag, the spirit inside Bishop Horne, contacted Light—his master, Beelzebub.

"The Mormons have captured Horne," it cried.

"They have Dimirag," Light told his master, Belial.

Perez's eyes glowed red with anger. Spirits placed within human flesh were as vulnerable as the flesh was weak. Somehow, human adversaries were discovering them and destroying his minions.

"Where do they keep him?"

"Deep within their tabernacle. The Navajo shaman and a Mormon holy man are there, and others he cannot clearly see."

Perez counted his losses: Swain, Foster, Claremont, Smalls, and now possibly Horne. His loyal Paronto, Cherry and Macack, had reported the Navajo and a stranger observing the rock. Perez deduced it was Rabbi Isadore Vogel. Goode had mentioned that Benjamin, the FBI Jew, and Ruiz, the Mormon Mexican female detective, were investigating the origins of the stone knives. They had translated the golden plates, with the help of that damned Mormon Weber. Yet no one other than that pest Weber had yet to confront him directly. And pressure was being aimed at the spirit servants of his sub-princes, Amaimon and Beelzebub, not him. Yet what Bertha Smalls had revealed disturbed him.

A visit from the CIA? Why? How did they find Smalls? They do not get involved in domestic affairs. Why had they talked to the supervisors at the nuclear plants? How much did they know? Were the secret contents of those shipments compromised? Had Foster and Claremont talked? Perez sensed a noose tightening around him. He would not tolerate interference.

"Give me ten Paronto to move the nuclear waste into the shafts. We begin tomorrow. It should take no more than a few days. I will bring your brother, Amaimon, to supervise. It is time to handle these meddlers," he told Light, "and show them the end of their kind."

"Yes, master," Light said, pleased that Belial was angry. He felt an immediate surge of power in his own being. Suddenly, a bolt of heat shot through his body. Light screamed in pain.

"The Navajo has driven Dimirag out. Aieee … Oh, master. And the Mormon holds him. He commands your servant to speak his name."

"Stop him!" Perez demanded.

"I cannot. The Mormon has a parchment. A holy thing, from the hand of the prophet Joseph Smith. Aieeee… " The pain was torturous. Light fell to his knees. He concentrated all of his powers on destroying Dimirag before the spirit spoke his master's name. But it was too late. Dimirag's words echoed in the throne room from Light's open, tortured mouth.

"I am Dimirag, servant to Beelzebub, sub-prince to the archangel Belial. He will make barren your Earth. He will destroy all that lives. He, and his brothers, will reign forever!"

"Kill him!" Belial ordered. But Beelzebub was powerless to do so.

"Another has come forward," Beelzebub within Light cried. "He holds… Oh, master. It is the gold and bejeweled breastplate of Aaron and the twelve tribes! Dimirag has been sealed in Horne's body." Belial reared his head and roared like a puma. He then grew calm.

"Very well. If they want to fight, we will show them the price they will pay." Perez stepped from this throne. "I want Allen Weber killed. I want his family killed. And be sure to find his wife and the new baby. I want them bloody. Have Cherry and Macack do it. You, my sub-prince, will make sure it happens. No mistakes this time."

"Yes, master. It will be done," Light promised. Perez, pleased with his sub-prince's subservience, rewarded him with a rush of pleasure. Light arched his back and shuddered with delight.

"Now bring me the pentagram from my office," Perez ordered.

CHAPTER FORTY-TWO

A PLAN OF ACTION

"I am Dimirag, servant to Beelzebub, sub-prince to the archangel Belial. He will make barren yourE. He will destroy all that lives and reign forever!" These were the words that the servant Dimirag, residing in the Horne's body, had spoken through the bishop's mouth. It was a detached and inhuman voice that sounded like speech through a ring modulator used by rock musicians. The words reverberated off the walls of the secret room, deep under the great Mormon Tabernacle in a part of the building that few knew of and even fewer had ever seen.

Bishop Horne lay flat on his back, bound tightly to a cedar board that rested on an oak table. He was gagged and naked. A bright, sharply focused overhead spotlight shown directly in his eyes so that the others in the room were not visible to him.

Jacob Yahze was positioned close to one wall, at Horne's feet. He chanted softly. On a table in front of the medicine man was a large turquoise stone, a bowl of white corn, a crystal flask of spring rain, and a small pile of ground boysenberries, bluebird eggshells and wet birch bark.

Vernon Flood stood to the left of Horne. He wore a white, silken robe and held an ivory frame with a parchment from the original Book of Mormon in it.

Rabbi Isadore Vogel stood against the wall opposite Yahze. He wore a long black robe, an ancient woolen prayer shawl, and a black miter. He clutched Aaron's breastplate to his chest.

Standing in a corner of the room, in the shadows, was Allen Weber, with a video camera, and a transfixed Michael Benjamin. The FBI agent could not yet grasp the ramifications of what he had just seen and heard. For the first time on the case, he felt he was in over his head.

After the spirit Dimirag's revelation, driven out by the same ceremony Yahze had performed on Foster and Claremont, it would not leave Horne's body.

"This one is different," the shaman said softly.

Vernon Flood walked forward, into the light, and raised the Book of Mormon parchment over Horne's. His body stiffened and his eyes rolled back until only the whites were showing. The cedar board began to shake.

Rabbi Vogel stepped into the light on the other side of Horne, facing Flood. Horne's eyes flashed angrily as he glared from one to the other. A deep, guttural growling sound, like the warning of an angry beast, filtered through the bishop's gag. His body rocked up and down, nearly levitating the cedar board from the oak table. Horne's pupils were dark black pools without an iris. They widened and filled with panic as Vogel lifted the breastplate above Horne and brought it down onto the bishop's chest, slamming the board back onto the table. The spirit Dimirag moaned with pain. Horne's body went limp, and he fell into a deep sleep.

"This will keep the evil within him and block those who control it from destroying the body, his vessel," the rabbi said. He opened Horne's mouth and pulled out his tongue, twisting it so the underside was visible. A black dragon with red eyes was imprinted there.

"This spirit, Dimirag, is a servitor of Beelzebub, sub-prince to Belial, the brother of Satan, whose face I have seen and whose fury I have battled. We must strive to identify Belial and capture him. But before we can do that we must locate his earthly home, which is also his tomb. Then, when captured, we will seal him within and he will plague mankind no more."

"But if it is his home, how can it also be his tomb?" Weber asked as he stepped forward, still recording with the camera, with Benjamin following behind.

As members of The Vigilant, Yahze and Flood knew the answer. Vogel decided to take a moment and explain to the young man who had suffered so much loss, and whom they had taken into their confidence. It was also time for the FBI Agent-in-Charge to be told about what they were really up against.

"Please. No camera," Vogel asked. Weber turned it off. "There was a time when the four now fallen archangels were in the grace of God. They were among His most beloved. We are told that before he was born to walk among men, Jesus was also beloved of God, and destined to be His son. And when God made the Earth and man, a dispute arose between Jesus and these four archangels as to what man might be. The archangels wanted man to be ingrained with God's law and His word. Jesus wanted man to have free choice. In the end, God sided with Jesus. The archangels were angry and denounced Jesus and the Father. They were unrepentant. So God cast them out of His presence to the Earth, and there they were entombed, each in his special place."

"Perhaps the domed rock?" Benjamin asked.

"Perhaps. In time, God took pity on them and freed them from their prisons, hoping they would repent. But instead, the four joined forces and plotted to destroy God's Earth and all that lived upon it. Each went forth to work his particular evil. When Jesus came to walk among men, the story is told that he imparted knowledge to very holy men. These men were priests, eventually known as rabbis, who lived in Safed, near Galilee.

"The Lord said that should mankind resist evil by following God's laws, the fallen archangels would fail to corrupt. But should mankind, having been given free choice, become the instruments of evil, a battle would be joined. So it has been for the past two thousand years, with evil taking the upper hand, mankind suffering, and our planet disintegrating. God's message to those ancient rabbis was also that if the evil ones were to be sealed in their homes by man, their homes would become their tombs. There they would be bound for as long as mankind chose honestly to pursue peace and harmony on Earth."

"Do you know where these tombs are located?" Weber asked.

"Our Buddhist brothers found one—the home of Satan. So we knew of its existence, but until some years ago, we did not know where Satan lived outside it and in what form."

"So then is Satan in his tomb?" Benjamin asked.

"Yes," Vogel answered. "His disciples have made many attempts to free him, but so far we have successfully defeated them. Now we may be close to another. Belial. But without knowledge of his tomb's location, we cannot contain him, or his evil."

"He is here, in Salt Lake, isn't he?" Weber asked. It was more a statement than a question.

"Very possibly," Flood answered.

"And might that domed rock be his home?" Benjamin asked.

"Also possible," Vogel answered. "But we must be certain. The evil ones use decoys and obfuscation to trick and deter. What might seem obvious is often only a ploy to draw us into a trap."

For the rest of the evening, and well into the night, Flood, Yahze, Benjamin, Weber, and Vogel discussed all aspects of the problem that now confronted them. The clues left little doubt that Nicholas Perez and his assistant, Raymond Light, were prime suspects to be the sub-princes Beelzebub and Amaimon, one of whom is close to his master, Belial, at all times.

"One may well be Beelzebub or Amaimon. One is usually kept at a distance," Flood offered.

"True. We may be lucky and hope Belial himself is close," Vogel added.

"Might Belial himself be one of them?" Weber asked.

"It is possible, but we can know only when he is cornered and confronted. There he may reveal himself," Yahze said.

"Jacob is correct," Vogel told Weber. "The archangels are crafty and devious. They will sacrifice the spirits that serve them and the servitors that are their eyes and ears and do their bidding. They will even give up the vessels that contain their sub-princes. So we must be cautious and move against him only when we are certain."

Michael Benjamin had witnessed what his superiors would call, a strange, anomalous event—one that should, by FBI protocol, be thoroughly investigated. But he knew there was no time for that. The bureau was overwhelmed with national security investigations. Bringing the possibility of the "supernatural" to distract resources from the harsh reality of terrorism would be rejected. Benjamin made the decision to proceed without the full authority of the FBI director.

"We'll pick up Perez and Light," Benjamin volunteered.

"Just one of them," Vogel suggested. "The other may feel the pressure and lead us to Belial."

"I suggest we have a good look at that domed rock," Yahze said.

"Yes," Vogel agreed. "The obvious. But remember what I said. It may also be a decoy—a devious trap to destroy us. We must be careful."

"My brother-in-law told me that until the floods, it was hidden beneath the Great Salt Lake," Weber offered.

"Which was once part of the Pacific Ocean," Flood added. "Submerged, it could have offered access to the rest of the world unseen. It's possible. Water is the domain of Leviathan, another of the four fallen archangels."

"That rock? That's where Perez is now," Benjamin offered. "He's with the DOE woman Bertha Smalls, Raymond Light, and a stranger we could not identify."

"Perhaps the stranger is this Belial," Weber said.

Up to now he had been bent on revenge. But if the Christensens had been slaughtered by supernatural beings, evil spirits, fallen archangels with earthly tombs, there was more at stake than his revenge. He looked at the bejeweled breastplate lying on Bishop Horne. The voice of Dimirag had emanated from Horne's lips. How could mere human beings combat archangels, sub-princes, servitors, and evil spirits? His thirst for retribution was replaced by fear.

Benjamin looked at his wristwatch. "Our helicopter team will have to refuel soon. I have two teams on the ground outside Perez's property. Which one do you want me to pick up, Light or Perez?"

"Let's have a look at Mr. Perez," Vogel said. "And the Smalls woman. Bring her in too."

"I'll get a room ready," Vernon Flood offered. He gestured to Weber to follow. "Come with me." Benjamin started to leave, then paused.

"Perhaps you'd like to come with me, Rabbi Vogel? In case we have the real thing and, well …"

"Vogel nodded. "I understand. But the breastplate must remain here."

"Take the parchment," Flood offered.

"And the turquoise stone," Yahze added. "I will watch over the bishop."

CHAPTER FORTY-THREE

AN OFFENSIVE

The chill in the air was a sure sign of autumn's approach. Daylight no longer lingered, and dusk moved quickly into night. It was at twilight that Benjamin ordered the two units waiting outside the gate to Perez's property to arrest him and Bertha Smalls.

"Don't enter the property. If they haven't left yet, they probably won't move until dark," Benjamin told his men. "See if you can ID the fourth person—the one who came in earlier with Perez."

As darkness descended, the surveillance team in the helicopter switched to night vision. A few minutes later Raymond Light emerged from the domed rock with another man. They got into his car and drove off the property. Using a low-light-level camera and an ultraviolet-sensitive filter, they were able to photograph the two men. One FBI unit outside the gate followed at a safe distance. Since there was no sign of Perez or Smalls, the second team waited. Fifteen minutes later, the helicopter pilot reported that he would have to refuel, and left the area.

Ten minutes later, neither the pilot nor the other agents in the chopper noticed the condor circling above them. In its claws it clutched a large rock. It suddenly dove at the chopper, but a moment before colliding, the bird spread its five-foot wings, applying them like air brakes, and released the rock.

The pilot, sensing movement above him, looked up. He was momentarily confused, frozen in time, as the huge bird peeled away and the rock smashed into the main rotor, then down, shattering the hard plastic cabin bubble. The helicopter spun wildly out of control, rolling, tumbling, and then falling like a huge wounded bird. The pilot and two FBI agents were dead on impact. The fireball that engulfed the chopper destroyed the images of the mystery man who had left with Raymond Light.

Grace Miller was home alone. Her husband, Ronald, had gone to pick up their nephews, Michael and David Weber, in Park City, where they had been visiting with their mother and newborn sister. Grace was preparing a roast chicken dinner in the spacious kitchen of the split-level ranch house in the quiet suburb of Millcreek, on the western edge of Salt Lake City. Her back was to the window that overlooked the backyard. A noise outside made her turn, and she saw that a peregrine falcon had landed on the sill.

"Now what on earth do you want here?" she said playfully to the bird of prey.

At the same time, Alex Cherry, the Paronto servant to Belial, was at the side door of the house. He tried the doorknob. It turned quietly in his hand. He slipped into the mudroom that was adjacent to the kitchen, closing the door behind him. He saw Grace Miller in the kitchen and then stealthily checked out the rest of the house. No one else was home.

In the kitchen, the falcon strutted back and forth on the windowsill, pecking at the window, flapping its wings, and holding Grace Miller's attention.

Cherry quietly slipped a deerskin glove whose fingers were tipped with four razor-sharp eagle talons and one deadly eagle beak, onto his left hand. Silently, he moved toward the kitchen.

"Do you want something to eat?" Grace asked the falcon. "I bet you'd love to tear into this chicken," she said, lifting the plump roaster for the falcon to see. Those were her last words. From behind, Cherry grabbed her hair with his right hand and pulled her to the floor. He then lifted her head to stretch her neck and slashed her carotid artery and trachea with the eagle beak, then ripped at her shoulders and face with the talons. Her cries of shock and pain were stifled by gushing blood, coming out only as an intermittent, gurgling sound. After watching Cherry's performance, the satisfied falcon transformed into Raymond Light and came into the house.

"Where are the others?" he asked his Paronto servant.

"The rest of the house is empty."

"Wait for them. Two boys and a man. Destroy them as you did the woman. Make it as bloody as you can. I will join John Macack."

Agent Benjamin was anxious and worried. The FBI helicopter was long overdue and could not be raised on the radio. According to the FBI team still outside the property,

Perez and Bertha Smalls had not left. His first team reported that Light had driven directly to Victory Development's headquarters with the unidentified man and parked in the building's underground garage. No one had left the building. Benjamin requested that the Utah State Police dispatch an air unit to the last known location of the FBI helicopter, ten miles northeast of the Christensen farm.

Two state troopers were on duty outside Susan Weber's suite at the Carlisle Clinic. The exclusive rehabilitation center, best known for its programs for injured skiers, was situated below the downhill and slalom venues that had been built for the 2000 Winter Olympic Games. It was close to seven thirty in the evening. The outside temperature was a chilly forty degrees. At this elevation—over seven thousand feet—the temperature dropped rapidly after sundown. Soon it would be below freezing.

John Macack, another Paronto servant of evil, pushed a hospital cleaning cart slowly down the hallway toward Susan Weber's suite. In the utility closet at the other end of the hallway, Pedro Garcia, a Guatemalan immigrant who had recently obtained his green card, lay dead—his neck snapped like dry tinder by the thick-necked, burly Paronto.

Macack parked the cart along the wall about thirty yards from Susan Weber's suite. He glanced at the troopers outside Weber's door, then took a mop and began to slowly push it along the edge of the hallway toward them. When he was just a few feet away, he leaned the mop against the wall and went back for his cart. He wheeled the cart, its wheels squeaking, close to the suite. The state trooper closest to him glanced at the Paronto, giving him and the cart the once-over. Macack smiled and nodded hello. The trooper acknowledged him and turned his back. In one swift movement Macack pulled a sawed-off twelve-gauge shotgun from under some towels on the cart and fired at the trooper, blasting a huge hole in his back and tearing out the front of his chest. His partner reacted surprisingly fast, dropping to the floor while opening the safety snap on his holster. But it was too late. Macack jumped over the first slain trooper and fired point-blank into the second trooper's forehead, killing him instantly.

Above the clinic, a lone peregrine falcon circled in the thin, cold air, watching and listening.

Susan Weber was nursing her daughter in the bedroom of the suite when the two shotgun blasts rang out in the hallway. Her bodyguard, Sergeant Clara Williamson, a ten-year veteran of the Utah State Police, immediately appeared at the bedroom door with her gun drawn. She gestured for Susan to get down behind the armchair she was sitting in. Susan pressed the baby to her breast and followed the officer's orders. Williamson, a thirty-five-year-old black woman, the mother of three, dropped to one knee in the bedroom doorway and pointed her weapon, a hefty .45 Smith and Wesson Magnum, at the suite's only doorway.

John Macack stepped over the prostrate bodies of the two troopers and kicked open the door. Sergeant Williamson unleashed a fusillade of four shots that slammed into the Paronto's chest, driving him backwards out the door and into the hallway. He was dead before he hit the floor. Special Agent Benjamin's tactic of keeping Officer Williamson's presence in the suite a secret had paid off.

Light and the Falcon, circling above in the night, saw Williamson too late to warn Macack. He cursed his own carelessness in not being more thorough. As he backed away from the clinic to return to his master, he dreaded the report he was obligated to make. But he hoped that with Alex Cherry killing the two Weber boys and the Millers, Belial would be somewhat mollified.

Ronald Miller had chosen to take Route 224 from Park City to Interstate 84. Unlike the straighter Route 40, which went due north to 84, this road wound through the mountains. After spending the day with Michael and David Weber's mother and new baby sister, Miller had left the clinic with his nephews an hour before sunset, promising them a spectacular look at the setting sun and the mountains. He had called Grace before they left for home and told her his plan. She had urged him not to dally too long, as she was making the boys' favorite dinner, roast chicken.

Miller and the boys watched the sun descend toward the mountaintops, an orange ball dipping behind some thin clouds just above them, turning the clouds into orange and pink slashes. The sun then emerged below the clouds as a fiery red ball that slowly disappeared into the nearest mountaintop—a celestial coin being slipped into a cone-shaped bank.

When they were three miles from the interstate, they came upon a jackknifed tractor-trailer blocking the narrow mountain road. The police were on the scene. It was going to take an hour or two to clear the way. If Miller turned around and went back to Park City, and then to Route 40, it would take at least an hour, not to mention a ride in the dark through the mountains. He decided to wait. The boys were fascinated by the process of clearing the accident. A monster wrecker arrived on the scene. The operators first had to detach the cab from the trailer and then maneuver the wrecker into position to lift the cab. After that was done, they lifted the trailer. All this, on a dark mountain road, took skill and care.

Miller's cell phone was without service up there, so it wasn't until two hours later, when he was on the interstate, that he was able to call Grace to advise her of their delay. But there was no answer.

Miller, nearly forty, had served six years in the army. He had seen action in the first Gulf War as a navigator/gunner on an army Warthog tank-killer aircraft. He was a cautious man who was always aware of his surroundings and wary of out-of-the-ordinary events. When Grace did not answer the phone he became concerned, since Allen Weber had told him he was helping in the investigation of the Christensen murders.

"There are some very dangerous people involved," Weber had told his brother-in-law. So keep your eyes open and always know where the boys are."

"Grace should be home," Miller thought, *and if she went out, the answering machine would be turned on. But it wasn't. Maybe she was in the bathroom.* He waited ten minutes and called again. Still no response, and no answering machine. Miller keyed in a call to Detective Andrea Ruiz. Weber had told him that she was the liaison person to contact in case of an emergency.

Ruiz was concerned when she received Ronald Miller's call. She contacted Special Agent Benjamin.

"Mrs. Miller's probably just out somewhere and forgot to turn on the answering machine," Ruiz told Benjamin. "But I thought you'd best know about the call." She tried to sound casual, but she had a bad feeling in the pit of her stomach.

"I've sent a patrol car out to the house. I'm heading out there now." Benjamin thanked her. He was relieved to know that the Weber boys were with their uncle.

Then, five minutes later, he received a call from Trooper Williamson in Park City. "The attacker appears to be alone," she told Benjamin, "but I've brought in two patrols units. They are searching the grounds now. Our forensics team is on the way. I've moved Mrs. Weber to another part of the clinic, under heavy guard." Benjamin called Ruiz back immediately and told her what had happened.

"Got it," was all Ruiz said. She was already in her car. She turned on her siren and flasher and notified the officers she had dispatched to the Miller house to wait for more backup, which she then ordered from Salt Lake City Central Command.

Meanwhile, Benjamin called the Utah State Police commander and asked that Ronald Miller and the boys be intercepted on the interstate and escorted home.

Beelzebub, as the falcon, flew through the cold night to Alex Cherry at the Miller house. He needed to know that his orders had been carried out.

Ruiz approached the Miller house silently, with her lights out. One of the two Salt Lake City officers that she had originally dispatched was standing by his patrol car when she approached.

"My partner's gone around back," he told the detective. "There are no lights on."

Ruiz glanced at the house. "I've called for more backup. You keep the front covered. Tell your partner to be alert. I'm going to see if anyone is home." She unsnapped the leather gun guard on her holster and walked toward the front door.

The officer keyed his radio and passed the word to his partner at the rear of the Miller house.

Inside the dark house, Alex Cherry was getting nervous. Miller and the Weber kids should have been home by now. His instincts told him something was wrong. He thought a few times about leaving, but he feared his master would be angry if he did not complete the mission. Then he heard someone cross the porch to the front door. He slipped into the living room and peeked through the curtains. The doorbell rang. Cherry saw it was a young woman. She rang again. He kept quiet. Then he saw her draw a Glock 9mm. A cop, he thought. He silently cursed because he had not checked to see if the door was unlocked.

Detective Ruiz saw two more patrol cars arrive at either end of the street. The officers approached the house with guns drawn.

"Mrs. Miller," Ruiz called out. "It's the police, Mrs. Miller." There was no answer. She reached for the doorknob and turned it slowly. The door was not locked. She pushed it open and went in. "Mrs. Miller?" she called out again.

Cherry slipped on his beak-and-talon glove, and drew a hunting knife from a sheath in his boot. Suddenly the lights went on in the hallway, and Ruiz, her Glock cradled firmly in both hands, stepped into the archway entrance to the living room. Cherry moved quickly away from the window and rushed at her.

Ruiz, sensing movement, swung her pistol in that direction as shots rang out. She saw three bullets hammer the man who was coming at her—one in the hip, one in the gut, and one that tore through his neck, nearly severing his head. Cherry's blood spurted out across the room. She then saw that the officer, who had been at the rear of the house, was the shooter. He had come in through the kitchen.

The officer kept his gun on Cherry, who was on his knees, and glanced over at Ruiz, eyeing her gold shield dangling from her neck.

"There's a dead woman in the kitchen," he said. The officer was a short, stocky man of fifty, maybe more—obviously a veteran cop. "I saw her on the floor through the window, so I came in."

"I'm sure glad you did," Ruiz said. "Is she dead?"

"I'm not sure. I was about to check when you turned on the light and I saw this creep about to attack you." Cherry slumped forward. His head hit the wooden floor hard. The blood that had been spurting from his neck was now flowing slowly. Ruiz was sure he was dead. She holstered her gun.

"Stay on him," she said. "I'll check the woman."

As Beelzebub, the falcon, approached, he saw the police in the street rush toward the house yelling to one another and radioing in "shots fired." He was not in time to save Cherry, but the sub-prince reached out to his servant and gave him momentary strength.

Cherry rose to his feet. His head hung to the side at an impossible angle as blood continued to flow from his wounds. Amazed at his strength, the officer pointed his gun.

"Stay where you are," he demanded in a loud, firm voice. The Paronto smiled an evil grin and raised the beak-and-talon-gloved hand in a threatening manner as he came toward him.

Astonished, he gritted his teeth and fired five rounds, point-blank, into Cherry's chest and abdomen. But Cherry kept coming, even as the bullets spun him one way and the other as they struck. Hearing the shots, Ruiz came running from the kitchen.

She fired four shots rapidly into Cherry's head, spinning him toward her. As he moved forward, he slashed out with his clawed hand.

Two cops arrived at the door and immediately assessed the situation. They emptied their guns into Alex Cherry. One blasted his body while the other's bullets tore into his knees and legs until Alex Cherry had no bone or tendon left to hold his torso upright.

Circling above the house, Beelzebub gave up the fight and released Cherry's body from his control. His Paronto servant collapsed to the floor at Andrea Ruiz's feet.

CHAPTER FORTY-FOUR

A TIME TO ACT

With the FBI surveillance helicopter out of the way, Belial the condor had resumed the form of Nicholas Perez and returned to the tomb. He then walked through his tomb, gathering power and planning revenge on the Navajo, the Mormons, and the rabbi who were interfering with his plans.

After the nuclear waste was dumped into the aquifers, he mused, *he would proceed with his next attack, a major chemical spill in the pristine Johnston Straits, a body of water that stretched between Vancouver Island and the British Columbia mainland.*

It was rare for a fallen archangel to keep both of his sub-princes so close to him, but with the power that the shaman, the Mormons, and the Jew were wielding, and the arrival of Aaron's breastplate, he had decided he needed them now. He summoned his sub-prince Amaimon, dwelling within the body of the Salt Lake City businessman Melvin Plotter, and instructed him to gather immediately ten Paronto and meet him at the flood-control tunnel before first light. As he left the tomb, he buried the entrance and stairway, leaving the soil as smooth as the rest that surrounded the domed rock.

A few hours later, when Melvin Plotter and the ten Paronto arrived, Nicholas Perez led them down the finished mine to the main chamber. There, he issued orders for the nuclear fuel waste containers to be opened. These Paronto were loyal followers of Jim Swain. They worshipped Belial and, through Swain, did the archangel's bidding, although they themselves were not possessed by spirits. A few of them hesitated, voicing concern that the material was dangerous. Perez angrily opened one container and lifted a spent fuel rod in his bare hand, showing the Indians that there was nothing to fear. They did not know his true identity and that he was not human, and thus invulnerable to the deadly radiation.

"You see, there is nothing to fear. Mr. Plotter will show you the work to be done. I want all these containers emptied by tomorrow." The Paronto were convinced, and got to work. Perez then left Plotter in charge and headed back to his office. As he drove through the gate, the FBI unit watching him called in to Benjamin.

"Perez is leaving, but he is alone. Should we proceed to arrest him?"

"No," Benjamin told them. Just stay with him and keep me informed."

Benjamin had received the state police report that his helicopter was down. The pilot and two agents were dead. The investigation as to cause was proceeding. There was nothing to report yet. He met with Andy Taft, who had just arrived in Salt Lake City with a CIA team. Andy and Benjamin were joined by Detective Andrea Ruiz, who had returned from the Miller house. The three assumed that the helicopter had somehow been forced down, and that Perez was responsible.

"Grace Miller's killer was a Paronto named Alex Cherry," Ruiz reported. "I've got to tell you that those last few moments, when he came at me, were totally unreal. I mean, he was dead. I saw him die. And yet, he got up and somehow… " Her voice faltered. "God's honest truth, he came back to life with a vengeance, like some kind of zombie." She raised her hands before either agent could respond. "I know I know. But it really seemed like something or someone was controlling him. I'd swear to that. I mean, how do you fight dead people?" For a moment, neither man knew what to say.

"You did good, Ruiz," Taft said. Ruiz was not aware of The Vigilant, so Taft could not confide in her that he had seen that kind of thing before when they battled Satan. "I don't know what to tell you except that we have to fight them with everything we have."

Fifteen minutes later, Rabbi Vogel and Allen Weber arrived at the FBI command center. They had left Jacob Yahze and Vernon Flood to watch over Bishop Horne. Benjamin was informed, and came out of his meeting with Ruiz.

"I've got to see you for a moment, Rabbi," Benjamin told Vogel. They left Weber in the small conference room and went back to the room where Taft and Ruiz were waiting. "Weber doesn't know about his wife or the kids. And the dead woman."

"Grace Miller was his sister," Ruiz informed them.

"Dead?" Vogel asked. "Who is dead?" Benjamin and Ruiz filled him in. "Poor Mr. Weber," the rabbi said. "His family has paid such a terrible price. Who will tell him?"

"Listen," Benjamin said softly. "I'm a field agent. This kind of stuff, you know, telling someone a family member is dead, just isn't my forte."

Ruiz nodded. "Yeah. Okay, I'll tell him. I've got the update on his wife and kids, and Ronald Miller."

"Thank you," Benjamin told her, relieved.

"Sure. But from now on, I want in on nailing these killers. I don't mean a collar. I mean I want to be there to see them go down." Her voice was quiet and firm, but her anger was obvious. "And, I imagine Mr. Weber is going to feel the same way."

Ruiz left the room. She needed some time to prepare herself to face Weber. Benjamin, Taft, and Vogel discussed the relevance of Bishop Horne's capture, and the trapped spirit Dimirag, servitor to Beelzebub, sub-prince to the archangel Belial. They agreed that that event, plus the attack on Susan Weber and the murder of Grace Miller, had brought things to head. Action was now called for.

Benjamin directed his staff to secure the necessary warrants from a federal judge, and to equip an assault team. Andy Taft moved to fly CIA agents in from their base in Twenty-nine Palms, California. The team following Perez reported that he had returned to VDC headquarters. It was after midnight.

Allen Weber sat on the edge of the conference table and observed the uptick in activity in the command center. He was feeling left out of things as he sipped a cup of freshly brewed hot coffee. He checked his watch. Then he saw Detective Andrea Ruiz coming down the hallway toward him.

"She's really pretty," he thought. As she approached he realized that with all the fantastic happenings of the past weeks he not had one sexual thought.

"How are you, Detective?" Weber asked as she entered the room and closed the door behind her. She smiled.

"Okay. It's been a while. I hear you've been in the thick of things. How are you?" He took a deep breath and smiled.

"Okay, I guess. Some pretty weird things going on, huh?" She nodded. She lowered her eyes to the floor and then slowly raised them up to look at him. "Something's wrong," he said, picking up on her body language.

"Yes."

"How bad?"

"Bad. It's your sister, Grace." Weber's shoulder drooped. He slumped back against the table, put down the coffee, and steadied himself. Then he looked up quickly, his eyes burning into hers.

"My boys?" he asked.

"They're fine. They're safe with Mr. Miller," she told him.

"Where are they?"

"With your wife in Park City."

Ruiz went on to relate the whole story. Weber listened without interrupting. She withheld the gruesome details of his sister's murder. She ended by telling him that the state police had cordoned off the Rehab Center. "Your wife and children are safe."

Weber stared at Ruiz for a long time, and then beyond her to a place, a state of mind, where he could gather the pain, anger, sorrow, and rage within him. His sister was dead, and he was sure Perez was responsible. His wife and baby had been attacked by Perez. His brother-in-law and his entire family had been murdered by Nicholas Perez.

"I want to see my wife and children now," he told the detective. After a brief conversation with Benjamin, Ruiz and Weber were in a patrol car speeding north, through the night, to the Carlisle Clinic in Park City.

CHAPTER FORTY-FIVE

ASSAULT

The FBI assault team, led by Agent-in-Charge Benjamin, was divided into three units. The first would enter Victory Development's headquarters from the main entrance—a frontal assault. A second unit, comprising marksmen, was positioned in a perimeter around the building. The third special unit, five former Navy SEALs recruited by the FBI, would be delivered above VDC's rooftop by a stealth helicopter and would assault the target from there. It was nearly dawn.

The Christensen farm was a hive of activity. Two paramilitary squads from the CIA, led by Andy Taft, went through a final check of their equipment. One unit would be transported by Blackhawk helicopter to secure the so-called flood-control tunnel on Perez's property. The other squad's mission was to surround the domed rock and secure a perimeter.

The FBI and CIA attacks were coordinated. All units struck at the same time. The FBI frontal assault unit entered Victory Development unopposed, knowing that Perez, Light, and a third man were inside. As they broke in to the building's main entrance, they divided into four three-man squads. Each took a floor, including the basement. They swept down hallways and through the offices, room by room. They disabled security cameras wherever they encountered them. But the building's security system had built-in redundancy. The obvious cameras were backed up by state-of-the-art micro cameras, implanted and camouflaged in the walls and ceilings.

Perez and Light observed the attack on video monitors from the third-floor communication center. Raymond Light was concerned.

"This intrusion is of no matter," Perez told his sub-prince. He touched Light's shoulder, spreading calm through his body. "We no longer have need of this place. By now your brother and the Paronto have moved the nuclear waste material into the aquifer. Let us deal with these fools."

They calmly set destruct devices on the files and safes. There was no way to get Professor Goode, who was confused as he watched the activity, out of the building.

"We will have to find another home for you, Trisaga," Perez said to the professor. He then slit Goode's throat with a sacrificial stone knife and then plunged it into the man's heart. That freed the spirit Trisaga, who disappeared into the ether.

"Thank you, master," the spirit communicated as it departed. "I await your pleasure." Perez's keen hearing picked up the stealth helicopter rotor above them.

"They are coming from the roof," he told Light. "Put the nerve gas release on thirty seconds." Light went to the main console and set a timer, then pressed a large blue button labeled "Sarin." The digital clock next to it began to count down: …29, 28, 27…

The FBI teams slid down ropes onto the roof and blasted open the locked roof doors. With Uzi's at the ready, they rushed down the stairs to the third floor. The chopper hovered above the roof with a 5,000-watt halogen light illuminating the area.

At the same time, an FBI squad entered the third-floor corridor with automatic weapons locked and loaded. The moved quickly, checking every office and room.

Perez and Light entered the small, windowless room adjacent to the VDC communication center. In the dark, they transformed: Perez into a condor, Light into a falcon.

Outside the room, the deadly nerve gas was released through vents in the ceiling on each floor and in the basement. The lead agent from the roof team saw his chemical indicator start to glow a bright red.

"Gas!" he yelled into this microphone. Everyone in the building heard the warning and reacted immediately. Gas masks were put on, and everyone checked that no skin was exposed.

"Withdraw immediately," Benjamin ordered. He called the nearby FBI communication truck to request a decontamination unit immediately.

The doorway in the wall of the small dark room slid open. Condor and falcon, Perez and Light, left the building, soaring up and away into the early-morning sky. From above, the FBI assault teams exiting the building looked like black ants leaving their nest.

In the chamber in the flood-control tunnel, Plotter and the Paronto were behind schedule. Even though Perez had demonstrated that handling the nuclear waste was not hazardous, a few of the men were skeptical and afraid.

As Plotter urged them on with threats, Taft's CIA team swooped down in their Blackhawk and dropped from ropes at the tunnel's mouth. Heavily armed men wearing protective gear—chemical, biological, and radiological—secured the entrance and then moved down the tunnel, surprising the Paronto. Plotter, who had gone to the rear of the chamber to survey the shafts that led to the aquifers, hid when he saw the black-suited CIA team. A few of the Paronto tried to run but were immediately cut down. The rest, seeing there was no hope of escape, surrendered.

One of them told the soldiers where Plotter was, and two men were dispatched to bring him in. As they searched, Plotter, the sub-prince Amaimon, hunkered down in the shadow of an outcropping. As the soldiers approached, he transformed into a spotted hyena. He leaped out, surprising the two men. He soundlessly killed one soldier by crushing his neck in his powerful jaws and pushed the other down one of the shafts. The attack was so swift that neither soldier was able to fire his weapon or sound an alarm. Amaimon then threw the first soldier's body down the shaft and resumed the form of Plotter. He hid and waited.

The Paronto had all been secured. When there was no sign of the two men sent to find Plotter, two more CIA operatives and an officer went looking for him. They found blood on the cave floor. The officer called for more men. They all spread out. Seeing that there were too many soldiers to kill and elude, Plotter surrendered.

"Don't shoot," he called out. "Please don't shoot." He crawled out from under the outcropping, pretending to be frightened as he raised his hands. "I'm only the foreman here. I had my orders." He knew that all he had to do was bide his time until he could make his escape—either by himself or with his master's aid.

The second CIA unit, led by Taft, had moved under cover of pre-dawn darkness into hidden positions close to the fence between the Christensen farm and the domed rock. As the other two attacks proceeded, Taft's squad remained hidden, waiting. The hope was that the other attacks might drive someone here, perhaps a sub-prince of Belial.

A message from Benjamin came in. No one had been captured. The Sarin gas had claimed five FBI agents. VDC headquarters was quarantined. A hazmat team had discovered Professor Goode's body. He had been murdered. A BOLO—Be On The Lookout—was sent out. An arrest warrant for Nicholas Perez and Raymond Light had been issued. A four-state search was now in effect.

The officer leading the CIA unit in the tunnel radioed in that all was secure. Taft then ordered his squad to move in. They cut through the fence and surrounded the domed rock. There appeared to be no entrance into or under it. Having heard about the Sarin gas, Taft feared booby traps, so no digging was instigated. While they carefully searched, no one took notice of the condor and the falcon circling high above.

CHAPTER FORTY-SIX

CONTAMINATION

After a few hours, it was apparent that Perez and Light had somehow fled. The BOLO was expanded to a nationwide FBI alert, stating that the two men were wanted for questioning and were presumed armed and dangerous. The hazmat team vented and secured Victory Development Corporation's headquarters. The building was searched from top to bottom. The first filing cabinet that was forced open exploded, injuring two agents, but not critically because they were wearing protective clothing. The nearest available explosives experts were with Taft's CIA units. They were brought in to defuse the rest of the files and safes.

FBI forensic, accounting, and computer experts were flown in from Denver, Portland, and Los Angeles to sift through VDC'c papers and collect evidence against Perez and Light.

Outside the tunnel, Melvin Potter and the eight remaining Paronto were processed through a mobile hazmat detoxification facility supplied by the Salt Lake Office of Emergency Preparedness and set up under FBI supervision.

Andy Taft moved his CIA unit away from the area and back to California, as operating domestically was outside their legal jurisdiction.

The Paronto told the hazmat team that Perez had handled the nuclear waste material to show them it was harmless. But the reality was they had been exposed to far too much radiation. By mid-morning, all except Melvin Plotter were feeling ill. A few already had lesions and painful rashes. Plotter showed no sign of radiation poisoning. When questioned, he said he had arrived a few moments before the soldiers.

After as much decontamination as possible was done, and a complete change of clothing supplied, Melvin Plotter and the Paronto were moved to a safe house in nearby Layton, just north of Salt Lake City.

The Paronto were first confronted by Jacob Yahze, who again wore his beaded antelope jacket and his headband with the nine-pointed yellow star emblazoned on it. One golden eagle feather hung from the headband, one on each side of his braided gray hair. The necklace of bear claws and orca teeth hung from his neck down to his waist, but attached to it was the skull of a sidewinder rattlesnake, the most powerful symbol of the ancient Paronto medicine men. Yahze had arrayed on a table in front of him the required ingredients for driving out spirits: a polished piece of brilliant turquoise; a blue clay bowl filled with white corn kernels; a grinding stone with dried boysenberries, bluebird eggshells, and strips of wet birch bark in it; and a crystal jar of clear water, gathered from the first spring rain. As Andy Taft brought the ailing Paronto captives into the room, Yahze chanted.

"He made it. He made it. He made it.

At the place where the people
emerged from the underworld,
Near the Lake of Emergence, he made it ..."

Upon seeing the shaman, and the items prepared on the table, the first Paronto stepped back and tried to get to the door, but in his weakened condition he was no match for Andy Taft's strength.

"Take him away," the Paronto pleaded. "His magic is evil."

"It is you who are evil," Yahze shouted, pointing his finger at the frightened man. "It is you who worship the white man's devil!"

Cowering, the Paronto watched as the shaman mixed the ingredients on the table. Yahze then brought forth a fetish doll made of the skin of sidewinders and whose head was that of the great horned owl, a hunter of snakes. The Paronto dropped to his knees quivering with fear.

"Help me, master," the Paronto howled.

"Your master cannot help you here," Yahze exclaimed. He thrust the fetish doll down in front of the Paronto's face. The man fell to the floor, paralyzed. But nothing more happened. Yahze held the turquoise stone against a radiation lesion on the man's cheek. Nothing happened.

"He is not possessed by any spirit," the shaman told Taft. "He is just an unfortunate follower. A pawn of the evil ones."

After all the Paronto had been confronted, and none of them proved to be servitors or possessed by spirits, Taft questioned them and confirmed that their leader had been Jim Swain. They were all worshipers of Belial, whom they had never seen. Two of them, older than the rest, understood that they had been fatally poisoned. They each told Taft that when Perez had handled the nuclear material it was clear he had not been affected.

"He is superhuman," one told the CIA agent. The other, older Paronto went further.

"He was without fear, and so was the other, named Light."

"What about Mr. Plotter," Taft asked.

"The same," the man answered. Taft then had the eight Paronto moved to a secure hospital facility at a secret CIA army training base in the mountains. Their prognosis was hopeless. They would die.

Eight of Taft's men, all in protective gear, had remained behind after the raid to return the materials to their canisters. But the entire chamber and the lower part of the tunnel had already been contaminated. Bulldozers were brought in to seal off the tunnel and chamber, and the area was fenced off. The Perez property would be guarded until Department of Energy and the Nuclear Regulatory Agency could devise a solution to the contamination. Until then, the problem would be kept top-secret, and the property off-limits.

CHAPTER FORTY-SEVEN

FAMILY REUNION

Allen Weber sat beside of his wife's hospital bed, holding her hand. "Here we are again. I can't shake the feeling that this is my fault," he told her. Unable to look her in the eye, he turned his gaze out the window at the mountains, topped with early snow, rising above Park City and the Carlisle Rehabilitation Clinic. "If I had talked Bob out of starting that flood-control project, or maybe refusing the loan, then all this, and dear, sweet Grace … it wouldn't have happened. He sighed deeply. "Dear Grace. And Ronald, alone now." He winced. Tears flowed down his cheeks.

Susan squeezed his hand. The baby, nestled next to her, moved slightly and cooed. She kissed their new daughter's forehead.

"What you did was right, Allen. My brother, may he rest in peace, was a hardhead. Stubborn as my dad. Once he set his mind to do something, there was no discussion. And Grace … " She also sighed and teared up. "Who else would we trust with the boys?" Weber shook his head slowly and wiped his tears with the palm of his hand. He looked at his wife and then their baby daughter.

"She's beautiful," he told Susan. "Just like you."

"She has your eyes," Susan told him. "And your smile." She lifted his hand to her mouth and kissed it. Filled with love that overcame his sorrow for the moment, he took a deep breath and smiled.

"I love you, Susan. With all my heart and soul, I love you." They were words he had said to her often, but now they triggered a new emotion that rose from deep within. He kept it to himself; waiting to be sure it was what he wanted. Like his late brother-in-law, once Allen Weber made up his mind on a course of action, he was unwavering in its execution.

"What did the boys say?" Susan asked. She and Allen had discussed what to tell their sons: Michael, age seven, and David, age nine. They decided not to tell them about their Aunt Grace just yet. Ronald had gone back to Millcreek to make arrangements. He had wanted a quiet family funeral and agreed that the boys should not attend. They would be told about their aunt after things had settled down and everyone was home.

"Michael was excited by the state police activity around the clinic," Allen said. "They're all very nice to him. David was sort of quiet. He's a smart kid. I think he suspects something bad has happened. When I said goodbye to Ronnie in the parking lot, he was at the window. I think he saw Ronnie cry when we hugged."

There was a knock on the door, and Sergeant Clara Williamson, Susan's state police bodyguard who had so ably protected her from the attack, stepped into the room.

"I'm sorry," she said. "I didn't realize you were in here, Mr. Weber. I just wanted to tell your wife that I'm back on duty. I filed my reports, and my boss, along with FBI Agent Benjamin, put me on permanent assignment here with you."

"This is the woman who saved my life," Susan told her husband. Allen Weber stood up and shook hands with the trooper.

" 'Thank you' is nowhere near adequate," he said. "Susan told me what you did. It was very brave of you, and—"

"Please, Mr. Weber," Williamson said. "That's my job. I am glad I was here to help. And I want you to know that I'll be here until all this … until things are settled and safe." Her words confirmed the course of action he would now take.

"That's good to know, Sergeant Williamson. And a comfort."

"I'll be outside with Detective Ruiz," she said, and left the room.

Allen sat back down next to the bed. The baby began to whimper. Susan gave the infant her breast to nurse.

"There is something I have to do," Allen told his wife. His tone of voice was firm. She had heard it before when he had made important decisions—unshakable decisions. She was afraid.

"What's that, Allen?"

Weber had not told her anything about his experiences with Yahze, Vogel, and Flood. Susan was a woman of faith, with a strong belief in God. Allen knew the idea of evil archangels and spirits and possession could frighten her, even to the point of refusing to allow him to do what he now knew he must.

"I've been working with police," he began. "I helped them with some translations of the, uh … the things that were on the children at the farm." It was difficult to speak about his young nieces. The imagined images of how they must have suffered were still with him. "I want to continue to help. They asked me to be a sort of liaison between our church and some of Bob and Carole's neighbors," he lied.

"What about the boys? And your job?"

"The boys will stay here with you. I want all of you protected. The FBI and the state police feel this is the best situation. Here in Carlisle."

His words and demeanor were upsetting Susan. She felt that there were things he was not telling her, but Allen was so determined, that she kept it to herself.

"As far as my job is concerned," he continued, "I'll talk to Dale Richards. Desert Management can get along without me for a week or two. He's already told me to do what I must. And not to worry. He was adamant that family comes first."

"He's right. Be sure you remember that, darling," Susan said softly as she adjusted the baby at her nipple. "We all need you."

Weber was silent on the way back to Salt Lake City as he considered what might lie ahead. Detective Ruiz, feeling that he had something that he needed to discuss, searched for the words to start a conversation. But Weber spoke first.

"Did Benjamin tell you what happened with Bishop Horne?" he asked.

"Yes," she answered quietly. "He showed me the tape."

"What did you think?"

"I think we're up against something I don't understand. He didn't himself. It requires an act of faith that I'm not sure I have."

"I guess seeing is believing," Weber answered as he gazed out the window. "I've seen other things that Yahze, Vogel, and Flood had to do. Ancient ceremonies, prayers— weird things." He wasn't sure how much to tell Ruiz, but then again, if Benjamin had confided in her, then she was part of the team. "I don't think it's an act of faith that's needed. I'm pragmatic. This is some kind of evil and it must be defeated."

Ruiz was silent for a long moment. They were coming down out of the mountains. The night was clear. The air was crisp. A chilly northern wind had temporarily swept away the normally polluted atmosphere. The lights of Salt Lake City spread out before them.

"Then we'll beat it," she finally said.

"Yes. I surely will, or I'll die trying," he answered, emphasizing how personal the battle had become.

CHAPTER FORTY-EIGHT

AN INNOCENT BYSTANDER

Vernon Flood, who knew Melvin Plotter to be a Mormon businessman of some note, interviewed him, along with Andy Taft, in one of the upstairs bedrooms of the CIA safe house. The conversation was low-key, with Taft playing the role of inquisitor and Flood as Plotter's fellow Mormon protector. Plotter maintained that he had been in Victory Development Corporation's underground facility as a potential investor in what Perez had described to him as a DOE pilot project for the disposal of nuclear waste.

"Mr. Perez showed me that he had the authority of the Department of Energy for the project. He said it was approved at the highest levels," Plotter offered as his defense for being in the chamber. "I had arrived very shortly before you came in with guns and all. I was frightened. I didn't know who you were, dressed in those protective suits. I panicked and ran away to the back of the chamber." He was still playing the role well—a meek executive caught in something violent that he didn't understand. The fact that the FBI had observed him entering the property with the

Paronto Indians was not mentioned. Taft led Plotter along, but softened his tone.

"I understand. That makes sense. So what happened to the soldiers who came to find you?"

"I don't know. Like I said, I was scared. I saw them coming… I thought they were coming to kill me. I didn't know who they were. So I hid. Then there was an animal of some kind back there. I don't know where it came from. It was large and fierce. It attacked the soldiers."

"What kind of animal?" Taft asked. He was getting more suspicious of Plotter's lies, and wary that he might be the evil archangel Belial himself.

"I couldn't see. I was hiding." Taft took another tack. "Mr. Perez was not in the chamber. You said you had just arrived. Didn't he bring you there?"

"No. I came by myself. I was surprised to see he wasn't there. In fact, I was asking about him when you all charged in.

"How close to the open canisters were you?" Taft asked. The hazmat people had reported that Plotter showed no symptoms of radiation poisoning or illness.

"Not close at all. One of those Indians said Mr. Perez had just left. I was confused because I didn't pass him in the tunnel, so I decided to leave. Yes, thank the Lord I never got close to those containers."

"Thank you Mr. Plotter," Taft said. "We won't keep you much longer. How long have you known Mr. Perez?"

Plotter was noticeably relieved. "For a few years, I guess. He's an immigrant, you know. He came here from Cuba for political asylum. We've done business before. This is all very upsetting to me."

Later that day, Taft, Flood, Yahze, and Vogel visited the domed rock. They had kept out of sight of the prisoners, observing the interviews through one-way mirrors. They examined the area where Perez and the other visitors had seemed to enter, but the sandy soil was solid against the rock and no entrance was apparent. They then walked the domed rock's entire circumference, carefully searching for an opening or sign of where the entrance might be hidden, but without success, keeping in mind that the threat of booby traps was still very real. Vogel and Yahze still sensed a strong presence of evil in the area. The four Vigilant members grew more convinced that this location might very well be the archangel's tomb.

On the way back to the safe house they discussed a plan of action. Perez and Light had disappeared. Plotter and Horne were in hand. The Paronto unfortunates who had been used were now awaiting their inevitable, painful death.

"We know that Horne's spirit Dimirag is controlled by Belial sub-prince Beelzebub," Vogel began. "It is trapped and, for the moment, in our control."

"True," Flood added. "The breastplate contains him. Otherwise Belial would have freed him by now."

"Correct," Vogel said.

"But we don't know who, or what, Plotter is," Taft said. He was at the wheel of the specially equipped black SUV. Vogel, in the front passenger seat, turned to Taft.

"Yes, Andy. But we know he was somehow immune to the radiation. I believe he is not just a human body possessed by a spirit, like the bishop."

"Then maybe it's time to drive whatever he is out into the open," Flood suggested. They all were silent as each man considered Vernon Flood's proposal.

"We must be careful," Vogel began. "Dimirag's declaration that Beelzebub is his master is an important key to our discovering Beelzebub's identity. If that evil sub-prince is identified and captured, he can lead us to Belial or his tomb—or both. Perez or Light or Potter could be Beelzebub, or Belial himself."

"There is a way," said Yahze, who had been silent up to now. "We can use one to reveal the other."

CHAPTER FORTY-NINE

THE HOGAN

Jacob Yahze and Taro Heart flew to the Utah Navajo reservation in a CIA helicopter. More than four months had passed since Yahze had been home. There was much to prepare. When he was ready, Vernon Flood and Isadore Vogel brought Bishop Horne directly to the reservation, also by helicopter.

"You will be the maiden in this ceremony," was all that Yahze told Heart. "There will be some danger, but now I know this spirit Dimirag. It wants to be free of the bishop's body. It does not know all the powers we have to control it."

Yahze and Heart then prepared to enter the ceremonial hogan, used only by the Navajo medicine men on special occasions. Yahze removed his clothes and unbraided his hair, then washed his hair and body with spring water from a colorful Navajo pot. Heart also undressed and washed her hair and body. They dried themselves off with cornmeal—Yahze used white while Taro used yellow. Their hair hung loose. Yahze was dressed in his full Hatali—medicine man—costume. It was made of fine buckskin and white beads. He hung a bearskin pouch on his shoulder. His weathered face was powdery white from the cornmeal.

Heart dressed herself in a full-length white cotton robe. Her shoulder-length, straight black hair was an ebony crown. Her pretty oval face, colored slightly from the yellow cornmeal, glowed. Yahze handed her offerings—two white shells and a large blue crystal from the river shore—and threw an ancient buckskin shawl over his shoulders. They both entered the hogan. Once inside, Yahze unrolled another, longer buckskin shawl and spread it out on the ground.

"Place your offering there," he told her, pointing to the buckskin. "Sit there," he said, indicating a spot next to her offering. He then sat down to her left and opened the bearskin pouch. From it he took a buffalo horn, an exquisite turquoise, a white bead, a white shell, a black stone, a red stone, a small pot of spring rainwater, and blue pollen, placing them all on the buckskin. He began to chant:

> Mountains of the East:
> The Dawn Mountain,
> The White Corn Mountain,
> The All-Water Mountain,
> The Pollen Mountain,
> Gather to me and this maiden,
> Gather the strength of the ages.
> Bring us the power you gave to the Diné,
> To the first people.

The Shaman then motioned for Heart to go to the hogan doorway. She opened it. Three CIA soldiers and Rabbi Vogel brought Bishop Horne inside. He was awake and blindfolded. His hands were bound tightly behind him, and the Breastplate of Aaron was attached to his chest. The soldiers left. Vogel remained.

"The doorway faces east," Yahze said to Heart. "Seal it." She obeyed. The only light came from a small opening in the roof. Horne was frightened, but within him, Dimirag had not lost his arrogance. When Yahze removed the blindfold, Horne's eyes quickly adjusted to the dim light.

"Pagan scum," he muttered when he saw where he was and who was there. "Filthy Jew," he spit at Vogel. The rabbi remained impassive. Yahze lifted the buffalo horn from the basket and shook it at Horne.

"Silence!" he demanded. Horne's mouth clamped shut involuntarily. He was unable to open it. "You have given your soul to evil. I will cleanse it and free it." Yahze took the blue pollen and sprinkled it on Horne's head. It turned red as it touched his hair. The bishop's hair turned snow-white and his eyes closed. "Remove the breastplate," Yahze told Vogel.

As that was done, Horne's body shuddered. He fell backward onto the buckskin. Vogel moved to a place in the rear of the hogan and sat down with the breastplate in his lap.

"Place your shells upon his eyes and your crystal upon his mouth," Yahze told Heart. Once she had done that, Yahze then took the turquoise, white bead, white shell, black stone, and red stone and prepared to place them, in that order, in a line down Horne's body, from his sealed mouth to his groin, chanting as he did so.

The mountain to the South is Tso dzil.
It is standing out.

266

The strong Turquoise is standing out.
The mountain to the East is Sis na'jin.
It is standing out.
The strong white bead is standing out.
The mountain to the West is Dook oslid.
It is standing out.
The strong white shell is standing out.
The mountain to the North is Debe'ntsa.
It is standing out.
The strong jet-black stone is standing out.
The mountain in the center is Dzil na'odili.
It is standing out.
The strong beautiful red stone is standing out.

As each item was placed and each chant completed, Bishop Horne's body shuddered, then arched on the buckskin. When the last item—the red stone—was placed, the blue crystal on his mouth shattered. The shards from it flew and imbedded themselves in the four poles supporting the ceremonial hogan. A black mist seeped out of Horne's mouth and spilled into the buckskin, surrounding his body.

"Ahhhh," the spirit Dimirag sighed. It was a voice from within the dark mist. Yahze took the small pot of spring rain and handed it to Heart.

"Pour this on the mist." She did so, and the mist gathered into the water until it was black and muddy and had a foul smell. Heart backed away. "No!" Yahze commanded. "Stay there and keep the water ready. We may need more." He then took more blue pollen and threw it at the dark mud. "You call yourself Dimirag, servant to Beelzebub," Yahze said.

"I am Dimirag. My prince is Beelzebub," the mud answered.

"Where does this prince of yours dwell?"

A deep, guttural laugh came from the mud. "Wherever man allows him."

"Now. Where is he now?"

"He is far, but always watching." The spirit laughed again.

"Do you wish to be free of this body?" Yahze asked, indicating the now sleeping Horne.

"I wish to serve my master."

Vernon Flood listened outside. Earlier that morning, Flood, along with Andy Taft and a few of his men, had moved Melvin Plotter from the safe house to a position close to the ceremonial hogan. As Yahze drew the spirit Dimirag from Horne's body, Flood signaled to Andy Taft to bring Plotter, guarded by four burly CIA operatives, to the hogan's entrance.

"I will bring your master to you," Yahze said in a loud voice. He gestured for Heart to open the sealed doorway. As she did so, Plotter's body stiffened. Flood and Taft watched him closely, but his face revealed nothing. "Here is your master," Yahze said to Dimirag. The spirit did not respond. "He is our captive too."

"He is not my master," Dimirag said. Then he laughed.

"Who is he?" No response. "Pour more spring rain, the water of our Mother, on this abomination," Yahze told Heart. This time, as the water touched the mud on the buckskin, it sizzled and bubbled.

"Aiieeee!" Dimirag's voice was filled with pain. Outside, Plotter tried to back away from the door, but the guards held him fast. A deep growl emanated from his throat. His lips curled, revealing yellow fangs. His nails thickened and his hands began to transform into large, flat paws. Taft, observing the transformation, recalled that Plotter had said in his interview that a "large animal" had attacked two of his men in Perez's underground chamber. He had a syringe filled with a powerful tranquilizer ready. He plunged it into Plotter's neck. The transformations immediately reversed, and Plotter collapsed in the arms of his guards. For a fleeting moment Taft wondered if the chamber was Belial's tomb.

Inside the hogan, Dimirag wailed again. "Aiieeee!" Yahze moved next to the spirit, which was still being held within the dark bubbling mud on the buckskin, and took the red stone in his hand.

"Who is he?" Yahze demanded, holding the stone above the mud. "I will ask again and then no more."

"He is my master's brother. All serve Belial."

Yahze then dropped the red stone into the mud. Dimirag issued one more moan, which died away as the mud was absorbed into the stone. Yahze picked up the stone and put it into the hollow of the buffalo horn. Then he added the turquoise, the white bead, the white shell, and the black stone. Finally he poured the remaining blue pollen in top of that. The pollen blended with the stones and formed a seal. Bishop Horne opened his eyes.

Yahze turned to Vogel, who was still seated with the breastplate in his lap. "You know the brother of the one we seek?"

"Yes. Rabbi Abraham identified him as the sub-prince Amaimon. If you drive him out, it is possible that the Mormon parchment that Vernon carries will hold him. But when we are finished with him, he must be destroyed. These

269

sub-princes are foul vermin. They do their master's bidding, but they also make mischief themselves. They are dangerous. Merciless."

"Yes," Yahze said. "I understand."

They called Flood and Taft into the hogan and explained what had transpired.

"Do you think the Joseph Smith parchment hold Amaimon?" Flood asked Vogel."

"I cannot be certain. A sub-prince is not a spirit like this Dimirag was. He gets his power directly from the archangel. If Belial is near, then Amaimon's power may be greater than we can control."

"We've got to try," Taft said. "The nuclear material that was in that chamber could be elsewhere." The others nodded their agreement. "The chamber might even be Belial's lair and tomb. We have to know."

"Agreed," Yahze said. "I must go to the tq'ache, the sweat lodge, to prepare."

"What about the bishop?" Taft asked.

"With the spirit out of him, he is of no use to us. He will remember what he did, what he was. That will be his burden," Vogel told them.

"I will notify the Quorum of the Twelve Apostles. They will deal with him," Flood announced. He glared at Horne, who was now awake but confused. "And when he leaves this earthly life, our Lord will decide his eternal fate."

CHAPTER FIFTY

THE SWEAT LODGE

When Jacob Yahze's father, Hash'ke, the Utah Navajo tribe's medicine man, was teaching him to take his place, he sent his son north to spend time with the Haida people, a coastal tribe located in western Canada, and the Tlingit people in northern Alaska. Jacob integrated the Haida's ability to commune with the natural world and animals, even the Old Ones" known as Sasquatch. Though their numbers were few, many still roamed the dense forests of the northwestern mountains. He also learned to use the Tlingit ability to summon powerful spirits. Jacob Yahze's powers were many, but they were not often called on in the modern days.

Long before the white man set foot in the Americas, the Navajo, a deeply religious tribe, practiced their most sacred ceremonies in specially constructed sweat lodges, tq'ache— hollowed mounds built by arching cedar frames sunk into the ground and covered with earth. A fire is kept going nearby, where round, sacred rocks, taken from holy mountains, are heated until they glow red-hot. They are placed in the northern corner of the lodge to hold back the north wind, which the Navajo believe carries disease.

Jacob Yahze stripped naked and entered the sweat lodge first to make sure that the temperature and conditions were correct. He then signaled for Isadore Vogel, who held Aaron's breastplate; Vernon Flood, who carried the parchment from John Smith's original Book of Mormon; and Andy Taft, who held the naked, bound, and gagged Plotter, to strip naked themselves and enter.

"Think of this lodge as our church," Yahze said as he spread an ancient woven red and black blanket on the earthen floor. Then he closed the sweat lodge door. It was dark. The rocks in the northern corner glowed a faint red as they gave off heat that caused everyone to sweat profusely. Plotter twisted in his bonds, fear flashing in his eyes. Yahze poured onto the hot rocks a brew of water, cedar bark, and pine needles from a silver spruce that had been struck by lightning, creating a rush of vapor that dispersed rapidly and left a pleasant aroma of pine in the heated air. As the steam rose, he began to chant:

> Far in the distance the black cloud rises.
> I am he who killed the monsters.
> Far in the distance the black cloud rises.
> The Male Rain rises up from the far horizon.
> Lightning rises from the far horizon.
> The rainbow rises from the far horizon.
> They rise like the Most High Power Whose Ways Are Beautiful.
> They rise far in the distance.

Yahze was calling spirits of earth, air, and water, as the Haida and Tlingit had taught him, blending souls with these basic, natural elements. They would not, he explained, enter upon the body and soul of evil. Yahze lifted a wooden bowl with the liquid in it and passed it to Andy Taft.

"He must drink this," Yahze said.

Taft removed the gag from Plotter's mouth and took the bowl. Plotter turned his head away violently, refusing to drink. Taft grabbed Plotter's hair and pulled his head back, then put the bowl to his captive's lips and poured the resinous liquid into his mouth.

"Prepare the parchment," Yahze told Flood. The shaman then began to chant again as he doused the rocks with more of the liquid:

> I am he who came to Earth with the lightning.
> The black vapor rises far in the distance.
> The Female Rain rises far in the distance.
> The lightning rises far in the distance.
> The rainbow rises far in the distance.
> They rise like the Most High Power Whose Ways Are Beautiful.
> They rise far in the distance.

The heat in the lodge was intense. His chant was meant to urge the men to be as brave and strong as the great warriors of old. He then blessed Vogel, Taft, and Flood so that no harm would come to them.

Belial, as condor, had fled from Salt Lake City and flown north, across the Canadian border and up to the northernmost tip of Vancouver Island, close to Port Hardy. Without his pentagram to observe his sub-princes and

273

servants from afar, Belial had left Beelzebub, as falcon, in Utah to be his eyes and ears.

The four CIA guards outside the sweat lodge did not notice the peregrine falcon observing the lodge from the top branch of a nearby dead cypress.

Inside the sweat lodge, Plotter's hair began to change, growing longer in Taft's grip. The captive's naked body began to change shape. The hair coarsened and turned brown. Black spots appeared in it. Potter's bound hands and feet took the shape of large, clawed paws. He was transforming into the spotted hyena.

"Now, quickly," Yahze urged Flood when he observed the hyena emerging. Flood took the sacred Book of Mormon parchment and placed it on Plotter's hairy chest. It had no effect. The transformation continued. Long yellow fangs protruded from the hyena-man's mouth.

"He is a powerful animal spirit," Vogel whispered. "He cannot be broken this way, Jacob."

"Shall we use Aaron's breastplate?" the medicine man asked.

"First let us try this, along with your words," Vogel said as he took the dragon amulet that had been found buried in David Christensen's heart and pressed it against the hyena's forehead. Yahze chanted:

> He made it. He made it. He made it.
> At the place where evil emerged from the underworld,
> Near the Lake of Emergence, He made it.
> He made it with the North Mountain silver.
> He made it with the Black Mesa rock.
> The-Most-High-Power-Whose-Ways-Are-Fearful.

The dragon amulet glowed and burned through the hair of the man-hyena into its flesh. It screamed. The sound was blood-curdling, but to the Vigilant members present it was a positive sign. Then, suddenly, the beast twisted, and with agility and unexpected strength, lunged forward and plunged its long, sharp fangs into Rabbi Vogel's neck. Taft reacted as fast as he could, reaching for a syringe of tranquilizer he had brought. But the hyena's crushing jaws clamped down and his massive head twisted, tearing through Vogel's neck and severing his head. Taft plunged the needle into the animal's side. The hyena turned to him snarling, mouth dripping with blood. As the tranquilizer took effect, it collapsed onto the rabbi's lifeless body. Vogel's blood continued to seep from his severed blood vessels onto the drugged hyena and the ancient Navajo blanket. The beast did not return to the human form of Melvin Plotter.

"We must bind the beast," Jacob Yahze said, visibly shaken. "Do it tightly. Keep him sedated. We will take him this way to the domed rock."

The three men pulled the hyena away from Vogel's corpse. "Now this dear man is with his ancestors—with all of our ancestors," Yahze said softly. He placed the rabbi's head back in place. Vernon Flood took Aaron's breastplate in hand and placed it on the drugged hyena.

"Perhaps this will help."

"Perhaps." Yahze sighed. "Now let us enfold our friend in this sacred blanket and return his body to his people."

Afterward, Taft and Flood dragged the hyena out of the sweat lodge. The CIA unit bound it in chains.

Yahze remained behind in the sweat lodge, where he chanted a prayer over Vogel's body, now wrapped in the blanket. He asked the spirits to help guide him in the quest to find, and capture, Belial.

CHAPTER FIFTY-ONE

GATHERING AT THE ROCK

Beelzebub, as peregrine falcon, watched as the spotted hyena, his brother Amaimon, was taken from the sweat lodge and put in chains. It was a disturbing sight because both sub-princes were now far from their master's power. Then, when he saw the blanket that held Rabbi Vogel's body carried out of the sweat lodge, his spirits were lifted. Amaimon had destroyed an old foe of the fallen archangels.

The drugged hyena and Vogel's body were put aboard a helicopter with the Mormon, the Navajo, and the CIA men. Beelzebub followed it to his master's tomb.

From the helicopter, Taft contacted Michael Gross and Rabbi ben Abraham of the Ben Zimrah sect. Rabbi ben Abraham asked that Taft arrange to have Rabbi Vogel's body prepared for travel. Diplomatic clearance would be arranged for an Israeli military transport to land at the old Fort Douglas military reservation northeast of Salt Lake City.

"A plain pine coffin is all he needs," ben Abraham said.

"Jacob Yahze offers the sacred Navajo blanket as his shroud," Taft told ben Abraham.

"That will be a great honor. You will find a blue and gold robe among Rabbi Vogel's possessions," ben Abraham told Taft. "It is one of Aaron's holy robes. Please wrap the breastplate in it carefully. It will be of no further use to you. Be sure that the twelve jewels of our tribes are covered by the robe."

Taft promised to do so. He then told the rabbi that they were going to try to enter the domed rock.

"You must be extremely careful," ben Abraham warned. "I will send four of The Vigilant on the plane that comes for our brave Vogel's body. If this is the archangel's tomb, they will know how to prepare it to receive Belial when you find and capture him."

"I understand," Taft responded. "But neither the Mormon holy parchment nor Aaron's breastplate were able to control this sub-prince, so what will contain Belial?" There was a long pause before Rabbi ben Abraham spoke.

"We are not sure. Belial is not like Satan, who profaned the word of God and turned man against man. This one is a despoiler of the Earth. The key to his capture must be in that world—the natural world."

"Any thought about our entry to the tomb?" Taft asked. He knew he was involved in something beyond his experience and ken.

"No. What we learned in Xian was that the dragon sealed the tomb. The key was within the dragon. All I can do is promise that if this is Belial's tomb, then when it is opened it will be prepared by the Vigilant holy men to receive him and imprison him forever."

As the chopper landed close to tomb, two black Chevy Tahoes, loaded with CIA operatives, and a flatbed with a backhoe on it arrived and parked there.

Beelzebub circled above and saw the hyena taken from the chopper, in chains, and carried close to the domed rock. The falcon considered how he might help his fellow sub-prince, Amaimon, without risking his own capture.

Agent Benjamin had reported developments in the case to his superior in Washington and was ordered to go to the federal court in Salt Lake City and get an order giving the FBI control over the Perez property.

The attorney general was apprised of the situation. He called the director of central intelligence and asked that Taft desist from any further involvement in the case. Benjamin was being told of this development when Taft called in and told him what had happened, and that they were presently at the domed rock. Benjamin was confronted with a dilemma. He was not a politically motivated man. He loved his job and was a loyal American. He had served meritoriously as a tank company commander with the First Marine Division in Kuwait and Iraq during the first Gulf War. Disobeying a superior's orders was not in his lexicon. On the other hand, Taft's call was startling. The CIA agent had made important discoveries. He decided that before he went for the court order and blocked Taft from the case, he would drive out to the domed rock and have a look for himself.

Allen Weber was at the farm going through more of Bob Christensen's papers when the helicopter and the vehicles arriving near the domed rock got his attention. He drove down to fence, where he was stopped by CIA operatives. He asked for Andy Taft.

"How're your wife and kids?" Taft asked from his side of the fence.

"They're okay, thanks. What's going on?"

"Just trying to figure a way in," Taft said, being casual.

From this position, Weber could not see the hyena. Then the helicopter lifted off from behind the rock, carrying Vogel's body to the Fort Douglas military reservation.

"Sure. Now, are you going to tell me what's going on, Andy, or do I have to get the media over here to find out?"

Taft was surprised to hear the anger and threatening tone in Weber's voice.. "We won't let you do that," he said.

"Then either take me in with you or kill me," Weber responded. "I've seen the spirits. Damn it man, I taped them. Did you forget? I was there. Now you freeze me out?"

"No one's freezing you out Allen,"

"The hell you're not. Listen to me carefully. All the Christensens are dead. My sister is dead. My wife and kids have been attacked. I'm into this up to my eyeballs. I want my pound of flesh, or spirits, or whatever the hell this evil is. Now either cut me a hole in this fence or kill me."

Taft stared at Allen Weber long and hard. The man was serious, and he did have a stake—a big stake—in the battle to be waged against Belial.

"Okay," was all Taft said. He waved to a CIA officer, who trotted over to the fence. "Chop a door here and let this gentleman in," he ordered.

A half hour later, as FBI Agent-in-Charge Michael Benjamin arrived at the domed rock, Andy Taft had finished another conversation with Rabbi ben Abraham and had received permission to invite Allen Weber to join The Vigilant.

CHAPTER FIFTY-TWO

BREAKING THE SEAL

The drowsy, chained hyena was placed next to the domed rock. He was guarded by several CIA men. Yahze and Flood watched the animal closely as it came back to consciousness. Taft was ready with more tranquilizers, should they be needed. Weber and Benjamin, who had both been briefed, stood out of the way. The hyena shook its head and growled. It opened its mouth wide and let out a screech that sounded like a crazed laugh and echoed back from the far-off Wasatch Mountains. Above, the falcon, silent and unobserved, heard his brother's cry.

On Yahze's signal, the CIA men dragged the hyena around the perimeter of the rock. It struggled fruitlessly against the chains that bound it tightly. Flood and Yahze watched the animal's reaction as it was dragged. When it reached one place where the rock was very smooth, it became extremely agitated, which broke one of the five locks that secured the chains.

"Stop!" Yahze shouted. He pointed to a spot in the earth. "We will try here," he told Taft.

The backhoe operator maneuvered the machine into position and began to dig. Four CIA operatives, with shovels and picks, moved in to help. Amaimon, still the hyena, screamed and fought against his chains during the excavation. A half hour later, the stairway and door to the tomb were exposed. Beelzebub, circling above screeched to Amaimon, as hyena, below, "Shall I go for our master, brother?"

"No!" roared Amaimon. "I have a plan. They will not know how to enter. I will show them. Once we are all inside, I will gather our master's power and destroy them all."

Taft, Yahze, and Flood studied the sealed golden door. They tried to force it, but it did not budge. They probed under, over, and on both sides of it. They searched every nook and cranny of the great dragon emblazoned on the door. They examined the ruby eyes and the upside-down pentagram. But they found nothing helpful; no sign of any keyhole or opening. The door seemed impenetrable.

"We cannot break it down or try to use blowtorches," Flood said. "When the evil one is captured, the door must be intact to be sealed as it is now."

Above the excavation, Amaimon, as hyena, listened to the frustration in his captor's voices. It was time. He began to change back into Melvin Plotter. The chains that bound the large animal were becoming loose.

"Something's happening, sir. It's changing," the guards called to Taft. He bolted up the steps. Flood and Yahze followed. By the time they arrived, the hyena was Plotter.

"I know the way in," Plotter said in a teasing way, grinning like the Cheshire Cat. The three men were wary. "Ahhh, he said. "Now I have your attention, don't I?"

"You do," Taft said as he took a syringe in hand. "But we are not here to play games." He signaled to the CIA agent, who chambered a round in his Uzi and aimed the weapon at Plotter's chest.

"No need for that, Mr. Taft. I have no games to play."

"Why would you show us?" Yahze asked.

"To live! I know the Jew wanted you to destroy me. But I killed him first, didn't I?" He smiled. "You can't blame me for a little self-defense, can you?"

Jacob Yahze felt rage welling up within him as he recalled Rabbi Vogel's violent death. But capturing Belial and sealing him his tomb was what Vogel would have wanted, not revenge.

"What's done is done," Yahze told the sub-prince. "Open the door and you will live."

"I must hear it from the others," Plotter demanded. "I must know that you will release me if I open the door."

"You have my word," Taft said.

"And mine too," Benjamin promised.

"What about the Mormon?" Plotter questioned. Flood studied the man he had known as an upstanding Salt Lake City businessman before being revealed as this evil being.

"Rabbi Vogel was my friend," Flood told Plotter. "He was a good friend to our church. But vengeance is not our way. I would not kill you." Plotter smiled and nodded.

"All in character. But what about the other Mormon?" he gestured toward Allen Weber. "I feel hatred emanating from him."

"He's a civilian," Taft offered. "He can't do anything."

"Do not lie to me. He helped to drive out my servants. He is one of you. And his hatred of me is greater than all of you." Taft turned to Weber.

"Allen, we need you to assure this creature that you will not harm it."

In the few private moments that Taft had with Weber after Rabbi ben Abraham had given permission for him to join The Vigilant and Weber had accepted, his loyalty to the cause became paramount. "Our mission is to capture Belial and seal him in his tomb. Everything else, including revenge, must be set aside. Is that clear?" Weber had agreed.

"I will not harm Mr. Plotter," Weber stated, as he glanced at Taft, assuring him that he honored the vow he had taken when invited to join The Vigilant.

"Then all of you promise before your pitiful God?"

They all nodded.

"Take me to the door."

Above, the falcon circled lower, his sharp eyes watching every movement, his ultrasensitive hearing listening to every word.

Plotter, held by Flood and Taft, who had a syringe in his other hand, was brought down to the golden door, while above, at the top of the stairs, a CIA officer kept his weapon trained on Plotter's back. Yahze walked behind them.

Once in front of the door, the sub-prince bowed to the dragon sculpted within the inverted pentagram emblazoned on it. The whites of his eyes turned coal black. He breathed heavily, sensing his master's power that lay beyond the door, power that he would use to slaughter these meddlesome humans who held him captive.

"Give me that amulet you burned into my skull," he demanded from Jacob Yahze. The shaman opened his buckskin pouch to get it. "And remove those fetish dolls of yours, savage. They give me a headache." Yahze went back up the steps and slid the pouch off his shoulder. He took out the silver and onyx dragon amulet. He then slipped something else into his belt behind his back and went back down the steps to Plotter and the others.

Two more CIA operatives had joined the officer with their weapons aimed at Plotter. Yahze handed Plotter the amulet. This time it did not burn his flesh.

"Ahhh!" The sub-prince sighed as he caressed it. "In my hands this gives great pleasure." He slowly turns his head, revealing that the yellow fangs of the hyena had grown smaller but had not disappeared. "Now to keep my end of our bargain." He took the silver dragon amulet and pressed its onyx eye onto the ruby eye of the dragon on the door. There was a slight rumbling, followed by a hiss like the seal of a vacuum being broken. The door opened by dropping down and disappearing into the earth. Inside it was pitch-black. Then several things happened in rapid succession.

Plotter, swelling with evil power, surged forward to enter the tomb.

In a flash, Andy Taft knew they had made a great mistake. He grabbed Plotter's arm and felt a rush of searing pain tear through his body. He was forced to let go.

Weber reached out and grabbed Plotter's other arm, with the same result. He was a smaller man than Taft and not as physically fit. The shock of touching Plotter threw him to the ground.

Yahze, who was behind Plotter, threw out his right leg and kicked sideways, cutting Plotters legs out from under him. The sub-prince fell to the ground and rolled over on his back. He glared at the shaman and bared his fangs.

The officer at the top of the steps, whose line of sight had been blocked by the scuffle below, now had a clear look at Plotter. He raised his weapon, set on semiautomatic, and fired four quick rounds into the fallen sub-prince.

Yahze saw the rounds tear into Plotter's chest. They had no effect on him. Plotter laughed and rose to his feet. Several more rounds tore into his body. There was no blood. There were no wounds, only holes that remained in his clothing but disappeared from his flesh. He arrogantly turned his back on Yahze and the CIA officers to enter the tomb.

Yahze reached behind his back and gripped the bone handle of the Aztec stone sacrificial knife that he had taken from his pouch and hidden in his belt.

"Amaimon!" he shouted.

Plotter stopped and turned to face the shaman. "You will die now, savage, as did so many of your kind who refused to worship my master." He stepped out of the doorway and reached out with his left hand, which had now become a hyena's clawed paw.

Yahze stepped to his right and plunged the stone knife's sharp point into Plotter's neck, twisting and slicing, over and over, until he had beheaded Amaimon, sub-prince of Belial. The flesh, blood, and bone of Plotter turned into a black, powdery substance and sank into the sandy soil at the entrance to the tomb. A gust of foul-smelling air swirled above the black soil and disappeared.

Beelzebub, the falcon, felt the pain of Amaimon's beheading and his separation from the body—Plotter—that their master had fathered. For unlike the spirits that could be called to enter a human body, a sub-prince could only possess human form if fathered by his master.

The falcon rose rapidly into the warm air currents above the tomb. It headed north to warn Belial of what had happened. A new vessel for Amaimon would have to be created. Only Belial could do that.

CHAPTER FIFTY-THREE

WHERE EVIL DWELLS

There was no doubt they had discovered Belial's tomb. Everyone was elated. Before exploring it, Andy Taft reported their finding to Rabbi ben Abraham in Safed. He warned Taft not to remove anything from the tomb.

"Disturb as little as you can, Andrew," Rabbi ben Abraham warned. "While Belial is not sealed within, he can use the power of these things if he gets them. And when he is captured, he must be sealed in the tomb with everything intact."

Powerful battery lights from the CIA helicopter were used initially for illumination as they cautiously explored the catacomb-like passageways and chambers of the tomb. As Andy Taft realized the size and scope of this underground hideaway, he thought it might require more people than their small group plus the four Vigilant members soon to arrive. But he couldn't expose anyone new or uninitiated to the battle. He considered bringing in Sasha Andreyev, who was a Vigilant member and still in Washington, and Detective

Ruiz. He decided to keep exploring the tomb before putting either one of them in harm's way.

In addition to other logistical matters, much more lighting would be required. A gasoline-driven electric generator was brought in and set up at the top of the stairs. Heavy cable from it snaked down the steps into the tomb. All available lighting the CIA troops had was connected, but a search of the construction equipment found outside the sealed flood-control tunnel uncovered more lights and wiring that was designed to be used to illuminate the rear of the chamber where the shafts to the aquifers had been excavated. It was pleasingly ironic that those lights, meant to help wreak death and destruction, would be used against Belial.

The first room they explored, more like a chamber hewn out of the rock, contained records of ecological disasters that Belial had caused and/or encouraged. These were inscribed in large, leather-bound books, written in the language of the country or land in which the activity had taken place: the Chernobyl nuclear contamination in Cyrillic; the Exxon Valdez oil spill in Atkan; the Bhopal chlorine-gas release in Dravidian-Tralugu; the Brazilian rainforest destruction in Portuguese; the Indonesian rainforest rape in Papuan; the Montana strip-mining blight in English; the thinning of the ozone layer above Antarctica in Maori; the world's fish stock decimation in Japanese; the acid rain blight in the northeastern United States in English; and the burning of the Kuwaiti oil fields in Arabic. It was a long and tragic series of mindless exploitation, plunder, and misuse of precious natural resources. Belial's mischief was worldwide in scope as he encouraged and manipulated greedy, shortsighted profiteers.

There were hundreds of these books—a sad testament to the failure of human stewardship of the planet.

Taft, Flood, Weber, Benjamin, and Yahze made note of the writings they could not translate, knowing that the four Vigilant members coming from Safed could read and speak several of these languages and would be able to translate many of the records.

The second chamber was a repository of charms, implements, amulets, statuary, paintings, carvings, and weapons—all expressions of man's attempt to identify and combat Belial, as well as an indication of humanity's fear of the evil archangel's power. On the opposite side of the chamber was a record, also bound in leather books, of those enlisted or possessed through the ages who had joined Belial's evil crusade.

The third chamber they came upon was much like the ancient room deep in the cellars of the Ben Zimrah compound in Safed. It was small, and oppressively hot and humid. There was no indication of where the heat and moisture came from. On its walls, written in Aramaic, were the names of the evil ones. Each wall was devoted to one archangel and his minions. Allen Weber, the only one among them who knew the ancient language, read their names aloud—a roll call of iniquity. At the top of each wall the archangel and his sub-princes were named:

Satan: Asmodee and Ariton

Belial: Beelzebub and Amaimon

Leviathan: Magot and Paimon

Lucifer: Astarot and Orines

Beneath those were the names of the spirits and servitors bound to them, which numbered in the hundreds, and the functions they could perform.

Weber identified those they had already encountered: Hamaculi, the spirit that withers life, who had possessed Lincoln Foster; Orgosil, the spirit of tumultuous events, who had possessed William Claremont; Dimirag, the one who drives forward, and had possessed the body of Bishop Horne. They did not know that it was Trisaga, Ruler of Triads, who had possessed Bertha Smalls. If ever there was testament to the existence of organized and deliberate evil, it was inscribed on these walls.

In the center of the chamber was an altar carved out of one huge piece of pure jade. Upon the altar, next to a bloodstained stone Aztec sacrificial knife, laid the putrid, decaying remains of Bertha Smalls.

The next chamber, the fourth, was divided into quadrants. One contained bones, heads, claws, and skins of animals. Agent Benjamin suggested that his forensics experts examine these as possible weapons used in the Christensen murders. Taft repeated Rabbi ben Abraham's admonishment that nothing be removed from the tomb.

"I still have two murder cases to pursue," Benjamin reminded the CIA operative who seemed to have had taken charge of the operation. "The Christensens, Grace Miller, and the state troopers in Park City."

"Let us not forget Rabbi Vogel," Flood reminded them.

"Amen," Taft said. "But now there are priorities that go far beyond murder cases. The nuclear waste we found in Perez's so-called flood-control tunnel and the horrors we saw in that first chamber make that clear." He turned to Allen Weber. "I know how you feel about your family. But now we must be concerned for the lives of millions—perhaps all of mankind."

Weber nodded his understanding and acceptance, although the heat of revenge against Nicholas Perez still boiled in his belly.

No matter how conscientious Michael Benjamin was about his duty, in this netherworld of an archangel's tomb, it all seemed distant and removed. He decided, for now, to accept Taft's evaluation of the situation.

In the second quadrant of the fourth chamber they found many identifiable body parts of extinct species such as wooly mammoths, saber-toothed cats, Tasmanian devils, and the remains of what must have been experiments to cross-breed species, resulting in bizarre and abnormal creatures—serpent-birds, scaly mammals, and ferocious, two-headed shark snakes.

"These are abominations," Vernon Flood remarked.

"The unnatural always is," Yahze said.

In the third quadrant of the chamber were remains and body parts that were unidentifiable other than they appeared to be humanoid. They were very large beings, with enormous skulls and bones.

"These are Old Ones," Jacob Yahze said softly as he examined one of the skulls. "They are the first mother of the Diné, the first people brought up from the center of the Earth."

"They must have been special to Belial," Flood remarked to the shaman. "He has separated from the other animals."

"No," Yahze said firmly. "These are not animals." He respectfully lifted the huge skull and showed it to Flood. "It is as man is. And see how it is crushed on the side? That is a blow from a weapon. This being was murdered."

"Perhaps it was an enemy to Belial," Taft suggested.

"Yes," Yahze agreed. "That is the legend. A fierce enemy of evil ones." *Yahze considered telling his companions about the Haida's interaction with these creatures—that they still existed—but he hesitated. No point in confusing matters, he thought.*

As the others moved on to the fourth quadrant, Yahze lingered to utter a prayer chant for the souls of the Sasquatch remains. When finished, he chanted one for Isadore Vogel. Somehow it seemed appropriate, for these creatures and the good rabbi had battled evil.

The final quadrant of the chamber had wall paintings, much in the style of those done by Neanderthals in France, or by the aborigines on the red rocks of central Australia. They depicted a few recognizable animals: puma, condor, falcon, hyena, and a great white bear. There was also one that appeared to be a winged serpent.

"Is this a dragon?" Benjamin asked.

"Quetzalcoatl," Yahze answered. "The plumed serpent-god of my Aztec and Toltec ancestors. Yes, you might call him a dragon."

"I wonder why there are only these few animals here?" Benjamin remarked. "Might it be a clue for us? Something to look for?"

"We saw Amaimon take the shape of the hyena," Taft said.

"This suggests that if we find puma, and those birds—"

"Peregrine falcon and condor," Yahze interjected.

"Or a bear," Weber added.

"Yes. A white one."

"Then," Benjamin continued, "we may find Beelzebub and Belial."

"And the flying serpent?" Weber asked.

"That I do not know," Yahze answered.

"Whatever he is," Taft remarked, "I'd sure hate to meet him a dark alley."

The fifth chamber housed corruptions of the sacred writings and symbols of many of the world's religions. Among them were seven more golden plates, like those found hung around the necks of the two young Christensen children. They too were based on the Book of Mormon, but corrupted to glorify evil. For Benjamin and Weber, this discovery solved one of the puzzles of the Christensen murders—the source of the plates.

Other corrupted religious items in the chamber were a Torah—the Five Books of Moses—written in blood and reading left to right, the opposite of Hebrew; the Hindu Vedas, books of knowledge directly from Brahma, extolling the demon king, Ravana, and Rakshasas, malevolent imps that serve him, as well as the serpent Vritra, enemy of the Hindu gods; Sutras, Buddhist scriptures written by Siddhartha Gautama, the Buddha, which spoke of the glory of him as the son of a rich man, caring little for his fellow men; the Koran, rewritten to encourage the murder of infidels, all non-Muslims, and the glorification of using murder and suicide to that end; twisted and corrupted writings of Confucius and the Taoist founder, Lao Tzu; and the New Testament in its original Greek, as well as desecrations of the writings of Martin Luther, John Calvin, Simon called Peter, John Wesley, and many more. The chamber was a repository of lies and corruptions designed to contradict and reject all religion.

The group identified as many of the writings as they could. Since nothing could be removed from the tomb, a list would be hurriedly prepared and flown up to nearby Fort

Douglas military reservation, where the plane from Israel was due to land. It would be sent to the Ben Zimrah in Safed, along with Aaron's breastplate, robe, and Rabbi Vogel's remains.

"The linguists and scholars from The Vigilant will have much to study here. Careful copies and recordings must be made," Flood said. "It is possible that there are clues here that we can use to locate the other two fallen archangels, Leviathan and Lucifer, their sub-princes, and their tombs." That thought lifted their spirits as they moved to the sixth and final chamber.

Here was Belial's throne room. It was the largest chamber and its purpose was obvious. This was Belial's lair, his physical seat of power.

"Satan's throne was also gold," Taft remarked as they approached Belial's golden throne. He looked up to the high ceiling. One word was emblazoned on it, as it had been in Satan's tomb. Taft knew the Aramaic writing and its meaning.

"Yahweh," Weber said respectfully. "It is the ancient name for He who has no name. God."

Taft nodded and smiled. "You know, in Xian, when we locked Satan away in his tomb, Rabbi Vogel said that even there, at the very heart of Satan's power and evil, God was watching."

"And so He watches here too," Flood said, more a prayer than a statement.

"And over our lost friend," Yahze added. "His efforts also brought us to this place.

"And his sacrifice," Taft added.

They moved forward and examined the inverted pentagram that framed the throne. It was bejeweled with glittering lights whose power source was not evident. Most of the lights were flickering, but some had been extinguished.

Andy Taft recalled that a similar pentagram had been described to him by Peter Somoroff, the KGB colonel with whom he had worked in the Soviet Union to capture Satan. It was in that Evil One's office in the Kremlin.

"It may be a device to describe the status of his sub-princes, servitors, disciples, and spirits," Taft offered.

After they had explored all the chambers and many of the passageways, Taft stepped outside and called Rabbi ben Abraham again to report their findings. He requested that the Ben Zimrah send as many linguists and scholars as possible.

"You have done a wonderful deed, Mr. Taft," Rabbi ben Abraham said. "I will send four others, along with the four of The Vigilant who will assess what must be done to prepare the tomb. Taft suggested that he would bring Sasha Andreyev and Andrea Ruiz into The Vigilant to help explore.

"Until the four arrive, no one should go into the tomb again except Jacob Yahze, Vernon Flood, Mr. Weber, and you," Rabbi ben Abraham continued. "And beware. Belial must certainly know of your discovery. He may try to gain entry. Guard the doorway well." He then asked to speak with Jacob Yahze.

"You must gather the black dust that was Amaimon's human body and place it in the fourth chamber near the bones of the Old Ones," the rabbi told the shaman.

"Yes," Yahze answered. "I understand. The Old Ones will watch over these evil remains."

"And they will deny Belial access to their spirits, even afterward, when he is sealed within. Now tell me about the drawings of the animals."

Jacob described the hyena, falcon, condor, puma, bear, and Quetzalcoatl. "The plumed serpent is familiar to me," he told Rabbi ben Abraham.

"You must watch for these animals. It is possible that Belial will use them to gain access to his unholy lair."

Yahze said they would keep alert. But his heart was heavy for the loss of his new friend. "Please pass on my condolences to Rabbi Vogel's family. Tell them he was a very brave and special man. I will always chant for his soul."

"Thank you, Jacob Yahze," Rabbi ben Abraham said. "Isadore Vogel knew the dangers of our work, and accepted them willingly. His family will honor your remembrance."

The exploration of the tomb lasted through the night and well into the morning. As they walked out and up the steps, Andy Taft took Benjamin aside and explained his conversation with Rabbi ben Abraham.

"No offense, Michael. These guys in Israel, and the rest of the group, have a task ahead of them that can't be messed with. They asked that things be this way for now, and I agreed."

"I hear you," Benjamin said. "Just keep me in the loop. I'm here to help as much as possible." But he wondered how long he would stall the people at the Bureau and Department of Justice. As long as it takes, he decided.

Taft then spoke to the CIA officer in charge, ordering him to double the guard on the tomb doorway and establish a perimeter defense around the domed rock. He gathered

Vernon Flood, Allen Weber, Jacob Yahze, and Michael Benjamin to him.

"No one comes in or out except these three men," pointing to Flood, Weber, and Yahze, "and me. Is that clear?"

"Yes, sir. Absolutely, sir."

"If I may," Yahze began. "Will there be a service for Rabbi Vogel? He was a good man, and my friend."

"Not here," Taft told him. "There is a plane coming from Israel to take him. His family is there."

"In Judaism, it is important that he be buried as quickly as possible," Benjamin added.

"I understand. It is the same with my people. Tonight I will chant for him for a safe journey to his Father."

The group was exhausted, overwhelmed by what they had discovered in the tomb, and aware that there was still much to be done. In addition, they were on edge with the thought that Belial might be lurking nearby, aware of their intrusion into his seat of power, and plotting to destroy them.

CHAPTER FIFTY-FOUR

NAN AND SAK

Autumn is a short but brilliant season in mountainous British Columbia. The Canadian Rockies are mostly wilderness. Much of it is still not topographically mapped or explored in detail. The winters are harsh. Spared the polluted imprint of man, it is one of the most pristine places left in the hemisphere. On the western side of Mount Silverthorne, where, over many millennia, the Seymour River has chiseled away the land, a small, verdant, sheltered valley is tucked between the mountain and the river's fiordlike shore. It is a remote, self-contained ecological system.

Nan crouched down behind a mossy granite boulder, his keen eyes observing the two strange birds of prey as they circled above, searching for a good place to land. Normally, Nan lived harmoniously with the creatures of the forests and mountains. This hidden valley, in the time before winter, gave him easy but protected access to the river and to the salmon run that had just begun. Instinct and cunning told him to hide and observe this strange pair—a large peregrine falcon and a very large condor. They had flown into the valley three weeks ago.

Nan knew that it was the wrong season for the falcon to be passing through. And the condor did not belong this far north. These birds had no mates. They did not nest and they did not hunt. From time to time, the falcon would fly off and be gone for two or three days. One of these disappearances had occurred a few days ago. Now the falcon had returned, and they both seemed agitated, swooping over the treetops in crisscross patterns. It was strange and unsettling to see such unnatural behavior.

Nan was a young male solitary. His kind had once roamed throughout all the mountain ranges and deep valleys of the world, meeting females once every five years to mate, and then moving on. The females reared the young in secluded mountain caves high above valleys such as this one. Nan's kind had lived harmoniously with the tribes of man. The Indians revered and respected them, as they did all of nature. But when the white man arrived, and multiplied, those intruding populations devoured and destroyed much of what was natural in their path. Nan's kind diminished in numbers and range. Now they survive solely in the most remote parts of the Andean, Rocky, and Himalayan mountains.

The North American Indians called them Sasquatch—the Old Ones. In Nepal and China they are known as "Yeti," and in Andean Peru, Chile, and Bolivia, "El Viejo Grande de las Montañas. The Old Man of the Mountains. Bigfoot is the name the white man gave them. Having seen the disrespect the newcomers had for nature, and their thoughtless destruction of habitat and species, the Sasquatch realized they must remain hidden and elusive for their survival. The air smells foul, the water is dirty, and the fish are dying. The thoughtless white man is nearly everywhere. As more of the wilderness is opened to mindless development, these large, gentle mammals retreated deeper and deeper into seclusion, sensing that, in time, the extinction of their race will come.

Most white men doubt their existence. But from time to time, a few have been observed, usually by individuals trekking far off the beaten path.

Today, most Sasquatch on the North American continent have retreated into the wilds of British Columbia, the Yukon, and central Alaska. They have lost contact with their brothers and sisters in Andean South America and mountainous Central Asia.

There are fewer adult males and breeding females, and so fewer children to be reared. The dwindling wilderness is their last refuge.

The strange birds of prey landed in a small, grassy clearing. Curiosity and concern drew Nan to have a closer look. His eight-foot, three hundred-pound body moved with unusual agility and grace along the forest floor with a his stealth that was impressive for his size.

By the time he arrived close to the edge of the clearing, the condor—Belial—and the falcon—Beelzebub—had taken their human forms, Nicholas Perez and Raymond Light. Nan knelt cautiously on the mossy carpet of the forest. *How had the two birds become men, he wondered?*

The Sasquatch communicated with a simple language consisting of sounds that represented their physical world, such as sun, direction, wind, rain, snow, mating, food, baby—a lexicon of about one hundred words and thoughts. They also used scent, touch, and high-pitched wailing that traveled many miles, mostly at night, in the thin mountain air. It was a songlike communication not unlike that of wolves, dolphins, and whales. They modulated their cries with others, from mountaintop to mountaintop, producing pleasant harmonies that expressed their thoughts, feelings, as well as information.

Nan had frequently hidden and listened to white men converse as they hiked in the deep woods or scaled remote mountainsides. As he crouched lower among the cedars and giant ferns, he watched and listened, but the two men spoke in a language he did not know. Straining to understand, he concentrated on their tone of voice and gestures. Something in his atavistic memory warned that these men were dangerous. They were certainly not ordinary white men. Their scent was evil. And if they were capable of transforming into birds and yet still be men, they could pose a great threat to Nan and his kind. The young Sasquatch decided to delay feasting on the spawning salmon and remain hidden until the strange man-birds revealed their purpose for being in the valley.

Perez listened as Light related the discovery of Belial's home, and Amaimon's failed plan. The death of his sub-prince, as Melvin Plotter, angered the archangel. Amaimon's spirit was now in limbo and would stay there unless Belial prepared another human body for him. That required mating with a human woman, a disciple of Beelzebub or Amaimon. The chosen woman would bear a child that Amaimon's spirit could enter, and as the child grew—more rapidly that a normal child—Amaimon's power would grow inside it until he was able once again to be of service to his master.

"I have a disciple prepared," he told Light. "The woman I have chosen is in the north. She is an Alaskan Aleut. Within her resides the spirit Effrigis—the one who quivers in a horrible manner." Light grinned and nodded, enjoying his master's cunning. "Her tribe believes the woman has a nervous disorder, a brain function gone awry. They have placed her in an institution in Nome. The staff there is small. Only a few caretakers. It will be easy for me to spill my seed into her."

"You have put her far from prying eyes," Light told Belial.

"Man is easy to deceive. Like the Aleuts, many tribes rejected my offer of power. They have grown weak and lazy, distracted by the ways of the white man."

Nan knew the word "Aleut." They were a tribe of hunters and nomads, far to the north. What did these creatures want with them? As night approached, Nan continued his vigil, noting that even though the temperature had dropped to near freezing, the hairless men/birds did not seem to feel the cold. They made no fire. They put on no fur. Nan's coarse, hairy coat, and a thick layer of fat beneath, protected him from the elements. His stomach begged for fresh salmon, but he remained patient, watching and listening.

"In the morning, I will go north," Perez said. "You will return to my home and collect certain things that I need." That worried Light.

"The tomb is guarded by the soldiers who captured our Paronto servants, and my brother in the chamber."

"You will find a way in. These intruders will be curious, so they will come and go."

"More soldiers have arrived, master." Perez glared at Raymond Light. This was no time for caution. Action was required.

"The dragon entrance door will be open. You have swift, strong wings and powers I have given to you. Use them."," Light said, lowering his voice as though he were telling a secret. Nan's keen senses enabled him to hear the hushed words. "The farther I traveled from your home to this place, the more difficult I found it to fly. And when I changed to this human form, I felt pain and weakness."

"I have these sensations too. It is because my home is disturbed. The human scum have defiled my possessions. They say the words I have written in the old tongues. They put their dirty hands upon my pentagram and throne. This saps my powers. But when you bring me what I need, we will have all the power required to destroy the intruders." Perez's words reassured Light.

"Yes, master. I understand."

"Now we must rest. Our journey continues at first light."

While Belial and Beelzebub rested in the clearing, Nan pondered the situation. As he did, he grew aware of the presence of another Sasquatch in the area. Normally, this was uncommon, but their mating time was approaching, and breeding males were on the move. This was Nan's first trip to the far-off mating grounds. He sniffed the cold night air to be sure, then sang out a greeting, a mournful wail that might have been a wolf's, across the valley. An answer came back shortly after his song's echoes faded. Nan knew it belonged to Sak, an older male, who was wise in the old ways before white men had come to the new world. Nan called out again, this time howling the meeting sound. Sak responded. They would meet at the end of the valley where the river forked.

Perez was awakened by the Sasquatch calls. He shuddered, and then sniffed at the chill air. Light was awake now too.

"Those calls. They are not wolves, master."

"The Old Ones. There are two, calling to meet."

"Are they following us?" Perez sniffed the air again. "No. They travel to mate." He listened again. His body relaxed. "They are moving away now."

Belial had not encountered Sasquatch for more than a hundred years. They were his mortal enemy long before the Navajo, at a time when other tribes, such as the Paronto, worshipped him. His comfort was that soon the world would be rid them because, encouraged by Belial, the white man continued to destroy the environment, and with it the Sasquatch habitat.

In the morning, Beelzebub, as falcon, flew south toward Utah, while Belial, as condor, flew out of the British Columbian valley in the opposite direction. Nan and Sak, who had met earlier that night at the river, watched both humans transform. Sak knew who they were.

"The most evil one goes north. Very dangerous." The message from the wise solitary was respected by the younger Nan.

"We go north. For mating," Nan said.

"They fly. We walk. Tonight, call a warning to our brothers. Now we go to Haida."

Nan had never revealed himself to any human before, but Sak had, during the time of a great earthquake. He had been moving south at night, along the rocky coast, when he felt the earth tremble slightly. Fearing a tidal wave, he rushed into a sheltered cove and came upon a Haida village. He stood at the edge of the village and wailed an alarm, waking the Haida and saving many lives. The earthquake hit with incredible force. The Haida homes, made of saplings, bark and thatch, were destroyed. Sak entered the village and helped carry many injured to safety on higher ground before the tidal wave rushed ashore. The chief and the medicine man were, of course, very grateful, though fearful of the heroic gentle giant whose existence until then had been only a myth. Since that encounter, Sak had stopped by the village from time to time to visit with the elders. There they learned the rudiments of Sasquatch language, and he some basic Haida. Sak also learned that the Haida medicine man possessed powerful amulets.

"With these, and an ancient tongue," the Haida told him as they sat before a fire, "we can call to the bear, the raven, the eagle, and the great orca to come. They help us as you Sasquatch do."

Sak waited until nightfall before announcing his presence to the Haida village elders. It was an icy, cloudless night of the full moon. As they had in the past, upon hearing Sak's cries, the chief and the medicine man left the village after they was sure all were asleep. They went to a large flat rock on the northern shore of the cove, where they waited until Sak emerged from the woods and joined them. Greetings were exchanged. Then Sak called out to Nan, who joined him at the rock. Nan, larger than Sak, was an imposing figure in the blue-white light of the moon.

"My friend, Nan," Sak told the Haida. The chief and the medicine man stood and bowed their heads in greeting. Nan responded in kind, and then sat next to Sak on the rock. The tide was rising, gently lapping against the shoreline below them. A small band of wolves had gathered at the forest's edge, attracted by Sak's cries. Nan sniffed the air and grunted a concern.

"Wolves guard us," Sak said. Nan relaxed. Sak turned to the medicine man, who wore only a waistcloth and moccasins. His body was heavily tattooed. On his chest was the bear; orcas decorated each arm, and a giant eagle head adorned his broad back. He did not appear to feel the cold.

"We see great danger," Sak began. His words were a mixture of Sasquatch and Haida. He used his huge hands to make signs and gestures that helped tell the story. "We have seen white men who change into birds of prey. One is a falcon. The other is a large bird from the land of our brothers to the far south. Condor is its name. These things are dark and evil."

The chief turned to his medicine man. "Do you know of this?"

"Yes from long ago. These are the ones who brought the white man to us. They are dark spirits who wish to destroy our land, our air, our fish and our game. They are our enemies. They possess great power." He turned to Sak. "Forgive that I speak rapidly to my chief. I tell him of these evil ones. We know them."

"Do you still have power to call the eagle and the orca?" Sak asked the medicine man.

"Yes."

"Will you call these to this place now so that Nan and I may speak to them?" The medicine man related the request to his chief.

"Do as he wishes."

The medicine man opened a sealskin pouch that hung over his shoulder and removed two amulets carved out of jade. One was adorned with the neck feathers of the bald eagle, the other with a piece of black-and-white skin from the orca. He placed both amulets on the large, flat stone that was their meeting place. He lifted the eagle amulet and tapped it three times as he raised his head to the sky and opened his mouth. On the third tap, an extremely high-pitched, screeching sound emanated from his throat and pierced the still night. He then placed the eagle back on the rock and took the orca amulet in hand and walked down to the water's edge. There he plunged the amulet into the water three times, sending ripples out onto the still waters of cove. On the third plunge he put his face into the water and opened his mouth. As before, a high-pitched sound came out—more of a whale's song than the screeching call of the eagle. It traveled away under the water.

By the time the medicine man returned to the flat rock, a giant bald eagle had landed there. Sak thanked the eagle for coming and told him about the large dark man/bird they were seeking. He asked the eagle to call to his kind and have them search for the condor.

"Nan and I will travel to the north. Send us messengers if you have found him. But take care. Keep your distance. He is very dangerous."

Then they heard an increased lapping of water against the shore. In the moonlight, the high, stiff dorsal fin of a large male orca cut through the water as it swam toward the rock, pushing a wave in front of him. The rushing sound of its breath, exploding from his blowhole, echoed in the cove.

"Orca comes," the medicine man said. The sleek, black-and-white orca, not a whale, but a member of the dolphin species, slid up on shore. His body rose nearly completely out of the water as his eyes intensely scanned the group on the rock.

"Who calls?" the orca asked. Sak jumped off the rock and walked over to him. He then knelt so that he was face-to-face with the great ocean hunter.

"We call you," he said in the orca's tongue. "The Old Ones." He then related his story of the evil man/bird.

"We know of him from his hated brother Leviathan, who brings evil to the seas. We will search for this one from the water," the orca announced.

"And we from the sky," the eagle called down to the shore. Both then left to spread the word of the mission to their kind.

"There is more we can do," the chief told Sak and Nan. "I will send messages to all Haida, and to our brothers the Comox, Tlingit, Eyak, Unangan, and Yup'ik. You will have their eyes and ears to hunt for this evil one as well. He then offered a swift Haida fishing boat to take the two Sasquatch to Alaska.

On his way north, as Belial crossed into Alaska over Haida Gwaii—the Queen Charlotte Islands—he encountered an early winter storm. The condor landed and changed to Perez, where he seeking sought in Rose Harbor. When the storm passed, Belial, once again as condor, followed the coast north and then west, resting at night until he reached the mouth of the Yukon River at Alakanuk. Along the way he took little notice of the bald eagles that cruised below him, apparently fishing the late salmon run.

But those eagles took notice of the strange, large, black bird they had been warned about. They sent word of his movements, via the orca, to Nan and Sak, who were now traveling rapidly along the coast in a new Haida copper hulled twin-engine halibut trawler.

Belial glided north to Stuart Island just off the coast of the town of St. Michael in Norton Sound. There he stopped to rest and make final plans to mate with his special disciple, the Aleut woman in the Nome institution.

Once again, the eagles tracked his movements and sent word of Belial's location to Nan and Sak, whom the Haida had put ashore near the village of Kwigillingok on Bristol Bay. They were only one hundred fifty miles south of Belial's location.

CHAPTER FIFTY-FIVE

FOUR MEN FROM SAFED

The Israeli transport, looking strikingly similar to the British Canberra night bomber but with twice the speed and five times the deadly weaponry, appeared like a giant black bat as it swooped down out of the inky night and landed. As it taxied to the hangar, its drooping wings bobbed up and down with the weight of its engines while the windows of the illuminated cockpit glowed like golden eyes. Fort Douglas was supposed to have been decommissioned, and inactive. The single runway, nestled between two six-thousand-foot mountains, had recently been extended and repaved to handle large aircraft. For the past five years, due to their growing involvement in actual battlefield combat, it had been secretly used by the CIA as a training facility for its elite soldier corps.

Rabbi Isadore Vogel's plain pine coffin was draped with an Israeli flag. Four CIA soldiers, in black battle dress, stood guard, ready to escort the remains to the plane.

Vernon Flood and Andy Taft welcomed the four Vigilant members as they deplaned. The visitors wore jeans, sweatshirts, leather jackets, and work boots. At first glance they appeared to be nothing more than four construction workers arriving at a job site.

The delegation was led by Shariat Khawaja, a Pakistani sunni Imam from Karachi. He was a tall, stoic man of forty-five, with a coal-black beard and brown, weathered skin. The imam had been a fighter with the Mujahidin against the Soviet Union in Afghanistan, but he was opposed to the Taliban and their brutal fundamentalist ways. They imprisoned him, but he escaped to Pakistan.

Next was Father John Apostolopoulos, a Greek Orthodox priest with a Ph.D. in antiquities. Father John was a native New Yorker who had reluctantly left his pulpit in Manhattan when the head of the Greek Orthodox Church, the archbishop of Istanbul, had requested his assistance. Becoming part of The Vigilant turned out to be part of that request.

Rahman Chandri, a sadhu—a Hindu holy man—with long, black dreadlocks, came next. Although dressed in nondescript Western clothing, his years of living in a cave with only a bowl and a trident as his earthly possessions, and spending his days in prayer, shone through as serenity on his handsome, weathered face. In those days of solitary contemplation, sustenance was provided by the charity of other Hindus. He is said to have heard a voice commanding him to set aside the life of a sadhu and join The Vigilant in their battle against evil.

The final member of the group was Kwame Dombo, the third son of a sub-chief from northern Ghana. He was a teacher in the Baha'i faith. Founded in the early 1860s in Persia, Baha'i is one of the world's newer religions. Its basic tenet is the spiritual unity of all humanity.

As the four men exchanged greetings with Vernon Flood and Andy Taft, the CIA soldiers escorted Rabbi Vogel's flag-draped coffin to the plane. As it passed by, the six Vigilant present bowed their heads and each put a hand on it, reciting his litany in his native tongue for the rabbi's soul. Afterward, they stood and silently watched as the casket was loaded onto the Israeli plane.

"Where is Aaron's breastplate?" Imam Khawaja asked when the plane's rear door was closed. Andy Taft opened a leather bag he was carrying and produced the breastplate, wrapped in the gold-and-blue robe that Rabbi ben Abraham said he would find among Rabbi Vogel's possessions. The imam held the breastplate while the Greek Orthodox priest and the sadhu carefully wrapped it in the robe. They ceremoniously passed it to Kwame Dombo, who took it aboard the aircraft, handing it to Ling Chow Sung, a Buddhist monk and Vigilant member who was onboard to escort Vogel's remains and bring the sacred breastplate home to Safed.

The Israeli flight crew locked up and began their taxi to takeoff. They would be refueled in flight by a U.S. Air Force tanker over the Caribbean.

Jacob Yahze had remained in the tomb, studying artifacts and what records he could decipher. The temporary lighting had been upgraded by two additional generators that had arrived with twenty CIA reinforcements. A satellite communication link between the tomb and the Ben Zimrah compound in Safed had been installed. Taft also cleared access to North American CIA satellite observation.

When the group from Israel arrived at the tomb, Yahze was proposed a plan of action. Among the eight Vigilant members there—Taft, Flood, Yahze, Khawaja, Apostolopoulos, Chandri, Dombo, and the newest, Allen Weber—they spoke twenty-nine languages and fourteen dialects. Yahze led everyone on a tour of the six chambers and then suggested that they first familiarize themselves with the chamber that contained the records of ecological disasters. The group was able to translate or decipher thirty-six more of the record books. Since nothing could be removed from the tomb, the four Vigilant members from Safed insisted that all documents and artifacts be photographed in detail. Yahze then led the group back to the chamber of corruption, as Andy Taft had named it.

"Here we will miss Rabbi Vogel's expertise in Aramaic," Shariat Khawaja remarked as they opened one of the three ancient torah scrolls in the chamber. It was written left to right, the opposite of Hebrew. Blood had been used in place of ink.

Allen Weber, who had been quiet for most of the tour, stepped forward. "With your permission, Imam, I had the privilege to study Aramaic with the Ben Zimrah in Safed, and at the Hebrew University in Jerusalem."

"Then we are blessed to have you with us," the imam said. Father Apostolopoulos knew some of the basics of the ancient language too. He was able to confirm that only three such torah scrolls—written backward and in blood—had ever been discovered. They had been found in archeological digs in Iraq, Australia, and China. Two had been preserved and stored in Safed. The third had been stolen from the Museum of Antiquities in Cairo in 1966. He suspected that this was that scroll. Rahman Chandri was thrilled to see the Hindu Vedas.

"These are surely ancient," he told his colleagues. "In fact, their existence is not known. Most Vedas were handed down orally through the ages. And these—glorifying the evil Ravana, Rakshasas, and the serpent Vritra—are the most offensive.

"In just a brief study of this Koran," Imam Khawaja announced, "I can see the basis for much of what troubles Islam today. The corruption announces that the word of Allah gives license to murder and terrorize. This is not Islam. It can be used as the seed of its destruction."

Father Apostolopoulos said the same about the twisted gospel of early New Testament parchments written in classical Greek. All of the material was photographed and would be forwarded to Safed as quickly as possible.

They then moved on to the throne room. Yahze guided them to the pentagram with its glowing lights.

"They are not electric," he explained. "They burn but consume nothing. They have no wick, nor gas, nor oil." Imam Khawaja, who had been in Xian when Satan was entombed, examined the light closely.

"The pentagram is identical to the one the archangel Satan, in the guise of the Soviet colonel Nickolai Valarian, had in his Kremlin office. This one must give Belial the power to communicate with his remaining sub-prince, Beelzebub, and the disciples and spirits under their control.

"Perhaps we can figure out how to use this device to locate Belial," Allen Weber suggested.

"Or, now that the nuclear waste is safely controlled, distract him from whatever new ecological disaster he is planning," Kwame Dombo added.

"We will try everything we can," Imam Khawaja told the group. "There is much to learn here, but locating Belial is most important."

"And if we find him?" Taft asked, knowing he would be the one to lead a capture team. "What then?"

Imam Khawaja was troubled. "We know now that the breastplate and robes of Aaron have little power over this archangel. Rabbi ben Abraham hopes the answer lies within these walls. We will search. We must find a way. Pray that God will provide."

"Based on what we've seen here, the rate of ecological disasters is accelerating," Vernon Flood added. "That, my friends, bodes ill for humanity."

"Yes. And triumph for Belial," Kwame Dombo added.

Andy Taft, who had the greatest respect for those in The Vigilant who represented organized religion, was a pragmatic soldier. He had different concerns.

"The FBI has a bulletin out for Nicholas Perez and Raymond Light," Taft told the new arrivals. "But if they are able to transform themselves the Amaimon became the hyena, well then, they could be anything and anywhere."

It was clear to all that unless the evil archangel was somehow captured and entombed, his goal of a dead, uninhabitable planet could be realized, perhaps even in the twenty-first century.

As the group discussed how Belial might be located and captured, Imam Khawaja's gaze drifted to the ceiling above the throne, where he saw the word "Yahweh" inscribed.

"Allahu Akbar. God is Great," he uttered. Andy Taft heard him and saw what Khawaja had seen.

"Just as it was in Xian, Imam," he said. The others all looked up.

"God is above, and here with us," Vernon Flood said softly.

CHAPTER FIFTY-SIX

BEELZEBUB'S MISSION

Two days after the men from Safed began their work in the tomb, Beelzebub, as falcon, circled high above the domed rock. His sharp eyes zeroed in on the comings and goings of those who had destroyed Amaimon, as well as on the four new foreigners. He counted the CIA soldiers and saw that many more had arrived. His master sought only two things from inside. The sub-prince could enter as falcon, but to carry away these things, he would have to be in his human form, Raymond Light. That troubled him. The image of the medicine man plunging the stone knife into Amaimon's neck, and severing his head, gave him pause. As falcon he could elude. As man he was vulnerable.

"Once my pentagram is in your hands, it will be in mine as well," Belial had explained. "Through it I can destroy them, and you will be free to escape. But first you will hide it where it cannot be found. The other item, the one I need to protect us, you will be able to carry to me in your talons."

It was time to tend to his master's needs. No one paid any attention to him as he pretended to hunt in the area.

Beelzebub took note that the guards outside the tomb followed a predictable routine.

At dusk, as the early winter sun dipped lower in the sky before setting, its rays touched the tomb door, illuminating the gold and causing a bright reflection. At that time of day, the one Belial had identified as the CIA agent Taft, the one who questioned Bertha Smalls at the DOE, would emerge from the tomb and go into a military trailer parked nearby. That would be his best chance. He could fly into the tomb as the door opened. The falcon perched on a tree limb to the west of the door and waited.

As Beelzebub had suspected, Taft opened the door of the tomb from the inside and began to ascend the stairs. With a powerful surge and a strong flap of his wings, the sleek falcon left his perch and swooped down toward the door. The setting sun was behind him. Before anyone could see him coming, he flew past the guards and into the tomb, timing his arrival just after Taft had cleared the stairs and was on his way to the trailer.

Andy Taft had a lot on his mind as he walked toward the communications trailer. The four Vigilant from Safed had determined which light on the pentagram represented Belial and which was his remaining sub-prince, Beelzebub. They identified them by the size, placement, and intensity of the glow within the inverted pentagram. They also saw that while some were dark or flickering, several smaller lights were active. Those, they reasoned, were servants and disciples, possessed by spirits such as those found in the DOE people and Bishop Horne. But they had no plan yet for finding Belial or Beelzebub.

Taft heard the whoosh of wings before he felt their wind. The sound alarmed him. He spun around and caught a glimpse of the raptor entering the tomb. As he ran back toward the tomb, he shouted for the guards to close the door immediately.

Inside the tomb, the falcon glided down the main passageway into a side tunnel. His keen sense of hearing told him that men were working in the throne room. He heard the tomb door slam shut and the men in the throne room comment about that. He landed softly, just short of the entrance to the first chamber, the library of his master's deeds, and listened. He heard the sound of pages being turned. Someone was working in there. How many? Then he heard the door of the tomb open and shut again. Had someone seen him enter? There was no time to waste.

Being close to Belial's seat of power gave him strength. He transformed into Raymond Light and peered into the library chamber. He saw a strange-looking man, dressed in dirty jeans and a sweatshirt. He had long dreadlocks and a heavy black beard. The man was bent over the book describing the 1984 Union Carbide hazardous chemical release in Bhopal, India. It related how his master had manipulated safeguards at the plant that caused the death of thousands. The man was able to read the Dravidian-Telugu language.

"He is an Indian holy man," Beelzebub thought. *"This will give me pleasure."* He transformed one of his hands into the falcon claw with its sharp talons. Then he silently came up behind the studious man and in one swift motion put one arm around his head and pulled it back while, with the claw, he slit open the throat of Rahman Chandri, the Hindu sadhu.

Once Taft was back inside, with the door sealed behind him, he made his way quickly to the throne room. He alerted the other Vigilant from Safed that someone, or something, had entered the tomb.

"It was flying. One of my men said it was a large bird." Taft was excited and worried.

"A falcon?" Shariat Khawaja asked.

"Like the one drawn on the wall in the fourth chamber?" Kwame Dombo interjected.

"Or maybe it is the condor that is drawn there too," Father John Apostolopoulos said. He had been working at the back of the pentagram and now came around to the front.

Taft knew that Allen Weber and Vernon Flood were in Salt Lake City at the tabernacle, and Jacob Yahze had received an urgent call to meet with Taro Heart. That left only one Vigilant unaccounted for.

"Where is Rahman Chandri?" he asked.

"With the books in the first chamber," Khawaja answered.

"Oh, God," Taft said as he drew his Glock and chambered a round. "You three stay here."

"No," Imam Khawaja said. "If it is the evil one, he must not escape. We must try to hold him here. Perhaps the weapons from the second chamber can subdue the intruder." Taft kept a cool head. He knew that all The Vigilant, like Rabbi Vogel, had prepared for confrontations with the evil ones.

"Okay. Go and gather them. I'll get Chandri and meet you back here. Keep together and stay alert."

As Taft ran to the library chamber, and the three Vigilant rushed to the second chamber, Beelzebub, now Raymond Light, gathered what Belial had instructed him to get from the fourth chamber. He had no difficulty in finding the large, hairy, pawlike hand next to the battered skull of the Old

One. It was light and dry and had hardened like stone from centuries of aging. The hand was from, Nii, a Sasquatch leader that Belial had fought and killed.

"These Old Ones are a curse that God put upon the Earth against me. But with Nii's hand, I can defeat any who try to interfere with my plans," Belial had told his sub-prince on the night he had sensed the Sasquatch presence. *"In times past they hunted me. But now they are almost extinct. I have seen to it that their habitat diminishes. Soon it will be gone and I will be rid of this curse."*

Light slipped the hand under his shirt and headed for the throne room. He felt his power grow. He moved cautiously down the passageway from the fourth chamber. He heard the sound of people coming down the tunnel ahead of him, so he hid in an alcove and watched as the three Vigilant from Safed hurried down the tunnel toward the second chamber.

"They go away from the throne room," he muttered aloud. "It will be easy to get the pentagram." When he was sure that the men were gone, he slipped out of his hiding place and hurried to the throne room. Success within his grasp, he felt his master's power surge throughout his body.

As Light had suspected, the throne room was deserted. Without hesitation he rushed behind the throne and removed the pentagram from is place. It felt warm and comforting, filling him with Belial's strength.

Taft had found the slain Rahman Chandri, who had bled out from a severed carotid artery. There was no sign of the bird, or of anyone else. Leaving the sadhu for the moment, he hurried back to the throne room just as Raymond Light was leaving. "That's as far as it goes," Taft said as he stepped out of the shadows with the red laser beam from his Glock nailed to Light's chest.

"You cannot harm me," Light said, laughing. "I am immortal." With the pentagram in hand, he walked toward the doorway leading out of the tomb.

"If you say so," Taft answered. "I've got hollow-points in this weapon. Let's find out how far you can go without a head." He moved the laser pointer to Light's skull.

Light rapidly calculated his options. He could transform into the falcon and avoid this fool pointing a gun at him. But that would mean abandoning the pentagram and the hand. He could attack the man, who he knew to be Andrew Taft of the CIA. He could feign fear and wait for another opportunity. But he worried that there were people in the tomb who had driven out spirits and destroyed the human body of his brother, Amaimon. If he could touch this man, he could call upon the power in the tomb and destroy him.

But rather than fight, he had a better idea. He put down the pentagram and raised his hands.

"I do not want to die."

Taft wasn't sure what to do next. The man in front of him had entered the tomb as a bird. He wondered anxiously where the three Safed Vigilant men were. At that moment, Light opened his mouth and let out an ear-breaking screech—the sound of the falcon amplified twenty times. It shot through Taft like a mass of hot buckshot, sending him across the room in agonizing pain. He could not catch his breath. Raymond Light leered at him, then picked up the pentagram and ran toward the tomb exit with Nii's petrified hand still hidden in his shirt.

A few moments later, the three Vigilant, armed with ancient knives and axes, rushed into the room. Taft was on his knees. Blood streamed from his nose, ears, and eyes. He pointed toward the tomb entrance. Kwame Dombo came to his aid while Imam Khawaja and Father Apostolopoulos raced toward the tomb entrance, wielding their weapons.

After meeting with Taro Heart, Jacob Yahze had hurried back to the tomb, anxious to share the startling news she had given him. The guards stopped him as he started to descend the tomb steps.

"Mr. Taft wants the door kept sealed," the officer in charge told Yahze. "There was an intruder. A large bird, we think."

A chill traveled down Yahze's spine. Falcon or condor? he wondered. A that moment the tomb door opened, and a man holding the pentagram rushed out. Yahze recognized him as Raymond Light, Nicholas Perez's right-hand man. Yahze didn't hesitate. Before the CIA officer could draw his weapon, the Navajo shaman launched himself into the air, down onto the man who was about to ascend the steps. Both men crashed to the ground, with Jacob Yahze on top. He already had the stone Aztec ceremonial knife in his hand. Light saw the knife as Yahze raised it.

"Nooooo… " he begged.

His plea fell on deaf ears.

As Imam Khawaja and Father Apostolopoulos arrived at the doorway of the tomb, they saw Jacob Yahze plunge the knife into Beelzebub's neck. The shaman twisted and sliced furiously, as he had done with Amaimon. Then, with one powerful final stroke, he severed Raymond Light's head from his twitching body. It rolled across the stones next to the golden door. Light's limp body turned into black dust, just as Plotter's had. Some of it swirled, emitting the foul odor, and disappeared. The rest settled into the earth. All that remained was Nii's petrified hand, and the pentagram, which had fallen from the sub-prince's grip. It rattled and shook on the ground. Then one of the brighter lights in it guttered out and was extinguished. But the brightest light, the one at the tip of the pentagram's bottom star point, remained lit.

"This was not Belial," Imam Khawaja said solemnly.

"Yes," Jacob Yahze agreed as he got to his feet. "But the light that went out is opposite that of Amaimon, the sub-prince we destroyed. This must have been his brother."

"Beelzebub!" Father Apostolopoulos said. "God be praised." The other two holy men echoed his prayer.

"Should we dispose of the evil dust as we did the other?" Yahze asked.

"Yes," Imam Khawaja said, "next to the bones of the Old Ones. And then let us concentrate on how we might use the pentagram to locate Belial."

"That, my dear friends, may not be necessary," Yahze said.

CHAPTER FIFTY-SEVEN

MOVING NORTH

Belial felt Beelzebub's demise instantly. From his hiding place on Stuart Island, he cursed God and the relentless group of men who served Him. Without the eyes and ears of Amaimon and Beelzebub, Belial knew he would have to keep his wits and senses sharpened to their maximum. Not having the pentagram was a serious blow to his power. He knew it would have to be in his home in order to make it his tomb. He was now certain that that was his pursuers' plan. And not having the ancient hand of the Old One Nii made him uneasy. He vowed to create new human vessels for his sub-princes. His anger toward The Vigilant swelled.

"By my brothers Satan, Leviathan, and Lucifer, I swear to destroy these meddling humans. And when that is done, with Beelzebub and Amaimon returned to me, I will wreak havoc and death using the greed of humans to destroy their environment."

His body began to change from Perez to the condor. His extended arms morphed into wings. His legs shortened and grew long, curved talons. Long, black wing feathers sprouted to cover his compressing body, and his head shrank and became covered with feathers. His eyes moved from the front of his face to the sides of his head, while his mouth and nose crunched together and emerged united in a long, sharp, black beak.

"I curse you God, and I curse the faith you have placed in these humans to whom you granted free will. It is my work on Earth, not Yours, that will prevail."

The metamorphosis was complete, and the condor rose into the sky, heading north toward Nome, Alaska, just fifty miles across Norton Sound. As he took flight, he took note of two bald eagles that rose up from the tall cedars of the forest to the south. Later, one peeled away when they were halfway across Norton Sound, and flew rapidly to the south.

Nan and Sak continued to travel on foot, from Kwigillingok to Alakanuk, through the shortening northern days and the lengthening nights. The winter ice was forming rapidly along the shore of the Bering Sea. At dawn, they were met by a lone bald eagle, who reported that as of yesterday the condor was heading for Nome.

The two Sasquatch knew they would not be safe near the city. There were too many people. They might be seen. They decided to attempt to make contact with a reclusive Tlingit shaman they knew who lived in the Bering Land Bridge National Preserve. It was a mating site for their kind.

Central to Tlingit beliefs is that people and animals are relatives, with common ancestors. Each can, under certain condition, cross into the other's world. There were many cases of animals appearing in human form and interacting with the Tlingit people. But the reverse, to observe humans who became animals, was rare.

Sak and Nan wanted to hear what the shaman had to say about the condor and the falcon, whom they had seen transform. They hoped he might also help them find the condor, when and if it left Nome.

CHAPTER FIFTY-EIGHT

UNHOLY CONCEPTION

The Seward Peninsula is westernmost land on the North American continent. It pokes out of northwest Alaska in the shape of a huge arrowhead pointing toward Russia. Nome lies to the south, at the bottom of the arrowhead. No roads connect Nome, the transportation and commerce center for northwest Alaska, to any other major city, so almost all entry is via boat or plane, with the exception of the competitors in the famed Iditarod dog sled race from Anchorage to Nome, 1,050-mile course, every March. Then Nome, the normally quaint town of thirty-five hundred stoic, weather-hardened souls, swells with race fans and continues for a month of post-race celebrations.

It was a sunny day, with a slight breeze. The brightly painted houses of Nome, set on a hillside above the harbor beneath a brilliant blue sky, glistened in the clear Alaska air. Although winter's crunch was fast approaching, the people of Nome, more than sixty percent native, mostly central Alaskan Yup'ik, enjoyed the break in the weather. They moved about outside with a bounce in their step.

Jane Borovski, was a twenty-six-year-old Nome resident, whose ancestry was a typical mixture of native Unangan, sometimes called Aleut, and Siberian Russian, a group that settled much of this part of Alaska for the fur trade. They introduced their Russian Orthodox Church to the natives, who embraced it in great numbers. Intermarriage was common. Jane's high cheekbones, Asian features, and jet-black hair blended with her tall, slim European body. The visual effect was stunningly beautiful. She was also a kind and caring woman, who had been at the top of her class in nursing school. To all who knew her, she was called an Inupiaq—a genuine person.

Jane stopped by the Saint Sergius church to drop off some discarded clothing for the indigent, then walked three blocks to Nome's small but well-staffed eighteen-bed hospital. The two-story wood frame building had recently been painted, and it sported a new, bright blue roof. In Jane Borovski's care were the four long-term-care patients housed in two rooms at the far end of the second-floor hallway.

Because of the unusual break in the weather—a balmy Alaskan thirty degrees—she was going to take her charges out onto the hospital's patio, two at a time, for a few hours of sun. Two of them, indigenous Aleuts, had advanced multiple sclerosis. The third was a retired man from California making a slow recovery from a severe stroke. The fourth was a Tlingit woman who suffered from Alzheimer's disease.

Jane took the two MS patients out to the patio first. One of the Aleuts was a sixty-year-old man. The other, a thirty-five-year-old woman named Lilly Tupiq, was her most difficult patient. She had violent episodes of shaking. When their hour outside in the warm sunshine was over, she took the two back to their rooms and dressed the other two patients for their outing.

The hospital was not a heavily trafficked institution. When she returned to the patio a second time, she took notice of a rather short, squat man who seemed to have emerged out of the conifer forest behind the hospital. She thought it strange because she knew there were no paths or houses back there.

"Now where do you come from?" she muttered aloud. As she watched the man walk quickly, and with purpose, to the main entrance of the small hospital, the Tlingit woman suddenly got up and began to quiver and babble in a tongue Jane did not understand. Her patient seemed frightened. Her eyes widened and then shut tight. Jane put her arms around the shaking woman and comforted her until she calmed down. A while later, Jane took both patients back to their rooms. She then gathered the stroke patient from California and the Tlingit woman with Alzheimer's and took them to the patio.

Lilly Tupiq liked being alone. The time she had spent outside made her sleepy, so once Jane had tucked her into her bed, she nodded off for a nap. Even in sleep, her body continued to shake and shudder, as it had for the past twenty years. But then, ten minutes into her nap, the shaking suddenly stopped. The change was so radical that it woke her.

Lilly became aware of a presence within her body and mind. She was alert. She was excited. Her thoughts were of long-suppressed erotic and sexual desire. The Aleut woman's body housed Effrigis, the servitor of Belial, "the spirit who quivers in a horrible manner." Sensing Belial's presence, Effrigis was preparing Lilly Tupiq, a chosen disciple, to receive her master.

The man that Jane Borovski had seen emerge from the forest was Nicholas Perez. He entered Lilly's room and closed the door behind him. There were no locks, so he wedged a wooden chair under the knob. He said nothing as he undid his pants and stepped out of them, leaving them on the floor. He removed his jacket and shirt. Then he removed the down comforter that covered Lilly Tupiq. She smiled at Perez as he pulled aside her nightgown. As she tilted her head back, the spirit Effrigis, as a pale blue wisp of smoke, left Lilly's body through her mouth and nostrils and gathered in a cloud above her.

"You are free, Effrigis," Perez said. "I thank you for keeping my disciple safe." The cloud moved to the window and passed through the glass into the air. "And now we shall create a new human body for my sub-prince, Amaimon." Perez mounted Lilly and impregnated her without sound or emotion. Lilly lay there, confused. She had never experienced sexual intercourse. The sensation of Belial's penetration did not give her any physical pleasure, yet there arose within her a grateful and joyous feeling. She had become a vessel that would bear a child who would, in time, become the receptacle for the spirit of the sub-prince, Amaimon.

Lilly Tupiq fell asleep when Perez was finished. As he dressed, he felt deep satisfaction that he had begun to fulfill his vow by taking this first step toward bringing back his sub-princes.

"Now this is done, Amaimon, my son," he said, knowing the sub-prince's spirit would hear him.

His other disciple, a Mongolian girl of sixteen, lived far away in Choyren, a town on the Trans-Mongolian railway, in a bleak north edge of the Gobi Desert. Her body was guarded by the spirit servitor Raderaf, the Rose Bearer. That child was to be kept a virgin for Belial when she was needed. He would impregnate her and she would become the vessel to grow a human body for Beelzebub.

Perez moved the chair away from the door and opened it. The hallway was deserted. He went into the room across the hall where the other MS patient, the sixty-year-old Aleut man, lay sleeping.

"Let my vow of vengeance begin here!"

Perez transformed into a large, ferocious puma. He leaped onto the bed and stood on the Aleut's chest. The man awakened but thought he was still dreaming. The puma's mouth opened wide and he sank his sharp fangs into the man's neck. Blood spurted. The man's body collapsed. The puma shook the body violently and then tore at it with his razor-sharp claws. He dragged the bloody remains onto the floor, smearing the blood and shreds of skin and bone around the room. Then the puma went from room to room, killing five more patients in the same violent manner, until he heard the voices of an orderly, two doctors, and a nurse approaching on rounds. Belial quickly morphed into the condor. He smashed out through a window, flapping his great wings and lifting up into the still, blue sky.

Nurse Borovski was bringing her two patients back to their rooms from the patio when she heard the glass shatter and saw the strange black bird soar into the sky above the hospital. The sight frightened her as she recalled Unangan stories of the raven, another black bird, who played tricks on humans and was driven by greed and selfishness.

By the time Jane reached the second floor with her two patients, all hell had broken loose. The hospital staff worked feverishly, but to no avail, to save the savaged patients. Within fifteen minutes, the hospital and the surrounding area were crawling with the local Nome police and the Alaskan state police. An hour later, troops from a nearby army base were pressed into service to seal access into and out of the small city. But it was all an exercise in futility.

Belial was gone, heading north toward Little Diomede Island and the town of Wales. He noted again a bald eagle trailing him, and his suspicions grew. But he was so exhilarated by the mating, and the kills he had made, that he put off investigating the eagle, opting to savor the sensation of power that surged through him.

One of the Nome detectives, Jerry Kotchev, interviewed Jane Borovski. All the patients attacked, including one of hers, were dead. Miraculously, Lilly Tupiq was untouched and fast asleep.

"That may be what saved her," the detective suggested. "Perhaps she was under the covers and the killer missed her."

Jane was not so sure. "Lilly's MS makes her shake uncontrollably. Even under the covers, she would have been noticed," Jane explained. The detective looked at the notes the uniformed police had taken when they had first interviewed Jane.

"You mentioned a bird," he said. "And a man who came out of the woods."

"Yes. The man was short, but looked strong, like a wrestler or something. Athletic." The detective made notes.

"And the bird?"

"You are?" she asked.

"Half. And half Tlingit. My father. He still lives up north. Says we have to preserve the old ways, you know?"

"Yes. My grandfather is the same. So you don't hold with the old ways?" she asked.

"Not exactly. But I respect them. What about this bird?"

"It came from up here. This floor. I heard a window break, and I saw it fly out and away. It gained altitude very fast. It frightened me. I felt... You know about the raven?"

He smiled and stopped writing.

"Yes. A nasty fellow to the people...at times."

"This bird was larger and jet-black and...well, it seemed unnatural. I felt evil in it. Is that strange?"

The detective put away his notes. He liked the pretty nurse, and he made a mental note to stop by when things had settled down to ask her out. He got up.

"No. Not strange. It just surprised you, and a black bird, like a raven, makes the thought of evil seem natural. So, thanks, Ms. Borovski. We'll be back to you about that man if we find him." She eyed him carefully. He was nice-looking, kind of attractive, but she felt he was patronizing her.

"You don't believe me, Detective Kotchev. I mean about the bird."

"It's not that I don't believe you. Like I said, it was shock. But the old stories about the raven? Well, this is the twenty-first century, and... " Jane got up and cut him off.

"And you are a fool." She stormed out of the room.

Later that night, when she went home, Jane called her oldest brother, who lived farther north, in the village of Teller. He was in touch with their grandfather, who at that time was out on the growing pack ice hunting seals. Jane told her brother what had happened and asked him to tell their grandfather the story as soon as he could.

"I saw the black bird fly north," she told her brother. "Be sure to warn Inupiat—the people!"

CHAPTER FIFTY-NINE

A MESSAGE FROM THE NORTH

After Raymond Light, Beelzebub's host, had been destroyed, the dust that was his body and severed head was brought into the tomb's fourth chamber and buried in the third quadrant next to the dust of Amaimon, where the bones and skull of Nii, the ancient Sasquatch who battled Belial long ago, would watch over it. Nii's severed hand was also returned there. All of this was done precisely as Rabbi ben Abraham of the Ben Zimrah had instructed.

Afterward, Jacob Yahze, Andy Taft, Imam Khawaja, Father Apostolopoulos, Kwame Dombo—along with Vernon Flood and Allen Weber, who had both been summoned from the Mormon Tabernacle—gathered in the throne room. They first prayed for the soul of Rahman Chandri, the Hindu sadhu Beelzebub had slain. His body was removed by a CIA paramilitary squad. The Vigilant holy men would prepare it for the journey back to India, and cremation. His ashes would be scattered in the Ganges River.

Imam Khawaja held the pentagram in his hands, studying it, turning it various ways, rotating it so that each star point faced downward for a moment.

"You mentioned that we might not need this to locate Belial," Khawaja said to Jacob Yahze.

The shaman, although anxious to relate his news, had remained silent, respectful of the prayers for Rahman Chandri. "Yes, my friends," he said. "I have good news. I was with Taro Heart, our Navajo attorney. You will soon meet her. Aside from handling tribal matters, she keeps us in touch with the national and international affairs of the native peoples. It is not widely known, but there is a continuing dialogue among many tribal leaders around the world. Mostly, these days, it has to do with protecting our heritage and our land."

"This is true," Kwame Dombo confirmed. "During the height of apartheid, I attended a secret meeting in New Zealand, hosted by the Maori. More than two hundred indigenous peoples were represented."

"Yes. I heard about that gathering," Yahze confirmed. "It is where the first boycott plan was discussed and developed. Now to the business at hand. Ms. Heart has received a communication from my close friends the Haida people of western Canada. It came from a Haida chief and a medicine man I spent some time with before my father died. There was an encounter with two men who could change into birds. A falcon and a condor."

"Beelzebub and Belial," Flood said.

"Yes. I would think so. The falcon, Beelzebub, we have dealt with."

"Amen," Father Apostolopoulos said.

The others repeated "Amen."

"And the other. Belial? A condor, you say. Where did it go?" Imam Khawaja asked.

"To the north. The Haida alerted the tribes there—the Unangan peoples. Aleut, Tlingit, Yup'ik, and others. They are tracking him."

"Tracking a bird? How is that possible?" Weber asked.

Yahze now had a problem, as he feared he might. The Haida had asked Taro Heart that their interaction with the Sasquatch be kept a secret among the native peoples. But these men, The Vigilant, now present in Belial's tomb, were not tribal, with the exception of Kwame Dombo from Ghana. If Yahze revealed Sasquatch communication, and that with eagles and orca, he might run up against Western religious beliefs that denied such things exist. He decided to let the matter slide for the time being. If necessary, at the right time, he would reveal all the facts.

"The northern tribes have an extensive network. Many of these are nomadic people—hunters and fishermen. They are spread out along the Alaskan coast, and far north, up into the Arctic Circle. They have been told what to look for."

"So it is a condor we seek," Flood said. "I saw many when I did my missionary time in Chile."

"In fact," Yahze went on, "this bird was spotted on the Queen Charlotte Islands a day ago." He then told of the brutal killings at the hospital in Nome, and the sighting of the black condor leaving the scene and heading north across the Seward Peninsula.

"Such slaughter could not be done by a condor," Father Apostolopoulos remarked after hearing of the carnage.

Apostolopoulos"You are correct," Yahze told the priest. The Royal Canadian Mounted Police believe it was a large carnivore."

"The puma," Allen Weber blurted out, interrupting the shaman. "Or the bear. They are on the chamber wall with the condor and falcon and, uh, what's his name?"

"Quetzalcoatl. The plumed serpent," Yahze said patiently to encourage the enthusiasm of the newest member of The Vigilant.

"Then Belial is the condor and the puma," Weber stated with conviction.

"Or the bear," Yahze said. "Or others we do not know. Anything is possible. We must keep an open mind."

"That is the truth, shaman," Kwame Dombo agreed. "These archangels are masters of deceit and disguise."

"Well," Imam Khawaja said as he put aside the pentagram. "It seems we have this evil one on the run."

"I agree," Father Apostolopoulos said. "What shall we do?"

"Capture him, and bring him back here to rot forever," Andy Taft answered.

CHAPTER SIXTY

PLANS AND PURPOSE

The problem of what to do if and when they found Belial remained an obstacle. Concentrated studies of the tomb's chambers and artifacts and of the pentagram had revealed nothing about how The Vigilant might capture and entomb Belial as they had Satan.

Flood and Dombo were intrigued by the large petrified hand that had been in Beelzebub's possession., Of all the artifacts in the tomb, why had Beelzebub chosen that, and the pentagram? Remembering Rabbi ben Abraham's admonition not to remove anything from the tomb, they had Agent Benjamin's forensic expert examine a tiny sample of the nearly petrified flesh, along with some hair. Preliminary tests showed a remarkable similarity to human DNA, even closer than that of a modern chimpanzee. Additional tests would have to be run before a species or genus could be determined. In passing, at one meeting, Benjamin joked that perhaps it was Bigfoot.

Fortunately, he laughed as he said it. Jacob Yahze laughed heartily with him—perhaps a little too heartily. For a fleeting moment, Vernon Flood saw a flash of concern cross the shaman's brow.

The Vigilant were stumped. Nothing in the tomb or on the pentagram gave them the confidence that they could capture Belial. But the tribes were tracking him traveling north, and they felt they could no longer ponder the problem sitting in Salt Lake City.

"We cannot wait," Yahze told the others. "Winter is coming to the north country, where the condor is going. Soon he will be lost in that vast icy world."

"How will he survive in that harsh environment?" Father John asked.

"If he is a condor, and has been the puma, then let us remember the white bear," Yahze answered. "An animal highly suited for the Arctic winter."

"A polar bear," Kwame Dombo said. "Of course."

"Then perhaps it's time to move north and track down that condor," Taft suggested. The others nodded their agreement.

Imam Khawaja had an interesting thought that had been troubling him from the time he first heard where Belial was headed. "I believe the direction that he goes has purpose," the imam said. "Across the Bering Sea from Alaska is the shortest distance to China, and Satan's sealed tomb in Xian."

"But that is guarded by the terra-cotta army," Dombo reminded him.

"True. Many attempts to open it have been made by disciples and servitors. Possibly even sub-princes."

"And all failed," Father Apostolopoulos added.

"Yes. So Far," the imam agreed. "But we do not know what special powers Belial, a fallen archangel himself and a brother to Satan, might have, should he get to the tomb door," the imam warned.

That idea convinced Taft of their next move. "I'll make arrangements to get us going north," he offered. "The last thing we need is to have Satan free again."

They discussed transportation and logistics—aircraft, satellite surveillance, arctic clothing, helicopters, and what they might need for a capture.

"We must also choose who will go on this mission, and who will remain behind to prepare the tomb," Khawaja said.

The discussion went on for more than two hours. In the end, it was unanimously agreed that Andy Taft would lead the party. Michael Benjamin would go because he was the strongest link they had to the Salt Lake City area. He would be needed for future security and secrecy if they were able to bring Belial to his tomb.

Jacob Yahze and Vernon Flood would represent religious people in The Vigilant. Yahze would use his contacts with the Haida to bring amulets and fetish dolls. Flood would bring whatever Mormon religious objects he determined might be of use against the archangel, such as the Joseph Smith parchments.

Kwame Dombo and Father Apostolopoulos would represent The Vigilant in preparing the tomb, getting instructions via the closed-circuit link with Rabbi ben Abraham in Safed.

Taro Heart, who was in contact with the far northern tribal peoples, would be asked to join them as liaison and translator.

Imam Khawaja would remain in Salt Lake City at the tomb to continue studying the artifacts. Several CIA paramilitary were added to the traveling group, while a contingent of CIA guards would remain, trained in the use of the stone knife, should anyone unauthorized try to enter the tomb.

"So, who will record this journey?" Allen Weber asked. He had sat quietly throughout the discussion, patiently waiting to hear his name mentioned.

Taft realized that they had forgotten him. "Good point, Allen. You've done a darn good job with that digital video camera. You're hired." Weber was satisfied that he would have a chance to fulfill his promise to be there when the killer of his relatives was brought to justice.

Using the facilities and assets of the CIA, it took only a day for Andy Taft to conclude the travel and logistical arrangements.

The day before departure, Allen Weber spent a few hours with his wife and children, still ensconced and under guard in the Carlisle Clinic in Park City. Susan had fully recovered, and the baby was thriving. The boys were being tutored privately. They seemed to be coming out of the trauma of losing so many members of their family.

Allen told his wife what was going to happen next. "This is something I have to do," he said. "Please understand." She was frightened for him, but saw there would be no convincing him otherwise. In the end, she embraced him tearfully.

"Be careful, my love. Come home to us."

"I will. I surely will." He hugged her tightly. "I love you forever," he told her as he felt her warm tears trickle down his neck.

That night before they left, Fairchild Ballard, the president of the Mormon Church, who had been kept apprised of developments by Vernon Flood and Allen Weber, asked to meet with the group in the elegant conference room in the offices of the First Presidency of the Church of Latter-day Saints. With him was Jeremy Cabot, Second Counselor of the First Presidency.

"The mission you are about to embark upon comes as no surprise to this church. It was foretold millennia ago. After the destruction of the Temple in Jerusalem, some of the people of Israel, namely, the tribe of Joseph, were instructed by God to come to this hemisphere. They were the forefathers of today's Native Americans."

Jacob Yahze was uneasy. Living among the Mormons, he had heard this story before, but it did not jibe with his beliefs.

"From the tip of Tierra del Fuego in South America to the northernmost reaches of the Arctic tundra, all native peoples are God's chosen people, the Israelites. But as time passed, they forgot their roots, and their God."

Imam Khawaja wondered what Ballard was driving at.

"It is revealed in the Book of Mormon that when the Rabbi Jesus was resurrected, he came among these native people to bring them the word of redemption, and to have them prepare the New Jerusalem in this land," Ballard went on, sounding to Michael Benjamin like a Sunday morning televangelist. "His second coming will not take place until the way is prepared. Our mission is to convert all to his true church. Your battle against this evil Belial is a glorious chapter that precedes his return."

President Ballard then peeled back a portion of a red velvet cloth that was draped on the massive mahogany conference table, revealing a parchment, framed under glass.

It was similar to the one that Vernon Flood had used to control the servitor spirits of the sub-princes of Belial.

"We possess many writings and artifacts that are unknown to the public," he said as everyone examined the parchment. It was written in a flowing hand like the other parchments attributed to Joseph Smith, the founder and organizer of the Mormon Church in Fayette, New York, in 1860. "The Vatican in Rome, the Great Mosque of Haram in Mecca, the Forbidden City in China, the compound of the Ben Zimrah in Safed, and many other sacred places also hide great secrets." The Vigilant were surprised at the mention of Safed, but they said nothing. Many religious leaders have speculated about secrets unearthed by Israeli archeologists, and their locations.

Ballard continued. "This parchment is one said to have been given to Brigham Young by an angel, sent by Joseph Smith, upon our arrival in this place, the Great Salt Lake Basin." He carefully lifted the parchment and read: "In the time of great nations and a new millennium, evil will rise up. The people, those descended of the chosen of God, will confront this evil." He then gestured for Cabot to lift the rest of the velvet cloth. Under it, on a blue cloth similar to fabric of Aaron's robe, lay a small golden plate like the ones found around the necks of the dead Christensen children. "This was given with the parchment." Ballard read from the parchment again. "Seal this evil behind the dragon door, but beware of the dragon's eye, for through it the evil one will call to another." He put down the parchment and lifted the blue cloth and golden plate, which he handed to Jacob Yahze. "This is not a corrupted plate. It is a gift from God, delivered by the angel Moroni. When the day comes that you have Belial sealed in his tomb, place this over the ruby eye of the dragon and the archangel will be blinded to the outside. He will be unable to call to his evil brothers."

Yahze carefully took the golden plate, enfolded it in the blue cloth, and put it into his buckskin pouch.

"Have you another?" Imam Khawaja asked Ballard.

The Mormon president was taken aback. He frowned. "For what purpose?"

"I suspect you hold four such plates," the imam said. "We have need for one besides Belial. Satan is already entombed in China." President Ballard and Jeremy Cabot looked at each other.

"Satan is entombed?" Ballard asked, shocked.

"By my own hand, and the hands of my brothers and sisters," the imam answered. "Our meeting has purpose beyond Belial." Ballard nodded to Cabot, who left the room.

"Thank God for his church," Ballard said.

"Our church is the Earth," Yahze said, moved to respond to Ballard's parochial pronouncement, something that men of the newer religions were quick to proclaim. "Its roof is the sky above. My people believe we have been part of this land from the beginning. Our Mother brought the first man and the first woman up from the Earth's center to be the people."

"Forgive me. You are correct. Our church and yours are one and the same," Ballard answered. "Ours is based on the revealed word of the one God," he continued. "He guides us for his purposes. We will all join together and celebrate on the day of resurrection."

"There are ancient stories about a man who walked among the tribes to the East—the Iroquois, Mohawk, Algonquin, and Cherokee," Yahze continued, choosing to ignore for now this attempt at his conversion. "It is said he was a holy man who spoke of one God. Perhaps that man was this Rabbi Jesus you mention. He spoke of love and good will to all, and for all. Then the white man came and killed us, took our land, and tried to destroy the culture of those of us who respect and protect the Earth."

"It was a great injustice," Ballard said. He looked down, unable to face the shaman, because he knew the history of the Mormons and their zeal to convert the native peoples, first the tribes in this area, and then sending missionaries all over the world.

"Yes, injustice, surely," Yahze went on. For years he had wanted to have this conversation. "Your bible says God granted man dominion over the Earth. But that sacred stewardship has been abused and ignored, even by those who proclaim great faith. And now evil rushes in to exploit your rejection of God's word. Belial, destroyer of the environment, has found a fertile atmosphere here for his deadly work. We have seen this evil destroy species, and poison the water, air, and soil."

"But if Belial exists, that is proof that God does also," Ballard answered. "And is that not a joyous message?"

"Is it proof you need? Did you have doubts? For us, all the glory of Nature is proof. The wonder of birth and life is proof. The Earth that sustains us is proof. The Creator, our Mother, made it so. We know evil demons are here, as spirits and as men. We see the filth and death they leave in their wake. We see their distain for the future—for the world they corrupt for our children. You cannot deal with evil using words about God that are written by men for their own power and convenience. We here, this brave group, will confront Belial to keep our covenant with the Creator on behalf of all on this Earth."

At that awkward moment, Jeremy Cabot retuned to the room carrying another golden plate wrapped in a blue cloth like that of Aaron's robe. Ballard indicated for him to hand it to Imam Khawaja.

"This will be used to seal Satan's tomb as you have described. We thank you for revealing it to us. We were only the custodians," Ballard said. "You are God's right arm. Go with our hopes and blessings."

CHAPTER SIXTY-ONE

UP AND AWAY

An hour before dawn, the sleek CIA Gulfstream V lifted off the main runway of the Fort Douglas military reservation, banked, climbed and headed on a northwest vector. The state-of-the-art aircraft was outfitted with sophisticated communication and satellite-linking equipment. Its ample cargo bay held all the necessities for an Arctic expedition, including a newly improved set of landing skis. The flight plan would take the group of eight north to Nome in a little over four hours, cruising at thirty-eight thousand feet northwest over Seattle, Vancouver, and then Sitka, Valdez, and Ruby, Alaska.

The Gulfstream was followed by a retrofitted Army C-17. The big jet transport won this trip was three teams of sled dogs, their handlers, and teams of CIA and Arctic-trained scouts from the Special Forces base in Fort Huachuca, Arizona.

As dawn broke, the Gulfstream V glided past Pike's Peak and up over the Rockies into Canada. All the members of the party sat alone with their thoughts.

Andy Taft, who had previously confronted Satan and had seen many people destroyed in the process, knew that violent and sudden death always lurked in the presence of the evil archangels. He would be alert for any eventuality when Belial was confronted, but he was troubled that The Vigilant—Yahze, Flood, and the men from Safed—had not yet discovered how they might capture and hold him.

Vernon Flood studied the secret texts and prayers that Ballard had entrusted to him for the mission. But the church president had forbidden Joseph Smith's jacket or any of the parchments to be removed from the Tabernacle.

Taro Heart, having been made aware of all the recent events, found that the excitement of being along on the journey, tempered her fear.

Father John Apostolopoulos and Kwame Dombo prayed silently, preparing for the mission. This was what The Vigilant had all trained for and dedicated their lives to do. They knew a great struggle might lie ahead, one that held great danger that would test their mettle.

Michael Benjamin pondered the supernatural forces that had brought him here, tens of thousands of feet above the Earth, streaking toward a dangerous unknown. He recalled Ballard's remark that the existence of Belial confirmed the existence of God. But whose God—Mormon, Christian, Muslim, Jewish, Buddhist, Shinto, Hindu, or Baha'i? Or was He, as Jacob Yahze believed, the Navajo Creator, the Mother of all the people? Was ownership of the "right" God, as zealots preached, the way of things? There was no answer. But he believed that murder and destruction could not be God's work. Benjamin was a professional, and all he could do was his job—which was to try to catch a brutal murderer.

Allen Weber's thoughts were with his family, those alive back home and those lost to Belial's evil. If God had cast the archangels out of Heaven because they were against humankind's having free will, then fighting against them, rather than against other human beings, might find favor in God's eyes. That thought comforted the young Mormon who might some day be an important elder of his church.

Jacob Yahze sat alone at the rear of the aircraft, gazing out of the window as majestic snow-capped mountain peaks slipped by beneath him. He was not afraid. He had no confusion about the evil he pursued, nor doubts about his Creator and his stewardship of the Earth. He was proud that in such desperate circumstances, it was the old ways— harmonious commitment to life and Nature—that would confront evil. The power that had guided his hand when he held the ancient stone knife and beheaded the evil sub-princes was, he had no doubt, that of his ancestors and their Mother Creator. Also, the knowledge that his brothers and sisters, and the legendary Sasquatch, were now also in the fight gave him strength and hope. But the how of it, the capture and containment of Belial, eluded him. It gnawed insidiously at his undaunted resolve.

CHAPTER SIXTY-TWO

QUIPMIG AND PIAQ

The pack-ice east of Little Diomede, between that diminutive rocky island and the mainland, was freezing rapidly. But there were still some eddies, channels, and seal holes that could be hunted and fished. Soon the twelve-mile channel would be frozen solid. Then the Ingalikmiut Eskimos who inhabited the island would hunt during the four hours of winter daylight and sub-zero temperatures, traveling to the west, where the water flowed better. That was in the direction of Big Diomede Island, two and one half miles away, in Russian waters.

Nurse Jane Borovski's brother, Viktor, had called his grandfather, Quipmig, on Little Diomede via radiophone and relayed the story of the large black bird and the murders at the hospital in Nome. The old man was proud that Jane remembered her people's history and legends. He did not doubt her story.

"I am still hunting on the ice every day," he told Viktor. "I will watch for the large black bird."

On the northern shore of the Seward Peninsula, winter was tightening its frigid grip in the Bering Land Bridge National Preserve, where the North American continent was once connected to Asia.

During the last ice age, more than thirteen thousand years ago, much of the oceans' water froze, and their levels dropped. The submerged land between the two continents, called Beringia, was exposed for animals and humans to cross. Most biologists, anthropologists, and geologists agree that was the route that brought the first humans to North America. Their progeny eventually populated the hemisphere.

Nan and Sak had traveled night and day in their quest to find Piaq, the fabled Tlingit shaman, Piaq, hoping he could shed some light on who the condor and falcon might be and how they might be located.

As the two Sasquatch entered the preserve, an eagle, weary and half frozen, landed and reported that the black condor had left Nome, heading north.

"Soon it will be too cold and the wind too fierce for us to fly far. In the storms we will have to find shelter," the eagle said. "My kind may no longer be able to follow the evil one. But orca says he can find places to swim and breathe. He will continue to search." Sak thanked the brave bird and sniffed the air.

"The ice will be solid soon," he told the young Nan. "That is good in the mating time because it allows those from the other side to join with us." He was referring to their Asian cousins, the Yeti. "Some will make the journey across the ice to the mating grounds in the mountains far to the north. It is a place the white man calls Noatak National

Preserve. The harsh winter will keep humans away, giving us privacy for mating."

"But that iced may forbid orca from tracking the evil one," Nan said to the elder Sasquatch.

"Then we will track him ourselves." Nan was disappointed.

"I will miss my first mating," he said.

"What we must do is for those yet to be born. Perhaps if this one is captured they will have a safe place in the world." Sak placed his great hand upon Nan's shoulder. "Our ancestor Nii instructed us to do battle against this evil. And so we must."

Later in that brief gray day, as the twenty-hour Arctic night descended on the preserve's frozen landscape, Sak and Nan saw a fire burning next to a caribou-hide shelter. It was pitched near the Serpentine Hot Springs, whose steam was a silvery mist rising in the moonlight. They approached with caution, keeping their great frames as low to the ground as possible. As they came closer, they crawled on hands and knees.

An old man, sitting at the fire, looked up in their direction. They dropped flat on the snowy ground. Hidden by frozen vegetation, they observed him. His body and head were wrapped in caribou skins. He was roasting an Arctic hare, impaled on a rod over the fire.

"Come and join me," the man called out in the Sasquatch tongue. Sak stood, signaling for Nan to remain hidden. He approached the man with his right hand raised in a sign of friendship. The man signaled back. "You are welcome to the warmth of my fire," the man said, "and some of this hare, who has graciously offered himself." Sak moved closer. The scent of the meat cooking was good.

"I seek Piaq the shaman," Sak said.

"So I have heard from the otter," the man answered. "You have found him. Please sit. Be warm and eat." Sak bowed his head slightly and signaled for Nan to join him. Piaq looked past Sak at Nan. "Ah, yes. I thought I heard two. You are both welcome to share my fire and this brave and generous hare."

Sak and Nan sat with Piaq through the long Arctic night. They warmed themselves and ate a small portion of the hare while they related their story of the strange birds. When they were finished, Piaq remain silent for several moments. He stared into the fire and chanted softly. The Sasquatch sat respectfully and waited.

"I must bring something from my igloo." Piaq slid from under the caribou skins that covered his head and body. His hair, which had never been cut, fell like a long black mat down his back. He wore a hide apron and boots of sealskin. An impressive crown of bear and walrus claws encircled his head. He crawled inside his caribou-skin tent. A moment later, he crawled out holding a white rattle made of narwhal bone and filled with the teeth of the Arctic fox. He wrapped himself in the skins again and sat closer to the fire.

"Tlingit shamans have always known of the man-animal. From the beginning, our Earth Mother bound us to them. They are our yeks—spirits that serve. To find the evil beast you seek, you will need one yek to help. I will call him to you with his special song. I will tell him what you seek and where it was last seen. This will happen while I am in a trance. Follow the yek I call. Good hunting."

Piaq fed the fire and spoke no more. He stared into the flames and started to chant, shaking the rattle in rhythm to his chant. His voice grew stronger and louder, pleading for the yek to come.

Sak and Nan waited patiently by the fire. After what seemed a long time, they felt the breath of an animal behind them. It passed between the two Sasquatch and walked next to the fire. It was a sleek, white Arctic fox that bobbed its head up and down in rhythm to the rattle and Piaq's chant. Then the rattle stopped. The fox bowed his head once to Piaq and barked. Then it trotted off into the moonlit Arctic night. Sak and Nan stood up and followed the yek.

Nan gave one glance back at the fire. Piaq remained in his trance, chanting the song of the fox who now headed west toward Little Diomede Island.

Jane and Viktor Borovski's grandfather, Quipmig, was a tenacious, patient, and skilled hunter. He had hidden himself and his sealskin kayak between two large ice-covered boulders near the northwestern shore of Little Diomede. He was alone, the only hunter out this day. All of the one hundred seventy Ingalikmiut Eskimos who inhabited the island lived two miles to the south in a village on the leeward shore.

At first light, after twenty hours of darkness, Quipmig peered out from his hiding place and scanned the half-frozen Bering Sea. His view was across the two-and-a-half-mile stretch to Big Diomede Island, which was on the other side of the International Date Line, in Russia. *Over there, it is tomorrow. Here it is today. A strange, white man's rule,* he mused.

His experienced eye searched for a sign of life. There were a few seals active about three hundred yards out to the northwest. Then a swoosh of air caused him to turn his head southward, where he observed a large orca's dorsal fin cutting through an open channel in the icy water as it expelled breath through its blowhole. It was very odd for an orca to be here so late in the season. The Ingalikmiut venerated the orca, as did all of the tribes and clans on the northwestern coasts of the continent.

"Do not be trapped in the freeze, my brother," he uttered aloud, then silently wished the animal good luck and good hunting.

The orca stopped for a moment, as though it had heard Quipmig. Then, with a swish of its powerful tail, it slid his sleek black and white body out of the channel and onto the ice pack. The huge mammal rolled on its side and looked up. This strange movement drew Quipmig's gaze skyward to a black dot. It was a bird, a large back bird, descending toward the ice pack. Suddenly, as it gathered speed, it changed course and swooped down menacingly toward the orca.

"What bird hunts Orca?" a surprised Quipmig asked.

Orca, often called a killer whale, is actually a giant dolphin, and very smart, with a brain much larger than the human brain. It did not wait to do battle with the attacking bird. It flipped its powerful tail and slid off the ice, causing a great splash that threw a wave of icy water up onto the floe. To Quipmig's surprise, the bird continued its diving attack. The orca disappeared under the ice to safety. The strange bird followed, crashing into the icy water, beak and extended talons.

"Ahhh," Quipmig sighed as he pulled himself back into his hiding place. "You are what I seek, killer bird," he whispered.

The condor emerged from the water and hopped out onto the ice. He shook his wet feathers and looked around.

Satisfied he was alone, he spread his wings as if to dry them, but instead, to Quipmig's amazement, he began to change. His feathers dropped away, black slashes on the white ice. His body swelled, and his head along with it. His beak elongated and began to lose its point. White fuzz grew out if it and became fur. The claws and talons became flat paws and claws, as did its wings. It continued to grow in size, and yellowish-white fur spread out of the now-huge bird body, as if someone had poured heavy cream over a black tablecloth. The condor was changing into a giant polar bear, the top hunter of the Arctic north.

When the transformation was complete, the bear slid into the frigid water and slowly swam from ice floe to ice floe, in Quipmig's direction, toward Little Diomede. Each time the bear entered the water and was out of his view, Quipmig took the opportunity to back away from the shore.

There were times, out on the ice, when Quipmig had encountered a polar bear. Usually these bears avoided men. But this huge one, he sensed, posed terrible danger. And it was swimming directly toward him. He had to find help. All of a sudden, dark threatening clouds, a drop in temperature, and strong winds announced a fast-moving early blizzard approaching from Siberia.

CHAPTER SIXTY-THREE

STORM

As the CIA Gulfstream approached its checkpoint near Valdez, Alaska, a weather update was received in the cockpit. An unexpected early-season low was rocketing in from Siberia. It was a famous "Siberian Express," bringing with it gale-force winds and heavy snow. Nome would be socked in for the next twenty-four hours.

Andy Taft, leading the expedition, made the decision to change the flight plan and land at Elmendorf Air Force Base, the largest military installation in Alaska, and home to the 11th Air Force, just south of Anchorage. The slower C-17 transport, an hour behind them, was notified. The weather delay was now an enemy.

While Taft met with the commanding general of Elmendorf AFB, the others in his party, and those from the C-17, were billeted in the BOQ, the base officers' quarters.

"Our mission is of the highest priority," Taft told the brigadier general, a seasoned veteran of Vietnam and the first Gulf war. "We've got to get to Nome as quickly as possible."

During the Vietnam War, the general, then a young lieutenant flying reconnaissance support for an F-105 fighter group, had dealings with the CIA who were operating out of the Tan Son Nhut Air Base, where he was stationed. At times, they called in targets that were questionably nonmilitary. He didn't like them, and he didn't trust them.

When the Gulfstream requested permission to land, the general had checked with the Pentagon, who checked with Fleming, the director of central intelligence. Taft's boss gave him and his party the highest clearance, and requested cooperation with whatever the mission required.

"I am aware of the priority, Mr. Taft. But we do not control the weather. Most of our forces up north are grounded because of the storm."

"Most, but not all," Taft replied. He knew of aircraft that were designed for such weather, and worse.

The general, not anxious to commit to turning over the newly redesigned Chinook choppers, waited to see what the CIA agent knew.

Taft smiled. "I was DIA before I was CIA," he said, speaking of his days doing defense intelligence. "I saw the prototype for the MH-47E—the all-digital, terrain-following and terrain-avoidance radar, long-range fuel tanks, incredible GPS capability and—"

"Okay." The general cut him off. "So you're informed." He paused as he toyed with a fifty-caliber-bullet paperweight on his desk. "I've got one here, but the crew isn't checked out on it yet. Sorry."

"Just one is all I need to get to Nome. My C-17 can follow when the weather clears."

"I said the crew isn't cleared."

Taft smiled and stood up. "But my guys were six months ago," he said. He looked at his watch. "And we're losing valuable time."

Two hours later, the six Vigilant, Taro Heart, Michael Benjamin, a handful of CIA and Special Forces soldiers, and the three dog teams and their handlers were on board the Chinook MH-47E, traveling at a maximum speed of nearly 150 miles per hour toward Nome. They flew into heavy winds and snow, but the sturdy helicopter, with its high-tech avionics, plowed through the stormy night like a determined homing pigeon seeking its roost.

CHAPTER SIXTY-FOUR

THE FOX AND THE BEAR

While the storm threatened, the Arctic fox went on relentlessly, homing in on Belial's location. Even with long strides and capability to run for hours, Nan and Sak strained to keep up with the determined yek. Impervious to the cold, they trailed the fox down the shoreline of the already frozen Chukchi Sea to the westernmost tip of the Seward Peninsula. But when the Siberian Express hit with full force, the yek stopped at a rocky beach a mile north of the village of Wales and sought shelter. He hunkered down in a shallow depression beyond the beach, curled up in a ball, and disappeared from view as the snow built up around his thick white fur.

The Sasquatch sought refuge further inland among a copse of conifers, where they could wait out the storm and keep an eye on the fox's hiding place, in case he suddenly decided to continue the hunt.

The Siberian Express hit Little Diomede Island. Just before Quipmig returned to his village, he watched the large polar bear come ashore and take cover in the rocks not far from those where Quipmig had first hidden. He hoped the bear, which a short while ago had been a bird, would not discover his kayak.

Once home, Quipmig radiophoned his grandson, Viktor, who then conferenced the call with his sister, in Nome.

"I have seen the bird you described," Quipmig told them. "He is a powerful spirit and has now become the great white bear of the north. He rests on our island in the storm."

"You must be very careful, Grandfather," Jane said, the brutal murders at the hospital uppermost in her mind.

The Ingalikmiut are a proud and tough people who live off the land and sea on that godforsaken island just ten miles south of the Arctic Circle. And it was now winter.

"I am always careful, Granddaughter," the old man assured her. "I have hunted around the polar bear all my life. I know his ways and, if necessary, how to kill him," he boasted. Then he hesitated. "But this one—I do not know what he is. In any case, do not worry. I shall watch and wait."

Jane was relieved to hear her grandfather's sensible words, but she was still concerned.

Nan, who was awake and watching the fox while Sak slept, felt the weather begin to change halfway through the long Arctic night. The winds diminished. The temperature rose slightly. The snow eased off and then stopped. The caboose of the Siberian Express passed. The fox was up and alert. Nan shook Sak from his slumber.

"The storm has passed. Our yek stirs." Sak sat up and looked over at the rock where the fox had sought protection from the storm. The animal, illuminated only by the emerging starlight, sniffed the air. It looked back toward the conifers and the two Sasquatch and trotted over to them. As it did, it changed into a beautiful, young Yup'ik woman. She was no more than twenty, with fair skin and dark, almond-shaped eyes. She wore a white fox-fur parka and white sealskin boots.

"Did you rest well, Old Ones?" she asked in their tongue. *The shaman Piaq had told them that yeks could assume animal and human form. But why had she changed now, they wondered?* "The storm has passed. The one you seek is close, out there," she said, pointing to the Bering Sea. "He is on Little Diomede Island. The northwest shore. He sleeps as a great white bear. He will move again when daylight comes."

Detective Jerry Kotchev called Jane Borovski at the Nome hospital to ask her out on a date.

"May I ask why?" Because you're, well... I don't know. I guess I like you," he told her awkwardly.

"Why didn't you ask me in person?" she teased. She was interested in him too.

"Well," he began, "I'd uh...oh, darn. I'll have to call you back." Andy Taft, Jacob Yahze, Allen Weber, and Michael Benjamin had just walked into the detective's office.

A half hour later, Detective Kotchev showed up at Jane's door. With him were four strange companions from Salt Lake City. At first she thought they were just doing police work, following up on the killings. She thought that perhaps a similar crime had been committed, because they were particularly interested in the method of killing—the savage, animal-like attacks.

"It was like a tiger or some large predator had torn them apart," she said, describing the carnage. "I've taken care of a lot of badly wounded people, but the thought of that attack still makes me cringe."

"I understand and sympathize," Taft told her. "Detective Kotchev said that you saw a large black bird go through a window." She glanced at Kotchev.

"Yes. But I don't think he believed me," she said, giving Kotchev a baleful look. "But I know for sure it was true, what I saw."

"And how is that?" Yahze asked her in the Tlingit language. Jane was surprised he knew the tongue.

"Aren't you Navajo?" she asked.

"I am. But many years ago I spent much time with the Haida and Aleut." Then he changed back to English. "It is very important for you to tell us what you thought you saw."

Yahze's speaking her native language put Jane at ease. "What I thought I saw, Shaman, is no longer important. Like I said, I know it is true. And now it has moved north. My grandfather has seen it, and he is very concerned."

"Can you tell us where he is?" Weber asked, excited. His blood was up for a chase.

"Take it easy, Allen," Taft said. "Go ahead, Ms. Borovski."

"He is on Little Diomede Island." They listened intently as she related what Quipmig had told her on the radiophone.

"And your grandfather said the bird became a bear?" Yahze asked, remembering that there was an image of a bear on the chamber wall in the tomb.

"He said it was a giant polar bear." Taft knew immediately that they had to get moving.

"Is it possible that you can come with us to see your grandfather?" he asked.

"When?" Jane asked him.

"Now."

It would be dawn in a few hours. Belial, as the polar bear, was pleased that the storm had passed quickly. Such storms arriving later in the winter might last for a week or more. Although he possessed great powers, he was still cast down to an earthly existence and thus subject to the elements when in human or animal form. During his rest, he had finalized his plan. He would cross the icy Bering Sea to the next island, Big Diomede. It was in another country—Russia. He would travel to Mongolia and impregnate his young disciple there. She would grow a child within her womb. The sub-prince Beelzebub would inhabit it. Then, he would travel to Xian and seek out his brother Satan, who, although captured, could still communicate through the dragon's eye on the door of his tomb. He might then call to Leviathan, who roamed the vast oceans and made his home in Africa these days. Lucifer, the most powerful among them, had remained hidden since Satan's capture. Lucifer was always the most secretive, Belial admitted to himself. And the wisest. Perhaps he should try to locate him first.

Jane Borovski had never been on a helicopter before, much less one as large as the Chinook MH-47E. She had only seen such weapons and soldiers in movies. The religious men were all very nice to her, especially the priest, Father Apostolopoulos, who was of the same church as hers, Eastern Orthodox. Most of all she enjoyed meeting Taro Heart. The two young women sat together and talked about the wondrous adventure they were involved in. But neither of them knew all the facts, or the dangers that might lie ahead.

"It is the old stories coming true. My grandfather is Ingalikmiut Eskimo," Jane told Taro. "He accepts such things with grace and unwavering belief." I am ashamed to say that I did not accept everything he tried to teach us. Now I believe."

"It's the same with me," Taro told her new friend as she glanced over at Jacob Yahze. "There is so much that was valuable and might have been lost were it not for a few."

Jane put her hand on Taro's arm. "Not really lost, just replaced by another culture. But those like my grandfather and Jacob Yahze know. Their memories, knowledge, and beliefs might well save the world."

At a table in the front of the powerful Chinook, Andy Taft sat with the Special Forces captain and studied topographical maps of the Diomede Island. If Quipmig's message was correct, the polar bear might still be on Little Diomede. The proximity of American Little Diomede, in America, to Big Diomede, in Russia, worried Taft. He placed a call to Sasha Andreyev in Washington. Through her efforts, he was connected to Colonel Peter Ilyavich Somoroff, Ret., Andreyev's ex-KGB boss. Before the Soviet Union dissolved, Colonel Somoroff had helped identify, track, capture, and entomb Satan.

Taft filled Somoroff in on the situation and asked him if he could advise the commander of Russian troops on Big Diomede that there might be an operation that could possibly spill across the International Date Line into Russian territory.

"I understand, Andrew," the retired colonel said. "I wish I were with you, my old friend. Life has been too dull since we locked up that devil."

"Yes. And now his brother is in our sights. I wish you were here too, Peter Ilyavich. No one here has seen what we have seen."

"I heard that Rabbi Vogel is dead," the colonel said softly. "Anya called me from Tel Aviv, but she did not elaborate."

"I will tell you everything when we next meet. I can say that he died bravely."

"He was a good man, Andrew. I hope someday the world can learn what he did for all of us."

"Someday, Peter Ilyavich. Someday they shall."

"Yes. But now to business," Somoroff said. "Let me see what an old retired hero of the Soviet Union can do to help you."

CHAPTER SIXTY-FIVE

THE SCENT

Quipmig was delighted that his granddaughter was on her way to see him. The group would be here at first light. But he was also worried, because she was with white men who would not understand what the polar bear really was. He could not sleep.

His wife, Catherine, made him tea and sat with him in the tiny kitchen of their cabin. Her great-grandmother had been Russian, and Catherine was named for the Russian tsarina. She and Quipmig had been together for forty-six years. She knew his every mood. But tonight he was different. He seemed disturbed by something he had seen out on the ice

"What is wrong, my dear?" she asked. Quipmig kept nothing from his wife. The basis of Ingalikmiut marriage is trust and respect, as well as love.

"There is a thing out there, my wife. I have seen a strange spirit that changes shape from the black bird who hunts the orca to a great white bear of the north."

"A bird that hunts the orca?" she said. There was a bottle of vodka in the cabin, and for a moment she thought he might have been drinking. But he never drank when he was going out to hunt. "Perhaps it is a Tlingit yek," she offered.

"I do not think so. It has evil about it. Jane says it kills like a lion."

"Stay away from it," the old woman warned. "We have lost our son to war. That is enough bad spirits for one family."

Quipmig loved Catherine deeply. She was a wise and good companion. But the polar bear preyed on his mind. He could not dismiss it, as she asked. He kissed her on her forehead.

"There is something I must do before Jane arrives."

"You will be careful," was all she said. He nodded and left the room.

When Quipmig had dressed and strapped on his snowshoes, he went out in the dark and headed south to where he had seen the bear seek shelter from the storm. About a mile from the shore, he became aware of a strong scent in the air. It was one he had experienced some years ago during an exceptionally frigid winter when the Bering Sea froze from Russia all the way to the Land Bridge Preserve.

He had been out hunting seal when the scent caught his attention. He dropped down low, next to the seal's breathing hole that he was watching. A huge white furry creature came by, and then another, and another. They came across the ice from Russia. They walked upright like men but were much larger. He did not fear them, and he did not wish to hunt them. He knew stories of such creatures from long ago. He let them pass without stirring. They did not see him, although one stopped and looked in his direction. He asked the village shaman about them, and the holy man confirmed that what he had seen were the Yeti, the Old Ones, who mated with the Sasquatch every five years, in a secret place far to the north.

The same scent was now in the frigid air. But the Bering Sea was not frozen, and the scent came from the land ahead of him, not from the ice. He tracked toward it, carefully keeping downwind. A faint brightening in the eastern sky proclaimed the dawning of the four-hour day. At that moment, he saw a creature standing next to an ice-coated granite boulder. It was well over eight feet tall, with coarse, dark hair that covered its entire body. Its hands were large in proportion to its thick, solid body. Its fingertips reached to mid-thigh. Its feet were broad and flat on the snow pack. It stood upright, scanning the horizon. Even from this distance, Quipmig could see large brown eyes that conveyed a high degree of intelligence.

"Sasquatch," Quipmig whispered to himself, confirming aloud what his eyes saw. Awed, he dropped to his knees, and then flat on the snow covered ground. He sensed a presence behind him, something alive.

Centuries of the difficult Eskimo life in this harsh land gave him instincts for survival that were imprinted in his genes. Here, fear was not an advantageous trait. It could kill you.

Quipmig gently slipped his rifle strap off his shoulder as rolled over on his back. He expected to find the evil polar bear above him, ready to pounce. But as he brought his rifle up to fire, he discovered it was not the bear but another Sasquatch towering above him and smiling.

CHAPTER SIXTY-SIX

A GATHERING OF WARRIORS

In his shelter, the huge white bear stretched in the dim morning light. It would be a clear day. There was only a light breeze from the northwest, barely a zephyr. The bear moved out from between the rocks and gazed across the sea toward Big Diomede Island. More ice had formed during the night, and larger ice floes drifted into a swift-moving channel in the growing ice pack. That stretch of water would make it harder for him to cross.

Belial, as polar bear, was hungry. If he was lucky, maybe he would find a seal for breakfast. The bear left the beach and lumbered onto the ice, unaware that Quipmig and his two new Sasquatch friends, Nan and Sak, lay hidden on the ridge above the frozen beach, watching.

The great bear stopped and looked to the north. He heard something. Quipmig and the Sasquatch also heard it. A helicopter was about to land on the ice near the village. The bear trotted away, hurrying to the place where the ice ended at the new swift channel. If he swam hard and used the ice floes to rest, he could get to Big Diomede, and Russia, within an hour.

Before the chopper's rotors had stopped turning, the Special Forces and CIA troops were out of the Chinook, deploying into defensive positions. The Vigilant then deplaned, followed by Michael Benjamin, Taro Heart, and Jane Borovski. The children of the village ran excitedly toward them, followed by several of the adults. Jane searched the crowd for her grandfather. She spotted her grandmother and ran to greet her. It had been six years since they had seen each other. The two women embraced. Tears of joy froze on Jane's face.

"Oh, dear Grandmother Catherine! How much I have missed you," Jane told the smiling, old Eskimo woman. Catherine took Jane by the shoulders and looked into her eyes.

"How beautiful you are," she said. She brought Jane's face to hers and kissed it.

The village elder offered his house to the visitors while the soldiers stayed with the Chinook and prepared their gear. The three dog teams were fed and harnessed to sledges that were loaded with ammunition, light ordnance, and medical supplies.

Taft and his party settled into the village elder's house. Father Apostolopoulos, Kwame Dombo, and Vernon Flood prepared the amulets, parchments, and other articles they had brought with them.

By that time, Quipmig was back. He too had an emotional reunion with his granddaughter in the village elder's house. "Too many years away," he told her. He eyed the strangers in the room with deep-seated suspicion.

To Quipmig, strangers—especially white men— represented decades of patronizing and sometimes brutal treatment and exploitation of the tribes and nomads of the north. Their livelihood and culture was threatened as the local species were decimated—the whales by the Japanese and Norwegians, the seals by the Russians and Americans, and the salmon by all nations that fished indiscriminately using high-tech methods. Birds, walruses, elephant seals, and many other species were being destroyed by oil spills, pollution, and senseless killing.

"These white men have come to ask us to help them," he thought, as he was being introduced. "But when will they help us?"

Then Quipmig met Jacob Yahze, Taro Heart, and Kwame Dombo, and his spirits lifted. Quipmig and Yahze spoke in Inupiaq, the Eskimo language of this part of Alaska, because the matter at hand, the evil bear moving out on the ice, could be better described in language that recognized and understood such things. Taro Heart and Jane Borovski translated the conversation into English for the rest of the group.

"After dawn I saw the spirit bear move away and swim toward Big Diomede," said Quipmig. "He heard your helicopter. He is strong and will swim fast. But he is blocked by a swift new channel with large ice floes in several places. That might slow his progress."

Andy Taft spread a topographical map out on a table. "Can you ask him to show us where the bear was last seen?" he asked Yahze. Benjamin and Weber leaned in.

Quipmig studied the map. "This does not show the ice," he said. "Only how it is in the summer."

"I understand," Taft said. "Ask him to guess how far from the shore, and where?"

Quipmig traced the shoreline south of the village with his finger, then slid it out into the water about one third of the way to Big Diomede Island.

"Here is the place, I believe. But there is ice from here to here, and then again here, and one channel here that is filled with fast-moving floes."

"Good," Taft said as he marked the map. "Then I believe we have time before he reaches Russia." Quipmig understood the positive tone of Taft's voice. He knew this man was the leader, and was preparing to kill the bear.

"Tell your friend he cannot kill such a spirit," Quipmig told Jane.

"They know, Grandfather," she assured him.

"We must capture him," Yahze told Quipmig in Inupiaq.

"My wife thought he might be a Tlingit yek," Quipmig responded. "But I have seen him. He is not a yek. He is far more powerful—and dangerous."

Taft had little time to discuss such things now. If Quipmig was right, and Belial made it to Russia, the biggest obstacle to overcome might be international politics. An hour earlier, his latest conversation on the phone with Colonel Peter Somoroff had been disappointing.

"I am sorry, my old friend," the Colonel had told him. "But for the moment, all I could do was alert the military commander on Big Diomede. His father was a friend of mine. He will stop all ship and air traffic in the area. You will be allowed limited operations in the water and on the ice, but there is no clearance for you to pursue onto Big Diomede itself. I will keep trying."

After a hasty hot meal, all weapons were checked and loaded. Special thermal clothing was distributed to all who would be out on the ice. With only two hours of daylight left, and satisfied that preparations for his plan were in order, Andy Taft gave the signal to move out.

One dog team with two Special Forces marksmen, two CIA soldiers, Father John Apostolopoulos, and FBI Agent-in-Charge Michael Benjamin, guided by an Ingalikmiut hunter, moved south and onto the ice at the place where Quipmig had last seen Belial. . Once there, they would be south of the bear and would await further orders as the situation developed.

A second dog sledge team and handler, with two CIA and two Special Forces soldiers, along with Kwame Dombo, left the village guided by another Ingalikmiut hunter. They headed due west onto the ice. That route would take them north of the bear.

The Boeing Chinook CH-47E was readied to carry the third dog team and its handler, plus Taft, Yahze, Flood, Quipmig, Weber, the Special Forces captain, two of his sharpshooters, and four CIA soldiers. Taft gave the thumbs-up to the pilot. The co-pilot started the two Textron Lycoming engines. The ordnance officer loaded and armed two side-mounted, fifty-caliber Gatling guns.

Taro Heart and Jane Borovski remained in the village with a squad of CIA soldiers and the Special Forces communication team to coordinate and translate as things developed.

As Taft's teams began to board the Chinook, Quipmig took Yahze aside. "We have to get the other two passengers, Shaman," he said.

"You are sure they are necessary?"

"Yes. I will bring them. You must prepare the others."

As Quipmig hurried to his cabin, Yahze filled Taft in on who was going to join them. Taft, who had experience with myth and the supernatural, was not that shocked, but he was displeased that Yahze, now a fellow Vigilant, had kept this secret.

"I cannot apologize, Andrew, other than to say we dared not risk exposing them unless we felt it was necessary."

"And why is it necessary?" Taft asked.

"Because Belial is the archenemy of their kind, and has been for thousands of years."

"The bones and skull in the chamber," Taft muttered.

"Yes. And the petrified hand that Beelzebub tried to take from the tomb. It must be very powerful medicine for Belial to take such a risk. They have asked to come along. Perhaps they can help us."

Quipmig emerged from his cabin, leading Nan and Sak to the Chinook.

"Oh, my dear God," Vernon Flood exclaimed.

"What the hell are they?" the Special Forces officer asked. His men chambered their weapons.

"Stand down," Taft ordered.

"These are my Sasquatch friends," Quipmig said. Yahze translated as Nan and Sak were introduced to the group.

Although the group was stunned by the appearance of the Sasquatch, something in their manner and body language told everyone they were of the human race, and to be trusted. When Nan and Sak met Allen Weber, Yahze quickly explained who he was and what had happened to his family. When Quipmig related this to the Sasquatch, Sak and Nan gently touched Weber's shoulders and head while they softly sang a plaintive song to him.

"They are expressing how sorry they are for your losses," Yahze translated "They say this evil one has caused many of their kind—their families—to die."

Nan and Sak bowed to the group and spread their muscular arms wide, turning the palms of their massive hands up in a sign of friendship and peace. Seeing this brought tears of joy to Jacob Yahze's eyes. To have lived to see this was a miracle to him.

"The Old Ones," the Navajo shaman whispered softly to Taro Heart and Jane Borovski, who were standing nearby. "Like us, they have been driven from their homes and their way of life. And yet, they have come to help us."

CHAPTER SIXTY-SEVEN

THE TRAP

Five minutes later, the loaded Chinook CH-47E lifted off and climbed rapidly at a rate of fifteen hundred feet a minute to an altitude of five thousand feet. It then peeled off to the southwest. The visibility was excellent during in these few hours of daylight.

Both Sasquatch peered out of the large aft windows and looked down at the Little Diomede Island. Their gaze then wandered across the water to the mainland, and the mountains beyond, the same mountains they had crossed with the white Arctic fox yek. Excited, Nan and Sak spoke rapidly to each other.

"What are they saying?" Yahze asked Quipmig. The Ingalikmiut hunter strained to hear over the noise of the rotors. He smiled.

"They say they are like those who fly. They now know why the eagles soar and the birds sing."

Belial, as the great white polar bear, swam around the pack ice, through moving floes and freezing water. He moved along steadily, with powerful strokes of his massive webbed paws. Big Diomede, was about one mile ahead across the ice pack. Its jagged cliffs rose like a fjord from the rocky shore. Climbing those cliffs would slow him down, but he did not want to change to the condor, a creature less adapted to this frigid climate. He would head farther north, where the topography was flatter. Then he heard dogs barking from that direction.

A dog team and sledge, along with several men, was moving toward him from the northeast. He noticed they were on the main ice pack from Little Diomede, but the new channel and ice floes cut them off, and they could not reach him. His attention was drawn back behind him to where he had first left the ice pack and entered the channel. More men had appeared with another dog team and sledge, but they too were blocked by the newly formed channel. He slid up and out of the channel onto the ice pack that led to Big Diomede Island and Russia.

As he contemplated his next move, the sound of the huge helicopter reached his sensitive ears. It was high above him, heading for Big Diomede. Then he understood his pursuer's plan. They would try to cut him off with the helicopter and drive him back into the channel toward Little Diomede. *"Fools,"* he thought. *"The ice and frigid water is my habitat."*

Another sound caught his attention. A large male orca, the one that he had chased yesterday, was now swimming in the channel behind him, unfazed by the freezing water and ice floes. Belial became wary. Could the orca somehow be helping his enemies? As he considered that possibility, the orca moved away toward a small herd of seals resting on a

DAVID SAPERSTEIN

large floe that had just entered the channel on the swift current. *"No,"* Belial decided. *"He is hunting."*

He turned his attention back to the northern tip of the island. Once there, he would be safe. Then it was only thirty miles of open sea to the mainland. Being away from his tomb and not having the artifacts he had sent Beelzebub to fetch had weakened his ability to transform himself quickly. But he still had more than enough power to do that once, and then fly to the Russian mainland as the condor.

Allen Weber's sharp eyes spotted the polar bear first. "There," he shouted. "On the edge of the ice." Quipmig confirmed it was the same bear he had seen. He pointed to the new large channel and ice floes.

"This is what your map does not show. The bear is past the channel," he told Yahze. "Those coming from my island are cut off. They cannot pursue him." Yahze translated the disappointing news to Andy Taft.

"Then we have no choice but to attack. Russia is just ahead of him. This may be the last shot we get at him."

"Maybe we can drive him back across that channel to Little Diomede," Vernon Flood suggested.

"Maybe," Taft answered. He turned to the Special Forces captain. Inform your men and the teams down on the ice of our situation. We're going down!"

The pilot radioed to the Russian airbase on Big Diomede that he was about to enter their airspace. The Russians, having been made aware of that possibility, cleared the chopper. Taft then took the radio mike and identified himself.

"We have sighted our target. Our plan is to land on the ice pack, close to the island. We will offload a dog-sled team

380

and soldiers. They will head east—I repeat, east—back toward Little Diomede to intercept our target."

"Understood," the Russian commander replied immediately. "Colonel Somoroff informed us of your mission. You may proceed. Good luck, and good hunting."

Belial watched as the helicopter landed close to the narrow beach on the ice pack. It discharged more dogs, a sledge, and several armed men. *"They cannot block my way,"* he thought. *"I can swim under the ice, or be the condor and fly over it."*

The helicopter lifted off and began to fly in his direction. They were less than a mile away, closing fast and low. The team it dropped off on the ice pack was also heading his way.

As Belial started to make the transformation to the condor he heard a high-pitched screeching. Four large bald eagles had appeared above and were circling menacingly. *"What are they doing here?"* he wondered. *He knew the condor could not get past them.*

The Chinook, with its powerful engines, rapidly headed toward him. He stopped his transformation, which had drained some of his energy.

"I will swim under the ice and elude you meddlesome God-lovers," Belial said aloud.

A large black shadow moved from out from under the edge of the ice pack. The bear peered into the gin-clear water. The black form showed a patch of glistening white on it. Then a cavernous mouth opened, exposing a row of deadly teeth. It was the male orca. Even the large bear, once in the orca's element, especially under pack-ice, could not escape that deadly predator. The orca was too powerful a hunter and swimmer.

The helicopter was almost upon him.

"I will run to the island on the ice," he declared. His claws and wide, flat paws gave him the needed traction and stability. "And if these fools think they can stop me I have a great surprise for them. They do not know to power of Belial!"

"He's moving west on the ice, sir, making for the Russian shore," the captain reported.

"Damn that channel. Once he gets on land we don't yet have authority to follow," Taft said, realizing that his plan to force the bear into his trap might now fail. "How can he know that?"

"Perhaps he can read our minds," Yahze offered. That idea sent a chill through the Chinook. Taft looked at Yahze and Flood. He was out of time. He had to make a move.

"You guys ready?" he asked. Both men nodded yes. "Then take her down," he told the pilot. "On the ice. In front of that bear."

The Special Forces captain had been told that what they sought could not die. Imam Khawaja had stressed that killing Belial in any of his animal forms would only free the archangel to take another form, or to flee. Rabbi ben Abraham had also said that confining him in any way other than alive as archangel would not be sufficient to entomb him.

But perhaps, Taft reasoned, bullets well aimed at the polar bear's legs and paws could wound him enough to slow him down. That might give the CIA sharpshooter who had been given the task of hitting the bear with a powerful tranquilizer time to accomplish his mission. Once the bear was drugged, they would apply the parchments and amulets that might bind the animal, as they had Amaimon, the hyena. But what to do to entomb him properly was still the most important and unanswered question.

CHAPTER SIXTY-EIGHT

BATTLE ON THE ICE

Taft radioed to the team of CIA and Special Forces soldiers who had been dropped off on the ice pack near the beach of Big Diomede and ordered them to push north and east to cut the bear off there. The other two teams had come from Little Diomede and reached the new channel of water and ice floes.

"Hold your positions and be prepared if the bear retreats in your direction," Taft ordered. "Wound and tranquilize only."

The bear was now surrounded on three sides. In a minute the Chinook would cut off his only lane of escape.

Belial watched as the helicopter descended rapidly toward him. He steeled himself for battle and noted that the four bald eagles that had been circling above him backed away so as not to interfere with the helicopter. *Changing form might yet be the way out, Belial reasoned, not to the slower condor but to the swift peregrine falcon. He was far from his tomb and the strength it gave him, but he could still change form, albeit more slowly.*

The helicopter landed thirty yards away from the bear. Having experienced some of the archangels' powers, Taft ordered the pilot to keep the rotors turning in case they had to take off quickly. The side doors of the Chinook slid open and four of the Special Forces and CIA soldiers jumped out. They slid about in the rotor wash on the slippery ice.

Belial saw this as an opportunity to kill these humans. The sharp claws and wide paws were an advantage he could now use. *"And,"* he mused, *"while they are licking their wounds and calling for puny reinforcements, I will have time to transform into the falcon and leave swiftly."* He rose up on his hind legs to full height—over eight feet. He roared and moved to attack. The soldiers, who had been ordered to disable the bear, were too unsteady on the ice to fire their weapons accurately. Belial swiped one of them up in his massive paw, slicing through the thermal clothing. The soldier was hurled away, bleeding, across the ice.

Taft and Flood jumped out of the chopper. Flood held one of the golden plates that Ballard had given to him to cover the dragon's eye on the door to Belial's tomb. Allen Weber followed with the second plate, which was meant for the door of Satan's tomb in Xian, China. Jacob Yahze came out next, holding the dragon amulet and a large fetish doll.

Belial, who had grabbed another skidding soldier in his claws, instantly felt the effects of the charms. He became dizzy. He released the bleeding soldier onto the ice and backed away from the group. The two remaining marksmen dropped prone on the ice and aimed their weapons.

Flood and Weber held the golden plates in front of them and advanced. The plates glittered in the orange light of the setting winter sun that was almost at the horizon. The long Arctic night was approaching.

Yahze came forward with the fetish doll in one hand and the amulet in the other. The doll began to smoke, and then caught fire. Yahze dropped it. He began to chant and scatter blue pollen in the air.

The bear became unsteady on his feet, rocking back and forth. Belial's anger grew. He gathered his strength. Suddenly, the ice beneath him shook violently, knocking him over. The bear struggled to get up, but the ice shook violently again. Then, like a sleek nuclear sub crashing up through the polar icecap, the huge male orca plowed up through the ice, snapping his powerful mouth of glistening white teeth at the bear.

Awed by the sight of the orca's sudden appearance and attack, Yahze struggled to his feet and reached for more blue pollen.

"Pick up your plate," Flood yelled to Weber who had dropped it when the ice shook. It was sliding toward the water. Weber lunged and grabbed it. The cool-headed Taft saw an opportunity.

"Now is our chance," Taft shouted to the soldiers, who had regained their position on the ice.

He raised the Uzi he carried and began to charge the bear.

The two soldiers got to their feet and followed.

The four bald eagles dove toward the bear, their sharp talons poised to tear into his thick coat and eyes.

The orca, now completely out of the water and on the ice, shook his body and slid, with mouth wide open, toward the polar bear, who was retreating toward the icy water and floes of the channel.

It was a three-pronged attack: orca, eagle, and man.

But then, to the amazement and horror of all, the bear took the form of Belial as Belial. He was evil incarnate, appearing like that evil monster depicted on the walls of ancient temples of the Inca, Maya, Aztec, Hindu, and Buddhist, in frightening legends and texts, in horrific paintings and statuary. He became a living gargoyle, a nightmare. The beast that is part human, part animal, part bird, part serpent.

He became the living plumed serpent—the dragon, Quetzalcoatl.

The stunning transformation stopped them all in their tracks. Belial spread his huge, scaly, green, batlike wings and glared menacingly at the eagles overhead. The four great birds hesitated and broke off their attack. The orca, confused momentarily by the sight of this strange animal, pressed his attack. But now he was no match for what confronted him. Belial slashed out with his claws. He ripped the brave orca's flesh to the bone with one stroke, and then tore the poor animal's gut open with another. Blood and viscera spewed out onto the ice. Mortally wounded, the orca slid off the ice pack, into the water and an icy grave.

The team of soldiers and the sledge that had been dropped off near Big Diomede arrived on the scene and proceeded to open fire. Taft and the two soldiers with him fired point-blank at the grotesque apparition, but bullets had no effect. Belial turned to the soldiers.

"How dare you!" he bellowed. His hot breath filled the air with a foul, nauseating odor. "I am Belial. You now see your destroyer as he was cast out by your God."

Yahze, Flood, and Weber recovered their senses and bravely stepped forward. The two Mormons held the golden plates out ahead of them, while Yahze, pointing the dragon amulet, scattered blue pollen into the frigid air. Belial did not retreat.

"Foolish toys," the archangel hissed. "You will die with them in your puny hands." He spread his wings. His green serpentine tail slid back and forth across the ice like an excited puppy. Thick yellow saliva dripped from his fangs and black lips. Belial, brother of Satan, Leviathan, and Lucifer, cast out of heaven by God, reared up and roared again. "You have defiled my resting place. You have murdered the vessels of my sons, my sub-princes. You have destroyed my disciples and servitors." He pointed a clawed wing at the three brave men who continued bravely to hold the plates and amulet in front of him. They stood their ground. "You and your God-loving kind have driven me to this desolate place and turned even the beasts against me." He gestured to the slick of orca blood that stained the nearby ice and water. "Now I will destroy all of you by—

Belial suddenly ceased his diatribe. His black, evil eyes widened. His tail stopped moving. His wings slowly folded. He seemed to grow smaller.

"You," he hissed.

Nan and Sak, led by Quipmig, had stepped in front of Flood, Weber, and Yahze. Their massive bodies blocked Taft's and the soldiers' view of the monster.

"I damn you and your kind!" Belial shouted in the Sasquatch tongue.

Nan and Sak roared and drove the beast backward, cowering.

"Silence, cursed of God!" They rushed forward and grabbed Belial in their powerful arms, holding him in a viselike grip. They roared their hatred of Belial up into the clear, blue sky. Their shrill howls echoed across the ice pack. All who saw or heard were awed. The eagles screeched. The sled dogs howled. Whales and seals in the area sang with delight. Quipmig chanted in celebration.

But the shock of being confronted by the Sasquatch began to wear off. Belial flexed his powerful muscles and tried to stretch his clawed wings. He bellowed in defiance and began to struggle.

"Now," Yahze shouted. Flood and Weber approached Belial, whom the Sasquatch still held tightly. The two Mormons and the Navajo shaman once again offered up the plates, the amulet, and the blue pollen. Yahze chanted and was joined by Quipmig. The combined powers of Mormon, Navajo, and Eskimo, along with the physical strength and fearlessness of the Sasquatch, weakened the evil archangel once again.

"Aim for his neck," Taft yelled to the Special Forces sharpshooter.

The customized bolt-action Springfield leaped to the sharpshooter's shoulder in a tight loop-sling. He raised his right elbow while pulling his left close to his body, and aimed through an infrared scope, placing the visible red dot on the beast's jugular. He squeezed the trigger and fired a huge dose of tranquilizer, a derivative of the potent curare used by South American Indians, into the plumed serpent's neck.

The effect was immediately calming, but it did not put him to sleep.

The Sasquatch saw what the men had done. "He relaxes," Sak told Nan. "We have a moment. Grasp his wings. I will hold his neck and tail." Nan did as Sak asked. "Now put him in the water … in and out … in and out." Nan understood immediately what his wise old mentor wanted to accomplish.

As the two Sasquatch began repeatedly to dunk Belial in the water and then hold him out in the sub-zero air, the last flickering rays of the winter sun left the ice pack. Taft told the chopper pilot to turn on the powerful halogen landing light on the Chinook, illuminating the area.

"They are freezing him," Yahze told an amazed Andy Taft. "He is now part reptile, like the snake and the lizard. His blood is cold. He will not be able to break free."

"They will make him like the bear in winter," Quipmig said to Yahze. "He will go to sleep." And he did.

In the end, it was neither religious objects, nor native prayers and chants, nor the weapons and technology of modern man that made possible the capture of Belial. It was an enemy of long ago, the Sasquatch, the Old Ones. They had never worshipped or feared the evil archangel. Only in the greed of humans did Belial and his followers flourish. Ironically, it was a species he strove to eliminate, the water he planned to pollute, and the air he wanted to foul, that subdued him.

As he was dunked into the freezing Bering Sea by the Sasquatch, and then held in the frigid air repeatedly, a prison of ice formed on his repugnant body. Layer by layer, the crystalline straitjacket grew thicker until the abhorrent beast, stilled and encased, could no longer be seen. Belial, as the dragon-beast Quetzalcoatl, was locked in a thick coat of ice.

It only remained to move him rapidly to Salt Lake City to be sealed in his tomb—forever, it was hoped.

CHAPTER SIXTY-NINE

FAREWELL

The Chinook CH-47E carried the frozen archangel, suspended by a makeshift arrangement of cables and hooks, to Quipmig's village. Two hours later, Andy Taft notified the Ben Zimrah and Michael Gross in Israel, and Imam Khawaja in Utah, of Belial's capture. Rabbi ben Abraham dispatched more of The Vigilant via a jet supplied by Mossad , to help Imam Khawaja make final preparations to receive the evil beast.

"This is a glorious day," the old rabbi told Taft. "You have worked a miracle."

"No, Rabbi ben Abraham," he said. "It was those whom the world had long ignored or forgotten who did it. They are the ones that now must be honored."

The C-17, left behind in Nome, was hurriedly equipped with landing skis flown up from Elmendorf AFB. The jet cargo plane then flew north and landed on the ice adjacent to the Ingalikmiut village on Little Diomede, where Taft's crew stood guard over their frozen captive. The plane's cargo bay doors were removed, and the block of ice that held Belial was secured onboard. The plan was for the C-17 to quickly climb above thirty-eight thousand feet and fly to Utah with an F-16 escort. At that altitude, the air temperature was a frigid minus 70 degrees, ensuring that Belial would remain frozen. They would land at the Fort Douglas reservation, where a refrigerated army tractor-trailer waited to receive the block of ice and transport it, with maximum security, to the tomb under the domed rock.

As final preparations to leave were made, Jacob Yahze, Taro Heart, and Quipmig's granddaughter, Jane Borovski, approached Andy Taft as he supervised loading Belial aboard the C-17.

"My grandfather informs me that it is the time of mating for the Sasquatch," Jane Borovski told Taft.

"They chose to help us instead of joining their kind," Yahze added. "It only happens every five years." Both Sasquatch and Quipmig stood off from the activity, staring northward across the thickening ice.

"Where must they go?" Taft asked.

"They don't say where exactly," Taro Heart said. "Just to the north. I don't think they wish to entrust that secret to us."

"Let's talk to them," Taft suggested.

The foursome approached Nan and Sak. Having seen their great strength and courage, Taft now observed something gentle, even sad, about these behemoths.

"I am told you must go north," Taft said. Quipmig translated. Sak nodded.

"We will miss the mating," Nan said.

"Let us fly you where you must go in our helicopter," Taft offered, pointing to the Chinook.

"Not to that place," Sak said.

"Then where?" Yahze asked.

"To the place called Noatak," Sak answered.

"I know the village," Quipmig told his granddaughter. "It is across the Chukchi Sea, maybe a hundred miles. If we bring them to that place they will be able to reach their kind in season."

"Then let's do it," Taft said, giving Nan and Sak a thumbs-up. "The ladies await!" When Quipmig translated, both Sasquatch smiled—a very human trait that was not lost on anyone.

When Sak and Nan were ready to board the Chinook, everyone gathered to say good-bye. Andy Taft extended his hand. Sak took it gently and enveloped it in his massive hand. Taft thought of the petrified hand in the tomb. A Sasquatch hand, as they all now knew, had belonged to an Old One named Nii. It was a hand that Belial had feared.

"Thank you," Taft said in their language. Quipmig had taught him the words and gestures. "Travel and live safely."

"You, too," Sak replied in a sing-sing voice. Both Sasquatch then reached out their massive hands and gently stroked everyone on the head, as if petting puppies. They made a cooing sound to the women and, once more, a special gesture and bow to Allen Weber for the loss of his family. They did the same for the CIA soldiers.

"They are blessing us," Quipmig said softly.

"We are honored," Yahze added.

Sak then spoke several Sasquatch words to the assembled group and boarded the helicopter. As the doors closed, Quipmig translated.

"They ask us to please leave their world unspoiled. They ask the white man to leave room for their children to live."

"I wonder if we'll ever see that day?" Vernon Flood mused as he walked with Michael Benjamin and Allen Weber to the waiting C-17 for the trip to Utah.

"I think we must," Benjamin answered.

"If we don't clean up our act for them," Weber added, "I believe we will be signing mankind's death warrant as well."

CHAPTER SEVENTY

BLINDING THE RUBY EYE

By the time the refrigerated military tractor-trailer, carrying its frozen cargo, parked as close as it could get to the tomb stairs, Imam Khawaja and the additional Vigilant from Safed—Rabbi Chaim Malachi, Father Colm McDonough, and Huan Chi Lo, a Taoist Monk—had prepared the tomb to receive Belial.

A light crane lifted the glimmering block of ice and placed it on a steel cart on tracks that had been laid leading down to the tomb door and into the tomb's throne room. However, at its present size, the block of ice would not fit through the tomb's doorway. CIA soldiers with blowtorches moved in to melt the ice down so that it could pass on into the tomb.

It was a nerve-wracking time for all. Out in the air, the thick ice that had been opaque was now clearing, and the beast that was Belial was almost visible. As the soldiers' work was nearly complete, Belial's eyes opened inside his icy prison. It was clear that he was aware of where he was. Anger and hatred surged in those terrible eyes.

"Okay, everyone. He's awake!" Taft yelled. "Let's try again." The soldiers pushed the cart to the door. It was still a little too big. "Clear the tomb," Taft yelled again.

The soldiers backed the cart away from the dragon door. Taft ordered all The Vigilant from Safed out. "There's no time for a ceremony inside," Taft told them.

"Then we will do it from out here," Imam Khawaja announced to his fellow Vigilant.

"Trim it a little more, but be careful," Taft ordered. This time the blowtorches shrank the ice so that it was close to being able to fit through the tomb door. The ice surrounding the beast was melting rapidly. Small cracks began to appear. Belial was somehow generating heat from within. Water was now pouring off his ice prison and pooling at the bottom of the stairs in front of the door.

The Vigilant began their ceremony of prayers that would remove Belial from the face of the Earth and sentence him to eternity within the very walls that had once been his sanctuary and seat of power.

Belial groaned inside the ice. What was left of the block shuddered.

"Try it again," Taft ordered. This time the huge, melting block fit through the doorway. "Okay! Give it a shove and then rip up the tracks in the doorway. Go! Go! Go!" Taft shouted. "Everyone back! Get out of the away!"

Three of the soldiers pushed the cart while four stood ready with picks and a burning bar to cut and disassemble the cart tracks that blocked the doorway. As the cart hurtled down the tracks toward the throne room, the tracks at the doorway were torn out. Just as the last section was pulled away, the cart derailed in a crash and the ice shattered, followed by a spine-chilling roar. Belial was free!

"Seal it," Imam Khawaja ordered. Allen Weber and Vernon Flood took one side of the door while Kwame Dombo and Jacob Yahze grabbed the other. The fury of Belial grew louder as he rushed from his throne room toward the door. The four Vigilant slammed it shut. It sealed with a hissing sound and immediately began to shake as Belial hammered from the other side.

Imam Khawaja stepped forward and removed the golden plate that Fletcher Bullard had given to Flood from its blue covering. As he placed it over the ruby eye of the dragon on the tomb door, the plate jumped from his hands and adhered itself to the door. The hammering from inside the tomb suddenly ceased.

"Now he is blind," the Imam announced. "Darkness is his eternal life, and may we finally see the light." From within the tomb a wail of pain and a roar of anger shook the Earth.

"Fill it in," Taft commanded. A bulldozer pushed the sandy subsoil down the stairwell, covering the door, and continued piling dirt and rocks until the dome was buried.

Eventually a wall would be constructed to block entrance to the property. Flood-control and pumps would be installed to stop erosion. The mine shaft was sealed. Nicholas Perez's land would become federal property and the sealed nuclear waste put under the control of the Nuclear Regulatory Commission.

The Weber family would cede the farm to The Vigilant. The fence between the farm and the Perez property would be removed. The farmhouse would serve as headquarters for The Vigilant to watch over the tomb, assisted by armed Navajo, chosen by Jacob Yahze. They would patrol the area, for although Belial was blinded by the golden plate and could not communicate with his disciples and servitors, The Vigilant knew that some of them would try to free him.

High above, in the Wasatch Mountains, overlooking the farm, a lone Paronto observed the Navajo through powerful binoculars. Effrigis, the spirit that quivers in a horrible manner, had come to him in a dream and told him of an Aleut child that would soon be born to Lilly Tupiq, disciple of Belial.

"Be patient and watch," Effrigis instructed. "Our master's sub-prince will come."

EPILOGUE

Imam Khawaja, Rabbi Chaim Malachi, Father Colm McDonough, and the Taoist monk Huan Chi Lo visited Satan's tomb in Xian and placed the second Mormon plate over the dragon's eye on the door. Like his brother Belial, Satan bellowed his protest, but to avail. He was blinded to the outside world.

The stoic terra-cotta horsemen and soldiers who guarded that tomb were ever on guard, and though many attempts had been made by his disciples to free him, Satan was still a prisoner.

Over time, real and lasting peace in some parts of the world had begun to seem like a possibility. The Cold War ended. The Berlin Wall came down. Tyrants were toppled. The prospects for freedom and democracy improved. Many of the world's leaders and politicians had begun to respond to their people's yearning for justice and a better life. But given the many despots, power-hungry tyrants, religious fanatics, avaricious businesspeople, and corrupt politicians, worldwide peace would take time. Mankind had been given the gift of free will. It was humanity's choice if they wanted to live free or oppressed.

With Belial's entombment and blinding, it was possible for
the natural and physical world to begin to heal itself as well.
Issues such as global warming and nuclear proliferation
were no longer "problems to be studied." The facts were on
the table. The ignorance, greed, and outright stupidity that
raped natural resources, man-made filth, mindless use of
finite resources, and the pollution of our air, water, and land
that belong to all humanity began to come into focus with
the evil archangel's imprisonment. Mankind had been given
the gift of free will. It was humankind's choice to survive or
to allow the Earth to be destroyed.

The other two fallen archangels were still at large. Their
location, and the site of their tombs, was unknown.

Leviathan, whose realm was the seas and oceans of the
world, plied his unique evil of fomenting hunger and
disease.

Lucifer, the most virulent of all, made his particular evil
known through what the world called terrorism. He spread it
in any way that he could. The egocentric of the world
supplied him with an endless list of corruptible souls.

In Nome, Alaska, Lilly Tupiq bore a son, the spawn of
Belial. Unlike ordinary humans, whose bodies could
unknowingly become vessels for spirits when placed there
by the evil archangels, and their sub-princes, this child was
aware of his lineage. His master was sealed in a prison. His
awaiting sub-prince Amaimon and Amaimon's brother
Beelzebub, existing in the shadowy, limbo world of spirits,
were also locked in the tomb. The child repeated daily the

vow made eons ago when God cast out the archangels and condemned them to live among men.

"I, conceived from the seed of Belial, will serve my master forever. We shall destroy God's Earth and all that dwells herein." Forever is a long time. Belial had patience.

"In time," the child thought, *"I will grow and gather strength to free my master. God has foolishly given humankind free choice. I will find ways to corrupt their weak souls to do my bidding."*

But The Vigilant had other ideas.

www.ingramcontent.com/pod-product-compliance
Lightning Source LLC
Chambersburg PA
CBHW071642260626
47170CB00001B/195